Love Is a Racket

Love Is a Racket

a novel by

John Ridley

Alfred A. Knopf

New York 1998

THIS IS A BORZOI BOOK
PUBLISHED BY ALFRED A. KNOPF, INC.

www.randomhouse.com

Library of Congress Cataloging-in-Publication Data

Ridley, John.
Love is a racket : a novel / by John Ridley. — 1st ed.
p.   cm.
ISBN 0-375-40142-3
I. Title.
PS3568.I3598L68   1998
813'.54—dc21   98-15879
CIP

Manufactured in the United States of America
First Edition

To

Lisa

To

Beth

To

Gayle

21498/831/∞

For Raider:

My Long Shadow

ACKNOWLEDGMENTS

To Adam. Thanks for all the sage advice, and thank God you're on my side. Your skills are amazing, like Hal Jordan except without the insane desire to resurrect Coast City.

To Judith, Linda, Peter, and everyone at Ballantine for giving the finger to Hollywood.

To Sarah, Janet, Chip, Paul, and all at Knopf for your hard work. Especially the copy editors who had to wade through the way I use the language.

To Sonny for showing me that tighter doesn't mean shorter, just better.

To my crew at Pine and Assoc.: Sarah for all you do, Lori for spreading the word all over the world, and especially to Richard for not just selling books, but making sure the books are worth reading . . . but the cash don't hurt. It don't hurt a bit.

First Things First

*K*raop was the sound that I heard. Heard it twice—*kraop, kraop*—one time each for my two fingers that got broke. I heard my bones pop before I felt anything, gunshot-loud they echoed in my ears. Maybe that was the tip-off what'd just happened was going to hurt like hell.

Wrong.

It hurt so bad, I didn't feel a thing.

The hands that held me, Ty's hands—big like bear claws, strong like presses—let me go. I twisted to the ground, slow, the way a snowman melts. Couldn't help from going down. Something about having body parts mangled that messes with your lucidity. I gave that a lot of thought as I lay on the hard, dirty pavement that felt feather bed–comfy to my fucked-up senses. If I slept a million years in this outdoor bedroom I couldn't care less.

"Sorry, Jeffty," Ty said from somewhere above me. He meant it, too. I could hear it in his voice. It almost made me feel guilty. It almost made me feel like even though he'd just busted my fingers, somehow I was the bad guy.

All Dumas had to add to things was: "Let's see if we can't get me my money, do you know, Jeffty?"

I heard the two of them walk away. I heard them get in their Benz and drive off, the sound seemed to drift from the other side of the planet.

I was alone. On the ground. In an alley. I thought about getting up, but the growing throb in my swelling fingers told me otherwise. It said I should relax, take a rest, pass out for a while. Why not? I didn't have any plans; nowhere to go except a little further down in life than I already was, and there was plenty of time for that. I got cozy with the dirt and rubbish, and remained undisturbed. People passed by the lip of the alley, but they paid me no mind. Just another black man stretched out near some garbage cans. So what?

So nothing.

So life went on around me. I took my fingers' advice and went to sleep.

Later, I came to. The same throbbing in my fingers that'd passed me out woke me up. Except sometime during my minicoma, the dull pain had gone through a metamorphosis into full agony. Agony that instructed me in the strongest possible terms to get to a hospital.

Hospital. That's what I'd thought. Free clinic is what I'd meant.

I made the long climb to my feet, the five-thousand-mile journey to my car, and drove. I did my best not to look at the fingers, but you got broken fingers, how can you not look at them? They were bloated and a deep black-purple. They twisted up and back away from the other fingers of my hand like decrepit branches on a tree that refused to grow right. It only took a second or two of staring at them before I started choking on my own vomit.

Fairfax. The free clinic. A nurse—a woman in a nurse's uniform—at the receiving window, neatly tucked away behind bulletproof glass.

"Here." She shoved a clipboard with a sheet of paper attached through a slot in the window. Her tone told me she was annoyed, like me showing up had interrupted whatever she'd been doing that was far more important than helping injured people. "Fill this out and bring it back when you're done."

The woman in the nurse's uniform spoke without looking up. She spoke as if she said the same thing every sixty seconds whether there was someone there to hear her or not.

I took a seat and went to work on the forms. There was a gunshot victim, a stabbing, and some guy with hedge clippers in his thigh ahead of me. Around this part of LA, a lousy twisted finger or two isn't much as emergencies go. I guess they figured trying to do paperwork with my busted appendages would just about eat up enough time for them to get to me.

It didn't.

I sat for I don't know how long, my arm raised, my fingers looking like I was trying to point up and around a corner at the same time, waiting. Just like Gunshot Guy and Hedge Clippers Guy kept waiting.

What health care crisis?

I took the opportunity to pass out some more. When I came awake again there was a nurse — another woman in a nurse's uniform — yelling at me for not finishing my forms and pushing me toward an examining table. As I walked, the world started to do funny things. It juked and jived and turned to soft matter under my feet. I thought, Rather than deal with the yelling woman and the liquefying ground, it might be better if I pass out for a while more. It was getting so I could do it on cue. There was a circus job waiting for me somewhere. Jeffty, the one-trick wonder. See him get roughed up. See him go down like a prom queen. Then witness the marvel of him going lights-out at the first hint of pain or bother.

A crazy dreamlike big top floated through my fuzzy mind. It was full of scary clowns, and lion tamers with nothing to do, and a guy sporting a turban.

Only . . . the guy with the turban wasn't part of the dream. The guy with the turban, as my eyes fluttered open, was standing over me. As I got my wits back, I figured Turban Guy, skinny and greasy-looking, must have been a doctor. At least, maybe he was a doctor in the country he came from which was probably the same as being an auto mechanic in the civilized nation that I called home. This one looked like he should be selling fruit from a freeway off-ramp as much as operating on people.

"It is bad. It is very bad," he said. I think he said. His command of English was about that of someone who had mastered it just that morning. "You should have had this looked at immediately," he scolded. "Why did you not have this looked at immediately?"

Sure. It was all my fault. Whatever. I didn't say anything to that. I just let Turban Guy finish setting my fingers with splints and medical tape. When he was done hacking around with my hand, he wrote out a prescription for painkillers, codeine, he wanted me to go have filled, as if I had the money to fill it. Twice as strong as aspirin at five times the cost. Nice racket.

But don't think I wouldn't find a way to come up with the cash. Codeine ain't heroin, but it'll get you high, and there's always a junkie out there looking for some kind of a fix. I could turn around and sell that shit on the street for a healthy profit.

What about my fingers?

What about them?

I could live with the hurt. Cash is my painkiller.

The Long Shadow

Morning. A new day.

Money. I needed it. Not just to have and to hold and to spend like normal people. I needed it in a near desperation that I went to bed with at night, and woke up to at dawn. More so now in the week since my fingers got broke.

My good luck was LA's a great place to work. Except for the smog and the gang violence, the brushfires in the summer, the rain and floods in the winter, it's great. It's a city of roads. Not just highways, and, yeah, LA's got lots of those. Roads: La Brea, Western, Wilcox, Sunset. The boulevards that made up Hollywood. At almost every intersection was a minimall, and in almost every minimall was a little mom-and-pop setup: liquor stores, drugstores, ninety-nine-cents stores, and their business was my business.

Highland and Santa Monica. I roll up in there to this dry cleaners. There's a man working the counter. Soon as I walk in, he's smiling at me. Smiles like he's got it tattooed on his face. Foreign guy. Not sure from where. Iran, or Lebanon, or Syria. I don't know. Just one of those Middle

Eastern countries where there's a war going on, and everybody's a refugee, and they still smile all the goddamn time.

"Good morning to you, sir," he says to me, thick with an accent from his yet-to-be-determined nation of origin. "What is it I may do for you?"

From my pocket: a twenty. "Got change?"

"Certainly," he says, or something that sounds like it. From the register he counts out a ten, a five, and five ones.

I keep the five, give him back the ten and the five ones, and ask for a five and ten ones, then tell him: "You know what? I'd rather have three fives and five ones."

As he does it I take a five and tell him that a ten and two fives would be best.

He gives it, I take it and go. Canadian buildup played low rent; I'm up ten as I'm out the door.

The guy behind the counter keeps smiling. Throws in a wave for good measure. Foreigners: They'd smile at you while you stole their teeth, then point out the ones you missed.

God love 'em.

Ten dollars in two minutes. I can do that at every dry cleaners, liquor store, and 7-Eleven there is, and there's one in every minimall, and there's a minimall on every corner, and there's nothing but corners in a city of roads.

The bitch of it was—and there was a major bitch to my life—all those corners and all those minimalls couldn't put enough cash in my hands to get me out from under Dumas's thumb.

The thought of it depressed me.

My depression asked for a drink.

I got in my car and drove. A Corvair I had. GM's little deathmobile. In LA you are what you drive. Me? I'm unsafe at any speed.

I headed the Corvair east, then north up across Sunset to Hollywood Boulevard, to the heart of Hollywood. Not the notional one of movie stars and beautiful people and ugly people with good plastic surgeons, but the one you can point to on a map. The one that runs from La Brea to Vermont, from Melrose to the hills north of Franklin.

Check the scenery: all along the boulevard sleeping bums puddled on the sidewalks. At a bus stop bench a man and a man trying hard as he could to look like a woman wagged tongues in each other's mouths. The rest was just boarded-up buildings, stores that saw more food stamps than cash, and a whole lot of people talking a whole lot of Mexican. Tinseltown. I couldn't stand the glamour.

Hollywood, the physical Hollywood with its low-rent lifestyle, is where you ended up when everything else you ever planned on, or dreamed about, or hoped for in life didn't pan out. The air stinks of desperation. Take a deep breath and see if you don't choke on the hopelessness.

Truth: About the only thing this city has going for it is the weather. No matter how bad you feel inside, it's always eighty degrees and sunny outside. I think that's just about all that keeps most of these people alive. Why kill yourself on a perfectly good day?

South on Cahuenga. The Regent. A bar. With movie stars and post-premiere parties that spilled over from the Pantages, at one time the Regent used to be stylin'.

Yeah, and at one time Al Jolson used to make for a sold-out show.

Not anymore.

No more limousines or black ties, and about the only star who ever came around these days was some soap throb who figured it was pretty much the safest place in town to rendezvous on the low pro with the guy he was fucking.

All the Regent was decent for anymore was drinking; for being left alone to stare at yourself in the bottom of a glass when you had to work things out. Good for me that's all I needed.

You've got to go through two doors to get into the bar. An outer door, down a short hall, then through an inner door. It's built that way so no sunlight leaks into the place. Sunshine never gets into the Regent. No windows, no skylights, nothing. High noon on the Fourth of July and the joint is black as a mine. That way you can drain your lunch without feeling like you're a midday alky. Not that any of the people in the Regent are the kind of drinkers who'd let a little thing like sunshine or time of day slow them down. Booze just tastes better in the dark.

"Hey, howzit, Jeffty?" Eddie's voice came at me from across the bar train-rumble deep and low. Eddie Gorodetsky was a wide guy. Five-eight, maybe, but as much around as he was tall. Not fat, mind you. There was just a lot to him. A lot to him except his left arm. He was a marine — and had enough tattoos to let you know so — and he'd lost his arm during the invasion of Grenada.

There's a bitch.

Bad enough getting hacked up, but it's not like you were in Nam or World War II. What are you going to tell your grandkids? You lost an arm protecting a bunch of American medical students who couldn't get into good schools?

"How about a shot of Jack?" I said as I dropped onto a bar stool.

"Ain't it a little early for that?"

"It ain't too early for you to be making money. You're open, and I'm drinking."

"So you're drinking, so have yourself a beer."

I felt myself starting to go a little stiff. I'd known Eddie for a long while, ever since things started going bad for me and I needed a place like the Regent to hide in. Like I said, a long while. I don't mind talking to Eddie, and I don't mind him messing with me from time to time. What I mind is a bartender who's got something against pouring drinks. "Something wrong with your Jack? You out of it?"

"I'm not out of—"

"Then what's the problem? Let's get to drinking." I threw a few bucks down on the bar in front of me. To a guy like Eddie, a guy who works for a living, the crash of money on the wood should have been car wreck–loud. Loud enough to get him to quit talking and start filling glasses.

Eddie didn't move. Not for the money anyway. With his right arm he scratched under the pit of the stump that hung from his left shoulder, but that was all he did.

I ran the back of a hand across my forehead. "What?"

"Not like you, drinking in the middle of the day. It's not like you."

"Jesus, Eddie—"

"It'd be different if you came in every day—"

"Then it'd be okay?"

"It'd be different."

"So I got to work my way up to an afternoon brace, that it? All right. Just give me a mai-tai, and make sure you put an umbrella in it."

"I'm just saying, Jeffty, I don't want to see you like that." Eddie ticked his head toward the back of the room. Dingy little people, men and women alike, hunched over their drinks. They looked like they were protecting them; like they were protecting little glasses of liquid gold.

Better than gold.

Gold was something they'd only lie and cheat for, but they'd beat their mothers to death for a sip of what was in those glasses.

"There was," Eddie said, "this studio guy in here the other day. Think he was trying to pick up a prostie. I don't approve of that shit, not in my place—"

"Eddie—"

"But he was buying top shelf, so . . . Anyway, this studio guy is in here drinking and yakking, and he's going on about this thing they got where he works. Some writer's thing."

"I don't want to hear about it."

"It's special for minorities, you know? Maybe he's just trying to impress the whore, but I'm thinking: Hey, Jeffty should—"

"I don't want to hear about it!" I exploded with that. I surprised Eddie. I surprised me, too. "I'm, sorry."

"S'okay," he mumbled. Big ex-marine all tattooed up, but he was still friend enough of mine to be hurt by my outburst.

I said: "Eddie, that shit's all passed up for me, you know? I can't . . . I don't . . . All I want is a little juice to help the afternoon go by. I'm having a bad week."

"I know. Dumas's been in here looking for you."

"Yeah." I rubbed at my busted fingers. "He's been finding me, too."

Eddie wagged his stump at me. "Trust me, Jeffty. Booze don't make the pain go away. And compared to me, what you got is a hangnail."

"Oh, for Christ's sake, Eddie! All I want is a drink."

Eddie didn't say anything to that; he just stared at me. I looked down at my palms and rubbed them together. I ran a hand over my scalp, looked back at the people sitting behind me—still dingy, still guarding their liquid gold. After all that, I looked back up at Eddie. He still stared down at me. You'd get more movement from a rock than I did from him.

Eddie said: "Why you do it? Why you get mixed up with a lowlife like Dumas?"

I didn't give it much thought, but I didn't need to. There really wasn't an answer. "Gambling's the only pleasure I got left. I don't pick which lowlifes come with the action."

"So you like to gamble. So you go to Vegas."

"Been to Vegas. Vegas don't give odds like Dumas."

"Vegas don't break fingers either."

"And the bartenders don't break balls; they just pour drinks."

I could hear Eddie's teeth slide against each other. He slapped a shot glass down in front of me, ripped up a bottle of Jack Daniel's, and threw some at the glass. Some of it made its way in. He took up the bills from the counter and offered no change, not that I had much coming.

Glass in hand, I went to a table that rested in a pool of dark at the tail end of the room. I looked back at Eddie, wiping down the counter where I'd sat as if wiping away the memory of me. In all the time I'd known him, I'd never known him like that: particular about who drank what when. Course, in all the time I'd known him, I'd never come in drinking in the middle of the afternoon.

So what? That didn't make me like them—like the rest of the ghosts who hovered nearby above their little tables and their little glasses with little drinks that fueled their little lives.

I looked down at my glass. A small bit of my face gave me a look back from the brownish liquid. Just a shot glass full of booze, but I would drink it slow, I thought. Nurse it. I would show Eddie; I didn't need this.

I made it about a minute, putting up a good front of not even thinking about the drink. But that's all it was was a front. Not a second ticked by that my mouth didn't seem to get packed fuller with cotton. But I didn't drink. I wanted Eddie to see me. I wanted him to get an eyeful of me just sitting there content as can be with that glass still brimming.

He wouldn't look at me.

He wiped the bar, chatted, counted change. Did everything but look at me.

I knew he was doing it on purpose. It was going to be a test of wills. I could do it. I could wait him out.

I almost made two minutes before I tossed back the glass and let the Jack run down my throat, a cupful of fire.

When my head came down I saw Eddie staring my way, smiling at me like he expected me to race back to him and beg for another round.

Fuck you, you one-armed bastard. I can wait you out. I can wait for another round.

"Wanna buy a watch, Jeffty?"

I hadn't seen her sneak up on me. Amber's breath filled my nose before her voice reached my ears. It was soaked in alcohol. A whiff of it was enough to send a reformed drunk back on a binge. I turned to her and got a faceful of some cheap knockoff Rolex. The gold on the band was chipping, and the silver—what passed for silver—was badly tarnished. Still, she held it there, full of confidence, like she was about to cut me in on the deal of the century.

"Wanna buy a watch?" Amber said again.

"Got a watch."

"But you ain't got a Rolex."

"If I bought that I still wouldn't have one."

Amber gave a little laugh. "C'mon, Jeffty. What do you think? I'm just going to sell you some crap? Is that what you think?"

Amber was such a pretty name for such an unpretty woman to own. She probably was pretty once, a long time ago, when she first stumbled into Hollywood wanting to be an actress, a singer, a model—anything other than what she was; anything other than the bum she'd become. She was probably a knockout back then. Tight, beautiful skin, smooth as ice and just as clear. Rich, flowing hair and the kind of blue pools for eyes you could swim in. Most likely Amber was the kind of woman who got invited to all the right parties, met all the right people. I bet she fucked like a hellcat, too.

Like I said: a long time ago.

The years had been about as kind to Amber as a whip to a dog. She was maybe fifty-some, but looked twenty years beyond that. Her face had furrows, not lines, and her flesh sagged and drooped away from the bone. Blotches dotted her skin like flecks of paint. And the veins—the thick red-and-blue drinker's veins stitched all across her face like they were the only things holding her features in place.

Sad. Maybe. Or maybe it was just pathetic: a worn-out beauty queen hawking cheap watches, or any other shit she could get her hands on just to make her booze money. That was her racket. I didn't know what drove Amber from where she was to where she is, and to be honest I didn't care. I just wanted to know what it would take to drive her from my table.

"Fifty bucks, Jeffty. I'm giving you a deal."

"Fifteen-hundred-dollar watch for fifty? Why you being so good to me?"

"I'm your friend, Jeffty. Ain't that what friends are for?"

I gave a little laugh and reached for my drink. I had the glass halfway to my mouth before I remembered I had already emptied it. My eyes shifted to the bar and I saw Eddie watching me with a shit-eatin' grin.

Fuck you, Eddie.

"It tells time real good. And it'll look good on you. Look at it on you."

She tried to work the watch onto my wrist. I swatted her back like I was swatting a pesky insect. And like a pesky insect she kept buzzing around for more.

"How you gonna pass it up? Forty dollars? How you gonna pass that up?"

"Forty?" I could feel the cotton getting packed back into my mouth.

"'Cause you're a friend, like I said. All I need is forty. That's all I'm asking."

My throat went bone-dry and started to itch. It was the kind of itch only a good shot of liquor could scratch away.

"Why you always got to put the bite on me, Amber? Place full of people, city full of souls, and you always got to try to squeeze me."

"Christ, Jeffty. Hot like hell outside and you want me to wander round looking for money?"

"I don't care where you look for it. I just don't want—"

"It ain't easy for me, Jeffty. There's nothing young about me anymore. I put in the hours—on the street, in the sun—but I don't make nothing for it. It seems like every year I got to spend more time making less."

"You and the rest of America," I said without thinking about it. I said it while thinking how I was going to get another drink without letting that bastard Eddie have his satisfaction.

"Thirty dollars. All I'm asking."

It was only because Eddie was giving me shit; that was the reason I was thinking so hard about another drink. I didn't need it. I didn't.

"I'm begging you, Jeffty. I can't go back outside. I been out there forever, and I can't do it no more. Look what it's done to me."

"Get yourself a new racket."

"Look at me!"

Her voice bit into me hook-sharp and whipped my head around. I looked at her, really looked at her for the first time since she'd come around my table. The side of her face was puffed and swollen. Where it wasn't bruised and ugly, crusted blood scabbed her flesh. It was bad. The fact that she was old only made it worse.

"This is what they did to me. Those sons of bitches out there; they see I got a little money, and they do this. They beat me in the street and nobody stop for me. Nobody give a damn."

A tear ran from her eye down the bruises and the blood and the swelling, mixed with snot from her nose, and dripped from her chin.

"I don't want to go back out there." Amber sounded scared and pitiable. She pointed at her face. "All that's out there is more of this."

She looked away ashamed. Ashamed of having gone from pinup girl to street hustler. Ashamed of letting some punks beat her for what little she had. Ashamed of having to come to a nobody like me for enough dough to make it through the day.

When she looked back at me, she saw the fifty bucks I held out for her. She snatched it fast like I might change my mind on the offer. And I might've changed it, too, except I was such a soft touch.

"You're gonna like this watch; look good on you. All the women are gonna love you."

She held the watch out to me, but I pushed it back. "Keep it, Amber. Pass it off on some other mark."

"You paid for it. It keeps nice time."

I shrugged. "The only time a watch tells me is how much time I've got left. Personally, I'd rather not know."

I felt something crawling up the back of my neck. At first, I thought it was a bug, but then I remembered it was that drink I'd been wanting.

Fuck Eddie. If I want a drink, I'll—

I'm not used to loud noises. Nobody in the Regent is. That's why you go to the Regent—for the dark and the quiet. That and the cheap sauce. So when the loud noise came rolling in, for a second everyone got real nervous and they clutched their drinks a little tighter. Then I saw what the noise was all about: Wesker busting through the door like he was leading a marching band.

"Line 'em up," he yelled at Eddie. "Line 'em up good an' long. Everybody gets a round on me."

Wesker tossed a hundred toward the bar carelessly, like it was wet tissue he'd finally shaken loose from his fingers.

Wesker. Just another con, just another heel grifter who spent every day trying to stretch a couple of bills into a party same as the rest of us. This time he was buying the party, and the way he was throwing money around it was a black-tie affair. It was pretty obvious Wesker had gotten lucky. Or gone stupid.

The second Wesker's hundred hit the bar it was surrounded by grabbing hands and empty eyes that wanted their free round. Most of them didn't know Wesker, and hardly a one of them said anything that came close to a thanks. That would slow them down too much; give someone else time to get the drink that was meant for them.

Wesker came over to my table. I guess I passed for a familiar face. He swung around a chair and sat, draping an arm around Amber and me like we were long-lost dear friends. Sad part is, for Wesker we were about as close to being friends as he had.

"I hit it this time. This time I hit it big."

"Hit what?" I asked.

Wesker just smiled at me and brushed back his long blond hair. Usually he wore it in a ponytail, which I always hated because it reminded me of the male models and asshole agents who crawled over every inch of this town. Wesker was a not bad-looking guy, just starting to get that "I spend too much time in a bar" pallor and the dry, flaky drinker's skin that goes with it.

"Hey, Eddie!" Wesker called across the room. "How about some service over here?" He shook a twenty in the air to let Eddie know he meant business. To Amber and me: "What do you two want, some wine?"

Wesker didn't even give us a chance to answer, but the fact is, if he was buying Amber and I were drinking.

"Eddie," Wesker yelled again. "Get some wine over here. Three glasses."

It would be a while before I got my lips on that drink. Eddie was swamped, doling out the free rounds Wesker had just bought as fast as his one arm would let him.

Amber: "I'll bite. You win the lotto?"

"Better than that." He drew us in close, the wise master about to impart the secret of life to his two favorite disciples. "A bank job. I pulled a bank job, and I got away with it."

"You didn't get away with anything," I told him straight out and unimpressed. "There's no getting away with a bank job."

Wesker had nothing but a smile for that. "I did. I walked in, and three minutes later I walked out with thirty-two grand. A little more. Thirty-two thousand as easy as that."

"The cameras—" I started.

He dismissed me with a shake of his head. "That's the sweet part. No cameras. I got a friend at that bank; he's a maintenance engineer—"

"He's a janitor."

"Yeah, he's a janitor. So what he's a janitor? But he's got a memo from the bank that says they've got to do some work on the security system at ten-thirty today. Ten-thirty." His mouth went wide with a grin. "That's just when I happen to roll in there."

Eddie came round with the wine and glasses. Wesker got quiet for a minute. Before the bottle touched the table Amber grabbed it up and started pouring.

Wesker put the finish on his story. "No alarms, no cameras, no evidence. Just thirty-plus thousand."

"Except if your friend decides to talk."

"Oh, no. Ain't no talking for him to do, Jeffty. He don't know I found the memo. It was in his trash."

That hit me sideways. "What are you doing going through your friend's trash?"

Wesker stopped cold and his eyes went narrow. He worked up a look that was somewhere between hurt and angry, like he couldn't decide how he should feel that I wasn't falling at his feet over his big score.

"It don't matter," he said, voice barb-wired. "It don't matter why. I just was."

"Okay. You were."

Amber hadn't said a word. She could give a fuck less where the money to buy the drinks came from. All she knew was talking slowed her drinking, so she opted for drinking.

"Thing of it is," Wesker went on trying to prove his brilliance, "I'm going through the trash, I see the work order, I know what time the system's going down, I hustle in, wave a gun, and I take the money just like that. That's how simple it is to get thirty-two thousand dollars."

I laughed. I didn't even mean to; I just did. "It's not that easy. You think they're just going to let that kind of money go?"

"They got no choice."

"They got cops that's all they do is look for guys who roll banks."

Smiling sweet: "They don't know who they're looking for."

The sweeter Wesker got on the deal, the madder I did. "It's a federal offense, you know that? You do time, you do federal time, and a fed pen is nothing but badasses and lifers. Jesus Christ, the warden's gonna rape you."

That got to Wesker, but only so much as a slap on the side gets to an elephant. He threw back some wine, and chased it with another glassful. "You don't get it." Wesker leaned deep into my face like he wanted me to see his words as he spat them out. "I'm not doing time. I'm not going inside, 'cause don't nobody know who they're looking for."

"You don't even—"

"Leave him alone," Amber busted in. "He pulled a big one, and you're jealous, that's all." She got all up on his arm and cooed. "I'm happy for you. To hell with Jeffty. I'm happy."

He kissed her. Full on the lips he did. With no regard to her dirt, her bruises, her smell, Wesker kissed Amber. Amber kissed Wesker right back.

That's what drunk people do, and these two were drunk as drunks come. He was full up on the money three minutes of flashing a gun got him, and she with the booze it bought. A perfect couple.

I wanted to grab Wesker by the shoulders and shake him awake. I wanted to tell him how bad he'd messed up, how soon it would be before a couple of cops not bright enough to light up a shoe box would stumble over a mistake he'd made big as a truck, then reach out and clamp a hand on his shoulder.

Only they wouldn't.

Only Wesker hadn't messed up. From the way he laid it out, there were no mistakes I could figure. Here he was just a cheap grifter, but he'd lucked right into the payday I'd been waiting my whole life for. Maybe it was like Amber said: Maybe I was jealous.

I thought about it—about the $32,000, about what kind of misery $32,000 could buy me out of. My bad fingers started to burn.

I'd had enough of the Regent for the afternoon. I crawled back out into the daylight. Back into the Corvair. Back into Hollywood looking for another ten dollars.

I drove. A lot.

I worked. Some.

I made money. A little. A very little. Enough to buy a few days' worth of food.

Sunset took me west past La Brea to Ralphs. The twenty-four-hour Ralphs. The rock-and-roll Ralphs where wannabe music stars went to buy their food, if they ate. Some of them were so thin—sporting that heroin look, which was apparently very popular among the rock set—they looked like the kids Sally Struthers is always whining about.

Grabbed up a basket, walked the aisles. Tossed in some rice, frozen burritos, canned chili: no-brainers. Nothing that would take more than a couple of minutes to make, and I could eat out of the pan I fixed it in.

Turned down an aisle. Soups, pasta. Stopped at a case of Ramen noodles. Ten packs to a case. Easy as hell to make. Boil water, drop 'em in, five minutes later you've got noodles in their own soup. Pour 'em over rice and you've got a bowlful of the hottest, steamiest, blandest shit you ever choked down. I hated it, but I could make it and I could afford it, so I lived off it.

My stomach started clawing at me, begging me not to buy the noodles. For the love of God, it churned, you got a whole storeful of food. You want to punish yourself, okay, but why you gotta punish me, brother?

Down the aisle and across were the meats: hamburger, pork. Steak. A big, juicy T-bone was sitting there waiting for me to pick it up, take it home, and treat myself right. And why not? Why shouldn't I just once, just one single time, be good to me?

A girl turned up the aisle. She wore cowboy boots and a sundress like a thousand other LA chicks who read the same fashion magazines. But she wore them over tanned flesh, tight muscles, a curved ass, and tits pushed up like someone had welded steel girders under them.

I looked at her. I looked hard. She saw me looking and she didn't care, so I looked more. I could have done it all day. Weak with hunger, dead tired, a bullet to the head. Didn't matter. I could've kept up a stare at that girl for as long as my eyes worked. She didn't hurt a bit.

That's when she did it. She didn't look around to see if anyone was watching, if anyone might catch her. Made her no difference. She grabbed the hem of her sundress and flipped it up. Flipped it so I could see her pussy. No underwear, not even a tan line. Just bronze lips framed by golden blond hair that looked better than what most women had on top of their heads.

It happened fast; her dress went up and down. So fast I could have missed it, except it burned into my mind branding iron–hot, and deep where it would probably stay for the rest of my life. A little longer even.

I opened my mouth, or rather it just fell open like I was a living cartoon. It opened not to say anything—what could I say? Thanks? Nice pussy? Where do you get your hair done? My mouth opened because you couldn't just stand there, see what I'd seen, and not do anything.

That's when he came around the corner. Jeans ripped in all the right places. Denim shirt hanging out from under a rumpled black sports coat.

Sunglasses indoors. The kind of guy who spent hours in front of a mirror trying to get that "disheveled look."

I would have figured him for a West Hollywood fag except for the way he grabbed up the girl, low near her ass, pulled her to him, tits pressing up over the top of her dress as their chests met, and slid his tongue between her lips. Yeah, except for all that I might have thought him for gay.

They headed down the aisle away from the soup and the pasta, and especially from me. As they walked on the girl tossed me a parting gift. A little smile that screamed: Fuck you, sucker. You can't have me.

I could have just gone in and out of that store plain and simple same as a thousand other people every day. I could have, but this happened. It happened so I'd know what I always thought I knew anyway: Some men were born to be with well-tanned, well-toned, big-titted, fine-pussied women. And some men . . .

I left the steak alone, grabbed up the carton of noodles, checked out.

The second I was out the door the sun, the smog, the noise, the bad karma that syruped over the city, they all went back to sanding away my humanity—mine, and the 8 million other people trapped in the gulag LA.

"Change," a voice said up at me.

Outside Ralphs, by the door, on the curb: a girl, a street tramp, a run-away. Dirty-faced with hair matted so that it hung in clumps. Two, three days without a bath? Still, with all that, she had looks. Decent body. Her skin was not quite tan, but of that color naturally, like she was Mediter-ranean, or something. No doubt, being a street girl, she sold herself to stay afloat. With a body like hers, I wondered, how come she doesn't live a little better?

The girl held out a palm to me. The girl said to me: "Change?"

I kept staring at her. While I was staring at her, I kept thinking she reminded me of someone. Not like someone I had ever met, but like someone I knew, or knew of, but right then I couldn't figure who. Or maybe it was with that body she just looked like a girl I'd want to get to know.

"Change?" she asked one more time.

Yeah, I had some. I kept it. I got in the Corvair and drove.

.　.　.

Yucca. My street. Home. Home being an apartment building of soot-covered walls, a funny smell, and a zoo of insects that could not be sprayed, stomped, or bludgeoned out of existence.

I parked on the street, went in, took the stairs up to the third floor. There was an elevator, but it wasn't working. Just like it wasn't working the day before, and the day before that, and every day since I'd moved in going on seven years prior. I'd complain to the landlord, but let's say I'm the type who doesn't always get his rent together on a fixed date.

The stairway was filled with the sound of screaming voices. Screaming because they were mad, or screaming because they were having great sex, or screaming because they were in the middle of getting killed. Whatever way it was, the screams didn't have nothing to do with me.

By the time I reached the third floor I had worked up a good sweat. The heat congregated up there at the top of the building and I had to push through it like it was some curtain that hung the length of the hallway.

My apartment was 316. One-bedroom. Small and cheap with cheap furniture to match, the black wooden crap that lasted just long enough for you to realize how very cheap it looked. But on the upside, the apartment came with a stunning view of the wall of the building right next to mine.

I fixed a drink, just a little something to fight back the heat. I reminded myself when I got through all this shit with Dumas, if I got through all this shit with Dumas, I should cut down on the booze. I reminded myself that as I fixed drink number two.

I stripped and ran an electric razor over my head. I used to be balding and worried to hell about how I looked as a balding guy. One day I decided: Fuck it; just shave your head. I don't worry about going bald anymore. It just gives me more time to worry about everything else in my life.

I showered up, but by the time I toweled off, I was sweating just as hard as when I'd come in. Over to a chair, I flopped into it with nothing but the towel wrapped around me and worked on drink number three. I was putting on pounds. With just the towel on, I could see that. I wasn't a fat slob yet, but I was creeping that way. I was tall, not too much so, just a little more than average so that the weight I put on ballooned around my waist. It wouldn't take but a little exercise, a few sit-ups, to work me into some kind of shape; to pull me back from the edge of plumpness. Just a few sit-ups, that's all.

I picked up *TV Guide* instead. *TV Guide* said *The Big Combo* with

Cornel Wilde was on tonight. *TV Guide* lied. Anyway, I found a show to watch. More rightly, I found a show that wasn't as loud, or annoying, or offensive as the others, so I left it on and stared at the moving images that swirled in a mixture of soothing blue light. TV was so comfortable, so dependable. TV was my friend. Thank you, God, for TV.

I sat there, me in nothing but a towel on a hot day in a third-rate apartment, drinking in front of the tube. I would've felt lonely and near terminally depressed, but I was so used to my life all I felt was content. The drink and the television numbed me well, and I decided it was time for sleep.

My bedroom. A futon, matted and years dirty with sweat stains. I crawled into it, not bothering with covers, and started to drift off. I thought more about Dumas, and the money I owed, and how I was going to pay it back, and what parts of my body were going to get busted up when I didn't, because I knew I couldn't. All that was my bedtime story.

I started thinking, or the booze started thinking for me, why: why at thirty-plus years of age all I've got to show for myself is a dirty bed in a dirty apartment, money that won't make it from hand to pocket, and a guy who slaps me around like I'm his whore in a city of heat and violence to call home. Why do I live like this? As I lay in my bed, I felt more like I was sitting in a tight, dark corner being punched and pummeled, but not knowing where from or who by. And yet, there in the other room was the door that would lead to the hall which I could walk to my car so I could drive this city of roads to someplace that was anyplace else, but not here. All that was just steps away. Steps I couldn't bring myself to take.

I remembered, or the booze helped me remember, a bird I once had. A parakeet. Kept it in a cage. For a long time, I never took it out because I always figured it'd get away. One day I decided to take the bird from the cage. I don't know, I was feeling generous. I closed all the windows in the apartment. It couldn't go anywhere; it couldn't fly free as it pleased. But I figured anything would be better than being stuck in a cage. The second I took the bird out of the cage, quick as it could it flew straight back in. I took it out again, but as soon as I let go it couldn't get behind those bars fast enough. I gave up. The cage was the only thing it knew, and that's where it wanted to be.

I fell asleep.

Or the booze did it for me.

Tiiin," he whined. He whined it again. "Tiiin." Some kind of accent obscured most of his English. A voice like a cat caught under a truck tire hid the rest of it. An Oriental guy, the market owner was, but not Korean.

Don't mess with Koreans.

Koreans got no love of black people. Out here a while back, a Korean shop owner shot a little black girl in the head for stealing a thing of orange juice. Judge gave the shop owner probation. Might as well have thrown in a foot massage with it. What's Korean for "open season on niggers"?

Once more with the whine: "I give you tiiin, you give me five and five single, riiight?"

He was following along. He was asking questions, slowing the whole trick down. From the street I thought he'd be an easy mark. Look at him: greasy hair, sweat-sheened face, Hawaiian-print shirt—washed dull—worn over a dirty T-shirt and pale gray pants. Sandals and black socks.

Sandals and black socks!

He wore stuff the Salvation Army wouldn't take, and here he was screwing up my grift.

Truth: People aren't always as dumb as they dress.

"You give me fiiive, and I give your tiiin back."

"Uh, yeah." I smiled. This was going nowhere.

The electric eye at the door buzzed as it opened. Someone else coming in. Someone else watching. Someone else rushing me along so they could get served, busting my groove. This I didn't need.

I didn't know how much I didn't need it.

"Let's go, Jeffty."

I went tight; my muscles stitched together. The voice plenty familiar.

"Dumas wants to see you." Ty. One of Dumas's boys. His best boy. The same one who took my usable fingers from ten down to eight.

"Give me a minute," I said. Cool, as if being cool was going to buy me anything.

"No minute. No nothing." Ty was cool, too; it's just his went further. His cool talked tougher. "Dumas wants to see you."

"Just let me—"

"Tiiin, tiiin." The Oriental worked his whine in.

"Yeah, I—" I started.

"Give me a tiiin."

I was fazed from the second Ty walked in. The last time Dumas went looking for me I got bones broken. I knew him wanting to see me now, there wasn't likely any flowers and thank-yous involved.

I handed a ten to the Oriental without even thinking about it. I was trying to work out other things, like if maybe I'd be alive at the end of the day.

Ty said again: "Come on, Dumas—"

"You said. He wants to see me." I turned and looked Ty straight in the eyes. Straight *up* into his eyes. Ty was big and beefy in a 100 percent muscle kind of way. I think he was born big, and I'm pretty sure he was one of those guys who didn't need a gym to keep looking that way. Some things came natural to Ty. His size, his ability to look good—despite his size—in a suit and tie, and, foremost, his ability to fuck you up.

I tried to give him a stare that was hard and cold and tough the way guys in movies looked hard and cold and tough. Imitating movie actors was the only way I knew how as I wasn't naturally hard or cold, and certainly not tough.

Ty smiled heavy, like this was the most amusing thing he'd seen all morning.

I walked out of the store.

Ty fell in behind me.

As I left, it came to me that I never took any money back from the Oriental.

Fuck.

In the midst of all my nervous jangling over how Dumas was going to respond to me not having his money—again—while I was trying to take the Oriental, the Oriental took me.

Fountain to Highland. South toward Century. Inglewood, we were going to.

Ty had a Benz. S-class. Snowflake white, like all Dumas boys rolled in. I sat in back, like I was getting chauffeur-drove to my own execution. I tried the little doohickey that worked the window and got nothing.

"Nice day out," I said, like I was saying it to no one in particular. "Sure would be nice if I could breathe some of it."

Ty looked up at me in the rearview mirror. Nothing in his eyes. No anger. No pity. No nothing. He just looked up at me like he was looking at a sack of food he was carrying home from the grocer. He reached over to the armrest and the window next to me sank. Not far. Not far enough for me to jump out, as if jumping out of a moving car into traffic is ever a good idea. I just sat there and sucked up lungful after lungful of that thick chocolaty LA air.

As we rode south into the shitty—even shittier—parts of LA, we passed some ghetto houses, which was a peculiar thing to Los Angeles: houses in the ghetto. Our poor had houses, and our bums had tans.

Outside one of the houses, kids played with a shipping box they had gotten hold of. A big box for a dishwasher or refrigerator or something.

And now what was it? A castle, a fort, a spaceship? Something out of nothing. The kids—they smiled; they laughed. They didn't have a thought about anything beyond that box. Not the people on the street, not the traffic, not the big white Benzes that took guys where they didn't want to go. They just played. Fuck Disneyland. Who needs that when you've got a box? That's the way it is when you're a kid: Nothing is ever just nothing, and everything is fresh with possibilities.

I don't know why I thought about that, about those kids as they played. I just did. And I thought about how I used to be like them—young and full of chances.

Used to be.

Maybe.

Before I even knew I was saying anything, I was saying: "Why do you do this?" Ty didn't know if I was talking to him. I didn't know *why* I was talking to him, but I was, so I said it again. "Why do you do this?"

Ty laughed a little, then came back with: "'Cause you owe, Jeffty. You owe big."

"I don't mean that. I don't mean why you taking me to Dumas. Why do you work for him? Why do you do this for a living?"

More laughing. "What should I be doing, Jeffty? Huh? Selling shoes, maybe? Maybe patio furniture? Or how about used cars? Same kind of business, sort of; milking people, I guess. You tell me: What should I be doing?"

"You're not like them."

"Who? I'm not like—"

"Dumas. His whole crew."

"I'm not Haitian. That what you mean?"

"I mean you're not a goon. They're goons—big, dumb, and slow. You're not any of that. Big, sure, but you've got a brain. You've got . . ." I caught Ty looking at me in the rearview; staring at me full of suspicion.

"What are you trying to do? Make nice so I'll go soft on you?"

"I'm just saying. You're different from them. So, why do you do it?"

Ty thought about it. He gave it more thought than most would a question I had no business asking. When he got done thinking, he said: "Compton."

"Whereabouts?"

"Alvaro. Near Central."   .

I knew that area. Knew enough to stay away from it.

"'Round there a brother just spends his days marking time. When you're a kid, you dodge bullets on the playground, and the dope dealers who line up for business outside the schoolyard. Get to be ten, eleven, twelve you got to start choosing sides: which gang you gonna run with. And soon as you're in one, you start watching the older kids, the soldiers, get killed." Ty made a sound, part huff and part laugh. "Older kids. Some thirteen, some almost fifteen. Yeah, but 'round there that's about as old as you get. I decided I wanted to get a little older."

"So you got with Dumas."

"Got with Dumas. Got paid well. Got an education. Took the money I made running for him and hooked up some extension courses at Cal State, Long Beach. Most of those niggas where I come from couldn't point to Long Beach if you opened a map right to it. Now look at me: I know shit. I speak right. I read. And I'm not just talking about titty magazines. You want to know who I'm not like, Jeffty? I'm not like those shines back where I grew up."

"And all that learning's kept you humble, too."

"It's kept me alive. I'm twenty-four, Jeffty. In my part of the world that's goddamn ancient. Dumas isn't a banger. He's a bookie, pure and simple. Bookies don't deal with hard-asses; no dope, no gangs—"

"What kind of people do they deal with?"

"People like you."

"And what kind is that?"

Without a thought: "Losers. Look at you, Jeffty. How old are you?"

"Thirty-five." I lied, short by two years.

Ty's head shook. "Thirty-five," he repeated, like he knew what he repeated wasn't quite true. "Thirty-five and you're nothing but a scared little con with busted fingers."

"Thanks to you."

"Sorry about that."

It was the second time Ty had apologized to me for breaking my fingers. And, as with the first time, I felt he sincerely meant it. All that sincerity wouldn't keep him from snapping them again, or any other part of me, if Dumas told him to.

Ty went on. "You've got to admit, Jeffty, you're a little pathetic. More than that. I whistle, and you come crawling into the car like a lost dog gone days without food."

"Go on," I said like I didn't care. But it's hard not to care when a guy is poking you with a knife.

"Fifteen thousand. How long did it take you to get that deep?"

"Year and a half. Not including how the interest built up, about that."

"I could understand that all at once: A bad run, and you drop that in no time. But to let it eat away at you for a year and a half. To see it coming and not put on the brakes . . ." He laughed again. He was getting his money's worth on this ride. "Hell, Jeffty, even a horse isn't so dumb it won't swat the flies biting it. You're not even as smart as a big dumb animal."

I couldn't argue with that, so I didn't. "Yeah. I'm stupid."

"You are. You're the kind of brother who gives the rest of us a bad name."

"Sure. If it wasn't for me you'd be a bookie's flunky people could look up to. A real pillar of society; a strong-arm thug and a credit to his race." It was my turn to laugh, so I let loose. "Yeah, I'm stupid, but I'm smart enough to know it. You're not even that."

I thought my words clever. I guess they were. But from there on in things got very unamusing.

"Shut up, Jeffty. Do yourself a favor and shut up, or—"

"Or what? You'll beat me? You'll kill me? Take a number and wait your turn."

Big talk I tossed him. Why shouldn't I? I was feeling tough. I was feeling unstoppable. I had no fear, because in my heart I knew I was going to die. When a man knows he's going to die there isn't anything he can't do.

We made the rest of the ride in silence. Ty rolled up my window to mess with me. It wasn't much, but it was enough to get me hot and bothered. It was enough to give me a sweat so that my clothes were nothing but wet rags.

Inglewood. We pulled up to the Hollywood Park Casino. I knew it well enough. My antes alone must have built the carport. At least that.

A little Mexican in a red vest hopped in the car and valet-parked it. Ty clutched at my elbow, an unwilling date being forced to the prom, and walked me from the casino to Hollywood Park.

Hollywood Park was neither. It wasn't in Hollywood and it wasn't a park. It was a horse track, but *park* sounded nicer than *track*, same as "I spent my afternoon at the park" sounds nicer than "I lost this week's pay in the third at the track."

Big and beige and freckled with palm trees, it was just about out of place with the hard, hot asphalt reality all around it. The park was like an oasis come up out of the urban desert. Drink our cool water, it said. Relax awhile out of the sun. Play your money and dream a little dream. We're the sport of kings.

Ty guided me toward the Turf Club turnstile. Fifteen bucks just to get in. It was supposed to make the Turf Club more exclusive; keep the dregs out. I'd been up there before, and it wasn't fifteen bucks' worth of a better way to lose money than betting at trackside, but I guess for some people a ten and a five is a small price to pay to feel superior.

Ty watched as I worked some crumpled bills out of my pocket and fed them to the ticket girl. Dumas wants to see me, Dumas wants to kill me, and I've got to pay fifteen bucks out of my own pocket for the pleasure. Ty got more laughs out of this. I was making his day.

We walked in, me and Ty, his hand still on my elbow, past a cheap little man in a cheap little tux. It was the park's attempt at a touch of class. Except that it was white-hot out. The cheap little man in the cheap little tux was soaking in his own sweat. He stamped our hands with one of those inks that only show up under fluorescent light. More of the exclusivity the fifteen bucks bought you.

We worked our way up the track: the grandstands, the clubhouse. Middle of the day, middle of the week. The joint was packed. Grubby little people who looked like they thought the sole function of the U.S. government was to write checks and hand out cheese bumped up against Yuppies who'd most likely told their bosses they were just going to the mail room to run off some copies. Pretty much anyone who had two bucks to rub together had a passport to the glamorous world of horse racing and daydreaming.

Check it out over there: a fat one-legged guy in a wheelchair working a crooked arm up to the window to lay a bet. Sad. That big stain spreading over his trousers where he'd just pissed himself couldn't even make it sadder. Sport of kings.

Sure.

Sport of stupid bastards who don't know that losers are always losers, and there ain't a trifecta in the world that'll change that.

The stamp on my hand glowed under the fluorescent lamp just like it was supposed to for the guy at the Turf Club door to see, if he had been looking, which he wasn't. The park's little con ran out of steam right there. This guy, the guy at the door, might work for them, but he's not buying into their show. Everything about him—the way he slouched against the door frame, the way his head lolled as if he was in the middle of a death-defying act of sleeping upright—everything said: Go on. Go on in. Upstairs, downstairs; I don't care where you lose your money. It's all five and a quarter an hour to me.

The stands of the Turf Club were less than half-full. Ty escorted me in just as a race started. The crowd, what crowd there was, let go with yelps for their horses as if with the shrill of their voices they could push the animals down the backstretch. Such a real thrill, such a genuine excitement for horses that weren't there.

It was off-season at the park. No racing. No horses. Just a flock of pink flamingos that soaked in the pond at center track, and a pair of water trucks that circled the turf wetting it down. Other than that, nothing. The races were being run at Santa Anita, or up at Golden Gate. Every single person at the track had paid their money and laid their bets to watch races run miles away on closed-circuit TV.

Dumas sat at a table, his usual table, eating his usual meal and drinking his usual cool drink. He was surrounded by his usual boys; hangers-on who yes-manned him to death and ate his shit for the money he paid. But he paid good, and the right amount of cash helped choke down even the unpalatable taste of feces. Most of his boys were interchangeable. Just scum that was dipped off the top of a Haitian cesspool, had made its way Stateside, and would make more dough working for their man than I could dream of in a week of fantasizing.

Dumas was too busy watching the race to pay me much mind. At least he was too busy acting like he was watching the race to pay any attention to me. Let me stand there soaking up the sun, waiting; that was Dumas's style, and Dumas was all style. Skin that was dark and rich and clean of defect. Get a load of the way he drapes it in a white silk shirt and white pants. Ninety-five, a hundred out, hot so you break a sweat just coming up with a deep thought, and not a drop of perspiration on him. Cool. Always cool. That was his style, too.

Hair cut nice and tight, clean shaven. Dumas even flashed a manicure. You can be that way when you don't have to lift a finger. Not to work, not to live, not to count your gambling money . . . not to get a man dead, which was also his style.

And his voice; his accent: French, or French-Haitian if that mattered, but French-sounding. Soft. Soft so you'd think he was a fag if you didn't know. Sweet. Sweet so that he could make anything he was talking about sound pleasant—beatings, torture, breaking limbs, which were all things he talked of often. His voice had a way of making them seem . . . not so bad.

Miles away, in Santa Anita, the horses rounded the far turn and thundered down the straightaway. Most of them, horses that ran like all they thought about was the day when they'd finally get to be put to stud, were out of the money. Most, but not two. It was more than close for a bit as the pair of beasts charged full out. Ever see a cartoon of a horse when it's racing hard and they draw steam puffing from its nostrils? Look real close at these two and tell me what you see. I didn't have dollar one down, and I could feel myself getting a hard-on for this race.

Maybe it was in my head—had to be, since they were running in Santa Anita—but I could hear the jockeys going to the whip. The jockeys flogged, and the horses worked it. Two dumb animals that didn't know any more than getting beaten every couple of days. They didn't know why; they didn't know what for. It's just get hit and run, get hit and run. And if you're a good boy when it's all over we'll set you in a field and let you fuck your brains out. But first: Get hit and run.

I could relate. Except for the getting to fuck your brains out part, I could relate.

One of the horses crossed the line first.

If Dumas won or lost, you couldn't tell. One of the horses crossed the line first, and Dumas didn't move, or flinch, or yelp, or tear his tickets, or give them to one of his boys to collect. One of the horses took a beating, blew steam out its nose, crossed the line first, and Dumas played it like it didn't matter. It didn't. If his horse won, then he made a little more of what he's already got a lot of. If his horse lost, then it lost for a whole lot of other saps who'd taken bets with him and would now owe. Inside and outside, coming and going: When you can't lose no matter what you try, that's when you can play all things cool.

After a while, Dumas got around to noticing me. "Jeffty," he cooed, French and island mixed winsome. "Why is it I have not seen you around, I suppose? Why is it I have not seen you when I know, and you know, you are in my debt?"

"I haven't got what I owe."

"And why do you suppose that is?"

"Can't earn much with these." I held up my invalid fingers to him.

Dumas curled a perfectly healthy finger toward himself. "Let us have a look."

I stepped to him. I held out my hand, my fingers. He took them in his. I got nervous, him holding what he had broken, but his touch was gentle like he cared for my hurting. Just like he cared.

The caring that I felt was in his voice as well. "Not so bad. Healed up rather nicely. Rather."

He looked my fingers over, slow and careful and full of concern. So very much like he cared. Dumas looked up at me. He smiled.

And smiled.

And smiled.

His fingers twisted a bit. Just a small little bit they twisted, and twisted my broken fingers with them.

A piece of metal that had been stoking on a fire for days got jabbed into my hand. It got jabbed all the way up to my shoulder, then curved around back down to my knees. My eyes shot back in my head, and I enjoyed a quick out-of-body experience as my mind tried to run as far and as fast as it could away from the pain. It couldn't beat it.

A sweet voice sang at me: "Where is my money?"

When I got back to my body it had been painted over with a nice sheen of sweat. A stream of spittle ran over my lip and dripped from my chin. Dumas's boys, all of them, were helping themselves to a good laugh. It was just one of those days when I couldn't help but entertain people.

Dumas: "I don't like having to do that. Maybe a little, but not really. Still, at times it has to be done, do you know?"

I gave a casual response. "Whatever." I was doing too much sweating and shaking for anyone to buy my faux disassociation with pain.

"So, then, where is my money?"

"Don't have it. If I did," wiping drool from my mouth, "I would have paid it, and I wouldn't be standing here letting you work me over." I was getting a little too sharp for my own good, but the smoldering in my hand and the just-now-fading snickers made me that way.

Dumas stared off a bit like something out on the track, like maybe those two water trucks just driving around and around were more interesting than what I was about. He stared off a bit, then he laughed. His boys, who had barely finished with their previous bout of hysteria, started up again. They laughed 'cause Dumas was laughing, and Dumas was laughing at me.

Between the laughs Dumas said: "I could kill you."

Goddamn his voice was sweet.

"I could kill you right here, right now, and no one in this place—no one anywhere—would have a care, do you know? I could kill you, and you talk as if you wouldn't die; you talk as if you were a man." He laughed again. His boys laughed some more, too. "And that is exactly why I do not kill you: You amuse me. You are like a little clown, do you know? That's what you are: a little circus clown."

A sip of his fag drink, a leg raised and crossed the other.

Continuing with his dissertation on the state of me: "Certainly I'll break a finger here and there. You don't pay, I must do something. But you are too funny to kill, and it is so difficult to find a good clown in this day."

Dumas smiled Times Square–bright. An "I'm better than you" smile. An "I'm better than you, and you're nothing but an ant and you know it" smile. So much for one smile.

He should have twisted my fingers again. Dumas should have hacked them right off with that dull, dirty knife sitting on his table. It would have hurt less than his grin did.

"It's a funny thing, no?" Dumas asked. "You have nothing, Jeffty. You are dirt-poor and becoming poorer by the moment."

If that was funny, I couldn't see how.

He went on: "Here I am, an immigrant to your country. People here, Americans, they hate immigrants. A nation full of them, and they all hate the next who come. But I work hard, I've made a . . . well, let us say a fortune. Yes, let us call it that. I pay taxes. Do you pay taxes, Jeffty? Of course you do not. You don't even possess enough money to bury yourself well. That is the problem with this country. It is you lazy natural-borns who are spoiling it for the rest of us."

On the TV, in San Francisco, at Golden Gate, they walked the horses toward the starting gate.

Dumas glanced at the screen. Through his many-meaninged smile: "Make a little wager, care to?"

My head shook. I held up my freshly reswollen fingers. "That's how I worked these in the first place."

"How deep are we now?"

We?

I shrugged. I knew how much I owed. I knew, and I knew he knew, and to hell with him if I was going to let him get a hard-on listening to me choke out the number.

Dumas to Ty: "How much?"

"Fifteen and change." Ty was there with the number same as a dog bringing slippers to its master, but quicker. "Fifteen and change up-to-date on interest."

Dumas rolled the number around in his mouth for a bit. "Now you have an opportunity to win it off."

"I got no taw."

"Double or nothing. What matters owing thirty when you haven't even got fifteen?"

Dumas flipped a finger. Another one of his lapdogs grabbed up a *Racing Form* from the table and jabbed it at me. Nobody said a word, but we all spoke the same language. Dumas wants me to play, I play, and nobody's trying to hear otherwise.

I took the form, fumbled the pages, and came up with the fifth from Golden Gate. The page was worked up, the margins bloated with notations, numbers, stats. . . . It was like Dumas was trying to figure cold fusion.

The sweet voice: "I prefer Weatherly, number three. I like her works. She's ready to stretch out on the grass."

Number eight was named Terri's Song. I knew a Terri for a day once. She didn't fuck me over. Just like that: "I'll take eight." I tossed the form back down on the table for punctuation.

More smiles all around. Big stupid grins. Grab 'em up, boys. They're on the house.

Dumas threw in a few shakes of the head. A few "Isn't this dumb fuck pathetic?" shakes. He spread his hands to his minions as if to say: You see how pathetic, don't you? You see that?

Their ignorant smiles responded: Yeah, we see, boss. We see.

After Dumas had enough head shaking and grinning he got around to: "You would bet against the chalk? Eighteen to one, your long shot."

"Like you said, what's it matter owing thirty when you don't have fifteen? I win and you're off me, and that's all I'm thinking about."

On the monitors, up at Golden Gate, they finished herding the horses into the starting gate. Number eight gave the boys a little trouble about it—rearing, fighting, acting up, as if to emphasize to anyone who was even thinking about betting her, Don't.

She got settled, finally, after giving everyone around Dumas one more thing to laugh at. The bell rang, and a guy with a bad English accent said: "And they're off," just like a guy with a bad English accent says at every horse race everywhere.

Dumas's horse was smooth in second; looked like water running over a fall. There were some other horses behind it. And then there was mine, number eight, in the back, making sure the rest of the pack wasn't being followed.

"What's the fun part of gambling?" Dumas asked to no one in particular.

I didn't figure he was talking to me, so I let it go.

He asked again. "What's the fun part of gambling?"

Now I knew he was talking to me but just didn't want to waste the energy looking in my direction.

"Winning," I said.

"Winning," he repeated. "But if you won all the time it wouldn't be a gamble." His face scrunched up as if to show all the thought he was giving this incredibly complex issue. "No, I don't believe so. I think what is enjoyable is that even though you know the odds are against you, you know you will lose, there is one brief moment when the dice is rolled, or the ball drops, or"—he raised a finger at the monitor—"when the horses crash from the gate; a brief moment, a rush of excitement, when you believe there is a chance you might actually win, do you know?"

Hebrew he might as well have been talking for what I got from it all. "So?" I said.

Dumas worked up the most bored voice he could find. "So, it is the expectation of winning in the face of losing, not the winning itself, that makes gambling exciting. What pleasure is there if you know you're going to win?" As if to punctuate all that, as if to explain it to me, Dumas's horse slid easy into first.

Condensation gathered on Dumas's glass. A droplet formed and ran down the side. It swallowed up other droplets, got bigger, ran faster, and swallowed up more droplets, on and on like that all the way down the glass, and when it was done there was nothing left behind it.

Out on the track, the water trucks didn't do much gaining on each other.

Something happened.

I wasn't looking at the monitor when it did, so I wasn't sure what, or why, or how, but in the instant I was watching the droplet devour all other droplets on Dumas's glass and the water trucks chase each other, Terri's Song, number eight, my horse, had swung to the outside of the pack.

The thing about horse racing is you can load up on all the homework you want. You can read the forms, watch a horse do her works, dig up the history of the jockey like you were going to vote for him, not bet on him. . . . But the one thing no one's ever been able to do, the one thing that would make racing a sure bet every time: You can't ask a horse if it feels like running. Sometimes it does, sometimes it doesn't.

This morning, number eight felt like saying a big "Fuck you" to the world. Fuck the odds; fuck the works; fuck the dirt or the weeds. This morning, Terri's Song felt like running the hell out of herself.

Even going wide on the turn she gobbled up the other horses two at a time. Dumas got all uncomfortable in his chair like he was sitting on hot tacks. It wasn't so much that he minded losing money; it was that he minded losing at all. He minded more losing to me and losing to me in front of his boys. That cocktail was a bit strong for him. He didn't have much time to get a taste for it. This was no neck-and-neck race, no photo finish. Terri's Song just blew up the stretch and across the line like she had someplace to be.

I didn't smile. I'm pretty sure a smile would have gotten me a bullet in the face. I took my horse kicking the shit out of Dumas's very matter-of-factly while fireworks went off in my gut.

The results got posted down on the totalisator at center track. All around us people were talking, or laughing, or tearing up their race tickets in disgust. But we—me and Dumas and Dumas's boys—were in a long tunnel of silence that seemed to go on and on. Who knew what to say? Not Dumas, and sure as hell not his flunkies. Finally, quiet as he could, but still loud as thunder, a word worked its way out of Dumas.

"Well . . ."

Yeah. Well. As in: Well, how's it feel to get your ass kicked, you stupid Haitian bastard? That's the thought that came to me, all full of myself as I bit at my lip to keep from grinning. Inside my head I was having my own little private party.

I thought again, How's it feel to be the bitch for a change, Dumas? You picked the wrong brother to mess with. Today you did. I made that horse win; you're goddamn right I did, you black whore. With force of will shooting straight out of my head I made that nag run. I'm only going to let you push me so much, Dumas. I'm only gonna let you and your girl-friends get so many laughs out of me. After that? After that, I'm gonna stick it to you where it hurts. All your fine clothes and fancy talk, and you're still just a loser like everybody else. Ain't ya, Dumas? Ain't ya?

That's what I thought. "How about that" is all I said. I started to inch my way back up the stairs. As casual as I could make it sound: "I guess I'll just . . . you know . . . go."

Something happened.

Maybe I half saw it, or maybe I sensed it, or maybe in my heart I was just waiting for it to happen, but my head jerked hard around and locked on the tote board. The results that had been posted were flashing. The guy with the bad English accent came on the PA and told me what I already knew.

"There's been a steward's inquiry into the fifth race," he said with heated needles that boiled the inside of my brain box. One of Dumas's boys stepped in front of me—a big tree in the road cutting off my path. I wasn't going nowhere.

Still in that long, quiet tunnel. Nobody said anything, and nobody had to. Something had happened in the fifth. Something like . . . I don't know, but the kind of something where the officials have to sit around and talk about it. Something where a horse could get itself disqualified. Real quick I thought about the instant number eight pulled to the outside. She didn't bump another rider. She didn't cut another horse off . . . did she? No, I was sure she hadn't . . . almost sure.

The board kept flashing. The results there one second, gone the next. My victory there, and gone. My freedom there, and gone. The longer the board flashed, the worse things were. Whatever happened on the track wasn't some little matter—some runner-up jockey making a complaint just to be a pain in the ass. This was a genuine situation. A horse was coming off the board.

Dumas finally drove us out of that quiet tunnel. "I remember a story," he started, detached from his own words. Didn't matter what was going on up at Golden Gate; Dumas sounded like he could have been getting ready for a nap: "When I was a child, maybe no older, I heard it. The story of a boy whose father was a killer. Two men, I think, he murdered."

It was a clean break to the outside—that's what my mind was on. Some other horse—the inquiry had to be about some other horse.

"And his father, the boy's grandfather, had also killed. How many, I do not know. It's not important, but he was a killer, do you know? People thought this child, too, might grow up to take blood as his father and father before him had done, so the boy was removed from his parents. Taken away to another city, another family. Taken away where he might grow up to be . . . normal, I suppose, but at least not a killer."

I heard Dumas, his voice a warm buzz in the back of my head, but that's all it was to me. I stared at the board as it flashed. There, and gone. There, and gone.

"The little boy became a man, married, raised children. He had no notion of his true father, his grandfather, or the blood that ran through him. One day, he was in a mishap. His car. A . . . what? Fender bender? Nothing really. But he got into an argument with the other driver. The argument became heated, not more so than one would expect after an auto mishap. Not so much that a man could not walk away from it. But not this man; not this child of his father, and his father's father. This man took up a tire iron and beat the skull of the other driver until his brain oozed like pink jelly from the pulped stump that now hung from his neck."

Even as I watched the board, this last bit snagged me. So awful it was, so pleasant Dumas made it sound.

"Go where you like, do as you please, pretend whatever you wish, but we are all who we were born to be. Some lovers. Some killers. Some winners. And some . . ."

The board stopped flashing. My horse, number eight, Terri's Song, was gone.

The bad-accented guy came back to explain things. I caught the words that mattered: *Illegal. Disqualified. Bets void.* The guy talked on. The world seemed to slip under my feet having turned into a viscid fluid.

As the ground melted away, Dumas said: "Thirty thousand dollars. Oh, what in the hell. Twenty-five. You make me laugh, do you know?"

Night.

The phone rang me awake. It rang like it had rung a thousand times before, but somehow just as different. Unsettling. Maybe it was the hour. A phone call in the middle of the night had never good-newsed me. Or maybe I was just being paranoid. I was being paranoid a lot lately. A matching set of broken fingers will do that to you. I was hoping eventually the phone would ring itself out, but it didn't so I picked it up.

"Hello," I said, and waited. "Hello," I said again.

Something like a voice came back to me. "Jeffty?"

"Nellis," I whispered, or breathed, or maybe just thought. I knew it was him. All he had to say was my name, and I knew. After that one word there was silence. A lot of years, so much between us, but nothing to say.

"Where?" I asked.

"Bus station. Vine."

"I'll come get you."

.   .   .

I showered myself awake, dressed, drove over to the bus station just south of Sunset on Vine without remembering any of it. One step inside and the sweet stink of fermented urine snapped me back to the real world. Otherwise, I was living seven years ago; living the last time I ever saw Nellis. He saved my life, in a way. I guess you could say that. I destroyed his. You could say that for sure. A question kept playing over and over in my head, heavy rotation on a continual loop: Why now? With everything else that's going so wrong in my life, why do the living dead have to come back to haunt me?

I saw her then: the girl, the street kid, the one I'd seen outside Ralphs. I saw her like before; like I was supposed to know her and knowing her was supposed to mean something to me. Something more, anyway, than wanting to hose her down and take a roll.

Just a dirty white girl sitting, hand out, looking for change.

Just a dirty white girl same as the thousand other dirty girls who litter the boulevards so much so you can't clean them away, only make room for the next batch.

Just a dirty white girl, but she tattooed herself on my mind.

I shook loose of her, spotted Nellis curled up on the floor as if the filthy tile of a bus station was the most natural place in the world to catch a nap. For Nellis it probably was. My foot nudged at him, and his eyes fluttered open. Strange, maybe, but I couldn't help think he was pretty for a man. Not the first time I had thought that about him. Soft features and longish hair on the blond side. A body that was sort of feminine in its frailty. I don't mean any of that in a fag kind of way, I'm just saying . . .

"Hey, Jeffty." Nellis seemed to float to his feet like he'd gone lighter than air. His eyes misted same as if seeing me was no different than seeing a twin brother who'd been separated at birth. "How you doing, Jeffty?"

He went to hug me. Jesus, he felt thin to the touch. What the hell is that? His ribs tight against his flesh. One deep breath I think they'd punch through his skin.

And the stench. The thick smell of a body long unwashed. His breath reeked, too, like he'd just had a big heapin' spoonful of warm shit. I would have choked on all his aromas if I hadn't pushed Nellis back off me.

We stood there, seven years apart. What had the seven years got us? I was getting by in life. Broken fingers and afraid to close both eyes at night, but getting by. Nellis was obviously cash-poor and dirty and slept on bus station floors, but he was smiling. Bad as what I had done to him, bad as things were, he could still dig up something to smile about.

Finally I got around to saying: "Let's go."

"Could we stop for a drink? A drink would help me sleep."

I wanted to laugh, him looking baby-in-a-crib comfy not moments ago on the floor. "You sleep just fine."

"A drink will help me sleep better."

As soon as Nellis shut the car door he was out. Dead asleep, and he'd claimed he needed a drink. I thanked God for him going shut-eye anyway. I didn't want to talk because the only thing to talk about was Vale. Well, Vale and me. That's the other part of it.

A few blocks' drive to the Regent. A couple of hard shoves got Nellis awake. We went in from the darkness of the night to the darkness of the bar, Eddie there to greet us with a "Hey, howzit?"

Over there's Wesker, all a sudden king of the joint. Thirty-some grand, and he's still hanging around like he doesn't know enough to get out of the rain. The places I could run to with thirty grand.

Australia. Lots of beach. Hell, it's all beach. And they don't drink beer down there; they drink lager. I don't know what the hell that is. Like beer, I guess, only better. All I know is they got lots of it. And the women down there flip for brothers; the darker the better. That's what I hear anyway. Heard the same thing about England. And Japan. I think Sweden, too. Being a brother is like the hottest ticket in town everywhere except in America.

My luck.

Anywhere else in the world I could be getting fucked instead of fucked with.

Wesker stumbled over to me, a girl wrapped up in his arms. She was cheap. The tight pants she wore that restricted her movement and made her ass appear bigger than it was left her looking all the cheaper. She was the same kind of low-rent glossy hag who built this town. A woman who passed for okay in the dark, but I'm guessing in daylight was black-velvet-art ugly. This was the best thirty grand could buy? Why is it only guys who are money-simple ever fall into dough?

Wesker got all up in my face, breath thick with booze. "Jeffty," he yelled at me even though our noses were only a slip of paper apart.

"Jeffty," he yelled again in case I missed it the first time. His washed-out eyes wobbled over to Nellis. "Who's your friend?" Without even giving me time to answer: "Come on, who's your friend?"

Wesker was big and loud, so much so that he scared Nellis. His little burned-out frame began to quiver. I pushed Nellis toward a table at the back of the room.

To Wesker: "Leave us alone."

"Let me buy you one. You and your friend. Let me buy you a drink. I got a friend. Meet my friend."

Wesker started to introduce the girl, but as soon as he opened his mouth, he lost her name. If he'd ever really known it. Didn't bother the girl any that she was nameless to him. Nothing could get her down the way Wesker had her liquored up. She was three steps numb and all ready for a night of sex she'd never even know she'd had.

Wesker went on: "She's my friend. Whataya say we all have a drink? I'm buying."

"No." I was that simple with it.

"Come on, Jeffty. Just one. Let me—"

I turned up on Wesker, quick and close. My eyes snapped narrow; my teeth didn't part when I said it again: "No."

This time it took. Wesker backed up scared. "Trying to do you a favor. Trying to be your friend. That's what you get for trying . . ." He went on from there, but it got sucked up in the dull lyrics of rambling drunks and the music of clinking glasses.

I went for the bar, blew some dollars on a bottle of Jack, then headed over to Nellis. Halfway to the table I thought maybe I shouldn't have gone in for a whole bottle. I didn't know what Nellis was strung out on: Meth, blow, crack, smack? Maybe all of that. I didn't want to make things worse.

Make things worse.

Look at him: thin, and pale, and sickly like he just got let out of six months in a box.

Look at him: gray flesh painted over weak bones, like he ought to have vultures swinging overhead marking time.

Look at him: seven-eighths dead. One more drink along the way wouldn't make any kind of difference.

Crossing to the table I passed Amber, boozing alone like most everyone else.

"Hey," I said. "How's the face?"

"Whazat?" Amber slurred back.

"Your face where those kids roughed you up—that healing all right?"

Amber waited a beat, then cut loose with a big broad drunk's laugh. "Oh, hell, Jeffty. I didn't get beat up. I was drinking and fell down some stairs." Her mouth gaped. Saliva draped between her near-toothless gums. "That story about the punks, I was just trying to sell a watch. Jesus, are you soft, Jeffty. Jesus, are you."

I walked away. Amber's laughter followed me.

When I got to Nellis, he asked: "Why that old woman laughing at you, Jeffty?"

Simple: "'Cause I'm a clown. Can't you see that?"

Nellis didn't even give me the queer look a remark like that deserved. Soon as I put the Jack down on the table, his hands raced to it like a pair of hungry spiders. He poured some of what was in the bottle into a glass, then what was in the glass into himself. One, two, three drinks so quick he ought to have just quit the glass and taken his liquor straight.

He slowed down for a minute, his whole body gone flush, looked up from his drink and right at me. I could feel the sweat forming on my forehead. It was time to talk.

"How you been, Nellis?"

"I guess I been okay. I guess. I'm alive, right?" A little laugh. "That's something, ain't it?"

"Where've you been? It's been a few years."

"A lot. Been a lot of years, and I've been a lot of places . . . after what happened."

"Nellis—" I started

He knew right where I was going. "Don't matter."

"I . . . I just want you to know—"

"It don't matter no longer."

"Nellis—" I started again.

"You don't understand. She's gone. She's gone from my mind. She don't exist no more. So what happened never happened . . . in a way. Never."

Nellis's nonchalance just made all the thoughts floating around in my head thrash harder. I poured myself a drink, long and tall, and kicked it back. Mr. Daniel's did nothing to ease my suffering. I gave him another chance and still he did nothing, the lazy bum.

We both sat and drank, me and Nellis. We finished off a bottle and another, neither one of us getting anywhere near being high. Nellis because liquor was like sugar water the way he was strung out, and me because it would take a lot more than a few drinks to put down what I was trying to bulldoze under.

We didn't talk any more. Nellis didn't want any "I'm sorries," and he didn't offer up anything else. We just took up space marking time in each other's shadows. I watched the rest of the people in the bar; watched them booze. Every downed shot was trying to smooth over something, and for a while I played a little game of tagging up stories to faces. This guy over here's drinking 'cause his girl left him for another chick; his sister. This guy has to polish off another bottle 'cause if he goes home sober tonight's the night he's finally going to take that kitchen knife to his wife's fat gut that's been getting fatter since the day they married. And check out that sister in the back. She's getting drunk 'cause she just banged her son . . . and it was the best sex she ever had.

The game got old after a minute, so I went back to just sitting, and drinking, and staring across the table at Nellis while he did the same back at me.

When we'd had enough of that, we left.

I lugged Nellis's duffel bag into what I called "the living room" and dumped it on the couch.

"You can have the bed." I tried to sound big about it, like giving him the bed might somehow be enough to square us. He wasn't going for it.

"S'okay. I'll sleep out here. It's all right if you don't have no covers."

"I have covers on the bed. Take the—"

"Couch is cool. It ain't the floor."

"Yeah, but—"

"I mean, even the floor is cool. I'm used to floors."

All those words got mixed up in my thinker: *The floor. No covers. I'm used to it.* "So take the bed!"

"Gotten used to a lot in the last seven years."

"Take the bed! Just take the goddamn bed, would ya!" I didn't even know I was yelling. I just heard an ugly shrill noise filling my head like steel wheels dragging along their rails way before I knew it was me.

Nellis just stood there. Long after the train wheels stopped screeching, he just stood there. After what seemed like quite some time he shuffled over to his duffel bag and started digging into it. Dirty clothes spilled out.

Some porn. What the hell is that? A half-eaten box of Lucky Charms . . . Jesus; a copy of the script. All this time, and he'd held on to a copy. I guess I should've felt good about that, but it only made me feel worse; added weight to the growing pile of guilt.

Finally, Nellis got to what he was looking for: a rusted tin. He clawed at the top and pried it open with his fingernails. It squeaked and yawned against itself. Inside was a tarnished spoon, a lighter, some cotton, a piece of rubber hosing, a needle and a plastic bag of white powder. Nellis made the hosing into a noose and slipped it around his arm. Stingy like a miser with his money, he carefully poured a conservative amount of the powder into the spoon and heated it with the lighter until it bubbled and melted into a fine liquid. The tip of the needle—through the cotton—into the spoon, his teeth to the dangling end of the hosing, a jerk of the head to pull it taught. He did it all with an odd/beautiful finesse that comes from countless repetitions.

Christ. And I was worried about feeding him some booze.

Nellis flexed his hand. The veins of his arm ballooned, highlighting his track marks like a topographic map of his abuse. He looked up at me smiling. Maybe. Or maybe it just appeared that way as he clenched the hosing in his teeth.

"You can't run from the past," he said, offering up some disconnected but pointed philosophy. "Only bury it a little."

I stood there. He slid the needle into his arm, mixed the solution with blood, forced down the plunger, and I just stood there and watched as all the pain and suffering drained from his face to be replaced by sweet nothingness.

I could have stopped him. Right then and for the rest of the day. I maybe could've stopped him from shooting up tomorrow, too. But what was the point of stopping him now if I couldn't stop him the day after tomorrow or all the days after that? Was it even my responsibility? I didn't put Nellis in this place; it's where he wanted to be. And if he wanted out, then he was the one who would have to drag himself from it. And with that I had myself convinced of my own guiltlessness. I guess maybe that's the good thing about me: Doesn't take much to clear my conscience.

With the hosing still around his arm Nellis sank to the floor. He curled up and drifted away on a hopped-up little cloud of dreams. A quick fix, a long trip. Shoot straight, fly far. Look at him go. Bye-bye, Nellis. See you real soon.

I walked through the next couple of days of my life. I worked, conned, grifted. However you want to call it. And when I wasn't doing what little I could to get by, I went to the Regent and lost myself in the drink and the dark. I spent more time there than I had ever before. People who were only my acquaintances all a sudden saw me as a friend, as one of them. But I wasn't their friend. I wanted nothing to do with those people, and better still if none of them got in any of my business. Whenever the subject came around to old Jeffty, old Jeffty lied.

"Me, Eddie? I'm fine, real fine. Just a shot for me today; I'll nurse it. Hey, make it two. It was a rough morning. But just the two. I have to be on my way soon. Helluva lot to do."

The lies came easy. I lied on.

"Yeah, Wesker, I'm getting it together. Had a bit of a lucky stretch. I'm going to pay Dumas off; should have plenty left over to do things with."

"Oh, I don't know, Amber. Maybe I'll invest. Land. I'm not talking about buying up West Hollywood. Just a little patch here, a little patch there. Can't hardly go wrong with land. Maybe you can even come in on it."

"Meantime, Eddie, how about that drink? Just the two. Maybe three, but then I have to be off. Helluva lot to do."

I lied, and lied, and lied some more. Lied to keep them an arm's length away. Lied to be better than them. And if just one of those lies turned out to be the littlest bit true, then maybe I really wasn't like them, a boozer. Maybe one day I'd find a way out of the pit I was sliding further into.

Maybe.

Meantime, the lies wore thin to them and me after a couple of days. And after a couple of days more it wasn't even worth the energy to go through the motions. A week's time, and it was just money on the bar and a drink in the glass. That simple. The only lie that remained was to myself: That I wasn't a drunk and a loser. That I wasn't taking a slow ride to the low end of nowhere. That I wasn't any worse off than the other denizens of a little dark corner called the Regent.

When I wasn't grifting or drinking I was home, but home is where Nellis was which was what had me drinking—drinking more—in the first place. I didn't know how long he was going to stay, and I didn't have it in me to make him leave, so I avoided him the best I could. When he was awake I pretended I was asleep. I'd lie in bed for hours, eyes closed and dead still, if that's what it took to keep out of his path.

When he wanted to talk or spend time I always had to rush off.

"Can't hang with you right now, Nellis. I got to go over to the place to see the people about the thing. But I'll catch you later. Later we'll talk."

Yeah. Later.

Later I'd be back in bed faking my sleep.

Sometimes, some blessed God-loving times, Nellis would just be gone. He would be gone, and he would stay gone for hours at a stretch. I hoped and prayed it was forever. But there was his duffel. And inside the duffel was the rusted tin. And inside the tin . . . Nellis wasn't going anywhere without that. Not anywhere he couldn't get back here lickety-split the second his body started yelling and screaming and begging and pleading for a fix. Naw, he wasn't much gone.

On those times when he was gone for a bunch of hours occasionally a thought came to me and said maybe something happened to him. Things happened to vagrants and junkies. A guy like Nellis—living in a haze, a foot in the grave anyway—something could happen easy to a guy like that. Crossing a busy street when he shouldn't've. Walking down the wrong dark alley. Hell, to a guy in Nellis's condition a slippery piece of sidewalk became a death trap.

I was ashamed when I thought that.

The first time.

Then I got used to the idea.

Then I even started to like it. I never wished for anything to happen to Nellis, I just liked the notion of it.

But whenever I figured this was the time Nellis managed to tumble down a flight of stairs, or stumble in front of a bus, or end up on the business end of a gun, the door would open and he would shuffle in. Sometimes run in if he needed to get high, but in he came. No regular timing to his appearance, no way to gauge when, always unexpected he'd just show up. He had a way of doing that.

Why? Why was Nellis here, now; an obelisk of prior misdeeds built up to cast a shadow over my life? Is this what they mean by karma, payback, or was it just more shit on top of the pile I was already being buried beneath? I thought: You have to be very careful of the past that you create for yourself. You never know when it's going to show up in your future.

*W*here the Sidewalk Ends was the second feature of two—the first having been Laura—at the New Beverly, a revival house that double-featured theme movies. Tonight it was a pair of sort-of-gems with Gene Tierney and Dana Andrews. They were a film couple, like Bogart and Bacall, Lake and Ladd, except their names didn't go together as well. The place was just shy of half-full. Film geeks who didn't own VCRs, or who owned them but thought watching movies on tape was beneath them. Overweight, physically unappealing, mostly boyfriend- or girlfriendless, they related better to scripted dialogue and stilted performances than they did to the real world.

Losers all.

I fit in quite cozily.

Both movies I'd seen too many times. But the choice being sitting through two too-familiar pictures or refamiliarizing myself with Nellis, the movies won hands down. I left Nellis to sleep, or shoot up, or whatever while I went off to watch some dead actors prance around on-screen.

Feature number two: Andrews was a cop who beat the shit out of crooks up until he accidentally killed one of them. I guess, in the fifties, cops who beat the shit out of crooks were like a novelty.

Twenty-some minutes into the film a hand fell on my shoulder.

I turned.

It was Ty.

I felt pain, and he wasn't even breaking things yet.

He read my look. "Take it easy, Jeffty." Ty's hand, one of the pair that had snapped my fingers, massaged my shoulder. His thumb worked a kink at the lower part of my neck. It was all so very gentle. "I'm here same as you. Watching movies."

My eyes asked a question, and he answered: "Yep, no shit, Jeffty."

Up till then, I'd been conducting the conversation with my face. I said, I asked: "You like noir?"

"I like movies, old shit. You?"

Up on the screen, thug friends of the dead crook were putting the screws to Dana Andrews. "I like anything where people got a worse life than mine."

From behind, a film geek shushed us. I looked at the geek, then looked away. Ty didn't look at all.

At the screen he nodded. "I dig that Gene Tierney. She was a piece of ass."

I agreed. "Women back then had it, you know? Sexier, tougher than anything they toss up on film now. Bennett, Lake, Scott—"

"'The Threat.'" The smile that came with the words was broad and delicious. "That's a chick that could take a punch."

"Sure she could. She was a dyke."

"You don't know that." Ty got defensive, obviously having a thing for that femme in particular. "Don't nobody know that for sure. Now Stanwyck—"

"All I'm saying is, dyke or straight, they were better than what we got now."

"Got that right."

A question came to me, and maybe Ty was the guy to answer it. "Hey, who was that European actress? Dark hair?"

"Lamarr?"

"No. Later than that. The fifties, early sixties."

"Lavi?"

Daliah Lavi. She was a hot one, but, "No," and I was pretty sure Lavi was from the Middle East. But as Ty and me were getting along okay I didn't think correcting him was much of an idea. I thought for a second, but, since I didn't know who I was thinking of, couldn't come up with any more clues.

"Why you ask?" Ty asked.

"This girl I saw. Twice I've seen her. She remi—"

Again the film geek: "Shhhh!"

All that got was more ignoring from Ty. He leaned back in his seat. "Don't care much for Andrews. He's a stiff."

Up on the screen, cops closing in, getting closer to the truth that he was a killer. Andrews as tense as a narcoleptic.

"He was a booze hound," I said. "A perpetual drunk. How the hell's he going to act when he's three bottles under? You know in *While the City Sleeps*, he was so boozed up they had to write it into the character. Every other scene is in a bar with him drinking."

"For real?"

"For real. They could get away with shit like that then. They could get away with anything when the studios ran the show. You know one time Clark Gable killed a guy drunk driving. So Louis Mayer just points at some guy, some duty bug at MGM and says 'You're taking the fall.' The guy goes inside for Gable, does the time, when he gets out Mayer makes sure the guy is set for life."

"No shit?"

"Did the same thing for John Huston. Back then it didn't matter what you did, or who you fucked, or how badly you fucked up. This town took care of its own. Tell you something, Ty. If I could be alive at any other time it would be Hollywood in the forties."

Ty gave me an eyebrow, and I modified myself: "If I could be alive and *white* . . ."

Film Geek, one more time: "Shhhhh!"

This time, Ty didn't ignore. This time, Ty turned and gave a look. That's all he did, just gave a look.

Film Geek got up and moved away like his life depended on it.

"How come," to me Ty asked, "you know so much about film?"

I sat a moment looking at the screen—not particularly aware that I was—looking at Andrews and Tierney in black and white, and very much dead, but larger than life.

"You know what," to Ty I said, "I hate?"

"What do you hate?"

"The wannabes. Wannabe an actor, wannabe a writer, wannabe a director, wannabe . . . They grow up believing all that bullshit Hollywood spoon-feeds you about fairy tales and happy endings is true. So they come out here from Iowa, or Wisconsin, or wherever because they wanna create something, or wanna get paid a lot for creating something, or maybe they just wanna round of applause every time they open their mouths. They come out here wide-eyed and head busting with dreams, and all they get is slapped down at every turn same as some boulevard whore too stupid to know she shouldn't backtalk her pimp. They get slapped down good with nothing to show for all their wishing. Not a goddamn thing but bruises and empty pockets."

Ty nodded to that.

"Know why I hate them?"

"Why do you hate them?"

"I'm one of them."

Ty nodded to that, too. "What did you come out to do?"

"I wanted to be a movie writer."

That got some laughing from Ty. Nothing mean or nasty, not particularly so. Just the casual laughing that comes with something funny said.

I said: "Every time I open my mouth I got someone busting up at me. Every time. Here you and me are carrying on just about like two regular people—watching a movie, talking about stuff and it's . . . well, it's nice. Then you ask me something, I tell you something, and you bust up no different than anybody else. So how about this: How about since we're acting like regular people, how about one time, just one time, you let me talk and you don't laugh? How about that?"

Ty looked at me in a funny way. Funny in the sense I wasn't used to getting looks like that. He looked at me with compassion and understanding. He looked at me like I was a human being. No, I wasn't used to that at all.

"Okay, Jeffty. You talk, and I won't laugh."

I went on. "Seventeen, and I decided to come out here."

"Home life no good?"

"Same as most, I guess. My father liked to drink; my mother didn't much like to get hit."

"Same as most," Ty echoed.

"I didn't need to be around to see them work things out. I liked movies, I had a head full of ideas, so what the hell? Hollywood. I came to write. Gave it a shot, a couple of years' worth. Then . . . well, I gave it up."

"Just like that?"

"I was flat broke, and my stomach was dead empty. How much more encouragement do you need?"

"How'd you start living on the easy?"

"Met a guy. He knew the rackets. Nickel-and-dime stuff, but when you got nothing you learn to like the way nickels and dimes rattle in your pocket. Got to be friends. More than that. I didn't know how to do shit else before I met this guy. He taught me how to turn a few dollars, how to put food on my table. It's funny."

"How's that?"

"He used to look up to me. He's the one who taught me things; he's the one who kept me alive—and I was so far gone that was honest to God what he did, kept me living—but I'm the one he looked up to because . . . I don't know why because. He just used to."

"Used to?"

"There was a time when I needed money bad."

"Things don't change."

I smiled, nodded. "Some things, I guess not. My friend's wife—she had money. I put the move on her."

"You tried to whore money out of a woman?" I could tell Ty wanted to laugh, but good to his word he didn't. I wouldn't have blamed him, this time, if he had.

Shrugging: "Why not? Love's as good a con as any. I hit her up, made her feel special. Same as any woman wants. Sweet-talked a few bucks out of her. Worked for a while."

"But your friend found out." Ty was digging this more than anything the two dead actors had to say.

"Walked in on us. Waltzed right in, me with her tits in my hands. Well, that was that for me and him, I don't have to tell you. I went on with the woman for a while. Then I quit her. Had to. How could I shack up with a chick who screwed around on her husband with his best friend?"

"And him? What happened to the guy?"

I checked my watch. "I'd say about now he's still doped out on my floor."

Ty didn't much get that, but he did say: "Something's missing."

"How do you mean?"

"Your story. It's good and all, but there're parts that don't make sense."

"It's life, Ty. Mine. Not a movie."

"But how does a guy go from wanting to be a writer, from being full of ideas, to banging his best friend's wife?" Ty thought for a second, shook his head. Again he said, "Something's missing."

Yeah. Something's missing.

To Ty I said: "That's it. That's all there is to me."

I left things there, and Ty had no follow-up questions. We watched the movie, talking back and forth just some, until its end. Its end being although Dana Andrews was a murdering thug cop, Gene Tierney couldn't get enough of him to the point they were going to get married. I was wrong about noir. Even in the bleakest most cynical movies Hollywood could muster, these people's lives were better than mine.

Movie over, me and Ty exited with the film geeks to Beverly Boulevard heading in opposite directions to our cars, his paid-for Mercedes and my beat-up Corvair.

"Oh, hey," Ty called to me, just then remembering something. He remembered that if I didn't have some money in three weeks, per Dumas's instructions, he was going to have to break some more fingers, or at least get busy on my face.

Ty went on for his Benz.

I stood where I was.

After a while, the lights of the cinema went out.

I think it had been two weeks, or near about that, before Nellis and I spent any time together. Together meaning just being in the same room at the same time for more than three minutes.

Nellis lay all oozed out on the floor, like someone had snatched every bone from inside him, watching TV. Maybe not watching, maybe just looking at it. From all he seemed to get out of the cascade of images he might as well have been staring at a pile of bricks. It was pathetic, the only thing more so was me sitting there watching Nellis watch TV, the cool light from the tube dancing off his skin. It was so pale, the flesh so white, I swore I could make out the reflection of the television from it. I tried. I actually sat there and tried to watch the TV off his body.

Then, something else. I tried to picture them together, Nellis and Vale, the way they used to be. Vale's looks had been good—a decent figure, plush lips and thick eyebrows that almost met in the center of her forehead which, for whatever odd reason a man finds such things attractive on a woman, I found quite so on her.

I saw Vale, but I couldn't see Nellis. Not the two of them as a couple. Not as he was now; thin and weak and broken. But wasn't he always that?

On the inside? When he was heavy and okay-looking to the world, wasn't he really just a thin and weak and broken man hiding in a shell? What other kind of man would let me get away with what I'd done?

I told myself that to make me believe I hadn't really destroyed a man, I had just revealed him.

It didn't work.

For seven years what had happened didn't matter. If I had ever once felt bad about what I di . . . about how things worked out, it had lasted for a minute and the minute passed. But now, every time Nellis walked in the door as he had back then, guilt would hit me the way O.J. hits women, and what happened mattered.

At those times Nellis would look at me and know everything I was thinking. All he would say is: "It doesn't matter anymore. She's gone. I got her out of my head. She doesn't exist." He would say that, then he would get himself good and high.

It took me about a half hour of watching TV off of Nellis and seeing only the past before I realized I had to get the hell out of the apartment for a while.

"I got to get the hell out of here for a while," I said to Nellis.

He moved for the first time in hours, and it was only his head he moved to look at me. The rest of his bones were still missing. "Where you going?"

"Get something to eat." I wasn't even close to hungry, but it was as good a lie as any.

"Bring me something, huh? Like . . . a subway. I could eat a subway."

"I don't have enough money," I mumbled back to him as I headed for the door.

"Hold on." Nellis got the rest of his bones back and made it to his feet. He went over to his duffel bag and started digging through it.

What the hell, I thought. I got to watch you get high again? I got to stand here and watch you get high?

Nellis came up out of the duffel. When he did it was like I took a slap in the face from a speeding Volvo. His hand was wrapped around a wad of cash. Naw, not a wad. It was a goddamn brick. It looked like the cornerstone of the temple of money. Tens, twenties, fifties, all bunched up in his fist same as autumn leaves. He tried to peel off some smaller bills for me to buy his food with. Clumps of bigger ones fell to the ground.

Look at that! Is that a hundred? A hundred-goddamn-dollar bill?

If Stepin Fetchit and Amos & Andy had had an illegitimate love child, it couldn't have done a bigger bug-eyed, head-snappin', jowl-shakin', flustered Negro double take than the one I put together. On top of that, if I didn't look fool enough, my lips flapped—yeah, actually frickin' flapped—in the air as I tried to grab on to a couple of words.

"Wh-wh . . . how did you—"

"Here's a ten. Ten's enough, right?" Nellis didn't even notice what he was doing to me. He just tried to give me money for the sandwich as if living like a jagged-up slug while you tote around more money than most small-town banks was normal as normal gets. "Is ten good?"

"Where did you—"

"Just get me, like, a club sandwich."

"How did you get—"

"With bacon, though. I want bacon."

"Nellis—"

"I got a taste for bacon."

"The money!"

"What? More than ten? You think it'll be more than that?" He went to peel off another five. A fifty floated to the floor.

I got control of myself and made things real clear for him. "Where did you get the money?"

"What? This?"

What? This? Yeah, that. That big fist of green you sprouted with the hundred-dollar fingers, you stupid bastard!

"Yes," I said very calmly.

"I won it."

"The lotto? You hit the lotto?"

Nellis shook his head. "Cards. Poker."

"What, you had a hot streak?"

"I guess. I suppose that's a lot to win, seeing as I've been here for— how long now?"

The Volvo come back around the block and let me have it one more time. "Since you've been here? You won all that playing poker since you've been here in LA?"

His shoulders hitched up slightly and fell in a small shrug. "Most all of it."

It's not that I hadn't seen guys win at poker before, or win as big as Nellis apparently had. But here was a man who could barely work up enough brainpower to figure out the mechanics of a doorknob, yet somehow he had enough to pull down how many hundreds, thousands playing cards? And this wasn't no lucky streak, not the way Nellis was talking; not the way he was so casual about his money. This was a guy who had gotten used to winning.

"How did you do that?"

"What? Win at poker?" Nellis kept on being casual. I might as well have been asking him the secret recipe for scrambled eggs. "I learned it when I left here. After . . . well, you know. The incident."

I knew.

"After that, I went east."

"New York?"

"China. Best heroin in the world, and all kinds, too. Asia Silk, Brown Tiger, Canton Spike . . . It's like the Baskin-Robbins of smack. They got girls there, too. Lot of Asian girls in China, but not as pretty as I thought they'd be. I needed girls to get my mind off of . . . things. So I left China and went to Thailand. Good smack, and the girls are pretty there, but they're all whores. That's a generalization. They're not all pretty, but the pretty ones are whores, 'cause in a place like Thailand that's the best way to make a good living."

I didn't give a good goddamn about his little travelogue. "The cards," I said, to nudge him back on track.

"Well, if you're around pretty girls who are all whores, you get tired of them after a while. What's the point of fucking any of them if you can fuck all of them? I started playing cards then just to give me something to do. My friend Pok, my friend at the time, he's the one who showed me the Single Light Hand."

"The single light . . ."

"What really helped my card playing is when I went to Japan. I met a Shinto priest who used to be a gambler. Became a priest to hide out from the Yakuza. He showed me a Zen technique—"

"Wait. What the hell is the Single Light Hand?"

"One path, one way, one ray of light . . . only one hand can win a game of poker. The winning hand is the light. You have to embrace the light and the truth, the truth being that only one hand can win the game."

I got that as well as most dogs understand rocket science. "Yeah, one hand wins the game. That's the way it's always been. What's so special about this Light Hand bullshit?"

"You see? That's why you can't win at poker. You can't accept the light."

I went over to a dresser, tore it open, pulled out a pack of cards.

"Oh yeah," Nellis started to say. "That's a good idea. I should show you how it's—"

I grabbed him up and sat him down hard on a chair at a table. "Yeah. You show me." I shuffled up quick and dealt.

"We playing for money?"

"We're just playing."

"Got to play for money. I don't know if it works if you don't play for money."

I scraped together some singles I had in a pocket and tossed one in the center of the table. "There. Happy? You ready to show me this light crap?"

Nellis rummaged through the wad of bills still sweating from between his fingers. He had a hard time finding a single. Finally, he came up with one and laid it on top of mine.

I turned up my cards. Sweet. Pair of queens, pair of sixes. I was going to take this smartass prick down. I called to myself for a card, tossed out a three and drew a ten. No help, but I didn't really need it.

Nellis glanced at his cards, then set them down. I looked at the cards on the table, up at Nellis, back at the cards, back at Nellis. "What?" I asked sharp.

"I'm out."

"What do you mean, 'out'?"

"I don't have the light. I don't have the winning hand."

"You didn't draw. You're just going to drop out, and not even draw?"

"What's the point? You got the light. Anybody can see that."

Hopped-up. That's what he was. That's what he had to be. He wants to drop, let him. I tossed down my cards and took his dollar. I was going to take him for his thousands if I had to do it one bill at a time.

Dealt again. I got a pair of fours and some garbage. Threw out the garbage, and pulled one more four. Beat that, you pincush—

He did it again; Nellis dropped his cards without even drawing.

"What the hell are you doing?"

"I don't have the li—"

"Knock it off with the light shit! Pull some cards!"

"I can't beat you. Why would I try to beat you if I can't beat you?"

"Yeah, that's right. You can't beat me. Where's your fucking light at?" If my words had any punch you couldn't tell by looking at Nellis. All he did was fish around for another dollar.

Again I dealt. More sweetness. Three kings. This was too easy. So what? Nellis had to learn a lesson. This time, he didn't go out. This time, he called for four cards. Four. He didn't have shit. Four he wanted, and four I gladly gave him.

"Feel like playing this time, huh?" He didn't so much as look at me. I tossed another dollar on the two singles.

Nellis tossed down a bill. A ten.

"I only bet a dollar."

He shrugged. "I raised. I didn't know there was a limit."

"I . . . I guess there isn't. I just—"

"You didn't say anything about a limit. I'm just playing bullshit anyway, right?" The way he said it, without looking at me, I couldn't tell if Nellis was just talking to talk or trying to needle me.

Didn't matter. He didn't have anything in his hand. You can't draw four cards and have anything. He was bluffing. All this Single-Light nonsense was just smoke for a bluff.

Sprinkles of sweat sprouted up across my forehead.

I saw his nine and raised five.

Nellis tossed back a five and a twenty. He barely even looked at the bills as they fluttered to the tabletop.

I felt myself go warm. "This is bullshit, Nellis. You know it's just bullshit."

Nellis didn't say anything to that. He rested his head on his hand, doing a real bored take on the whole process.

"Fuck you," I said, and I echoed it with the way I threw a twenty down on the table. "Call." I flipped my three kings out like I was throwing knives. I didn't say anything. I didn't have to rub it in. I knew the kings hurt enough on their own.

Nellis laid down his cards. Threes and fours. A full house. He scooped up his money, but that only seemed to make him all the more bored.

"You drew a full house?" That's all I could get out. "You drew a full house?"

"I had the three. I guess really I only drew two pair."

"You drew a full freakin' house? How the hell did you do that?"

"I'm trying to tell you. The Single Light—"

Before he even finished, I had the cards dealt. I had two tens and garbage. I was going to draw, and Nellis set down his cards. "Pick them up!" I screamed.

"Why? You have the li—"

"Pick up the damn cards!"

A queer moment followed where Nellis didn't know what to do. I couldn't make him stay in the game. Not technically. He wanted to drop. He could drop, so I let him drop. I scraped up the cards and dealt again.

The afternoon went on like that. Every time I had a good hand, anything that might end up being a good hand, or just something that might win me a couple of bucks, Nellis went out. But when he got a good hand, he got it big. He got them dropping three or four cards at a time. Sometimes, more than sometimes, he was just dealt the win. It's like he got every card he needed, when he needed it. It was like he knew just what I had, or what I was going to get, and didn't even bother with bluffing me or chancing a good hand against my better one. It was like . . .

Shit.

It was like there was a single hand that could win a game, and Nellis knew—*he knew*—just who had that hand.

Forty-five minutes, and he had taken me for sixty-four dollars. I'd never seen anything like it. Hell, I didn't even know what it was I was seeing, so how should I know if I'd ever seen it before?

Forty-five minutes, and all winning my money did was make Nellis that much more worn out. "I'm hungry."

"Explain it to me."

"You can't fight the cards. You can't try to win when you're not supposed to win."

"I've never seen a system like that before."

"It's not a system. It's a way of life."

It was heavy science Nellis was dropping, but the only thing that made an impression on me was that pile of green sitting in front of him.

"I'm hungry," he whined again. "You said you were going to get some food. Get me a subway, okay?"

I got up from where I sat, half-blind from all of Nellis's cash in my eyes. It took me a beat to remember a good part of that money was mine. The little demonstration had cleaned me out. I stood there like a fool. Not like one, I was a fool. After a second of looking at me Nellis caught on.

"Oh, hey, why don't you take your money back. I was only showing you how to play." He peeled off a hundred for me same as most people hand out Kleenex. "Just, like, a subway. With some bacon on it."

Forty-five minutes was all it took for a dirty little addict to shake me down as if he was smarter than me; as if he was sharper than me, or a better con. Maybe once he was. Years ago. Not now. Now this druggie shouldn't have been able to take me. But he had, and three-quarters of an hour was all he needed. I was angry, and embarrassed, and hurt, and ashamed. I was a lot of things, but I wasn't so much any of them to be above taking my money back.

I didn't go to eat; I went to drink. At the Regent I took up a seat at the bar to be closer to the liquor. Eddie tried to make some talk. I didn't want to at first. I just wanted to sit and drink and think about what Nellis had done with those cards. It didn't take long for all my thoughts to get too big for my head and I had to say something before my skull split open with things I couldn't understand.

"Saw a guy win at cards."

"What's that?" Eddie swung around to look at me. The empty sleeve on his left side flapped in the air.

"Saw a guy win at some poker tonight."

"That what got you drinking—a guy wins some poker? Doesn't take much to set you off, does it?"

"Not that he won. It's *how* he won."

"And how's that?"

How did Nellis win? And how do I break it down without sounding like I was hopped up myself? I couldn't. "He just did. He just won."

"He got lucky, that what you're saying?"

"I guess. But different. It was like he knew when he was going to be lucky. And when he knew he wasn't, he didn't even bother to play."

"So how's that mess you up?" Eddie topped off my glass.

As he did, I tried, probably not very well, to explain my malaise. "You spend most of your life around gambling—seeing people get beat every way there is, being the *get-beat* guy always—looking to just once, just one time make a score. . . . Then you see a guy win and win on purpose; win because he's making himself win, and acting like there's not a goddamn thing to it. Aw, hell, that hurts, Eddie. That's a shock to the system."

Wesker blew in loud and already drunk. He had a new girl under his arm, drunk, too. The pair made a big show of arriving, like they were the king and queen of England fresh back from a trip to the winter castle. They crowded up to the bar and ordered a bottle of something so out of my price I'd never heard of it before. They went off to a back table to be alone, but made a point to laugh and giggle noisy enough to remind everyone they were there.

Eddie got up a good sneer. "Jesus God Almighty. See what a little money does? Some people were never meant to have dough. They don't know what to do with it. If there's one guy who always should have been fifty cents short of a dollar, it's Wesker. Then he's got to go and win the lotto."

That threw me a bit. I started to say something, then I remembered me and Amber were the only ones who knew Wesker's lotto win was courtesy of a bank and the working end of a gun.

I kicked back my drink. Eddie poured me another. "You believe that?" I asked. "That a guy could just know when he's going to win, that he could have a system like that?"

Eddie shrugged with his good arm, his only arm.

"Personally, I think systems are bullshit when it comes to gambling. The dice, the ball, the cards—you can't make them do this thing or the other. They don't care what happened with the last toss or deal. They're going to do whatever they want, when they want. Fuck you one minute, forgive you the next. Hell, far as I'm concerned a pack of cards or a roulette wheel is better than a woman any day. A woman never forgives. Only dice forget."

I drank to that, and Eddie filled me again.

"Nah," he went on. "Only system there is when it comes to gambling is luck."

Luck. Sure. That's all it was. How could Nellis with his deep-fried brain and Zen mumbo jumbo ever figure out a way to work cards? He couldn't. He couldn't because it was impossible. There was no such thing as Single Light whatever. No such thing.

I kept telling myself that, shot after shot, one bottle into the next as if all I needed was enough liquor, then I would convince: What I thought Nellis had done, he hadn't, so why let my already fragile world crumble to its consternation? Eddie had said it. Cards are going to do whatever they want. Only dice forget.

It was truth. It was fact. But . . .

But so was all that cash Nellis had.

Jesus Christ!

I was out the door before I even knew I was moving, left Eddie standing there in the middle of a pour. I got in the Corvair and drove hard like I'd never driven hard in my life. I had to know. I had to.

When I got back to my apartment, Nellis was gone. Well, of course he was gone. He'd been going on about how hungry he was, and I'd been away for hours. Okay. Fine. He ran out to eat. He'd be back soon. I'd wait.

So I did that, waited, not making a very good job of it. I was okay at first, but as an hour crawled by—and that's just how it passed, at a crawl— I got antsy. The one time I need Nellis, the one goddamn time, and he picks it to pull a fade.

Where the hell was Nellis, how long could he stay gone?

One hour slid into two, and pretty soon every second that ticked off the clock was as prickly as a needle. I couldn't sit still, but wandering my tiny apartment just made me feel claustrophobic. A drink would smooth me out, but I had finished my liquor for breakfast, and running down to the corner for a bottle was out of the question. Just like the cable guy and the phone repairman, the second I was gone would be the second that Nellis showed up and left again. I was staying put. No matter how long it took I wasn't budging.

Seconds, minutes, hours.

Seconds, minutes, hours.

I was dry and sweaty, and I felt myself tremble a little. Was that the shakes I was getting? Couldn't be. The shakes are for drunks. The shakes are for when you bottom out. The shakes were for anybody but me 'cause I had enough problems right now.

Where the hell was Nellis, how long could he stay gone?

Then, real sudden, I knew where he was. He was somewhere that was anywhere that wasn't here. It didn't matter the specifics; if it was a crack den on Western, or a peep show on Santa Monica. He was somewhere else, and it wasn't by accident. Just like when he knew when to hold and when to fold, he knew I wanted him. He knew, and he was staying away to torture me on purpose.

The thought of it made me drier and warmer, and made me tremble just a bit more.

That son of a bitch. How dare he come to my house, use my space, eat my food, drink my drinks, and lead me on with this crap about Zen poker just to leave when I needed him? I'm going to kick him out, I thought. Soon as he sets one foot back in this place I'm going to turn him around and kick his milky little ass out of here.

I wanted to scream my anger, but the inside of my throat was peeling like paint in government housing.

Where was Nellis, how the hell long could he stay gone?

Then a new thought came to me: I thought about all the times Nellis was away so long I figured he might be dead, or at least in the process of getting dead. I thought about the times I wished it and hoped for it, only to have him come shuffling in just when it seemed my wish was closest to coming true. Well, what if this time it did? What if today was the day the dope and a crooked staircase or busy street corner caught up to him? I could see the headline, LA Times "Metro" section: MAN FALLS DOWN STAIRS, BREAKS NECK. Or ADDICT KILLED IN BAD DRUG DEAL. Or MAN HORRIBLY CRUSHED AND MUTILATED BEYOND RECOGNITION UNDER WHEELS OF SPEEDING BIG RIG.

Jesus Christ. If he's dead, I'm dead.

I'm sorry, Nellis. I'm sorry I ever thought that way before. That was just . . . that was the booze making me think wrong.

Going crazy with despair and sobriety, I shut my eyes and projected regret and blame across the city.

I'm sorry, Nellis. Don't be dead. I'll never ever do wrong by you again. I swear. Oh please, dear God, don't let him be dead.

Where the hell is Nellis, how long—

The door opened and Nellis came in. "Hey" was all he had to say. Then he started a slow sink to the floor for what would most likely be a long sleep. Before his knees touched down I was across the room. I had Nellis hard by the shoulders and yanked back up and into my face.

"Where the hell have you been!" I spat at him.

"The Wax Museum."

"The . . . *what?*"

"They didn't have Tom Selleck. In the brochure, they have Tom Selleck. I walked all the way over to the museum and they didn't have Tom

Selleck. I told the manager they should change the brochure. I didn't think they'd put Tom back, but they should at least change the brochure."

"Why didn't you call? You're going to be gone that long, you should call."

"I . . . I didn't—"

"How the hell am I supposed to know where you are when you don't call?"

"I'm sorry. I didn't think. You never cared where I was before. You never told me—"

"Well, I'm telling you now. Call. You gonna be out somewhere, you're going to be gone a long time, you call me and tell me where you are, and when you're gonna be back."

Nellis's head went limp with shame like he was the one who had done something wrong. Like it was him, not me, who was out of line. "I'm stupid; that's what my problem is. Just stupid. Gone too long, then showing up at the wrong times. Right, Jeffty? I'm always at the wrong place at the wrong time."

I don't think he even meant to, but if he had swung a bag of hammers he couldn't have hit me harder. Wrong place, wrong time. Me and Vale, and Nellis walking in the door.

"I'm sorry," I sputtered.

"Told you: nothing to be sorry about. She's gone now, gone from my mind. Vale doesn't exist."

He said it in an odd way, a way that made me know that for him Vale really didn't exist anymore. Maybe it was the drugs or his crazy poker that I was starting to think wasn't so crazy anymore, but somehow Nellis had gotten rid of Vale forever. I couldn't say the same for me. The snapshot of what happened among us was jammed in my mind like it was hot iron branded there.

Me and Nellis stood in the quiet awhile.

In the city, somewhere, a siren wailed. Somebody had been shot, or stabbed. Or maybe somebody's house was burning down.

Maybe not.

Maybe it was a good siren. Maybe it was a woman being rushed to the hospital about to bring a new life into the world. I doubted it. And if it was, the kid would probably grow up to be an addict, or a pusher, or a killer anyway.

I glanced through the window. It was dark outside.

"Come on," I said plainly.

"Where we going?"

"I want you to show me something."

My hand still on Nellis's shoulder, I pulled him all the way down to the Corvair. I tossed him in the passenger side, then got behind the wheel and started driving.

Nellis was beside himself with happy. It was like we were finally hanging out, he told me between giggles. It was like we were buddies all over again the way we were before Vale. He blamed her for what happened, not me, and didn't hold back at all from telling me about it. He had a few choice words for her, for women in general.

"They're all evil," he said. "All women are evil all the time." He looked at me with an empty face. "How can you trust something that bleeds for a week once a month but won't die?"

Whatever.

I didn't agree or disagree with anything Nellis had to offer. He wanted to hate women, fine. He wanted to think we were hanging out, that was okeydoke, too. I had something bigger in my head just then, and although Nellis was part of it, there wasn't much room for him in my thoughts.

Normandie Casino. A legal gambling joint in Gardena. No table games, no craps or roulette—you can't bet those in California—but what they did have were card games, poker, and right now that would do me fine. I needed to know if Nellis was for real; if he could turn over dollars sitting opposite some real sharps. At first Nellis didn't want to play any. He said he was tired of cards, been doing it since he'd gotten to LA.

I told him I wasn't trying to hear that he was tired. Play!

We bought into a game, Nellis did, and I watched from the rail as he went to work. He didn't give me time to think maybe what happened earlier was a fluke, or luck, or just my bad card playing. It was nothing but flashback to what I'd seen before. From the first hand, it was the cards he needed when he needed them. When he couldn't get them, when he *knew* he couldn't get them, he folded before he got started. Even when he had a good hand it was like he knew if somebody else had a better one. It was all very weird and complex, and it was just as simple. He knew he could win, or he didn't bother playing.

Inside half an hour Nellis was up a few hundred. An hour marked him pushing eight. Just over a hundred minutes and Nellis, who said he was worn-out and bored—and he said it loud enough to get snarls from the rest of the table—cashed in with somewhere around twelve hundred dollars. Zen, or a system, or luck, or whatever, it made no difference. Nellis could win, and win big.

The ride home, Nellis was as talky as a kid on a car trip. He had fun hanging out. Could we hang out some more? When could we hang out again? Could we stop for a chili dog . . . with bacon?

I caught about every sixth word, too deep in my bliss to know or care about his ramblings. My mind was juiced and racing at a hundred rpms. It was a human supercomputer that had all the answers.

"Let's go to the Auto Museum next time." Nellis's voice was a little fly buzzing in my ear. "I want to do that. I like cars. Maybe they got the one Tom Selleck drove. The Magnum car."

"How about this, Nellis? How about we take a road trip?"

It could have been Christmas the way his eyes lit up. "Are you serious? Where are we going to? Can I drive some? We're going to drive there, right? Where we going?"

Nellis could win at cards, but to win the kind of dough I had to have, nearly thirty long, and to do it quick, we needed to gamble outside one of the legal joints. We needed an underground game with a few high rollers, but not the kind of guys who would slit your throat just for thinking about winning a hand. I was looking for the kind who, win or lose, were only trying to get their gamble on. One place I know where guys like that are spread around as thick as the bathroom carpet Elvis choked on. I turned to Nellis.

"How would you like to go to Vegas?"

I had the best sleep I'd had in a long time. A baby's sleep. A sleep of the innocent by virtue of becoming a virgin again to guilt. I had felt so bad about Nellis, about what I had done to him. But now I saw I hadn't done anything. I hadn't destroyed this guy, I'd rebuilt him. It was me with Vale that sent him to Asia where he learned whatever kind of craziness it is he does with cards, given him the means to do good, so that he could come back now to help me just when I most needed helping. Really, when you think about it, when I did what I did with Vale I was shaping my own future—setting myself up for a save I didn't even know I was going to need. Life in a perfect circle. No losers here. The house pays on all bets. When I looked at all the good that'd come of it, I was sorry I hadn't gotten busy with Vale sooner.

Of course, Nellis didn't know how he was going to get my neck out from under Dumas's foot, but I figured it was only fair he pay me back for all the things I'd done for him. Maybe I should tell him. Maybe I should clue him in on the good he's doing. Might do wonders for him to know he's not a tripped-out loser after all. Yeah, let me do that. It'd be like I'm helping him again, instead of him helping me.

I jerked awake. Not because I heard Nellis come into my room, but I felt him: a spider creeping on exposed flesh. When my eyes came open, I saw him hovering above me. Cream skin lit by moonlight. Blurry vision made him look like the boogeyman, his "get high" hose tourniqueted his left arm. He stood there for a while, creepy-quiet, not making a sound. Then he said: "I lied."

"Wha . . ."

"When I said she wasn't in my mind."

"Vale?"

"I tried, tried to get her out of my mind. That's why I ran away. That's why I went east—to forget."

"Go back to bed."

"But I couldn't make her leave my head. Everywhere I went, my skull was full of her."

"Nellis, for crying out loud . . ."

"That's why she couldn't exist . . . why I couldn't let her exist any-more; it was the only way to get her out of my head. I had to, Jeffty. I had to kill her."

I tried to say something, but my tongue caught in my throat.

"Snapped her neck. Snapped it, then crushed her head with a brick so she'd stay killed. Thought that would get her out of my skull." His right arm slithered up to his head and he massaged his face in his hand. "It didn't. Now she's in there all the time." His hand stopped massaging and started clutching. "If she would just shut up for a second. The bitch won't shut up!"

My hand hurt, and I realized I was choking the hell out of my blanket.

Nellis looked down at the hose dangling from his arm. "It's the only way to keep her quiet."

After that he didn't say a word. I had less to say back. Finally, Nellis left the room, swallowed up by the darkness behind him.

I didn't go back to sleep. I just lay, awake, strangling my blanket until dawn.

We left the next day for Vegas. I didn't pack much. I didn't figure it would take long to hook up a card game for Nellis to win me thirty thousand. More was fine, but thirty was my ticket to freedom. All Nellis wanted to take was his tin box. No change of clothes, no toothbrush, just the tin and what was inside. I convinced him, for my sake, to at least bring along a couple of extra shirts.

We left early in the afternoon to avoid the late exodus from the city to Orange County, and Whittier, and Pomona, and anywhere else that wasn't LA. I had the oil checked in the Corvair, pumped a little air in the tires, and took the 10 to the 15 to Las Vegas.

What happened the night before when Nellis showed up in my room wasn't mentioned. I knew it wasn't a dream, not on my part. Maybe it was for him. A dream, or a piece of one of his needle rides. A trip so deep and fine he just thought he . . . did what he said he'd done. He could feel his hands on Vale's imaginary throat as her neck twisted and cracked. He could see her head. . . .

Jesus.

Crushed her skull with a brick.

I looked at Nellis, next to me, sleeping like always. I looked at him and wondered what kind of animal crawled beneath his flesh. What could drive a man not only to kill but to destroy?

I caught my reflection in the rearview mirror.

No. I had nothing to do with what happened. It was his own choice. So I made it with his wife? So he got cheated on?

So what?

That happens to a lot of men. They don't go out and get themselves hooked. They don't puree their wife's brains. They yell, scream; maybe a few of them throw a couple of punches their woman's way. I'm not saying it's right; I'm just saying that's what some guys do. Other guys will go out and get themselves a fast new car to cool the hurt, or, better still, a good young lay. But to kill, to murder . . . that was all Nellis's doing.

Just sitting there sleeping against the door, he began to make me sick. He irritated me like a rash making its way across my skin. I wanted him out of the car right then and there. No pulling over, no slowing down. Just a quick yank on the door handle and a glance to the rearview mirror to watch his useless body flipping across the road—a dumped sack of potatoes.

I would have done it, too, if I hadn't needed Nellis to win me money. But the second I got my thirty thousand he was going to be ass out on the street. I meant it. I didn't even know if I planned on driving him back to LA. I could slip out on him while he was sleeping, and he was always sleeping.

That's what I was going to do. Soon as I got my thirty thousand. Maybe fifty, or sixty if Nellis was playing hot. But then, like I said, he'd get kicked straight to the curb.

Maybe eighty . . .

The Green Felt Jungle

*I*t was a four-and-change-hour drive, LA to Las Vegas, that most people made in little more than three and a half. About halfway there is a patch of dirt someone slapped a few buildings on and called Barstow. It made a good business off Angelenos on their way to lose money or fresh from getting picked clean, who needed to piss or eat. I needed to do both.

We stopped at the Trading Post, a roadside gas/plaza thing. Inside was a restaurant, Kattie's Kountry Kitchen. A big bruiser did double shift as cook and counter guy. A Mexican girl worked the tables. Kattie didn't much seem to be involved in the establishment that bore her name.

I ordered chicken fingers, fries, and a shake—strawberry.

Nellis got twice that to start, then got more. I didn't understand how someone who wore their skin like it was paint on bones could eat so much. Must have been the drugs.

We got gas, I pumped and Nellis paid, then hit the road. The second the tires touched highway Nellis was out, dead asleep again. Nice trick. It annoyed the hell out of me.

The drive was mostly mountains and desert, and there was little outside the car but night. No cities. No lights. It was empty, and to me the empty was beautiful.

We made the Cal-Nevada border. Used to be not much there, but a couple of big casinos had sprouted up over the last few years. They thrived on the philosophy of: Why drive that extra hour to Vegas when you can lose all your dough so much closer to home? They thrived on that philosophy well.

I kept driving.

More desert. More dark.

A car by the side of the road, on fire. I didn't even slow down.

More dark.

More dark.

The radio picked up a staticky version of a sort of old Yolly Maxwell song.

More dark.

Then you see it. Not the city itself. Not at first. Just a glow over the horizon like an electric fire. The lights of Las Vegas, a warmth in the night, sucking you in.

Drive on a bit. Closer. Now you see Vegas. At least the Vegas they want you to see: a thousand-watt neon smile that go, go, goes day/night/day. The mother of all rackets. The hustle to end all hustles.

I pulled off the 15 onto State Highway 604. Las Vegas Boulevard. The Strip. Excalibur and Luxor to the left. MGM and Bally's to the right. The Flamingo Hilton over there. Newt at the DI. Catch him early when he's sober and it's a hell of a show. And, of course, the boys and their tigers across at the Mirage.

Stopped at a stoplight. At the corner some redneck, him and his whole redneck family wearing JESUS SAVES shirts, starts yelling at a guy handing out well-illustrated flyers for escorts, call girls, hookers, and better.

"Get that shit away from me," the redneck screamed at the peddler. "You keep that shit away from my family!"

He took his wife and kid by the hand and yanked them into Treasure Island, toward the craps tables.

I drove on past big casinos, casinos in strip malls, slot machines in 7-Elevens, wedding chapels, twenty-four-hour wedding chapels, drive-through wedding chapels, strip clubs, triple-X all-nude strip clubs, open-all-night bail bondsmen, and one, single sign above a shop that said it all: BOOZE, DRUGS, GUNS.

Downtown. Glitter Gulch. The old Strip lit up by all the neon and dancing lights on Fremont Street. The Nugget, the Horseshoe, Vegas Vic—the big cowboy with the big smile jerking his big thumb back toward the Gulch, as if to say the Gulch was the only place any smart guy would lose his money. You could call it all kitsch, but it had long since become part of the Vegas style. Just recently, someone got the idea to erect a steel canopy over Fremont just above street level. As if a bunch of metal blocking out this midnight sun would somehow lure gamblers from what passed as the glamour of the Strip back downtown.

Forget it.

All it ended up being was a couple million dollars' worth of bad idea. The tacky gets tackier.

We, me and Nellis, were staying at the California, just off the Gulch. It made its trade catering to Hawaiians, and a good trade at that. Them Asians love to gamble. Tropical motif, Polynesian food, lots of employees from the islands. Anything and everything to make the visitors feel comfortable while they're betting. It was an okay place as downtown goes, fairly upscale. They didn't have penny slots, which is when you know you're scraping bottom. I used to gamble heavy there—it didn't take much to be a heavy gambler at the Cal—which meant I could still dig up a free room. There's always a comp room and meal somewhere for you in Vegas if you're willing to lose enough.

As soon as we pulled into the parking garage, and I mean the second I shut the engine off, Nellis came awake. Made me think that maybe he didn't sleep as much as he made out, but just put on a fake act . . . like I did with him. In the end, I didn't much care. I didn't like chauffeuring Nellis, but it beat trying to deal with conversation.

The check-in was quick, things having slowed to a dull hum by this late in the day. Most everybody who was going to do any serious gambling arrived early and had already staked out a slot machine, or stool at the blackjack table. Me and Nellis carted our own stuff up to the room. The porter didn't even make a move for us. We didn't have many bags, and we sure didn't look like the tipping kind.

Our room was wallpapered floral. Birds of paradise. Orange and yellow once, now gray with age. The rest was Hotel Anywhere, USA: couple of beds, a chest of drawers that had to be wrestled open, a sink and mirror outside a small room with a toilet and bathtub. Over in the corner was a safe rusted open from disuse. Anybody staying here had nothing valuable to put in it, and if they did, sooner or later it would end up on red twenty-three.

Nellis bounced around all hyper like we had just gotten to Disney-land. "Let's go to Circus Circus. I want to see the acrobats. Let's go win a stuffed animal."

Jesus. How much horse do you have to do to get your brains this sizzled? When you're this crazy do you even know it? Are you really crazy enough to kill someone, or just so crazy you thought you had?

"Yeah, we can go to Circus Circus. But I have to go see somebody first."

"Who? Who you got to see?

"A friend of mine. I haven't seen him in a while. I promised next time I was in Vegas I would stop by."

"So stop by later. After Circus Circus."

This shit I didn't need. "Look, I'm going to go. I'm going to hang out a little bit; then you and me are going to spend the rest of our time here doing whatever you want," I lied.

"Whatever?"

"Yeah. I mean, you pick something you want to do; then"—I slid in this part real subtle—"I'll pick something I want to do."

Nellis gave a shrug. "Yeah, okay."

"You hungry? Want something to eat? Get yourself some room service."

"Maybe I'll go down and—"

"No. No." I didn't want him leaving the room. I didn't need him dis-appearing, or, worse yet, finally finding his way out into traffic. Not now. Not when I was so close. Few more hours and he could take a header from the top of the Tropicana for all I cared. "Room service is much bet-ter. It's, uh, special." I worked overtime to sell him on the idea. "How many times do you get to have somebody bring a meal right up to your room? Eat it in bed if you want. That's better than sitting in some stuffy restaurant with a bunch of people you don't know."

It took. "I guess," he said.

"Yeah, it's like a treat." I sat Nellis on the bed, handed him a lami-nated menu from the nightstand, and inched for the door. "Whatever you want. Treat yourself. You just stay here, and I'll be back before you know it. Just . . . stay here."

I was out the door. A beat later I was back in. One more instruction. "But don't spend too much. We've got to share the money, right?"

He nodded.

I left.

Down to the lobby and outside. I had to make a short walk to the Union Plaza hotel/casino at the end of Fremont. The Plaza was right on top of the train station and right next to the bus depot. Probably was a time when this seemed like a good idea—when trains and buses were still the way civilized people traveled, and having two modes of transportation flowing right to your doorstep made for pure profit. These days they would've done just as good to build on top of a homeless shelter with the derelicts and lowlifes who made the Plaza their establishment of choice. Still, the casino tried to look as glamorous as it could. A giant fountain of lights ran up the facade and spouted from the top. It showered down in faux elegance on THE PLAZA, lit a blinding white. But like an old woman in spike heels and a push-up bra, it looked more silly than sexy.

I passed a pawnshop. In the window was a prosthetic arm someone had given up for one more pitch of the dice. At what point do you need a win so bad you decide you can go through life with one good arm? I looked down at my broken fingers.

Inside the Plaza. As low-rent as any downtown casino, and doing just as brisk a business. A magician, Baxter Fielding, was headlining the show-room. I had never heard of him. The way people weren't lining up to catch his act, I guess no one else had, either.

Brunson was the guy I was looking for, a blackjack dealer. It was a small floor, and he wasn't hard to spot. I nodded at him, and he nodded back, but since he was working and I wasn't gambling, I indicated I was heading over to the bar to wait for his shift to end.

The Omaha Bar was next to the Omaha Lounge which is where a Filipino guy with an all-Filipino band was working his way through "Unchained Melody" for the dozen or so people who passed as an audience. A drunk couple up front—a couple of drunks—went all misty-eyed as the Filipino sang. When I got to the bar, I realized I hadn't had a drink in a while. At least not what added up to a while for me. Nothing since leaving LA. Nothing since the night before that. I didn't need to drink. I didn't need to be braced up, or evened out. Not anymore. Now I had a plan. For the first time in a long time I was in control of things.

I celebrated my elevation to a higher plane with a Coca-Cola, and sat and waited for Brunson.

All across the floor: Players, dead-eyed, hunched over slot machines, fed them coins and tapped away at the spin button. They reminded me of the people back at the Regent. The soulless were alike all over.

Twenty minutes, then Brunson came over. Tall, thin, more pink than white. Wrinkles deep like blade cuts that made him look years older, lots tougher. He sat on the stool next to mine and ordered water since he was still in uniform.

"Jeffty. Ain't seen you around in a while." His voice was two-packs-a-day hoarse.

"No money. No money in this town, not much reason to be here."

Brunson nodded. Yeah, there wasn't much reason to be here. "Thought maybe you picked up the pen again. Thought maybe that's why you've been gone.

My head shook no.

"So, what? Got some cash you looking to lose?"

"Got some cash I'm looking to make."

That didn't get any kind of a rise out of Brunson. I was just another man with a plan. "Jesus, Jeffty. You got a couple of bucks, why don't you wise up and hang on to it?"

"Couple of bucks doesn't do me any good. I'm in deep to a guy this time."

"How deep?"

"Twenty-five pushing thirty."

Brunson didn't take the news in any particular manner. A guy who owed a guy. Again nothing new. Just pure Vegas.

I said: "I need to get in a game. Outside the house. Something where I could pull thirty or forty. At least that."

This got a little laugh. "You're just going to win thirty thousand in a card game and wipe your debt. Easy as that. You're talking like a retard. That it—you get retarded since you was here last?"

"I know I can win."

Brunson shook his head: Pathetic.

"I got a friend with a system."

More laughter.

"He can't lose."

Brunson's eyes got narrow until they were just more hatch marks on his face. "Aw, for the love of Pete, Jeffty. How long you been away that you got so stupid? The ground out here is filled with guys who can't lose, and the monuments over their graves read: Sahara, Mirage, and Golden Nugget."

Brunson pushed aside his water and ordered a whiskey. The bartender gave him something about employees not drinking while in uniform. Brunson cut him off with a "Shut your yap and just gimme the whiskey." The bartender just gave it to him.

Brunson said: "Thirty thousand down, and you show up begging for more. What happened to you? For a while, used to be you'd breeze in here all full of yourself. Gambling was something you just did to do; you were a winner before your money even hit the table. Now all of a sudden you come around sweaty and desperate like a guy who's betting with pawnshop money."

"There's nothing all a sudden about it. It's not an elevator down; it's an escalator, slow and steady, one step at a time till you end up here, right in this spot. Right where I am."

"Then do something. Something besides gamble one more time."

"I got a string of people between here and LA telling me what's wrong with my life—"

"I'm just saying, why don't you pick up the pen again?"

"Everybody's got the antidote."

"Remember that thing, the one you let me read."

I felt as if, like he was the Ghost of Shitty Life Past, Brunson was taking me back to a place I didn't want to be. "Yeah, that thing. That *thing*. The one time in my life that I ever did anything that was"— I tried not to sound like a little girl crying—"special."

"That's why I'm saying—"

"And what did I get for my trouble except beat? Beat up, beat down, beat every way there is. So, I'm not trying to go back to nothing. I'm trying to get ahead. Just for one time in my life I'm trying to get ahead, and all you can do is sit there and tsk-tsk me. You're a dealer, for Christ's sake. You stand around all day watching old ladies bet their government aid, now all a sudden you want to get religion with me."

"I know what I do, and I know what I see. Same thing every shift. People coming in thinking they got the house beat, and everyone of them walks out broke-ass and near butt-naked. And I don't give a damn about any of them. Two kinds of people in the world. The ones who take, and the ones who get taken, and the 'get taken' kind need to get their money pried from 'em."

Brunson took a long pull of his whiskey and went on. "You're not one of them, Jeffty. Maybe you're never going to do much with yourself, but you're not a mark. You con for a living; you know the score, so knock off this system shit. I can take it from the rest of the idiots who wander in here, but when the people who should know better start buying into the bullshit it's not long for any of us. Jesus. You make me mad, Jeffty. You make me mad."

Another tug of his whiskey followed that.

"It's a 'can't lose' situation."

"Tell me one I haven't heard."

"Then how about this: I can't lose, 'cause I'm betting my life on it. It don't work this time, it stops working forever. I need a card game, Brunson. That's all I'm asking for is a game."

Brunson sat there, drank a little; then he sat there some more. When he was through with all that, he said: "What kind of taw you got?"

"About twenty-five hundred."

"Day after tomorrow."

Day after tomorrow. Another day with Nellis. "Nothing sooner, like maybe tonight?"

"Not for your kind of money. This is all the game you need. You'll get some high rollers there—out-of-towners who want to see some off-the-Strip action, but not the kind who're gonna bust the rest of your fingers when you lose. And you will lose." He grabbed up a pen and wrote on a cocktail napkin. "Here's the address. Starts at eight. I'll let 'em know you're coming."

"Thanks, man. I'm going to do all right with this."

Brunson's head shook. "I had hopes for you. Yeah, I did. Wouldn't've had anything to do with you otherwise."

"I'm telling you, I'm going to do all right."

Killing off his whiskey, Brunson got up. As he walked away, without looking back, he said: "Break's over. Gotta go rake in some money from the rest of these people who can't lose."

Nellis wanted to go everywhere and do everything. The roller coaster over at the Stratosphere, the theme park at MGM, the pirate show at Treasure Island. Any of the new Vegas, the family Vegas, the "teach the kids to gamble so one day they'll grow up to lose their money here" Vegas, and we were there doing it. The guy was on overdrive. Dangle a shiny nickel in front of him and he'd jump for it. And just when I thought he was about to mellow out or fall into one of his minicomas, he would disappear into a bathroom, then bust out with his spring wound tight. I didn't know what he was taking hits of, but it kept him running on all cylinders.

I would have pulled my "I'm sleeping" routine, stayed in our room while he got his fill of this place, but I had to keep an eye on Nellis; make sure he didn't get hurt, make sure he didn't spend too much of my precious money. And at every place he dragged me to, every tacky tourist trap I had to endure, all I could do was count the seconds until I could jettison this lousy dope freak for good.

And the seconds crawled on. Time hung in the air like a drop of water that refused to fall from a leaking pipe. One o'clock, 1:05, 1:08. I had to take my watch off my wrist and stuff it in my pocket to keep from marking every single minute. I was a baby-sitter and a big brother and a thousand other things I had no desire to be with no end in sight.

Then it ended.

We were at the Luxor in Virtualand which is nothing more than a roomful of video games that someone had the bright idea to call Virtualand so you'd feel better about spending your money on video games. I had just changed a bunch of dollars into game tokens.

"I want to go back to the room." Nellis barely got that out, too lethargic was he to form words. He was a machine grinding down, but that was all I needed to hear.

I shoved my tokens into the hands of a nearby seven-year-old—his mom yanked him away like I was a perv scoping prepubes at a schoolyard to turn tricks for me—then hustled Nellis to the Corvair and back to the California.

Barely made it.

Whatever Nellis had been running on—drugs, adrenaline, a Vegas rush—it was gone now. This guy wasn't used to going, and living, and doing. He was used to curling up on a dirty floor and trying to shut out life as it passed him by. He was spent. Exhausted. I think it was all he could do just to keep his heart beating.

I fell back in a chair, worn to the bone myself. My eyes had just started to close a bit when a little voice called over to me.

"Jeffty?

"What?"

"Thanks for taking me around."

"Yeah."

Some quiet.

"Jeffty?"

"Yeah, what?"

"I had a good time. Not just seeing stuff. I mean I had a good time being with you. We haven't done that in a while."

"Nope."

"We used to have some high times, didn't we, Jeffty? Back before I took off. We used to . . ." He halted for a second; something caught in his throat. "We used to have fun. We used to live. I miss that."

His throat caught again; emotion was getting stuck in there. Then: "Never told you before, but you were my best friend. Sounds stupid, huh?

Like we're kids or something. But you were, Jeffty. You were my best friend. I used to look up to you, you know?"

"I know." I had to ask. "How come you did?"

"You could do shit, Jeffty. I mean, I could trick the half blind out of their pocket change, but you had honest-to-God real-life skills. You could . . . That thing—that movie script you let me read that one time . . ."

"You still have that."

"Yeah. I kept it all these years. It was . . . it was really pretty what you wrote. Except where that old man got gut-shot. I mean, that was a little . . . But other than that it was really . . . I always figured you'd be something; more than a con man, which is all I'd ever amount to. I always figured you'd be something for the both of us."

I looked at Nellis. He had been back in town for weeks, around me more than I could stand, but I didn't remember having once *really* looked at him; having once taken measure of this man.

I did now. I looked at Nellis, what was left of him, of what I used to know. When is it two people become friends? What is that moment when you choose to call another man so?

I looked at Nellis. He was right: We had had some high times. We'd lived our lives from sundown to sunup. Out when we shouldn't have been, and going places we had no business being other than it was where we wanted to go. But when you're young, you live a world without fear. Boozin' and cruisin' every track and card joint in LA. Laying down heavy bets, crazy bets, 'cause the young don't know how to lose. Naw, that you learn later.

Couple of girls in there, too. We found us a few. We hooked them not because they were of particular prettiness, or because we loved them, or wanted them to mother our children. We picked them up just to pick them up. We picked them up just to have something to fuck at night. And fuck them we did. Every which way and condom-free, then tossed them aside with all the indifference we could muster.

Yeah. The young live a world without fear.

I looked at Nellis. When is it you decide someone is no longer your friend; when you would treat them as you would a stranger, or even less so? Is it something that you plan, or is it something that just happens? Or maybe it's just that friendship, like everything else, has its own angles to be played. The time you spend with someone is just an investment in whatever it is you'll one day extract from them. That is, unless they extract whatever it is they need from you first. Is that all Nellis had ever been to me—not a familiar, but someone I kept in my pocket like a lucky quarter waiting to spend on a last-chance bet? Had I really used him? Had I really broken him? Had I really been the one to destroy him and in doing so . . .

I looked at Nellis. I asked him: "Did you do it? Did you kill Vale?"

Nellis looked at me. "Yes."

The California. Casino floor. I sat at a slot machine, feeding it nickels. I didn't care a thing about betting right then; I just had to be out of the room. "Yes," Nellis had said when I asked if he'd really killed his wife. "Yes," he'd said, casual, as if answering the most mundane of questions: Yes, it's raining out. Yes, this seat is taken. Yes, I strangled and bludgeoned the woman I'd married.

Another nickel in the machine.

I told Nellis I had to run out for a second. I told him I would be right back. I told him that more than an hour ago.

Another nickel in the machine.

I didn't even pay attention as the wheels spun. I thought of Vale. I thought of having sex with her. I didn't know it then, but all I was doing was killing her. As I moved my tongue in her mouth, kissed her nipples, went down on her, all I was doing was sealing her fate. It wouldn't happen until years later, but I was fucking a dead girl.

Truth: It's a weird thing to think about, but we're all the walking dead. Every single one of us. A car wreck, a bullet to the head, a slip in the bathtub—whatever the cause of our destruction is to be, it's already out there waiting for us. For Vale, it was me.

Across the way a change girl pushed her cart of hard count around the floor. Oriental. Oriental chicks have a way of looking young for a long time. I don't know why, or what it is, but you see an Oriental girl you got to know she's older than her face shows. They're lucky that way, I guess.

This one had empty eyes that looked right through people. If you didn't need change, she didn't want anything to do with you. Long hair tied back in a tail with streaks of gray. But all of that made her look, I don't know, not worn-out. Mature. It made her look like . . . not a girl, a woman. It made her look good. And the rest of her only helped things: an ass. Hard to find an Oriental with a decent ass, but she had herself a good one. Not flat, but tight and firm like the legs that stretched down from it. Up top she was all business, too. Maybe she was an old one, but she kept herself together. A heyday Nancy Kwan with a little extra sex slathered on.

I clicked on the change light above my machine and waited for her to come around.

She did.

Then she just stood, not saying a word, waiting for me to hand over a five, or ten, or whatever for her to break. I let her wait. I let her wait until she realized I wasn't handing her anything. I let her wait until she looked at me.

She had a little name tag: GAYLE.

With a twisted lip that was supposed to be a cool smirk I said: "Let me ask you something, Gayle. How old are you? You got that gray in your hair and everything like you're all old, but that body of yours says different. Not that it matters either way. You're a nice little package just as you come."

It was meant to be out of left field: Odd, with enough compliment to get her attention.

She kept looking at me.

Kept looking.

Then she said: "And you're an asshole."

I kept the twisted-lip smirk going and tossed in the best bit of clever I could come up with. "You're the change girl. Change me."

She reached over and turned off the light on my machine, then gave the coda to the end of our conversation. "You want something or not?"

I'd come with a good line, maybe not the best in the world, but a good one, and it bought me nothing. Not with this girl. In Vegas, in the casinos, guys want women for no other reason than they're women, and having one around fits right in with the loose money and high living. They're just a place to hang your arm while you're waiting for another free drink, or for your luck to change. And a chick like this, a chick more than halfway good-looking, had probably been hit on, come on to, and flirted with every way there was the first day on the job. I had nothing new to show her, so I thought I'd show her nothing to see how that grabbed her.

"What I want, you don't have, and what you have, I don't need." I tossed a nickel at her, injury to my insult, then walked away without looking back.

I kept walking over to the Market Street Café, sat down, and ordered myself the state special: prime rib on the cheap. As I waited for it, I tried not to look out onto the casino floor. I wanted to know what her reaction was to what I'd said and to the nickel I'd tossed. Women get hit on out here, but not many get blown off. Not many get turned down so bad, it makes them feel worthless and weak and cheap. Make a woman feel all that, then she'll need to feel wanted. So I'd used words like a fist and hit Gayle. One of two things happen when you hit a woman: Either she leaves you or she stays. If she stays, you own her forever. If Gayle was there for me when I went back out on the floor, she was mine.

So I waited. Same as if I'd laid a trap for an animal, I waited through my salad, and my rib, and a bad scoop of colored ice cream they hand out for dessert. Then I waited some more just to make it look like I didn't care one way or the other if I ever saw her again.

But the more I sat there, the more the waiting needled me with fine points, and I knew I did want to see her again with a need that, for whatever reason, crept toward desperation. I tried to sit five minutes longer. I made three, paid, and left.

Casino floor. Nickel slots. Same one I was at before. If she was around, she'd see me there.

If.

I hadn't lost more than two dollars when I heard her behind me.

"You didn't have to be so rough about it."

Her voice was soft and slow and weak, like I had hoped. I would have been proud of myself for having beat her down, except when she spoke her breath rubbed at the back of my neck. I felt myself go flush, and had to work hard to keep steady. I turned to her, taking my time about it, tossed a five on top of her cart. "Nickels."

"I said you didn't have to be so rough about it."

"And I said nickels."

She got mad for a second, but only for a second. Then she looked like she might cry. Her figurative skin was tough as leather, but I had long since gotten under that. She ripped open the top to her cart, grabbed up a five's worth of nickels, and shoved them at me.

"You're a real hard guy to be gambling nickels all by yourself at night."

"And you're a hard girl to be making change in a small-time casino."

The second I said that, I was sorry I had. I didn't want to be tough with her. Something about her made me want to be tender. But tenderness wasn't what got me in the door.

She said: "I get off in an hour."

Gayle pushed her cart on. I watched her walk away. I watched her gray-streaked hair and her tight ass get swallowed in a sea of gamblers. All the while I thought: I own that.

I hung back a ways from the employees' entrance to the casino. I was there well before the hour ended to make sure I didn't miss Gayle coming out. Better she didn't know that. Maybe that's what she wanted: to make me wait like a dog; to hit me like I hit her, then quit the game altogether. So I hung back.

Just past the hour, she came out. Uniform gone, skirt and blouse now. Legs better than I could have hoped.

I started for her, then had another idea: Let her do some waiting.

I watched her under the dim lighting that reached down from above the door as she went through phases. She leaned against the wall for a while. Casual. Then she paced. Anxious. Next she looked at her watch every minute on the minute. She was pissed, but she burned that off quick. Then she looked sad. Hurt. I didn't mean for that. I was just trying to stoke the fire some; make her want me. Seeing her there alone, waiting in the bad light, eyes puffed with disappointment, it made me realize all I had done was leave her dangling so long as to shred her hope and expectations. She wanted to see me, and I didn't need to torture her about it. Yet, for some reason, making her hurt a little got me feeling excited.

I went to her.

"I told you I got off in an hour," Gayle said.

"I didn't say I was going to be here in an hour."

"Why you have to be so hard?"

I said to her: "You drive."

She started across the street to a lot where employees parked. She said: "We got to get something to eat."

"I already ate. I had prime—"

"Look, I'm hungry. Okay? If we're gonna do this, the least you can offer me is something to eat. And that's the very least."

If we're going to do this. Do what? What the hell were we doing? Me giving her a verbal slap every chance I could just to see what she could take; just to feel myself get hard. And her taking what I gave her just to prove she could; to prove she was more man than me. What is that? In the rest of the world did they have a name for what we were doing? And if I was going to do . . . *this* to her—with her—for whatever reason I thought I had to, couldn't I at least fill her stomach?

"Yeah. Sure. Let's get you something to eat."

Carrows. Tropicana, off the Strip. Brighter than any place in Vegas needed to be. Light was not welcomed in Vegas. Light revealed things, and Vegas had too much it wanted to hide. But the light did okay by Gayle. It reflected off her skin with a warm glow that made her look younger, softer.

It was late enough that breakfast was a good idea. Gayle ordered eggs, scrambled, and ham. I watched her eat over a cup of coffee. She only picked at her food. To her it was without flavor, without aroma. I know. It's the way my food was every day. To an empty soul there is no such thing as a feast. What you eat or drink, the air you breathe—it's just that which keeps you living from one miserable day to the next.

Sometimes I forget to eat. Truly. A day would pass where I would not have so little as a snack, or a swipe of bread. Nothing for hours on end, but even so I would not miss the act of consumption. It means that little to me.

And sometimes I think I should never eat again. Or drink. And, maybe, I shouldn't even bother drawing another breath. If I took away what sustained me, if I pulled my own plug, I wondered, would I be better off than I am now? If I died, would that somehow be an improvement over my current state of not being alive?

I watched Gayle as her fork pressed through her eggs, dragged a piece of it through a puddle of butter and grease, then left it on the side of her plate. Was she just then thinking the very same thing as me? Would she pull her own plug if she could? Would she rather be dead than live—half-live—one more sticking day as she did?

If I had tears left in my body, I might have cried for her. For me.

"What are you staring at?" Gayle asked.

I didn't even know my gaze had been that hard. I covered up with: "Where you from?"

"Carson."

"So . . . what are you?"

"I'm from Carson. I guess that makes me an American. Californian, if you want to get technical."

"Yeah, but I mean . . . you know. You're Oriental—"

"Oriental is a kind of architecture."

"Asian. Whatever."

"So that means I've got to be something? Korean, or Chinese?"

"Aren't you?"

"What the hell are you? Nigerian? Jamaican?"

My head lolled way back and I stared up at the ceiling. Packets of sugar stuck to an air vent, held in place by the updraft. "I'm just trying to make talk."

Sharp and to the point: "Why, so you won't forget me after we fuck?"

I let my head come back down. I looked at Gayle for a moment. I looked at her half-eaten food. "Your hair gray like that natural? If it is, you should color it. You're good the way you are, but without it you'd look your age."

"I'm older than you think."

"Then you'd be prettier than I could imagine." I surprised myself with that. I surprised Gayle, too. She'd gotten used to me hitting her, and she was used to men coming on to her. She wasn't used to someone being nice to her.

A waitress came round and warmed my coffee.

"I'm Japanese-Hawaiian. I was born in Carson, but my parents are from Hawaii." She said it *Havai'i*, which I guess is the way it's supposed to be said. "That doesn't make me blood Hawaiian, not Hawaiian by ancestry; my parents are just from there. There's a difference between being Japanese-Hawaiian and pure Hawaiian."

This was turning into one of those questions you were sorry you ever opened your mouth to ask.

Gayle: "Their family, you know, they're from Japan. On my dad's side. My mother's side is really from Okinawa."

I shook my head slightly, not knowing the difference.

"Okinawa is part of Japan now, but it wasn't always. Japan took it over; invaded it. Okinawans hated the Japanese."

"But your mom married your dad, so what does that mean?"

Without a moment's thought: "I hate myself."

Gayle finished doing whatever it was she was doing to her food. I let my coffee go cold.

We left.

We drove west, then north, away from the Strip and the lights and Vegas proper. As much as the city had grown, it didn't take much driving to get beyond it.

She had a place, a little ranch house. The dark didn't do much to cover the peeling paint and fading wood, but it was a hell of a lot better than a couple of shabby rooms off a broken-down elevator in Hollywood.

Inside was a mix of style—furniture that had been collected over years in drips and drabs as little bits of money came in. It was the cheap thin-wood stuff you get from discount warehouses and put together yourself. The kind of stuff most college kids use to fill their dorm rooms, then move on from quick as they can.

The house was papered with photos. Framed and unframed, hung, taped, and stuck to almost every free space. They were of Gayle as a baby, a child, her with her family, in high school and in college with friends. A life passed before me, chronicled in out-of-fashion clothes and once-hip hairstyles. I noticed: She smiled a lot in the pictures, in almost every one of them. I hadn't known Gayle for more than maybe two hours, but I don't recall having seen her smile once.

If Gayle had been anyone else I would have thought she just liked pictures. Nothing queer about that. But this girl . . . The pictures weren't hung for fond remembrance. They were a sleight of hand; they were there to distract her from the monotony with which she drudged through each day. They were plastered on the walls to hide the cage that her life had become.

"What did you come out here for?" I asked.

"Why do you want to know so much?"

"I just do."

"Is that what you want to do—you want to talk? Is that why you picked me up?"

"I'm just asking. That's all. Just asking."

"When I came out here first, I was a runaway. I didn't have a father. My mother molested me. Sometimes she would make me have sex with men for money. Not to pay rent, or buy food. For drug money. She used to make me suck men off just so she could get high."

"Is that the truth?"

"Maybe. Or maybe I was a rich girl who got sick of parents I didn't know 'cause they were always flying around the world, and the only time I ever heard from them was by telegram on a day somewhere close to my birthday. So I left home, came to Vegas, and haven't spoken to them in years. And the bitch of it is, I don't even know if they miss me.

"Or maybe I'm here for some really weird reason. Maybe I'm here because I'm just one more person, like everybody else in Vegas, who came looking for something better. I don't know something what, just something better. But unlike every other idiot on the Strip who goes home somewhere between broke and even, but at least gets to go home, I got stuck."

Gayle asked: "What about you? Why'd you come out here?"

Simple enough: "I came to gamble."

"From?"

"LA."

"What do you do there?"

I thought about lying, or thinking up some clever way to explain what I did, but it didn't seem worth the effort. "I'm a grifter."

From Gayle, that got a raised eyebrow.

"It's the colorful way of saying I'm a con man. Kind of like the way they call every bum who climbs into the ring and gets his head pounded a prizefighter when the only thing he ever won was a quick trip to the canvas."

That gave Gayle a little laugh. "I believe it—that you're a con man."

"How's that?"

"You're good with words; good at getting people to do what you want."

"You think?"

"You manipulated me."

"You don't want me here, all you have to do—"

"I'm just saying you *are* here. I'm not stupid, and I got enough guys trying to get in my pants I don't have to be thankful you even bothered to try. But you got this far, and that's more than most of the rest of them do."

"Most?"

"You may be a con man, you may be smooth, but don't think you're special. Don't ever get to thinking that."

I didn't.

A photo: Gayle with a guy, his arms around her. I asked: "That your man?"

She gave a shrug. "Sometimes he splits the rent, most times he doesn't, and on occasion he sleeps with me instead of other women."

I gave a glance around the place, trying to see if there was any more to it than picture-covered walls and cheap furniture.

"If you're looking for the bedroom, it's in there." Gayle pointed to a room beyond me.

"I'm not in a rush." And I wasn't.

"Maybe I am."

"Hungry for sex, or just want to get it over with?"

Another shrug, like she hadn't figured out what I was doing there. To give her an orgasm, to make her feel not so alone, to paint the house. Right now, as far as she was concerned, it could have been any of those.

"What makes someone want to be a con man?"

"A kick to the heart."

She didn't even begin to get that. "Do me a favor. Make sense."

"I con because I'm lazy."

Gayle shook her head like she was all disappointed in my reply. "Naw. Conning isn't a lazy man's game. Too much work, and not enough pay."

"And you know all about the grift."

"I know all I need to know looking at you. You wear cheap clothes, you stay at a cheap hotel, you waste your time gambling nickel slots. Either your cons don't do so well or you're the poster child for going straight."

I felt that. I felt it sharp as a pinprick, painful as a dagger. "It's not like I started out to be a grifter."

"And . . ."

"Why are we talking about this?" I blurted. "Can't we just fuck? You're the one who was in a hurry."

"For you, I'll make time. And . . ."

"And nothing. That's the point: Nothing happened in my life, not like I planned."

"So you decided to start ripping people off?"

"I needed to eat. I needed to live."

"Bullshit. Any job would do that much for you low as you're living. Sounds to me like you got slapped around some, so now you want to slap people back."

"Yeah. Okay, fine. I like taking a whole lot more than I like getting taken, but I'm just a con man. It's not like anyone's getting killed. I'm not turning out junkies. Hell, I'm teaching people a lesson; teaching them to smarten up. Half the people walking around are so easy you could sell them the teeth in their own mouth. If I take somebody for ten bucks and they get wise so the next time they don't get taken for twenty . . . when you look at it that way, I'm doing a good thing."

"Yeah, you're a good guy, Jeffty. A regular saint. Somebody ought to let the Pope know what you're doing."

"Not my fault the world is full of retards."

"Not like you. You're smart."

"That's right. I'm smart."

"Smart enough to get yourself into that?" She pointed at my bandaged hand, at my two mangled fingers. "That how smart you are — you got somebody to twist around your fingers for you?"

"It's got nothing to do with my business."

"So how'd you get 'em smashed?"

I chewed at my lip a bit. "I got a problem."

"I'll say. You've only got eight good fingers."

"I like to bet. I like it a little too much. Actually, betting's not the problem. It's winning I can't make a habit of."

"Not much of a problem. Just quit."

"Not that simple."

"I eat too much Doritos, but if someone busted my fingers I think I could pretty easy give 'em up."

"I quit gambling, you might as well cut out my heart. Same thing. That's all I've got left; all that makes me feel alive. The roll of a dice, the turn of a card — it's a rush, like a hundred percent pure heroin straight to the veins. Nothing dulls the feeling when you win, no matter how many times you lose."

"Or what you lose?"

"Or that."

If I was a street-corner prophet talking gibberish she couldn't have laughed at me more. "You're an idiot, you know that?"

"Oh, yeah. Coming from you."

"Look at how you live. Hustling just enough to get by hand-to-mouth. And when you're not doing that you're gambling because it's easier to blame bad luck for being a loser than it is to blame yourself."

"What kind of life are *you* living? Do your eight making change, then come home to four cold walls and stare at pictures of everything you used to be? What the hell is that?

"You don't like what I do, or how I live, so what? At least I am living. All it takes is one time; doesn't matter if it's on the grift or at the tables, all it takes is one hit and I'm in the big league."

"Sure. Couple of bucks and you're a player. Nobody's going to kick Jeffty around anymore."

"Yeah, that's right. Money talks, and I want to have enough to scream for days."

"Throw it around a little. The big man in town, taking steps a block long. All of a sudden you're holding court and taking tributes like you're some kind of Sinatra. Snap your finger and watch people come running . . . if you've got any fingers left to snap."

"Fuck you."

"No, fuck you. You are smart, Jeffty, so why you gotta be so dumb? You think that's what success is—chasing some money dreams? I've been down that road, and this is what's at the end of it. Everything you said: making change, and looking at pictures of what I used to be."

Gayle's body started to tremble. A little at first, then you could see it without even looking. "I came out here thinking things would be so easy. I had looks back then, and that would always buy me a lot: lonely guys with pockets full of money who weren't shy about giving it away. Problem is, guys like that get bored easy. After a while your looks start to wear out, and they want to trade up to a younger model. Happens quicker than you think. One day you're living high, laughing at some rich pug's stale jokes, next you're turning tricks just to make rent. You got no choice. You may not like the guys you're with, but it's real easy to get used to the way their money spends."

Gayle smiled. The kind of smile that holds back tears. She said: "I came out here thinking I had this town beat. Now I just try to make it through the day."

There was a photo on the wall, one in particular: Gayle with two people. A man and a woman, Orie—Asian like her. I wondered if they were her parents. I wondered if they missed their daughter at night, or if they were too busy jetting around and dining and being rich to even care. I wondered if the mother loved her daughter, or hated her for no longer earning her drug money.

I said: "You talk like you're an old lady."

"I'm old enough to know it's too late to change things."

"So you wanted to be successful the only way you knew how, is that so wrong? And you had it for a while; you lived with some money."

Gayle smiled harder and laughed, but she laughed at herself. "You know what success is? Huh? You think it's being able to bang every guy who's monied up and got a fast car, or to be that guy in the first place? No. Success is the one time in your whole miserable life that you're glad to be you. You ever felt that way, Jeffty? You ever once been successful?"

She looked at me, her eyes full of hurt—pain that had been self-inflicted.

Gayle was right: She was old enough to know it was too late to change things.

She was right about something else, too: Never once had I ever been successful. Not for a second.

I grabbed up a handful of her hair. "You talk too much. Shut up and fuck me."

Gayle fell into me. We didn't so much hold each other as we did cling to each other. We didn't so much kiss as we pressed our lips together as if to breathe life into each other's worn-out soul.

We fucked, and in our sex we searched with a furious desperation for hope and possibility and salvation. We wanted to feel alive with the passion that the touch of another brings. We wanted what every person in this city, in this state, every life on this planet wanted: to love and be loved, and to feel good, and special. We wanted to be grateful, for once, we were who we were, rather than be pitiable for what we'd become. Was that so much to ask? From two people, for one moment in time, was that so very much to demand?

But in our search we found nothing. In our sex there was only sex, and when it was over, that's all it was was over.

It was very late, or early, when we finished, so we slept. For me the sleep was deep and weary, and without a dream that I can recall. I think it was the same for her, as well.

I woke late in the day, almost evening. She was still sleeping, or at least, maybe, pretending to. I dressed with no particular quickness, or ease. I wasn't in a rush to leave, but was in no hurry to stay. I called a cab and drank orange juice from a carton in her refrigerator while I waited.

When the cab came she was still asleep, or still pretending, so I left.

The driver took me back to the Cal by way of the Strip. There was a red light at the corner of Flamingo Road. As we waited, as I looked at the road sign, feeling an odd sense of disconnected loss in knowing now that even though the Dunes was only recently gone—blown up and bulldozed under because it was old, and plain, and not tacky enough for the new Vegas—they had already changed the sign from DUNES/FLAMINGO ROAD to simply FLAMINGO ROAD, a thought came to me: I couldn't remember the girl's name. Moments later, and already I had forgotten.

The light turned green and we went on.

When I got back to the room Nellis was sitting on the edge of the bed with his head hung down all sad sack. He mumbled something at me. I hoped he hadn't asked me where I'd been, or what I'd been up to. I didn't much feel like sharing. I was set to ignore him, but he mumbled at me again.

"What?"

He mumbled one more time, a little louder, a little clearer. I could make out two words: Lost. Money.

I stopped fast and stared dead at him. "What?"

"I lost the money, Jeffty."

I wanted to say something. My lips moved, but no sound got past them.

Nellis went on. "You were gone. I got bored, so I went down and—"

"How much did you lose?"

"I was just bored, that was all."

"How much?"

There was a long quiet Nellis let pass, then: "I lost about . . . all of it."

"Twenty-five hundred . . . You lost—"

"It was more like twenty-eight. You were gone a long time. I got bored."

"But . . . that Single-Light . . . thing. You never lose."

"That's poker, Jeffty. I was playing roulette. It doesn't work with roulette. I don't think you can beat roulette, Jeffty. I tried, but I don't think you can."

Nellis flayed spastically across the room landing in a heap at the base of the far wall. I thought maybe he had tripped, but I remembered Nellis had been sitting on the bed. My palm began to sting, and I realized I had hit him.

Nellis put a hand to his reddening cheek. His eyes started to water. "That's okay if you want to hit me. I deserve it. I deserve to get hit."

I didn't want to hit him. I wanted to kill him. I moved toward Nellis, a single violent motion. He pushed himself up tighter against the wall—a little mouse trying to keep from being squished to death. I think I would have done it, too, pounded his head until his brains oozed between bits of skull, if I'd taken one more step. I forced myself to turn. Sheer effort compelled my legs to walk me through the door. It took every ounce of inner strength to do it, but being out of the room was the only thing that kept Nellis alive.

I hit the lobby of the California, and was swallowed under a wave of light and sound. It sent the world spinning around me like I was on some kind of carnival ride. I lifted my left arm to check the time. It felt like my watch was cut from lead. Six-eighteen. The game started at eight. I needed $2,500 just to sit in. No money, no game. No game, no chance to win my thirty thousand. No thirty thousand and I was a dead man.

I wondered if Nellis somehow knew that. I wondered if maybe it was payback time for what I did to him and Vale. I wondered if maybe, just maybe, he wanted to see me six feet down, and this was the best way he knew how to get the job done. I was getting juiced up with crazy notions, and that wasn't good. I didn't have time for wild thoughts, and they sure didn't help me get me any closer to the $2,500 I needed for the poker game.

I checked my pockets. Eleven bucks. I had to lay some bets fast. Maybe I could win myself up enough money. It was a long shot, sure, but the only shot I had.

Roulette. Six on black, five on red. Split the bet, let it grow. I could do it; I could win enough. A good streak of luck, and maybe—

Double zero. The hole that built Vegas. Just like that. All gone.

I wandered the casino like a pinball bouncing in a machine. My eyes swept the floor looking for dropped change.

Nothing.

My hands fondled the trays of slot machines searching for forgotten coins.

Nothing.

Nothing for me anyway. But everywhere I turned there was money. Money being spread across numbers and pumped into machines and dropped on roulette tables . . .

Fucking roulette.

The money flowed in, and the money flowed back out by the hundreds, thousands, millions. People were screaming and hollering and whoop-whooping and winning, and all I needed was one tiny piece of what they had. Why the hell can't I get a piece of it?

There, on the floor: a nickel. I dived on it the way a hawk dives on prey. A nickel, like manna from heaven. Into a slot machine, and a pull on the arm. The wheels spun around like my world. I hit three bars, and the machine spat back three nickels. All back in. Max credits this time. A pull on the arm, the spinning wheels . . .

The wheels landed. I didn't even so much as get two of the same anything. I shouldn't have bet all three nickels. I should've held one back. I should've . . .

As if it mattered. As if I could have done the alchemy to turn a lost nickel on the floor into $2,500 then into $30,000. That nickel wasn't there to save me; it was there to mock me. It was just another line of the same joke.

My arm lifted the lead watch back up to eye level: 6:40. The carnival ride got going faster and faster.

Like the living dead I was, I zombied for the door, for the street, for some fresh air. I went outside and sucked it in. Warm desert air. Clean. It made me feel better, not by much, and it slowed the ride down a little. I stumbled to nowhere in particular.

Nellis. It was his fault for losing the money.

The girl. The Asian one. It was her fault for suckering me away from him with that goddamn body of hers.

Vegas. It was Vegas's fault.

This place, this city, had been my only chance. I came crawling here with need and desire, the way most men go crawling back to an old lover. And likewise, I, too, had been slapped down and rejected. It was my last pitch and toss, my last chip played straight up, and I had bottomed out. No reprieves and no second chances. All there was for me to do now was lie down and die.

"Hey."

The first time I heard the voice I didn't think anything of it. I was taking too big a bath in my own self-pity.

"Hey, my man."

I turned around. There were three of them. Three white guys. Young, twenty, twenty-one maybe. Fat. Not the sweaty, obese kind of fat, but the pudgy kind that says: I'm too much of a lazy pig to get off my ass and lose a few pounds. They wore Docksiders sockless, button-down shirts and corduroy shorts in too-bright colors, one red, one yellow, and one green. All of it spelled easy life, rich boys and Ivy League schools, and everything I hated about a certain kind of person.

"My man," the first little piggy said again. "You from around here?"

If I could pick and choose the three people in the whole world I didn't want to be talking to, these were them. I didn't say a word.

The first little piggy, the one in the too-bright red shorts, went on. "We're, uh, looking for a little action."

The second piggy, the one in green, got close and went hush-hush with his tone, his breath painted thick with cheap house drinks. "We did okay at the tables. We're thinking, you know, maybe we could get a little something for it." He flashed a wad of cash my way. My heart started to double-pump.

The third one. The one in yellow: "Know where we can get some chicks?"

Somehow I managed to ask: "How much you got?"

The yellow piggy again: "About three grand. A little more."

I don't believe in God. If I did, I sure wouldn't believe that God saw fit, for whatever reason, to send these three fat, drunk jagoffs—pockets fat with money—my way. But here they were, like a host of angels, comin' for to carry me home.

Money. They had what I needed, all I needed, plus extra, as if for once life should be so good as to give me exactly what I required and then some. All there was for me to do was pry it out of their bloated pink fingers.

I gave them the once-over, big and broad so it was obvious I was checking them out. Then I threw a little laugh after it. "You kids ought to go back to your room before you get your fingers burned." I started to turn away from them, but I did it slow enough to give the little pigs time to stop me. The line was out; I was just waiting for them to bite.

"Hey, dude," Red Piggy said. Dude. If I didn't hate them before, I sure as hell did now. "You don't think we can handle ourselves?"

I turned back, and cranked up the con. "Look, you guys seem like nice boys. You ask me if I know girls, yeah, I know girls. But, well, they're not for you."

"What do you mean, 'They're not—'"

I rode right over him and kept on. "You want my advice, you should just hit a casino and try to pick up some women on convention. They'll give you a kiss, or whatever you"—I hit the word hard—"*kids* are into."

Green Piggy: "Hey, man. We're not kids."

Yellow Piggy: "We can like totally handle whatever you've got."

"The girls I know . . ." My lips twisted into something like a smile. "Let's just say I know them through friends. These girls are professionals. They do what they do to guys for a living."

"We can pay. Told you we had money."

"That's not the point. What I'm saying is, I know these people, and I have to see them after you're gone back to wherever. If, and I'm just saying if, but if I took you to them, I wouldn't want to be embarrassed. What I'm asking is . . ." A pause for effect. "You all have been with a woman before, right?"

I got emphatic assurances from all around, like that question was the biggest insult I could put down.

I poured it on now. "I'm just asking. I'm not trying to be embarrassed in front of these women. When they get with a guy, they expect a guy to go all the way. Know what I'm saying? No fear. They fuck like it's their business to fuck, and it is. Hell, two, three hours at a tumble . . . and whatever you want. Whatever. That's the wild part. Think of some shit. Go on, think of something—that one thing you always wanted to do to a girl but you never even let cross your mind 'cause the idea of it made you consider maybe there was something a little wrong with you; maybe you were a little twisted and sick and abnormal for wanting to do the very thing you were thinking of. Yeah, think of it, and tell it to these girls. The only word out of their mouths is: 'Okay.'"

You could just about see the drool hanging from their lips.

"For real?" asked Green.

"We're, like, totally there, dude," Yellow said. "You gotta help us out."

I made a big show of considering things. Let them think I'm the one that's getting strung along. "Well . . ."

Red: "We'll tip you, dude. Twenty bucks. Twenty-five."

Yeah, you'll tip me all right. "Ahhh, what the hell."

The three piggies went up in whoops and hollers and high fives all around. I joined in: We're all friends here. We're all out to have a good time. Don't worry your thick heads about a single thing.

Red could barely keep his hard-on in his corduroys. "C'mon, dude. Let's roll. We're parked over at—"

I put my hands up and waved him off. "Whoa, wait a second. You want me to ride with you? I don't know you."

"What?" Green whined. "What are you talking about?"

"Bunch of guys roll up on me on the street, start talking real fast, next thing I know I'm taking a ride with them and getting my pockets picked clean."

"Duuuude . . ."

If one more of them called me that I swore, money or no, I was going to kill them where they stood.

"Like, we're going to do anything. You think we're like thugs or something?"

"I think I don't know you, that's what I think. And I think maybe we better forget the whole thing." Again I made the slow turn away, and again they didn't let me get very far.

"Okay, wait, wait. How about like you drive? How about that?"

I gave them a little more of my thinking act.

"C'mon, you got to help us out, dude."

Oh, I was going to enjoy this. "Yeah, okay. Guess it'll be all right if I drive."

More whoops and more high fives. When they calmed down a bit I said: "Wait here; I'll pull my car around."

The three piggies grunted and slapped each other's palms silly as I walked. My racket, obvious, was obscure to them hidden behind a curtain of pussy lust. They were blinded by a starving need for affection they would take any way they could get. I headed like I was going for the Nugget; then as soon as I was out of their eyeshot, doubled back around to the Cal. No need for them to know where I was staying. I checked my watch; it felt much lighter now. Seven-oh-eight.

I could do this.

I got the Corvair out of the garage and took the long way around the block so the piggies wouldn't know where I was coming from.

When I got back, they were still doing their frat boys "we're going to get laid" dance. They piled in, throwing out bullshit compliments on my car. We took off. Bridger to Main, snaked over to Paradise. Eventually, I got on Russell, drove west, then shot out past McCarran. Planes still coming in, wheels hitting tarmac one after the other, loaded full with gamblers. People couldn't get here fast enough to lose their money.

We talked about it, the planes, the people coming to Vegas. I wanted to keep them talking, and keep their minds off of where we were driving to. The piggies were from Nashville. Not technically. Two were from Cincinnati, and one was from Tampa, but they went to school at Vanderbilt. Studying business so when they graduated they could take some soft spot at the company their old man was like chairman, or CEO, or some big dog at. No interview, no training program. An office with a view and a big leather chair just like that. The rich get richer, and all they had to do for a living was carry their daddy's name around in their pockets.

There was to be no guilt for me, not a bit, about what was coming.

We drove on. I kept talking, and smiling, and laughing at whatever stupid shit the piggies thought was funny enough to share with me. I kept on rapping about these wonderful mystical women who were waiting for them. Women who knew no sexual boundaries. Women whose only purpose in life was to bring pleasure to men. Women who were born and bred to service fat little eunuchs from bullshit wannabe Ivy League schools in the middle of redneck country.

Quick off on a dirt road. Houses in the distance. It looked like we were heading toward them, just like it, but they were a ways off. I kept on the dirt road a bit, still talking, still laughing; then, casual, I slowed to a stop.

"Okay," I said. I got out of the car real smooth and easy like we'd just arrived at the Hilton after a long trip, instead of the middle of nowhere.

The piggies got out of the car, not smart enough to know better, but with just enough sense to have a little suspicion.

"This is it?" Red asked.

"That house over there." I sort of pointed off in a direction. "That's my friend's."

"Why we walking?" Yellow this time. "Isn't it kind of far?"

"Not that house." I talked as if he was looking at the wrong one. "The one over there."

The piggies started to walk, squinting into the dark. "What house? I don't see another house."

I let them get a couple of strides in front of me. This was going to be the hard part. I jammed my hand into my coat pocket, extended a finger, took a deep breath. It was the crest of the first hill of a roller coaster; nothing but a wild ride from this point on. Here we go.

"Hey, assholes," I said, calm and confident. The three pigs turned and looked at me.

I'd arrived at the part of the plan I hadn't fully figured out. Not that I'd figured out any of it, but everything that'd already come was fairly straightforward. Three rubes, pockets full with cash, hot for girls. You bait them, you lure them somewhere way away from everything, then—and this was the bit I was just now working on, as well as the most essential part of my whole scam which, looking back, I probably should have thought out earlier—you rob them. So what do I do with my brilliant self? Stick a finger in my pocket and hope it passes for a gun.

Right when I did that, right when I said, "Hey, assholes," it occurred to me that even for rich, pudgy punks, they were kind of big and there were three of them. And more, it occurred to me that out here, alone on a stretch of dark road, they could just as easily beat the shit out of me as I could steal from them. Cool as the desert was this time of night, I felt my armpits go wet with sweat.

I followed their eyes, all three of the pigs: me, to my hand in my pocket, back to me. Green Piggy was the first to get it.

"Oh shit."

"What the—" Yellow started.

Green cut him off. "Oh shit! He's got a gun!"

Red just stood there, too bitch to say anything.

The dark and the desolation were working for me. They bought my gun gag. Now I just had to play this thing through quick as I could with nobody getting crazy. The only person out there who was a candidate for most likely to get hurt was me, and hurt I could get from Dumas. I didn't need it from these guys.

I threw a little method acting on the piggies. I tried to get it in my head I really was a jacker and not just some desperate con with a finger in his pocket. When I talked, my voice was steady and even, the way Dumas would've laid things on the line for me. I was the one in control. I was the one who had the gun, I was the one who didn't give a damn about killing anybody or everybody if I didn't get what I wanted.

I said: "Let's have the money."

Yellow: "What the fuck is this?"

Green: "Give him the money."

"I'm not giving up shit."

"Give him the money. Give it to him!"

Red just kept on standing still. He whimpered a bit now, teared up some, but, other than that, just stood where he was.

The only piggy who had any balls was Yellow. "Fuck this guy! He wants our fucking money? Fuck him!"

"He's got a gun!"

"Fuck him!"

"For Christ's sake—"

"Knew we shouldn't have trusted a goddamn nigger!"

Lickety-split, the world stopped dead. Yellow had used the N-word. Yellow had said what just wasn't plain good to say to a brother, let alone a brother with a gun . . . even though I didn't have one. Green and Red looked like they were about to puke, or piss, or both. Yellow just stood his ground, defiant. The glow in his eyes barked: Yeah, nigger, I said nigger. Now what are you going to do about it, nigger?

I got up close to Yellow, gave him a hard, cold stare that he handed me right back. A stare that traveled back and forth between us in a closed circuit what seemed like forever.

There was a tense stillness. I thought, way off, I could hear a train.

Between me and Yellow nothing happened. Then, more nothing happened. Yellow got it in his mind I wasn't going to do anything; I wasn't going to shoot anybody. Maybe I didn't have the guts, or maybe didn't even have a weapon in the first place. And when I knew he was thinking that, when I could tell by the little smirk that crawled its way across his lips he figured I didn't have it to pull the trigger of the gun I might not have, that's when something happened.

My left hand, my free hand, swung up across my body. Fingers into fist, I whipped it like a ball and chain. The smirk was the target. I back-fisted my hand on the left corner of Yellow's cheek and drove the blow straight across to the other side of his face.

The sharp crack of busted teeth, the whistle of them flying past my ear, a warm spray of blood on the back of my hand.

I thought, for a second, Yellow's head had spun 'round on his neck, but his whole body had twisted as he corkscrewed to the ground with a stream of red pumping from his nose and the hole torn in his lip by broken teeth. Never before in my whole life had I felt like such a badass.

The feeling passed quick.

The whole night went shrill with a siren: *aGadaGadaGadaGad.*

Awww shit! Cops! My frickin' luck, but it figured. Wherever there were white people in trouble, cops weren't too far to come to the rescue. My chest heaved like a piston. I caught some air; my racing heart slowed, and with it the siren.

"Oh God, oh God, oh God, oh God!"

It wasn't a siren at all. It was Green going hyperbitch, bawling like a little girl who'd just gotten mud on her pretty pink Sunday dress.

And look at Red: Now he's standing there puking on himself. Queerest damn thing. He's got blank eyes staring at Yellow on the ground, meanwhile he's heaving. Red thinks he's going to die, that's what it is. He thinks I'm going to shoot him. Nothing like the fear of a bullet to the head to bring your lunch back up.

One was spewing, one was on the ground bleeding, and one was crying like he'd just got pimp-slapped. And I didn't even have a gun, just a finger in my pocket. Think of what you could do with a piece. I was starting to get a hard-on for this kind of thing. I was starting to understand why some guys made it a habit. Crime don't pay, they tell you, but they don't tell you it gives you a rush like nothing I knew of.

"Oh God, oh God, oh God. You can have the money. You can have it. Please don't hurt me." "Me," Green said. Not *us.* It was every man for himself. He dug a wad of cash from his pocket. A quakey hand held it out. "Here. Take it. Take it." He put it on the ground in front of me the way frightened natives place offerings before a pagan image.

Green scrambled, field mouse–style, for Yellow's pocket and dug up more cash.

Yellow moaned and sputtered blood.

Green made a pile of all the dough.

Green went to Red's pockets, his shirt stained with a chunky bile, and got me more cash. On the pile it went. When he was all done collecting money, Green put the begging into overdrive. "That's it, man. That's all there is. Don't hurt me. Just please don't hurt me. Don't . . . I don't want to die, dude. I don't . . ." The last of that dissolved into sobs.

I took up the money off the ground. Three thousand dollars. It felt good to my hand.

Time to go.

I eased for the Corvair, got in, started up, and backed away with the lights on bright. It washed out the boys' eyes and kept them from reading my plates. My brain was revving on the red line, but I tried to think of every detail, tried to cover everything that could point a finger back at me. There was nothing that came to mind. My tracks were clean. My only thought was I hadn't done a half-bad job for a first-timer.

As the car backed away, the headlights faded on the three piggies: Pukey, Bleedy, and Bitchy.

My watch: 7:38. Time to spare. In spite of Nellis's best efforts I had saved myself. All there was to do now was get him to the card game and win, baby, win.

At the card game, except for fifteen dollars, Nellis lost everything. His supersystem for winning was, as it turned out, vulnerable to losing.

The night had started out good enough. Us making it to the dingy off-Strip dive Brunson had told me about. Nellis sitting down to poker with a fat guy, some gay guy, an Italian in a cheap-ass suit, slicked-back hair and a pinkie ring that said he figured himself for a made man. But he wasn't—they weren't—anything Nellis couldn't handle, and handle them he did for starters. Nellis won. When he stayed in, he won; otherwise, he dropped and dropped early, getting out with barely a scratch. It was perfect and beautiful, almost graceful to watch.

So much so that I almost missed what happened, as what happened was like the blink of an eye: Quick and gone, and if you weren't paying attention you wouldn't even know what you hadn't seen. Nellis lost a hand. Quick and gone, like I said, 'cause he won the next three in a row, so I didn't pay much mind to it. None at all, really.

Twenty-five minutes or so went by. Nellis lost another hand. Like before, it was quick and over, and he went back to winning after dropping out of a few rounds. This time, this time when he lost, something scratched at me. Something made me remember that I'd never seen Nellis lose a hand before. That was the thing about his bullshit Zen poker: You didn't lose. You weren't supposed to lose. You could drop out, sure, and he did that plenty, but you weren't supposed to lose, and here he was, losing.

I was nervous, but I didn't really notice that at first. Sweaty palms crept up on me instead of hitting me all at once with a dead panic. I tried to ask Nellis if everything was all right, but the other players frowned me off before I could barely get the words from my mouth. A guy who's been winning starts to hit the wall, and nobody else wants you to say, or do, or think anything about it.

Nellis smiled at me and nodded. The kind of smile and nod that said: Everything's okay. Don't worry about it.

My future, my probable existence, was in the hands of a strung-out dope addict who played some trippy kind of cards, and he was flashing a "don't worry about it" face my way. Panic stopped creeping and rushed at me full on. I counted up Nellis's chips as best I could from my angle. About nineteen thousand. Good enough. Way short of what I owed Dumas, but good enough.

"Hey, Nellis," I said. "We ought to be getting back."

"Your friend's okay," the Italian said at me. He said it in a way that made me think maybe he wasn't just playing at being a made man.

"Yeah, but you know what? He's on medication, and I forgot to bring it, so we really need to get back to the—"

"Your friend's okay," the Italian repeated. I got the idea he didn't like to repeat himself. It was in his voice. It was in the way his fingers clutched into a fist. So I did the Italian the favor of pretending Nellis was okay.

Nellis was not okay. He barely made ten more minutes before losing another hand. He lost another one right on top of that. And dig his eyes: all glazed up, blinding him to what he was doing. I'd seen that look before. You can find it sitting before any slot machine, Let It Ride table, or Wheel of Fortune in Clark County at 2:00 a.m., 5:00 p.m., or any minute of any twenty-four hours of any day. The look had a name and its name was Desperation.

Another hand lost.

Another hand.

Now he wasn't even taking time between losing, flowing money same as an open wound seeps blood. Yeah, just like it. That was my life he was spewing onto the table.

Another hand.

Another hand.

I counted down from the nineteen thousand Nellis had. Fourteen, eleven, less than ten. Inside twenty minutes, he was below eight. I looked at Nellis, eyes still frosted. He wasn't hopped up on horse, but he was tripping just the same. He couldn't have seen me if he'd wanted to, but I looked at him, long and hard, like maybe somehow I could reach him through whatever universe, whatever alternate reality, he was calling home. I wanted to tell him it was over. I wanted to tell him thanks a lot, but it's time to pack up and go home.

The Italian—like he was a mind reader, like he hung out with Dionne and her Psychic Friends, like he knew just what I was thinking—the Italian said to me one more time: "Your friend's okay."

Yeah. He's great.

I left the cheap room, went down the dirty hall, through the low-rent casino, out to the car. I chewed stale gum I found in my glove compartment and killed time waiting for Nellis to finish killing me.

A couple of minutes moseyed into half an hour. Somewhere along the way, I got hope. The longer Nellis stayed in the dive, the more I thought maybe he'd gotten his . . . his thing back. Maybe he was playing cards again like he used to: sharp, and wild, and fucked up, but winning. Always winning. Maybe—

Nellis shuffled out to the car, head hung—a puppy who just took a shit on the carpet.

"You done?" I asked.

"I'm done."

"How much you lose?"

Hand to his pocket, it rummaged around and came out clutching that last fifteen bucks.

"Get in the car."

He got in. I got in, drove, hit the 15 south.

Fifteen. Same as the little bit of dough Nellis had left.

Just past the on-ramp, Nellis started in. "Wanted to win."

I didn't say anything.

"That was the problem, Jeffty. I wanted to win. You start to feel it; you start to push. You can't push with this kind of poker. You can't. You can't make things happen. That's when it all goes wrong. You can't think you're lucky; you gotta let the cards tell you if you're lucky. I wanted to win."

"Shut up."

"Not for me. I don't care about the money. It was for you. You gave me a place to stay. You took me on a trip. . . . You're my friend, Jeffty. I wanted to win for you."

"Nellis, do yourself a favor. Shut up."

We drove in an angry silence. Twice now in one day he'd lost my money. The first time, okay, it was his money. But we agreed to go gamble it for me, so when he lost it, he lost my money. Then I get it back . . . I stole some back, and he loses it again.

Look at him slouched over in his seat: pale, strung out, with a "needs a hit bad" look. How could I have let myself trust this thing to save my life? I never had a chance because he never had a system. His Eastern Single Light blah blah was just luck riding piggyback on the rantings of an addict. I mean, yeah, it's obvious to me now, but seen through the eyes of hopelessness his card playing looked like a gift from God.

Eddie whispered at me from days past: Luck does what it wants, when it wants. You can't steer it, just ride it a little.

I whispered back to him the mantra he had given me: "Only dice forget."

On the way back to LA I got it in my head I needed to stop at a strip club; I needed a couple of minutes of a woman pretending she cared thing one about me. I didn't really have any money to get much out of a nudie bar, but I needed what I needed and turned off at the first one I saw before hitting the state line.

Ten bucks got me and Nellis in the door, which didn't even leave me enough for a table dance.

That was okay.

We hung at the rail by the stage where the girls worked their magic. A waitress made the rounds for drinks. I brushed her off with a "We're cool, sweetie." In a place like this, the price of drinks is jacked to the sky, and the five I had wouldn't cover two glasses of water.

I let the waitress break the five into singles and I handed them out, a dollar at a time, to a dancer with great legs and a bad tit job. I mean, I love a big rack as much as the next guy, but get 'em in your size, honey, that's all I'm saying. If she'd had wood shelves nailed to her chest, they would have been less obvious, and probably would've moved more than whatever it was she had installed under her nipples.

Screw it. Beggars can't be choosers, right? All I know is, for every single I tossed out, she tossed back a "yeah, I love you, daddy" look. She smiled at me; she paid attention to me; she made me feel like a guy who could actually end up with a girl like that. It was the kind of warm, personal loving you could only get a dollar at a time, or for twenty bucks a lap dance.

After a while, not much of a while, the waitress figured out the drinks me and Nellis kept putting off were never going to get bought 'cause we didn't have the dough for it. That got us tossed out on our asses.

That was okay.

By that time I'd given out my last single, and the dancer had moved on trading her "yeah, I love you, daddy" look to a guy who was flashing a ten.

No cash left. We weren't even in the joint long enough to get a respectable hard-on. We got back in the Corvair, back on the 15, and headed home. Things were as bad as they could get.

*A*round Barstow I had to panhandle gas money to make it to LA. I hadn't thought about that when I gave the last of the cash to the bad-titted chick.

Quarter of three. LA. Finally. The 10 to La Brea, north to Hollywood Boulevard. Four-plus hours driving. Not a word between me and Nellis. Nothing since the parking lot of that cheap hotel.

Up the stairs. The door of my apartment slightly open, lights on. Could've been some crackhead ripping me off, but I knew I wasn't that lucky. No point in running. Nowhere to run to. I pushed open the door and walked in. Dumas sat on my couch. Ty stood next to him, a curl of papers in his hand. What very little was left of my world fell away from beneath me. I was free-falling, my trajectory toward a terminal impact.

Dumas: "Ahh, just who I was looking for." Voice sweet as ever. "I was looking for you, do you know? Won't you come in?"

Real white of him to invite me into my own apartment. I could barely make it past the doorway, at that moment enjoying a level of fear I had never made acquaintance with before.

"Word on the street was you took a little trip. Take a little trip, did you?"

Word on the street? Like he's fucking Huggy Bear. A phrase like that makes a guy sound stupid. I didn't say anything about it. I just said: "Yeah."

It was just me and Dumas talking. Ty stood ready to follow whatever orders Dumas gave him, and Nellis was still working off my "shut up" instructions from back in Vegas.

"Thought you might've tried to skip out. You wouldn't skip out, would you? You wouldn't skip out when you owed me forty thousand, would you?"

"Twenty-five, you said. You brought it down from thirty at the track."

Dumas shrugged. "Another day, another dollar. That's what they say. Isn't that what they say?"

"That's what they say." I didn't argue the point. Forty, eighty, half a million. I had nothing, so what difference did it make how much I owed?

My nervous eyes again looked at the papers in Ty's hand. Not just papers. Him and Dumas must have been here awhile, looked the place over. In his hand was the script from Nellis's duffel. My script. A *Kick to the Heart.*

I lost control. For a second, after a day of highs and lows, of lost money/found money/lost-for-good money, I no longer had the ability to corral my emotions. I didn't even have the desire to try.

From Ty's grasp I hard/fast snatched my script. "You get your hands off that!"

"Oh, yes," Dumas said as if he'd just recalled to inform me of something. "Ty found your little movie play there."

Me still hot: "You want to come up in my place, tramp through it like it was a goddamn bus station, I can't stop you. But you keep your fucking hands off my script! You keep 'em off!"

My fire didn't last long, and it burned without use or purpose. Ty, I could tell by his look, was genuinely sorry for having invaded something that was obviously personal, and Dumas's level of interest in me was constant whether I was furious, melancholy, or hungry.

Nodding toward my repossessed script, "It's beautiful," Ty said. I hardly expected a guy like Ty to use a word like *beautiful.* "Kind of wild in parts; where he punches that pregnant chick in the stomach—but it's—"

"Jeffty . . ." Nellis started. We looked at him, all of us. Three sets of eyes told him to keep quiet.

Ty asked: "What happened with it, the script?"

I could hear the impending laughter in my head. "It's a story," I replied, not even beginning to want to have to go into that shit.

"I would like to hear a little story," Dumas said back.

I waited a moment; then Dumas prompted me on with: "No, really, Jeffty. I insist."

Yeah. Sure. What the hell?

Deep breath, then: "I came out to write. That I told you," I said at Ty. Ty nodded.

"I hacked away a bunch of years and never came up with anything. Not even close to anything except shit on top of shit. And then one day, I did. I mean, just like *that* a switch got flipped. One day I sat down and wrote, and it . . . it was there. Everything inside me; everything . . ." Used-to-be-writer me stumbling over words. "Everything I was, everything I felt, every emotion I had—"

Dumas snickered right on cue.

"I don't know why, but it picked that day to start spilling out onto page after page after page. My life was a free-flow event, creation in real time. Except for eating and sleeping, honest to God, I don't know if I did anything else for a month but write. When that month was up, I had something that was . . ."

"It was beautiful," Ty finished for me.

Nellis slumped against a wall.

"And . . ." Dumas wanted to know.

"And nothing. Beautiful as it might've been, nobody wanted it. Seemed like a day short of forever nobody wanted it. Then some producer bought it. Got paid some. Not much, but some. Enough that it made me think I might actually make it as a writer. Enough that I could start going regular to Vegas, live high and take gambling from hobby to habit. . . .

"Enough that it was supposed to make me feel okay to sit around while they changed the script, rewrote it, shuffled it up, tore out this, that, and the other so that if two words were left that were mine, I didn't know which. Then after a couple of years of fucking with it, they tossed it in a drawer 'cause they couldn't remember why they wanted it in the first place. They owned it . . . and they buried it."

"And that was the beginning and end of Jeffty the artist." Dumas chuckled, and the chuckle bled into a laugh.

I saw that in my short absence no one had filled my position as LA's most prominent jester.

Ty just smiled because he knew he should, because Dumas was, but I could tell he wasn't particularly in the mocking mood.

On top of all that Nellis was laughing. I'd have been pissed, except he was just laughing 'cause Dumas was laughing, but he didn't have a clue what he was laughing at.

"Don't have much of a constitution, do you? They take your little play from you, and you never write again."

"You don't understand. You don't . . . I . . ."

I started to explain to Dumas what it was like to create something and have it stripped away from you. I started to explain what it was like to invest in something all of your emotions and feelings, all of your self and all that you are, only to have others—others who don't possess one one-hundredth of the worst of your abilities—tell you your emotions are wrong, your feelings are no good. You are not worth their time.

But what was the point?

I could try to explain passion to a bookie, self-expression to a man who expressed himself by the breaking of limbs.

I could try to explain creativity to Dumas, and all he'd see was a guy going soft and weepy for words on a page.

I could try to explain things.

I'd have an easier time explaining blue skies to a blind man.

"Such a funny story." Dumas snickered on. "Such a very funny story. Always the loser, aren't you, Jeffty? Always."

I recalled then why I liked so little to be laughed at, besides why no one likes to be laughed at. It made me feel small and beneath contempt, yeah, but it also made me feel, again, how I felt when they—when Hollywood—took the one decent thing I'd ever done with my life away from me.

Dumas stopped laughing. He picked a single, tiny piece of dark lint from his otherwise white-white clothes. "So, do you have my money for me? Do you have my forty thousand?"

"No."

Ty set down the script. He crossed to the door, closed it.

I couldn't remember the last time I'd eaten, but all a sudden I wanted to puke. Before I'd even finished the thought, like there was some genie somewhere handing out fucked-up wishes, I was on my knees, clutching my midsection and listening to myself choking through a dry heave. I was just a frightened little bitch who didn't want to die.

More laughs, and Dumas's sweet voice. "Oh shit, Jeffty. You are funny. You don't even know how funny you are. Every time I want to kill you, you do something so terribly funny."

More, bigger laughs. Except for Nellis. Nellis wasn't laughing any-more. Nellis was saying: "Stop laughing at him. You stop laughing at my friend."

Bigger howls from Dumas.

"Why are you making fun of Jeffty? He didn't do anything to you. He's a good person. He's good." Nellis was talking crazy, bottoming out and in need of a fix. Only thing worse than being jagged on drugs is being dry of them.

More crazy talk: "He—he took me on a trip. He took me to Las Vegas, and let me play cards for him. I never been to Las Vegas. I lost his money, and he didn't even get mad at me . . . not too mad. He didn't hit me or nothing . . . not too much. He's a good guy."

"Nellis," I said from the floor. Where he was, my voice couldn't reach.

"And after what they done to him, what they done to his story—raped it, cut it up, and dumped it in a grave. I know how it hurt him. I know what it did to him. I know 'cause I was there. I was there for him." Nellis looked at me. "I was there 'cause I'm your friend, Jeffty."

Dumas busting up like Jerry fucking Lewis was in the room "Hey, lady"-ing it up.

"Stop laughing, you stupid prick! Why do you get to laugh? You're noth-ing. You're not good like Jeffty." Nellis going full with his craziness.

"Nellis, stop it!"

"You leave! You better leave now! I'll call the police. The police will come and take you away if you don't leave."

Dumas holding up his left hand that signaled: Stop, I can't take it no more. Giggling now, not laughing: "Wait, my friend. I want to show you something. May I show you something?"

Me on the floor, watching: Dumas's right hand swings up. Something queer about it: an extra finger. Silver. The finger points at Nellis, at his head. The finger coughed once, spat fire. The front of Nellis's head popped open a little hole, a small red dot. The back blossomed wide in a gush of brain matter that caked the wall behind him. Red fountains sprouted from the twin wounds as Nellis's body twisted down, a puppet with its strings cut, and thudded in front of me. In an instant, all that Nellis was was atomized into a fine scarlet cloud of skull tissue that misted the air. Nellis was diminished to that, then, by degrees, not even that. Dis-sipation reduced him again; the cloud blended with the dust and the cordite, the soot and the smog that, when summed, formed nothing more spectacular than a dirty film that fell about the room.

From the body, blood, still spraying, bathed my face. I went back to vomiting, this time working something up from my stomach. It mixed with what was coming out of Nellis's head and started me on a cycle of regurgitation.

Dumas: "Your friend became boring. See what happens when I'm bored? You didn't use to bore me, Jeffty. Always I used to have fun with you, do you know? Scare you a little, break a finger if I must, but I tell people, 'Jeffty is always such fun.' But now . . ."

Blood puddling on the floor. Brains painting the wall. Me, I'm covered. Not so much as one speck of red marred Dumas's pure white clothing.

"Now you are simply becoming tiresome. My money. I would like to be paid, and I would like to be paid quite soon."

I heard Dumas and Ty tramp across the floor. I heard Ty say, "Sorry, Jeffty" as they went. I heard the two of them pass through the door and close it as they left. I heard all that, but didn't see it. My chief occupation had become staring at the body on the ground. I would stare at it for the next hour.

Desperation's Angel

A little shy of four in the morning.

Me: Still on the floor, still throwing a dead stare at the body. At Nellis.

Nellis, through his deadness, looking shocked and surprised. I guess he wasn't expecting to take a bullet to the head.

Who is?

I wasn't sick anymore—not like when first Nellis got shot—or sad, but angry. Angry at Nellis for being so stupid as to mouth off to Dumas. Angry at Dumas for making Nellis swallow a bullet for no good reason. I sat where I was and threw around a lot of blame for the causation of this killing at everyone I could think of. Everyone but me.

An hour plus now since Nellis had been forced to die. No cops. No neighbors banging on the door. They must have heard the gunshot, but around here what's one more bullet in the night, and what's the use of calling in the police who don't give a damn about what Hollywood low-life shoots which Hollywood degenerate?

Now that the shock of witnessing a murder was beginning to ebb, a thought started to come to me: What do I do with the body? Call the cops myself? Lots of questions. I'd have to give up Dumas; Dumas—not liking the idea of going to prison because I pointed the finger at him—puts a slow bullet or two out for me.

No thanks.

Get rid of it on my own? How? LA: Eight million strong, miles of free-way, porn just a 900 call away, but the one thing she doesn't have is a dead body–removal service. I was beginning to think Dumas had killed Nellis for the express purpose of giving me the most fucked-up task in the world to perform.

Leaving Nellis for the moment, I got up, and showered, and washed the gunked-up blood and bile and brain matter from my face and hair, and dressed again. Nellis still waited. The dead are patient.

Down to the street, to the Corvair. Driving Hollywood. Top down. The cold predawn wind kept me focused, and I kept asking myself: What the hell do you do with a body? What the hell do you do? No answers. No ideas. Nothing. The only notion that came to me was getting rid of a body was not the kind of thing you did sober.

The Regent. Same as it ever was. Lookit Amber bracing a drink at a table in back. Lookit Wesker working a blonde who passed for good-looking in this dark corner of the earth. Lookit Eddie, the one-armed wonder, flying drinks around the room twenty-four/seven.

Nothing changed. A body in my apartment getting stiffer by the second, and not a thing changed for the rest of the world. No slowdowns, no work stoppages, no mothers crying in the streets, no Senate subcommit-tees launching investigations, and—to the best of my knowledge—not a single solitary person who knew and/or gave a damn that Nellis would not be joining us today, or any day hence until further notice.

I felt bad.

I felt bad that a man could die in such utter anonymity. In the hour and some since Nellis was killed, the world had passed him by, paved him over, didn't give him so much as a thought because it didn't even know that Nellis had ever existed in the first place.

I felt bad, but then it came to me the more anonymous Nellis was, the easier it would be to get rid of him and the fewer questions that would be asked if he was ever found.

I felt bad, but I got over it.

Walking to the bar, I picked up a world of conversation. A guy and a chick sitting at a table:

Her: "How long we been friends?"

Him: "I don't know. About four, five mon—"

Her: "And all that time I never asked you for anything, have I?"

Him: "No."

Her: "And I never would. You know that."

Him: "Yeah. Yeah, I know."

Her: "So, like, in a month if I asked you for, like, five hundred dollars, you'd know it's 'cause I really needed it."

Him: "I guess."

Her: "And you'd give it to me, right? I mean, lend it to me, the five hundred."

Him: "I . . . I guess."

She threw him a hug as if she liked him. As if, but not quite.

Her: "Thank you. You're such a good friend. And I might need a plane ticket. That's not a problem, is it?"

Truth: Whenever there are two people sharing space there's somebody trying to pull something on someone else. The plans aren't always big and grand, and the scam isn't always strictly illegal, but everybody's got a racket.

Everybody.

I made an empty stool at the bar mine. Eddie came over and what's-going-on-ed me.

What's going on . . . ? Nellis, Vegas, the Oriental chick with gray hair and a great ass, stealing from the three pigs, the card game, Dumas, a gunshot, a dead body. "Nothing," I told him. "Nothing's going on."

I ordered a shot of Stoli and barely worked up enough money to pay for it. Eddie poured and left me alone.

I nursed the drink with all the tender loving care you'd give a cancer kid. It was all I could afford, and it would have to stretch me a long, long way, until I could come up with what to do about my corpse troubles.

A couple of sips. My mind wandered. Not too far. Check the door: three guys, clean cut, bad suits. Across the room, they stink like cheap detectives. I smell them; the whole joint smells them, goes quiet, then loud again with a nervous murmur. A bunch of guilty minds at work, mine the worst of them. The apartment. The body. They spot my car out-side and swarm the place.

The cops spread out. One stays at the door, one goes to the far side of the room—those two are to cut off runners—the third starts to work the crowd. This one, the third one—him I don't like. Hands bunched up in tough-guy clenches, ready to do some pounding. Easy to read: hard-line cop. Perps are guilty until proved innocent, or until they plea to a confes-sion beaten out of 'em.

Dig him: white guy. Good-looking, but not good enough to skate on. Smart, but not smart enough for real work. Tough, but not tough enough to take on gang bangers, or dope dealers. Just tough enough to knock around Hollywood vagrants and Franklin Ave. winos. You wear colors and sport a Glock, you got right of way, but if you're a spic on a street corner trying to panhandle work, get ready for the ass-kicking of a lifetime.

Working the crowd, working the crowd . . . The cop looked down at a picture he carried—mug shot?—then around the room. Fist still clench-ing, itching to bust a head. Lookit the room flinch in front of him: Wasn't me, Mr. Policeman. I'm a law-abiding Angeleno, so I'll just look away.

The cop's eyes: down at the picture, around the room. Down, around. Down, around . . . Bingo! Dead stare, across the floor: Wesker! Sure. The bank heist. Thirty-two grand. The perfect job, only not so perfect. I'm feel-ing so happy all this isn't about me and the body I had cooling, I almost forget to feel sorry for Wesker.

Everyone near him feels the heat. Everyone near him slides away. Amber, his blond girlie, everyone. Wesker feels the heat, too. He busts out in sweats and shakes; he even goes bitch and sheds a few tears. Tears are wasted on Tough Guy Cop. I can see that. Wesker can see that through blurry eyes, so he bolts for the door. He never would have made it past the cop spiked there, but doesn't get close in the first place. Tough Guy gets to him, and gets to him hard: Gut punch, a couple of 'em. I can hear ribs cracking from a distance. Wesker still standing. Bent, but standing. You got to give it to him for being at least that sturdy. But all staying up buys him is his face getting smashed into a tabletop. A spray of blood fountains from his nose. Now he's down.

For a split second, in my mind, it's Nellis, bullet to the head, floating to the ground. I close my eyes, and when they open Wesker is on the floor, wounded-animal whimpering.

Behind the bar, Eddie: "Hey—"

Tough Guy Cop pulls his piece before Eddie gets another word out. "*What? What!* You got something to say." Gun dead at Eddie. "This is police business. You want some of it?"

Eddie doesn't want nothing of nothing. Eddie just stays still.

On the floor, Wesker screaming pathetic through busted teeth and gurgling blood: "I didn't do nothing. I didn't do nothing."

From the house, Wesker gets the big ignore. All eyes are on their drinks, on the floor, on the ceiling, anywhere but on him. The room in unison: That's right, Mr. Policeman. Us law-abiding Angelenos didn't see you beat the shit out of this guy. And if we did see it, he deserved it.

Wesker, one eye not swollen shut, catches me catching him. "Jeffty, I didn't do nothing, Jeffty. I'm your friend. You gotta help me. I'm your friend."

Yeah, like Nellis was my friend. You don't want to know where being my friend gets you.

"Jeffty, please . . ."

Tough Guy Cop grabbing Nellis by the hair. Tough Guy swinging his gun. Wesker eats Smith & Wesson. More teeth and more blood spill to the ground. More whimpers.

Tough Guy Cop holsters his piece. Tough Guy primps himself. Tough Guy Cop calls over his two cop buddies. They haul up Wesker and take him for the street.

I watch all this. Tough Guy Cop watches me watching. He throws me his tough-guy cop stare, his "you don't want to fuck with me" look.

Not hardly more than ninety minutes since I had to wash blood and brains out of my hair. You get real death on you, and tough-guy looks don't mean much anymore.

The cops, Wesker, gone. I went back to the high business of doing nothing, me and everybody else. What just happened was like vapor, like a dream, like some wild dinner show: Hey, how about that? Wasn't that something? Now, can we get another drink?

A guy beat up, laid out, dragged away, and no one left behind to give a fuck. Except for Eddie. Eddie gave a fuck.

"What the fuck?" Eddie said out loud to no one. "Coming in here beating up customers. What the fuck?" Eddie said to no one again. "And the one guy with money. Cops got to beat the shit out of my only customer who's got cash and ain't afraid to use it. Waving a gun at me. You see that cop waving a gun at me? I pay taxes. What the fuck?"

Eddie was just white noise. Eddie was just background music. I still had a problem I couldn't make go away. Not on my own. Eddie . . .

"Eddie, I could use some help."

"Pointing the gun at me like I did something. Don't he see I got one arm? I'm a goddamn veteran. . . . What?"

"I need help."

Eddie's face tightened up like he's got no time for me. "Jesus, you see how I got cops killing up my business, now you want handouts? You want to be a booze hound, do it on your own. You ain't getting no handouts from me."

"It's not like that, Eddie. I don't need a drink." Half a lie. I could have used a bottle of rubbing alcohol right about then. "That's not the kind of help I'm talking about."

"Yeah, well what?"

What? A dead body getting deader. A dead body that has to disappear. A dead body that, if cops like Tough Guy found out about, would send them on another beating spree through the bar. How do you explain that kind of what to the guy you're asking help from? You don't. Not straight away.

"Yeah," I said. "I guess another drink was what I was thinking about."

Eddie, confused, still pissed about the cops and Wesker, pours out a drink for me and starts to move on.

"Hey, Eddie," I stopped him with. "You getting off soon?"

Eddie, getting more pissed by the second: "What for?"

"Just . . . are you?"

"At five-thirty."

I check my watch. Forty minutes. A little more. I'll wait, then see what I can get out of him.

I kill my drink; the warm fills me and the booze works on me. I start to feel weak, dizzy . . . tired? How many hours since I slept? Vegas, the card game, the drive, Nellis getting dead . . . was that all one night? One lifetime?

Let me put my head down for a second. Just one little second . . .

That's all it takes, and I fall into a certain kind of nightmare. An endless river—not water, blood. Deep, I'm wading against it. Logs flow toward me, only they're not logs, they're bodies and they've got no features. At least none that I can see. The bodies slam into me. I get pushed back, carried out toward a bloody sea. No way to save myself, nothing to grab hold of . . . then I see it. Almost. My salvation. Odd. Like an angel, both pale and dark at the same time, waiting to pull me from the gore and corpses.

My salvation. It has a face. Familiar, but from where? I can't quite make it out. I struggle for it, but the river just pushes me back. Desperation. I have to see it. If I can just see what's going to save me . . . If I can—

Fast-pitch Mexican babble was my wake-up call. I was startled conscious by a little guy, black, black hair and creamy caramel skin, coming into the bar yelling blah-blah at some woman with hair and skin to match his. Short, dumpy, a gut that pushed out farther than her tits, the chick didn't look like anything worth fighting over, or with, or about. Course, the guy was no find either, and since she seemed more than willing to take his abuse, then maybe they were made for each other. Couple of the year. True love.

Eddie: "Miguel, you're late. I'm trying to get home for a couple of hours, fer chrissake. Let's get to pouring. Chop-chop."

The Mexican, or whatever he was, went behind the bar, took a drink order, started pouring, all without missing one hot word to the woman.

Eddie started for the door, urgently trying to get out of the bar same as a diver urgently trying to get out from under sixty feet of water.

I caught him with: "Eddie . . ."

Angry and annoyed: "*What?*"

"I . . . I need your help."

"Jesus, buy your own damn drinks, okay?"

"No, not like that . . . I need your help."

"You said. You said that. What do you need, Jeffty? What?"

Still no way to put it into words. "I just . . . Could you come home with me?"

"Oh, Jesus, Jeffty—"

"Just . . . look, you need a ride, right?" I knew he did. One-armed guys aren't much for driving on their own. "Takes forever to get a bus this time of morning. I'll give you a ride, take you home, but . . . we just gotta stop by my place for a minute." More than a minute, but Eddie didn't have to be hip to that.

Eddie thought. Yeah, late/early, LA, waiting for a bus versus getting dropped at your door. That and my pathetic look and sound swung him over. "Okay. But just for a minute at your place. Then home. I gotta go home."

We drove. Me, in a haze, somehow managing to navigate to my apartment. Eddie, still going on about Wesker getting busted.

Home, I parked, led Eddie upstairs. Key in the lock, I paused, last chance to do some explaining.

"What?" Eddie asked harsh, sick of my shit. "What!"

Still no way to say it; no way I could think to soften up what was behind door number one. I opened up.

There was a beat while Eddie took in things, which gave me a second to close the door and shut out the world from my little drama. Eddie looked around, then looked down to the floor, to Nellis, to Nellis's body. I could see it in his eyes; see his mind doing the dark arithmetic as he added up the pieces of the scene. Body + brains + blood. Murder.

"Jesus Christ! Jesus! Jesus God!" Eddie's one good arm did windmills in the air. "You killed a guy! What the hell did you do?"

"I didn't do anything."

"You got a dead body on the floor. How you going to say you didn't do anything? Sweet Jesus Christ almighty!"

"It was Dumas. Dumas—"

"Christ! Jesus—"

"*Will you listen to me?* Dumas shot him."

"I don't want to know! I don't want to know who shot him! What the hell do you want from me? What'd you bring me over here for?"

"I gotta get rid of him. I gotta do something with the body."

"Jesus—"

"Keep it down!"

"Christ!"

"Will you help me?"

"Help you? Help you what? What the hell do I know about getting rid of bodies?"

"I don't . . . nothing. But you're the only guy I know, Eddie."

"The only?"

"The only one I could think of to help me with something like this."

"My luck."

"Well, Wesker, maybe. But Wesker got hauled off, so . . ."

"My good luck nobody thinks of me when they come into money, or got an extra woman hanging around. But you got a stiff cooling on your floor, Hey, Eddie, come on over."

Eddie's arm finally took a break from swinging around. Things got calm for a minute. After you introduce someone to the dead, life has a way of slowing down a bit.

Eddie stood there, and stood there, then he said: "Drink."

I knew what he meant, so I fetched him some old Jim Beam, which was all I had, and a glass that wasn't particularly dirty.

Eddie drank, and drank, then he said: "You got to get rid of this body."

"No shit I do. What the hell you think I brought you here for?"

"I'm just saying: That's what you gotta do." Eddie poured out more of the Beam and drank it up thinking all the while. "You got sheets?"

"Yeah."

"I got a friend who works at one of those concrete yards. They got a machine there, a . . . thing. A machine. Crushes stuff up. I mean, it crushes stuff up until there's nothing but nothing left. You get a sheet, we wrap the body in it, then we take it over to the concrete yard."

"How we going to get in?"

"My friend. I told you. He won't ask questions. He's not that kind of guy. Too early in the morning for most anybody else to be there."

"What if—"

"You want to lose the body, or don't you?"

The concrete yard was an idea, but it didn't seem like much of one. But right then Eddie was the only help I had, and a guy in my place was in no position to question that.

"Yeah. Okay. I'll get some sheets and we'll take him to the yard."

Bedroom, sheets, back out. Eddie had finished off the Beam and gotten himself a little glassy-eyed. Whatever, as long as he saw me through this. I laid out the sheets next to Nellis, hovered over the body, then looked at Eddie. Eddie didn't do anything, didn't move. I looked at him hard.

Eddie came back with a "What?" face.

"You gonna help me?"

Eddie's stump went up in the air.

"Aw, don't give me that."

"You show me what good I'm gonna be, one armed."

"You can get his feet or something. His foot."

"I can't get his foot. You get his foot."

"Eddie!"

"Hey, I had the plan. Who came up with the plan?"

Fuck it. I was just wasting time with talk, and time I didn't have. I took Nellis by the shoulders and lifted him toward the sheets. There was this sucking/slurping/cracking sound. The back of Nellis's head, where the bullet had pushed through—the dried blood was holding it to the floor and me pulling on the body was ripping his skull open.

Eddie: "Jesus!"

Me: "Shut up! You're not helping any."

Eddie: "Jesus!"

More pulling on the body. More sucking/slurping/cracking. Nellis came loose from the floor with a jolt. The back of his head and some of his brains stayed behind.

"Jesus!"

"Would you shut up with that Jesus shit!"

"Okay, but . . . Jesus." Nellis onto the sheets. Into the kitchen for a spoon. I pried up/scooped up what was left of him on the floor and tossed that onto the sheet, too. Rolled up like a dead meat burrito, I threw the body over my shoulder, no help from Eddie, and moved for the door. That Eddie opened for me. He looked around real careful.

Crack of dawn, empty halls.

We went for the stairs, down to the street, to the Corvair. I fished the keys from my pocket, the body still over my shoulder, and popped the trunk which, on the Corvair, was really the hood. I tossed Nellis down into it wanting at first to be careful, respectful. But he was heavy, and I was tired, and I figured if Nellis could take a bullet to the head, a couple of bumps off the side of a car wasn't going to be much worse.

Nellis hit the trunk. Big problem: He didn't fit. Limbs hung way out over the sides. I pushed at them, tried to force them. The body was already going stiff, and it fought me hard.

Eddie looked around nervous, but we had the street to ourselves. With nothing else for him to do, he got obvious. "He don't fit."

"Ya think, Eddie? Really?" Pushing, shoving, cramming. Nothing. Nellis was really starting to piss me off.

"He don't fit. I'm telling you, he don't fit."

"I know that, Eddie. I'm standing here looking at him hanging out of my trunk. I know he don't fit."

The body as it was, half in and half out of the trunk of a car on an LA street, wasn't doing anything good for either of our heads.

Eddie: "You got to do something."

"You're the idea guy. What am I supposed to do?"

"Well . . . you gotta make him fit."

"He won't fit."

"You . . . you gotta make him. . . . You gotta cut him."

A long beat.

"What?" I knew what, but it was the only thing that came to me to say.

"You gotta cut him up. Cut him up and he'll fit."

"I . . . I can't—"

"He's already dead."

"I can't cut him up."

"And you can't be standing around all morning with a body hanging out your trunk."

That, Eddie was very right about. It was just a matter of time before somebody stumbled onto me and him lugging a body—a shot-up body—around, which happened to be the kind of thing people tended to frown on.

Nellis: Up out of the trunk, back on my shoulder. I don't know if stiffer made for heavier, but it felt like it. Inside. Upstairs. Nellis's head banged the banister and scraped the walls on the way up. I didn't even pretend to care anymore. Inside my apartment and back onto the floor. Nobody saw us, not a person. That kind of luck in Vegas and I would've been able to pay Dumas off.

Eddie: "You got a saw or something?"

"No."

"Gotta cut him up with something." Eddie went into the kitchen, rummaged around, and came up with a butcher's knife.

"You're kidding."

"You don't have a saw. If you had a saw—"

"I can't cut a body with that!"

"Why the hell not? You can cut steak with it. A person ain't nothing but meat. And that guy there—"

"Nellis."

"There ain't much meat to him at that. Just cut him in half, that's all. Cut him in half, we can get him in the car."

Eddie held out the knife. All I did was stare at it. He gestured to me with it a couple of times, then: "It's only getting lighter out, man."

Lighter out. More people walking the streets as the morning went on. More people to see a guy and his one-armed buddy lugging bloody sheets to the trunk of his car.

I took the knife, went down to my knees, unraveled the sheets leaving Nellis's head covered—like there was a difference to be made there; like anything could make more tolerable such an unpleasant chore.

Eddie coached me: "Cut him at the torso. Right in half. Like that girl they found that one time. Way back when. Famous murder. They cut her in half."

Normalcy took a vacation. I was back up on that carnival ride going full out. Things rushed and whipped around me, but they were without form, shape, or substance. And that was fine. The crazier the world got, the easier it was to sink my knife into the body. The more wild, freaked-out, cuckoo things became, the simpler it was to put up with the tearing-fabric sound flesh makes when it rips from bone and the smells that creep out of a human being when torn open. They were all just part of a dream.

Miles away, Eddie said: "Gotta watch out for the spine. You'll get hung up on the spine. Gotta work your way right through that bad boy."

The cutting went on, me working up a frenzy to get the job done.

Spine: rough going, like Eddie said. I cut; then when cutting was no good, I hacked and chopped and whacked, the frenzy going fever pitch. Skin and bone chips kicked back into my face. My world spun out of control. I leapt into a tunnel and it closed into darkness on both ends. I screamed; rage and pain and anguish all stewed together. I wailed like a beast, and I thanked God for it—that I could not do this inhuman act without tasting emotion. It gave me something like hope to hold on to— the hope that I was not as soulless as I believed, if even for only a moment. I thought that as I went on cutting. I thought that as I went on wailing while I sliced and diced and tore and gashed and slashed and ripped and—

"Jeffty." Eddie's voice, his hand on my shoulder, bringing me back, pulling me out of the tunnel. "You're done, Jeffty. You're all done."

I looked down. I was done. I had cut Nellis clean through, only there wasn't much clean about it. I didn't look long, and I didn't much think about what I had done. The body parts got wrapped back up; I carried them awkward in my arms.

Eddie on the lookout. A few people, but they passed. Then nothing, no one. Still a little luck.

Nellis in the trunk, finally. Eddie piloted and I drove. Nice and easy. No need to attract attention. Just a couple of guys out for a ride first thing in the morning.

Longest ride of my life. A hacked-up body in your car has a way of making every moment last a little longer. A sweat every time a cop prowled by, and suddenly there was a cop on every corner. Each look from another driver, each glance from a pedestrian, every mother's son, eight million people—there wasn't one of them who didn't know I was up to something. Not a one of them who didn't want to point a finger in my direction. I felt each and every one of their eyes crawling over me, spiders to my flesh.

I wondered about Dumas. He was the one who had committed the crime, not me. Except for not calling the cops, and cutting Nellis up, and hiding the body, I hadn't done anything wrong, yet here I was nursing guilt and fear. I wondered if Dumas felt like I felt. I wondered if the guilt was sucking him under the way it made me feel like a drowning man.

I checked my watch. Six-twenty-six. I figured Dumas was fast asleep.

La Brea. The concrete yard. Still empty. Eddie's friend at the gate. They chatted up for a while, too long for my paranoid self.

"How you been?"

"Been okay."

"What you been up to?"

"Nothing much."

Finally, Eddie got around to how we had to do something out back of the yard and if he would mind just letting us in for a minute.

The friend was all easygoing: "Yeah, sure, go do what you gotta do." He wondered out loud, at the end of that, if he might come by the Regent for a couple of free drinks sometime, him and his girl. Eddie okayed it, and we were in.

We drove around until we came up on the thrasher, or whatever it was. A big-ass thing that ground up rock real fine to make concrete. Trunk open, I hauled the body parts over to the lip of the machine.

"Think it'll take care of things?" I asked.

"It tears up rock. It's not going to leave nothing of your pal."

I hesitated, which brought a prompt from Eddie.

"Go on, man. Toss him in."

More hesitation.

"What are you waiting for, an audience?"

I didn't know, and I told Eddie as much. I just figured this was like it for Nellis; this was his funeral. I was never much of a friend. Once you lie to someone, no matter how small the lie is, there can never be much between you. And every lie after that is like another brick in a wall you build between yourself and someone else. I had done so much more than just lie to Nellis. I had cheated him, used him, took him for all he was worth. And in the end, I had killed him. Same as pulling the trigger of the gun, I had. So now, at this moment, I figured Nellis deserved something out of me. I just didn't know what.

Eddie offered that we ought to have a moment of silence, and he stressed it should be a very short moment, as the yard would be opening soon. I yessed the idea, and me and him shut up for a second.

I didn't think of Nellis.

I thought of that dream — of seeing salvation for an instant before the river of blood swept me away.

And then I remembered. All a sudden when I dipped my head to pray, it came to me. Angeli. That was the actress the street girl reminded me of. Pier Angeli. Angeli, like the angel in my dream. How about that? Yeah. There was all that shit with her and Dean and Damone and Steinberg before she . . .

And then I remembered I was supposed to be having a moment of silence for Nellis. I quit thinking of other stuff and gave the dead his due.

After a minute Eddie and me stopped being quiet, tossed the two halves of Nellis into the machine, loaded up some rocks over him until you couldn't see anything, then got in the Corvair and headed out.

On the way home I took Eddie by Norms off La Cienega. He talked me into the strawberry pancakes. They were good.

When I finally got back home I dug an old .38 I had out of the closet. Watching people take bullets to the head makes you rethink your personal security. I tried sleeping with it under my pillow, but then I figured one bad dream might just kill me. I put it on the nightstand hoping I could get to it in time should Dumas come back around. Finally, I ended up admitting to myself I didn't have what it takes to pull the trigger, even if the difference was me or somebody else. Some people can kill; some can't. That simple.

I put the gun back in the closet and got some sleep.

Days were like waking dreams—they blended and swirled in their own little cocktail. I passed through them waiting for something—I didn't know what—but something to happen. I just figured you couldn't dump a body without an event occurring at your expense. The tap on the shoulder, the cops at the door, the crazies screaming murder, bloody murder, and pointing at you while you got hauled off. I waited for it.

Kept waiting.

Then the waiting got so bad I wanted it to happen just to get the whole business over with. It was the kind of unrelenting need for cleansing where every time you saw a cop you had to fight yourself back from crawling to his feet and begging him to let you confess.

Eddie was no help. I'd go to the Regent and drink, not to drink but to look in the eyes of the only other person on the face of the earth who knew my secret. Only, Eddie gave me the brush-off. Not straight out. He never said anything like "Get lost!" or "Stop coming around here anymore, you trouble-causing bastard I had to dump a body with!" He gave me the kind of brush-off that comes at the end of a laugh or a smile that reads like everything is perfect in the world: What happened didn't happen and I don't want you talking about what didn't happen. To me, it was worse than if he'd yelled at me, or told me to beat it.

All I needed from him was a "Don't worry about it." All I needed was to see him sweat, or at least flinch just a little to let me know I wasn't in things by myself.

I got nothing of the kind from Eddie. Just a smile and a change of subject anytime I got anywhere near talking about anything like Nellis.

Eddie made me feel alone. He made me feel I was living a conspiracy of one. I felt that way day after day after day. I knew I would feel that way forever.

Except I didn't.

All a sudden, very unexpectedly, my feelings of guilt and fear were gone. One day I woke up and showered and ate and went about my life for most of the morning before I realized I hadn't even thought about Dumas, or Nellis, or the queer silver finger that spat bullets, or the concrete yard. From then on, I didn't so much think about the incident as, if anything, think about how little I thought about it anymore.

After a while I didn't even do that.

After a while more my head was filled with questions: How am I going to pay for food? How am I going to pay rent? How am I going to pay off Dumas? And somehow, all that crap swirling around in my brain made life good. At least it made it normal.

That passed as well.

Normal has a way of wearing thin when you realize that your normal life is fairly shitty. Days dragging by were days closer to Dumas getting tired of waiting for his money and wanting me dead for sure. The fact of it, the oppressive weight of my situation, put me in a place where I couldn't so much as eat. Before where depression had only thinned my urge for food, now not even force of will could make me choke it down. Didn't have much money for food anyway. Couldn't bring myself to work to make money to buy food 'cause I knew I couldn't eat the food I bought, so what was the point?

Downward spiral. On and on. Didn't wanna eat/didn't wanna work. Didn't work/no money to eat. Didn't eat/too tired to work. Don't wanna live/waiting around to die.

Drink.

That's what I could still do: drink. I don't mean have a couple of high-balls down at the Regent. I mean drink myself right out of existence. That was the last bit of self-empowerment remaining to me: when and how I was going to kick off. I remembered Nellis's face—that look of shock and sur-prise that was burned there forever when the bullet took out the back of his head. That wasn't for me. I wasn't trying to go out with a glassy-eyed eter-nal "What the fuck went wrong?" stare up at the sky. Naw, if I was gonna go, I was gonna go my way and on my terms.

Drink.

Drink until I was dead—a slow, painless fade to black, just like the guy in that one movie that was a book that I didn't read.

Yeah, I had a gun. I could've just put a bullet in my own self and been done with it, but I thought it might hurt.

Funny.

I didn't mind dying. Didn't want to, but didn't mind. Hell, I was already dead. What I could do without was the pain. Maybe it wasn't so funny as it was telling. You die as you live, and I was trying to do it as softly as possible. Just like the guy in the movie that was a book that I didn't read. Cool. He was cool. The guy in the movie, anyway. I didn't know what the guy in the book was like.

A watch, a ring—about all I had left.

Pawnshop: forty-five bucks. That ought to do the trick if the booze was cheap enough.

Late, dark by the time I hit the 24/7 Mart. Bright inside. Nobody dug the light. Not the rocker/vampires who came down from their clubs on Sunset. Not the addicts who dragged themselves in for food to keep them-selves alive between highs. Not guys like me who were fixed on dropping into a permanent oblivion.

Me, going through the coolers: little this, little that. A mix and match of intoxication. Hard shit only, no money for the lighter fare. If it can't kill, it don't go in the basket.

At the counter: fifty-two dollars' worth of booze. A couple of bottles go back until I hit forty-five on the nose.

The clerk, his name tag: PARIS. How about that? I get to see Paris before I die.

I pack up and head out, thinking in my head, Who's the lucky one to get drunk up first? Smirnoff, Absolut, Jim, or Jack?

Behind me, a voice low and sweet: "Change?"

I knew before I turned. It was her, the Angeli-looking girl. She was curled up on the ground against the wall of the 24/7 Mart, hand out, just like she'd been curled up on the ground, hand out, in front of Ralphs and in the bus station.

"Change?" she asked again.

"I . . ." Forty-five bucks on booze. "No. But . . ." I held out some of the Jack as an offering.

The look she threw me was "What the hell do I want with that?" The girl rolled over, signaling me to go on with myself. Jack went back into the bag. I got in the Corvair and drove home.

My apartment smelled like puke. It smelled that way because I had puked all over the floor. A few times. That's one of the side effects of trying to drink yourself to death: You tend to puke a lot. The guy in the movie that was a book I didn't read didn't puke much, but that was a movie and he was a movie star, and movie stars have a thing about puking a lot on-screen. They got images. The guy in the book probably puked more, but I don't know.

The floor, where I lay avoiding the fermenting ponds of stomach juice and booze, was very comfortable. It wasn't really, but as the liquor melted my body and stole my sensations, it made the floor feel cozy to the extreme. Cozy as well as convenient. You don't have to look any farther than your feet to find ground, and when you're drunk it's a lot easier to hit than a spinning bed. I could see why Nellis found the floor his resting area of choice.

So I lay there, on the floor, still, my muscles having given up fighting the lake of alcohol in my stomach that made the world dip and sway.

I lay there knowing that to move was to slosh the lake, and that would just make me vomit again, and there was nothing left in me but bile, and the bile would scorch my throat that was torn and scarred from hours of dry heaving.

I lay there sensing my soul tearing from my self, trying to get the hell away from this hideous shell that had kept it trapped for so many ungodly and wasted years.

And as I lay there, feeling groovy but not glamorous, it came to me that I was going to die alone. It was an obvious fact, but one overlooked until that moment. The whole big city around me, and there wasn't a single someone out there to give a damn over my passing. I wanted to laugh, but the drink just made me mumble. If it was possible, I was going to die worse off than Nellis. At least when he was killed, I was there to give a damn. Mostly, sure, 'cause I was freaked about having a dead body in my apartment, but I did give a damn.

But me, I was as lone as alone is. Except for lying among a dozen or so empty bottles and my own puke, it doesn't get more pathetic than dying in isolation.

That was the other thing that was different from that movie. Besides the fact that drinking yourself to death involves a lot more throwing up in real life, I didn't have a really good-looking hooker with me in my final moments. The guy in the movie did. In the movies, all hookers are hot-looking. Hot-looking, drug-free, smart, not so much as carrying a cold, let alone some disease that'll stop you in your tracks.

And a heart of gold. Movie whores always have hearts of gold. The way Hollywood tells it, it's no wonder so many chicks are out tricking. It's like being a nun in a G-string.

I didn't have a hooker. For that matter, I didn't have any woman. Maybe it was the booze working, but I got to thinking I didn't know when was the last time I'd had a woman in my life. There was the girl in Vegas, the Oriental chick, but ten minutes after, I couldn't remember her name, much less now. And as it went, she wasn't much in my life. She was just a thing that happened. She was just sex. What had occurred between me and her was empty and useless, and about as fulfilling as masturbating during a rerun of *Ally McBeal*. And maybe that was okay then, in the moment, but looking back on it with the perspective of a guy dying of alcohol poisoning on the floor, it was those kinds of meaningless events, endless in number, stacked one on top of the other, that added up to my vacant life.

That other chick, that street girl, was more in my life than the Oriental was. My soul so close to a permanent sleep, I tried to think of her, her pretty face—the pale, dark angel who kept coming around and coming around, lying there in the 24/7 Mart parking lot with her hand out to me, wanting change. . . .

Change . . .

Her hand out . . .

Her hand out . . . but not wanting change; not asking for change. No . . .

Her hand out . . .

Her hand out . . . to *make* a change.

Ooooh shit!

An idea was racing at me locomotive-hard. A crazy swinger of an idea. An idea that could only be induced by a cocktail of booze and death. In a moment of high intoxication and crystal clarity, I was swept up in the rapture. Religion that had escaped me my entire life now overflowed from inside me, and with it a vision came and went like a sighting of the Grail: a perfect, shining scam. A con for the ages. And more than that. On the wings of an angel, God had sent me a bunko that would set me free—a way up and out from under the avalanche of all that I was, and passage to all I'd ever dreamed I could be.

Praise Jesus, I was saved.

Except I was dying. The hours of nonstop booze that flowed a river to my soul were taking their last swipe at me. I could feel life slipping away. Sure, God had tossed the perfect con my way, but He freakin' waited until I was five and a half feet under to do it.

My heart slowed. I began drifting up out of my own body to where I could look down on myself.

Christ. From my vantage point, I looked awful. Too late I had gotten wise, just a minute too late.

Bye, me. Nice knowing you. Have a good forever after. Tell Nellis—

No. No way. No fucking way! I wasn't going to die. I wasn't about to let myself kick off. Not when for the first time in my miserable, useless existence I was so close to something good; brushing right up against being able to buy myself a tomorrow, and a tomorrow after that, and all I needed until they added up to a life.

I reached out as much as I could control my drunken limbs and grabbed hold of my soul. I dug my fingers into it and held on. It bayed like an animal, leg snapped in a steel trap, that begged only its freedom. An ugly, desperate howl that ran razor-cold through my hollow self.

Too bad.

My soul whipped and churned, trying to break free, wanting nothing to do with me.

Too damn bad.

I never before had had any use for it, my soul. It could have left me at any time—every once in a while I thought it had—and I would never have missed it. I would have sold it on any number of occasions could I have found a buyer. But now I needed it. Now there was a little piece of brilliance to be done, and that brilliance had given me hope, and hope had given me a desire to live no matter how much part of me—nearly all of me—wanted to die.

So me and my soul rolled across the floor, grappling, locked arm in arm, doing battle. The stakes high as they get: life.

I woke up. I was still on the floor, where I had been for I don't know how long. All night, a couple of days. Time had turned to rubber. It stretched and bent and twisted into a shroud that clouded minutes and hours and days.

My hands ached, my fingers bent in stiffened curls. It got around to drifting back to me how they'd ended up like this; how I wrestled with my own soul, my own self. Just a dream fed by liquor, or maybe a manifestation of reality. I wasn't fighting my soul, not really, but I was fighting for my life, and somehow I had pulled it back from heaven, or hell, or some other place people like me deserve. I had gotten my life back, and now I just had to do something with it. To do something with it, I had to get off the floor. That was an event I hadn't undertaken for days, and one I sure as shit wasn't going to do soon.

I waited a while, time being abundant as it was. I waited till my fingers loosened, until they could help out in getting me to my feet.

First try: Got as high as one knee. Whole lot of booze still running through me, booze that didn't care much for the new angle at which it found itself. The wood floor popped as my head slammed it on my way back down, but that was drowned out under the dry heaves that hit me again.

I took a break from moving. A nice hour or so.

Second try: Didn't get as far as the first before the heaves came at me one more time.

Another hour relaxing. I took the time to carefully examine the many and varied details of the floor close-up.

Third time's the charm. Except for me. I hit the ground and took another break, but only a half hour this time.

On the fourth try, I did it. First up on one knee, then the other. I squatted, I struggled, I pulled myself into a standing—well, hunching—position with the same sweaty determination of a guy climbing Mount Everest. Sixty full seconds of fight, but I made it. Look at me, Ma, top of the world. I'm a big man. I can stand up.

Downstairs, shakily.

The street, barely.

The Corvair, thankfully. Took me another couple of minutes just to get all that little bit of nothing done, but I made it, the sunlight harsh and new to me. I drove to Hollywood Boulevard, headed west for a bookshop. One of the God knows how many in this town filled with stuff on moviemaking and biographies on actors and directors and anyone else who ever did anything to help get a picture made.

It wasn't a long drive; I could have walked it, but I was too fucked up to walk. I was too fucked up to drive as well, but half the people on the roads of LA were too fucked up to drive, so I fit in nicely. The other half may have been okay to drive; they just didn't have insurance.

I needed the drive anyway. The sunlight and smog helped sober me up, and the ride was just long enough I could ponder the oddities of life. Strange how something I'd heard or read once, so long ago that now I couldn't even think where, was going to save my ass.

Better than that.

Some words, some bits of trivia, a girl I didn't even know who kept popping up until she was able to pound her meaning through my dense head—they were all mixing together to hand me on a silver platter the one thing I never once had before: a chance.

I hit the bookstore running, as much as the leftover booze would let me run. A rack of old one-sheets, a cardboard cutout of Bogart. Over there: a couple of fags leafing through a book on Norma Jean.

What's that smell?

I went for the actor biographies, and there were a lot of them. Gig Young, Mariette Hartley, Stuart Whitman . . . Rows of pugs I didn't know, and faces I didn't recognize. I guess all you got to do is walk past a camera to rate a book on yourself. And it was the same story every time: They had a dream; no one else believed in them; they came to Hollywood and proved the world wrong by getting a couple of forgettable parts in some unmemorable movies.

I went through the A's. Nothing. Every other whoever, but not her.

What's that freakin' smell?

I started going through books on movies in the fifties, fifties actors. Nope, more nothing . . .

Yes. Found one. A coffee-table thing on Italian actresses. Tore the book from the shelf, flipped the pages until I hit some pictures. There she was, my dark angel—the girl from Ralphs and the bus station. Darken her hair, pluck her eyebrows, throw on some fake lashes and her face was the same—not kind of like, *the same*—as the one staring back from the picture in the book: Pier Angeli.

Italian, like I said. Born there. Her real name was Anna Maria Pierangeli. As beautiful as beautiful gets. Hair that was black silk running like a river over beige skin. Eyes that could drown a man, and lips that would talk him into diving in in the first place. Made a couple of films in Italy before Hollywood scouts found her. Must have been about as hard as finding a prayer in the Bible. They yanked her and her mom over Stateside, polished her up, then let her loose to be a star. Would have been one, too, except for the guy she fell in love with: James Dean. That mumbly little half fag who got himself into a car wreck that sliced off his head and turned him into a legend. He was what every wannabe that fills the coffee shops on Beverly Boulevard wants to be. A thing that defied death and time and the two dimensions of the silver screen, and even itself as there's no explaining how three movies—one good, two watchable after midnight—entitle you to live forever. Thing of it is, like with Elvis and Marilyn, that Mexican singer chick who took a bullet, even that English princess bitch, death is nothing but good PR.

The smell, that awful stench that had hit me since first I walked into the bookstore, was starting to get oppressive. That's when I realized the odor, the stink—it was coming from me. How many days of lying, drunk, in my own filth trying to die, then fighting to live? I was so hopped-up on finding my angel, I didn't even think to wash before I blasted out of the apartment. And nobody noticed, not a single person in the bookstore. Or if they did notice, they didn't pay me any mind. Jaded LA. What was one more stinking bum off the boulevard? If I'd walked in with a bloody ax in one hand and clutching a hacked-off head in the other, it wouldn't have gotten me second looks.

So, Pier I was talking about. Yeah, she was as fine as she wanted to be, and she hooks up with JD. Falls for him hard. Only her mom doesn't go for this. Doesn't matter Dean's a star. Like most moms, she doesn't dig her daughter hanging with dopeheads who beat their girls when they've got one on. Moms are funny that way.

Pier and Dean were like that—hot and angry and violent—and it filled their existence with the kind of sex and passion only heat and anger and violence can give birth to.

Pier's studio, MGM, didn't much dig their starlet hanging with Dean, either. Didn't fit the image they were building for her. Didn't fit the plan. So the studio teams up with mom and they arrange for Pier to marry Vic Damone. Italian. Catholic. Could sing, too. Not like the Chairman, but he could sing. Pier couldn't fight that; she couldn't fight her mom, and she sure as hell couldn't fight the studio. Your name's on a contract, your life is in their pocket.

So she married Damone. Dean showed up across the street from the church and blared a wedding march on his cycle as the newlyweds smooched on the steps for the press. Her and Damone went on for a while, just like her and Dean kept on screwing. Dig this: That kid Pier had with Damone? Word is it might not have been with Damone. See what I'm saying?

Then Dean died, the sham marriage with Damone went south, and Pier dropped out. It's been quite fun, Hollywood, but fuck you very much.

When she finally got around to it, Pier killed herself. Pills. That's what chicks do; how they check out. She left notes. Not *a* note. Notes. One of them went:

> *Today I am alone. I have always been alone. Always, except with Jimmy. I don't think anyone could save me now. It's too late. I believe I was meant to be alone and die alone. Love is far behind me; it was killed at the wheel of a Porsche.*

Some swinging shit.

Truth: The thing about love is no matter how twisted, or wrong, or evil, it never dies. Never. You can run, but you can't hide. Love stays with you like a cancer, working on you double shift, day and night, until it does whatever it was meant to do to you—shape or mold or bust up your life the way only love can, because nothing else is that powerful. Nothing else is that tenacious. Sometimes that's okay. Sometimes you end up with a decent relationship; wife and kids. That's livable. Sometimes you just end up dead. Pills were the way out for Pier, but Dean, from the grave, was the hand that popped them for her.

End of story.

Only, not end of story. Sometime between her crazy love of James Dean and the time when she ended things for herself, Pier had another lover.

Sort of.

Moe Steinberg was, is, the thing most indigenous, particular, and peculiar to Hollywood: the mogul. One of the rare breed of cigar chompers who ran the studios—he ran more than one in his time. Intimate to the tribe who built this town as far back as the forties, Moe was one of the guys who, depending on how he felt on any particular day, decided which waitress or busboy was going to go from nobody to household name by putting him in the next picture from the next script he'd already decided was going to be the next blockbuster. He'd made half his fortune that way. He'd made the other half buying up land in Santa Monica back when Santa Monica—hell, back when Beverly Hills was too far away for most Angelenos to even think about traveling to without making overnight reservations.

Moe was the guy who discovered Pier. He brought Pier to the States. He set her up with a phat studio contract and shoved her down the throats of producers who had other ideas about which female should take the lead in their movie.

Moe loved Pier. Not just in the "he wanted to bang a starlet" way. At his peak he could've had as many of those as he wanted. The way I hear it, he did. But then came Pier.

Moe *loved* Pier. It was the kind of love that consumed a man twenty-four/seven. The kind of love that burned and left a mark, that made you double up with pain at the thought of separation.

Unfortunately for Moe, it was also the kind of love that ran on a one-way street.

Moe loved Pier. Pier didn't love Moe. Imagine what it must have been like for the most powerful man in Hollywood—a guy who could make or break the career of any poor sap he wanted to just for the sport of it—imagine him having to sit on the sidelines and watch the girl he discovered, the star he created, go all soft for some skinny punk with a full head of hair. Imagine the kind of hurt that puts on a man. It cost Moe millions trying to prove his love for Pier. Cars, furs, diamonds and such. It cost him his wife, his family. . . . But who needs earthly wealth when you got Pier? 'Cept he couldn't get Pier because, instead of wanting to be with a guy that was mad crazy for her, Pier wanted to be with an alky who would get hopped-up, then beat the living shit out of her.

Go figure.

So Moe worked himself up a good hate for JD. Moe played things with Pier's mom so Pier would end up with Damone. Hey, if Moe couldn't have her, Dean sure as hell wouldn't.

And Dean? . . . I wonder. That crash out on a lonely stretch of road. That car slamming so violently into Dean's little speedster. Dean was the only guy of three not to walk away from the wreck. I wonder if Moe had the kind of reach to make an accident happen not so accidentally? I know he had the kind of hate.

Ironic. Moe breaks up Pier and Dean, Dean gets dead, Pier can't stand it so she kills herself, and Moe ends up, to this day, wandering around some Beverly Hills home longing for his eternal love. Nobody got what they wanted out of that deal, but it wasn't the kind of thing you could plan. Love, like luck, does as it pleases.

It was all there for me: Pier and Moe and a chance. Not much of one, but at this stage of the game, it was the only kind of chance coming my way. I closed up the book and thought about things as I went out of the shop and let the sunlight go back to pounding liquor-filled sweat from my pores.

I drove for the apartment. Blaring horns from cross traffic alerted me to the light I ran. My head was floating in vague ideas. There were things to get done—disparate items that had to be stitched together, and no telling what kind of time I had to get them joined up. How much longer was Dumas going to give me? Where was my dark angel, and could I get her into my fold?

Yeah, I could, I told myself, 'cause I had to tell myself something positive. I needed her and I could get her, but first I had to find her.

No.

First I had to get clean.

I parked and shot up to the apartment. Vomit that had been parboiling in the ninety-plus-degree weather hit me square in the face. I grabbed cleaning supplies, the few I had, and worked the apartment over. Wiped down the floors, washed off the puke. . . . There was a spot of red where Nellis's shot-open head had lain for hours that I couldn't get out.

Screw it.

Leave it.

Straightened, did laundry. The clothes I was wearing weren't good for much more than burning, so I tossed 'em. Showered, shaved, even found some cologne, but opted not to use it. Should I find my angel, I didn't want things to seem too set up, too planned.

Even rushing through it all—and believe me, I was hauling ass—it was sundown before I got the place and myself presentable. Downstairs and into the Corvair. This is what was facing me: I was in the largest city in America and I had to find one person I didn't know—didn't know her name, or what street corner or cardboard box she called home. And if I couldn't find her, if I couldn't convince her to help me, I didn't see much standing in the way of Dumas killing me.

It was gonna be a fun night.

First stop was a pawnshop. Again. I'd come up with a little more shit to sell off. Amazing what you can live without when you need dough. Bye, radio. Don't much like the music you play these days anyway. C-ya, electric razor. All you did was add to the electric bill I couldn't pay in the first place. Peace, blender. Blended drinks are for pussies. All pawned up, I was able to add another fifty-eight dollars to my personal fortune, which brought me to a grand total of fifty-eight dollars.

I went to Ralphs, to the bus station, to the 24/7 Mart—the three places I'd seen my dark angel. I went to them just like that—one, two, three. And one, two, three, I struck out. I figured I would. Prayed I wouldn't, but figured I would. What were the odds of finding this girl when I needed her? Sure, three times I'd seen her. Big damn deal. Think of how many times in how many places I hadn't seen her. Worse yet, think of all the places there were to look for her. I didn't have time to think about it. Time spent thinking was time spent not searching, so I just got to looking.

Hollywood Boulevard. Dirty. Ugly. Oriental tourists jump off buses, grab a couple of pictures at the Chinese Theater, then jump right back on again.

Up and down the boulevard, all along the side streets, nothing but kids. Runaways, dopeheads, some just kids whose parents didn't much give a damn and let them run loose at night—they were all here, commingling and infecting each other with a poison both physical and mental: Got dope? Sure I got that. Need crack? Got a friend who sells. Wanna fuck? I think I'm clean . . . I think.

America's future today. Almost made me want to let Dumas put a bullet in my head. It was a living graveyard, and it was also a good bet for finding a street urchin like Angel. Good, but not much good. I cruised from La Brea to Western and back. I went slow, zigzagging up to Franklin and down to Santa Monica.

Nothing.

Girl's got to eat, right? I checked out all the fast food joints, their parking lots. Figured she might be begging—money, food, sex for money or food.

Nothing.

It was getting late, or early. Either way, it wasn't doing me any good driving around Hollywood with the top down on my car, which is the only way the top was anymore. I bought food without blowing all my new bread, cruised back to the apartment, and ate. Eating for the first time after a steady diet of liquor didn't work out so good. I went back to throwing up, but this time I had the sober good sense to do it in the toilet.

After that little bit of fun I went to bed telling myself that tomorrow I would find my angel; tomorrow would be my first step on the road to emancipation.

I told myself that again and again, like I could make me believe it.

It didn't make me believe anything, but it did make me fall asleep.

I went back to work the next day. First time in a long while. I needed to get back in a groove. I needed to earn some dough. I needed to do something to get my mind off the "Will I or won't I find her?" tension that was bubbling up inside me.

Work didn't help much.

I found myself working angles anywhere I might stumble on the girl: convenience stores, Laundromats, taco stands. Nothing, nothing, and more nothing.

By midday, my body needed a drink. Not so much for the drink itself, but more for the couple of minutes of sitting over some booze in a dark corner of the Regent that came with it. A couple of minutes of cool, quiet womblike comfort in a place where depression and defeat were welcomed attributes in a man.

I fought the urge.

My body fought me back. A dry mouth and cold sweat told me I had it bad, worse than I ever figured. At some point, I'd gone alky. Maybe it had been slow, all the while Dumas'd been riding me. More likely it had come on during my suicide run. I'd tried to kill my body; now it wanted me to finish the job. It didn't come out and say that. All it was saying to me now, like a little nagging itch begging to get scratched, was, Just give me a drink. That was the deal I was trying to cut with myself. One drink, and I'd leave me alone, let me get on with the business at hand. It was a tempting offer. I knew how good a whiskey sour, a vodka and tonic—hell, how good a beer would feel right then.

It would have been nothing to give in. A drink, right? What's one drink? Nothing, really. But a symbol. That drink was everything I used to be: a loser, a lazy boozer. A guy who crawled through life small-changing it every step of the way.

Not anymore.

I had man's work to do, and to do it I needed to be sharp and pure, same as a boxer stepping into a ring. Maybe I'd lied that to myself before, but this time I had to make it stick.

So let my body ache and scream. Let me sweat and shake. That was part of the fight. It was part of the pain that let me know I was in the game. I was on a mission. No more doing things half-assed. If I took a step, it would be a block long. If I swung a bat, it would be for the fence. I was a winner now, and that's what winners did.

I big-talked and tough-guyed my way through the day. I made it through the night, too, looking for Angel every step of the way and coming up busted. One long twenty-four hours, and no closer to having accomplished anything than when I'd started.

Home. Bed. That's when things got tough. Alone in the dark, in the half-quiet of the city, that's where the hurt for a drink went bad. It got like the longing for a lover's touch from a woman prematurely kissed off. A gentle, soothing thing gone, and for which you'd do anything—murder and the trading of your soul not exempt—anything to get her/it back.

I not so quietly called to my former lover. I let her know I needed her by my moans and shivers and shakes. I let her know how much she was missed by the way my body wrenched and twisted over sweat-soaked sheets.

I wanted her/it, but I couldn't give in. I had fought too hard and come too far to slide back down. This was my last chance at everything—at a big con, at good money. It was my last chance at a good life. Life period. For me, it was win or lose, with no comebacks, and for once in the useless history of me I was going to do more than scam mom-and-pop joints for five bucks at a time. I was going to be more than a punching bag for some Haitian bookie, or some puking drunk on the floor. For once, I was going to amount to something; I was going to be glad to be me. For once, I was going to be successful. I dug my hands into the sheets of the bed, dug them deep, like I was trying to sink them through the mattress into the floor itself, and held on for dear life. I was going to make it through the night one second of one hour at a time.

I clamped my eyes shut, pictured my pale, dark angel, and howled.

The thing about LA, about Hollywood, is the sunshine. That's what it has working for it and against it. The sunshine, the weather, the two weeks out of the year that it rains—that's why people move here. It sure ain't for the earthquakes, or the gang violence.

But the sunshine is also what turns all the car exhaust into the smog, which keeps you from seeing the snowcapped mountains that rest behind the downtown towers, or hides the entire valley. Not that anybody is trying to see the fucking valley anyway. And the harsh white light of day only lays the city bare. It reveals it, not enhances it. The city doesn't match itself. Spanish next to Elizabethan next to prefab. It is cleaner than New York, but you don't walk around marveling at the ingeniousness of it the way you do the snuggled skyscrapers that make up the canyons of Gotham. LA wasn't planned; it just happened.

And Hollywood, these days, was unhappening, the sunlight making the slow decay of the city all the more visible to the naked eye. People, the glamour people anyway, were packing up and moving out by the limoful. That building there used to be home to a record company.

Empty.

The building across the way used to have a Mercedes dealership. Gone.

The producers who were in that building? Marina del Rey now.

In their place were the Mexicans and Koreans and Vietnamese. People who were too loud, too dirty, too poor. People who were just plain too not like me. I didn't care for them. I didn't care for what they were doing to this town, my town, with their signs I couldn't read and their languages I couldn't understand.

The other thing I couldn't do was stop them.

Nobody could. They wanted to be here in the worst possible river-swimming, fence-climbing, "inside the stifling trunk of a car on a hotter-than-hell day" kind of way because the shittiest job LA had to offer was better than whatever it was they'd been doing in wherever it was they were river-swimming or fence-climbing away from.

My city was changing. It didn't belong to me anymore, if it ever had. All there was for me now was to get out.

The morning gave no sign of Angel, and the afternoon was no different. She could be anywhere. She could be nowhere. She could be dead. It was very possible. Maybe between the last I'd seen her and now she'd been turned into a blot on the highway, or a body in a morgue. Maybe she'd fallen in with the wrong bunch and ended up in a big-ass rock crusher in a concrete yard and was right this minute being made into the cornerstone of some corporate headquarters next to Nellis. My mind ran with a hundred variations of a thousand ways my girl could have wound up a most excellent corpse. After a while I realized I was making myself depressed. Not so much because I cared about this girl maybe being dead, but if she was dead it really messed things up for me.

By the time it got to being the long part of the night, I'd made the rounds again to every place I could think of finding Angel. And just like the afternoon, and the morning, and the night before, I came up empty.

It's too bad I didn't just need a male prostitute who was supporting a drug habit, or a female one who looked twelve, or a female who was twelve. Plenty of those to spare. None of that came anywhere near doing me any good.

Time was running short. I knew that. What was worse was I knew
there was nothing I could do about it. I could feel Dumas's growing impatience seeping across the city. I started to think it wasn't destiny that had
crossed the paths of Angel and me three times before, just pure dumb
luck. I started to think my grand schemes were just the empty, drunken
musings of a guy whose dreams were too big for his little head. I started to
think for me the dance was just about over.

It was time to go home.

I parked around the corner from my apartment building and started
the walk when something tapped me on the shoulder. Across the street
was a liquor store. Same liquor store that had been in the same spot for
years. Even so, it had never been more noticeable than it was at that very
moment.

My body started talking to me. My body started telling me that I was
never going to find this girl; I was never going to be able to work an angle
that would set me free. I was a loser, it was saying to me. I went to bed a
loser and woke up the same way, and all the hard talk in the world wasn't
going to change that.

So, under the circumstances, being a loser and all, why not just give
in to the booze? I had a couple of bucks now. Not much, but enough to
get me good and soft with alcohol.

I started listening to what I was telling myself, and what I was telling
myself started to make sense. Getting drunk wasn't going to get rid of
my problems, but it would make them feel not so close. I'd been good
to me for a while; I'd laid off the drink. Wasn't that proof of something?
Didn't that mean I could quit—for forty-eight hours—anytime I wanted?
And if you're going to die, I said in my closing arguments, isn't it better to face things more drunk than sober? Isn't it better to go out on the
floor, tossing your guts, than look a bullet in the eye when it comes calling
for you?

The sweats started coming and the shakes were right next door. I was
standing there trying to rationalize and philosophize and intellectualize
things, but the fact was I needed a drink and I needed it right then.

I moved with a certain swiftness across the street, hand already in
pocket pulling up bills. I moved secure in the knowledge of two things: I
was, like I had told myself, a loser and always would be, and in a few
moments I would be too drunk to care.

"Hey," a voice said behind me. "Change?"

*I*t was her. The sound of her voice told me so. A look behind me only served to confirm it. Huddled up on the ground at the side of the building: Angel in the flesh. Seventeen, but she looked twenty-two. That was as good a state a woman could be in, would be in, until she reached thirty-six, full maturity. Thirty-six was when a woman, any woman as far as I was concerned, was graced with a breadth of life and mind and body that was still gilded with the hint trace of youth. It was a woman's last great flowering before years of wasting and the time when a man would toss her aside for a girl who was seventeen but who looked twenty-two.

Angel.

And under the dirt and the matted hair, it was Pier. I'd run the city for her, and here she was almost literally on my doorstep. Of course she was. She had found me the moment I most needed strength and salvation. I started thinking about destiny again.

A new thought: I found her, or she'd found me, so now what do I do? Take things slow, casual. Don't scare her off.

To her, I said: "I'll catch you on the way out." Let her wait a little. Let her think I don't give a damn about her. Let her think I didn't just spend the last day and a half turning over every rock in Hollywood looking for her, or that she is part of some grand scheme. Not that she would think that. Why would she think that? I was nervous, without a real plan. A confidence man without confidence is no good.

Liquor store. Inside. The jolt of seeing Angel shook the need to drink from me. Already she was working her magic. I walked around the aisles for a couple of minutes trying to whip together a strategy of some kind. All a sudden, I realized I'd been walking around the aisles for a couple of minutes, and for all I knew Angel could be gone again. Panic shot me out the door.

She was still there, still huddled and waiting. I stood in front of her, time ticking by, like something was supposed to happen. All that did was she said: "You didn't buy anything."

"Huh?" I dipshitted.

"You went in the store, but you didn't buy anything."

I tried to work up something that sounded reasonable, something that wouldn't make me come off as a complete idiot. Didn't need her thinking that. "Well, I was actually going in to check—"

"Change?" She got it in quick; apparently not being able to care less about the whys of what I did.

A couple of bucks from my pocket. Not too much, just enough for her to maybe take notice of me.

Nothing doing.

She took the money and rolled away from me same as she had the last time I saw her when I gave her nothing.

I kept on standing there for a minute. She kept on ignoring me. After another minute I said: "You got a place? You homeless?"

She turned a bit and looked at me, then turned back fuck-you pronto.

Another minute of standing there. Then, me: "Getting cold. Gonna be cold tonight."

No turning to me this time, but Angel said: "It's sixty degrees out."

For a guy trying not to come off as an idiot I was working overtime at it. "Yeah, but I just mean for LA. For LA, it's cold. Cool. Cooler than it—"

She turned. Sharp, direct, like even this little bit of talk had worn her out: "You want me to go home with you?"

I did, but do I say I did?

"Do you or don't you?" Even more tired of things than she was a second ago.

"Yes. . . ."

"Got money?"

I hauled out some bills, tried to puff them up in my hand to make myself look loaded. Apparently, whatever I had was enough.

Up off the ground, grabbing up a backpack. "Let's go."

Fast. All too fast. My brains sloshed around inside my head.

"We going or not?"

Angel took off walking. She didn't know where I lived, where we were going, but she led the way. She led, and I followed.

Inside my apartment. The second we were through the door she said: "It smells like puke in here."

"Yeah, well, I . . . I haven't been feeling good, and—"

Bulldozing by at eighty miles an hour: "You want to fuck, it's twenty bucks. I don't fuck for less than twenty bucks. Unless you got food. Food and a ten will get you a fuck."

"I don't want—"

"And you got to use a condom. I don't fuck without a condom. You got a condom?"

"No, I—"

"Okay. We can fuck without a condom, but you got to pull out. You better not cum in me. Ten bucks, food, and you gotta pull out."

"You're getting ahead of yourself. I don't want to fuck you."

That didn't trip her a beat. "Five bucks for a blow. No negotiating that. I don't go lower than five. Unless you got food."

"I don't want you to blow me, either."

"So what, you want to watch me masturbate? You want to like pee on me or something? You a freak . . . 'cause that costs more."

"I don't want any of that." Hell of a thing to say to a girl looking like she did.

That slowed her down. She was running low on offers, and she took a beat to try and figure me out. "You gay, that it? You're gay?"

"I'm not a fag."

"You don't want to fuck. That sounds like gay shit to me."

"I'm not—"

"You don't want to fuck, what did you drag me up here for?" I saw it in her eyes, her mind whipping up ideas. A guy picks up a girl; doesn't want to bang her, doesn't want her to blow him. Maybe something else gets him hard. Maybe he digs tying girls up, using them for an ashtray, poking them with sharp things, and then . . . then he really gets to work.

Angel was a hard girl, but what she was thinking made her go nervous. "You lay a finger on me, and I will scream so loud—"

Do something! Calm her down before you lose her. "I'm not going to hurt you, and I don't want to screw you. I want to help you."

Her face shifted to a curious neutral, but she kept edging for the door. "You want to help me?"

"Yeah, I mean, a kid like you shouldn't be sleeping on the pavement." I danced hard. "It's dangerous, and you obviously haven't got any money. I just wanted to give you a place to stay for a while . . . something to eat."

"All the street kids in LA, and you pick me out of the crowd? My lucky day." That came at the end of a laugh.

"I didn't just pick you out. I'd seen you around a few times."

She gave me a blank stare.

"Ralphs, the bus station . . . You asked me for money, for change."

"I ask a lot of people for change."

Part of me didn't want to hear that. Part of me really wanted to believe Angel was sent down for me and me alone. But the part of me that needed to get out of a jam didn't care how I'd stumbled onto her, and kept talking. "Okay, sure, you ask a lot of people. But you asked me a couple times."

"So you figured it was time for us to shack up."

"I figured it was maybe a sign I should get involved; I should try to get someone off the streets." I put a smile at the end of the lie.

"And it just happens when you turn Samaritan it's with a young piece of ass, and not some dried-up fat guy. Yeah, I buy that."

"Not too cynical, are you? You're pretty old for someone so young."

"I didn't get to be this age by accident." She matched my smile with a tough little smirk of her own.

I was starting to be able to read my Angel: Come at her soft and she had no time for you. Come at her hard and you might just be able to get something. "Look, you want the door, it's right there. You want to go back to sleeping on the street, you know where to find it. I understand the concrete is good and hard this time of year. Otherwise, I got food, booze, and a pillow. What's it going to be?"

Angel thought a bit. She laughed. I didn't know if she found the situation funny or if she was just plain laughing at me. "Okay, you want to be a good guy, be a good guy. Where's the bed?"

I shook my head. "You can have the couch."

That got a shrug from her. She tossed down her pack. "What about this food you were talking about?"

I flipped my head toward the kitchen. "Take what you want, but be quiet about it. I'm going to sleep." No more words. I went off to the bedroom keeping the tough-guy thing going. Truth of it was, I sat up the night, listening, to make sure Angel didn't leave.

When it got to be around seven o'clock I got up out of bed. I was whipped from not having slept. I was drained coming off the euphoria of finding Angel. I was sore from spending my nights fighting the urge to drink with every muscle I had. I felt bad, and I knew I looked worse. Avoiding all reflections, I went to the kitchen, made breakfast—eggs and some other stuff I could fry up. Eating didn't work for me; my stomach had too many other concerns to sit still for food.

Time went about its business very leisurely. I kicked it waiting for Angel to wake up, but tried not to look like I was just sitting around kickin' it waiting for her to wake up. It was a fine line I was walking between needing her and not letting her know I needed her; a narrow margin that ran along holding on to Angel too tight, and pushing her away too hard. I had to buy myself a couple of days to get her confidence, let her know I meant no harm. Then I was going to show her the way to the promised land for her and me both.

More time passed.

Angel got around to coming into the kitchen. T-shirt that ran down past midthigh. She hadn't bothered to take a shower, so her hair was one more day matted and the grime on her flesh was yet another night heavier. She didn't much pay attention to me, but she said: "You look like shit."

Happy day to you, too. "*You* look like shit," I sent back. Which was half truth. She was dirty, she didn't smell great, heavy gray under her eyes, but she had a body to go with her face. Package deal. She was young and firm, and living on the street didn't come close to taking that away. I didn't want to think about what six months in a gym would do for her, but I did and I got hard doing it.

She took a beer out of the refrigerator and popped it. Sitting at the kitchen table, she talked while picking food off my plate. "Yeah, I know I look like shit." The words came out as the food went in. "Sat up all night. Wanted to make sure you didn't roll up on me."

I made a dismissive little noise, a "You got to be kidding—why would I want to try to make you?" noise. I would have gotten up and walked away from her to drive the point home, but my hard-on would've shown.

She asked: "So how long is this thing supposed to go on?"

"Thing?"

"Me hanging out here, you making like you're the Pope doing me a favor. That thing. How long for?"

"For however long. Till you get a place to stay."

"And all I've got to do in the meanwhile is be my glamorous self?"

"For now."

"I figured you had a racket."

I liked the way things sounded coming from her. She had the kind of voice that translated everything into sexy. From her tough was a turn-on, and I'd bet she could make a man cum just reciting the alphabet.

She went on: "What is it? Porn films? What do I got to screw? Boys, girls, animals?"

"Slow down, you'll hurt yourself. First thing: What's your name?"

"What do you want it to be? Tiffany, Michelle, Lexi? What's the name of the girl you always wanted to lay in high school but she wouldn't give you the time of day? I can be her if you want." Her voice dropped on that line. Her eyes went wide, soft, sympathetic, and all a sudden the matted hair and dirt and smell fell away. What was left glistened and radiated. I felt myself going warm same as a solid drink makes you flush. And same as that, I felt myself being lost in intoxication.

She was working me. She did it because she knew she could; because it was fun to her. I could tell the instinct for it came to her natural. I worked hard to fake some disinterest. "Your real name'll do okay."

"Mona."

"Mona." I tried it out a couple of times. It didn't take. Not much to like in a name like Mona. It wasn't the kind of hot, tough name little girls who inherited Lauren Bacall's voice should have. Mona was old and tired and clunky, and if you yelled it out in a nursing home fifty or more geriatrics would start swarming at you with their walkers.

She smiled a little smile. "Bet Lexi's sounding a whole lot better to you now, isn't it?"

I liked Angel best. To her I shrugged. "How'd you end up here?"

"In your apartment?"

Wiseass. "In LA. On the street."

Mona hung her head, let her hair drop over her face like a curtain shutting me off. "Hey, if the price of a room around here is a Q and A, mark me absent."

"I'm just making conversation."

"Make it some other way. If I need a press I'll go to the cleaners. Otherwise, the sidewalks got all the space I can use."

She was for real serious about that. Mona would rather have a concrete pillow than so much as let me see the color of her blood. The past, whatever was back there and wherever she came from, was off-limits. For now.

"Fine." I got up from the table and made for the front door. "I'll see you later."

Mona said nothing.

That stopped me—the uncertainty of if she would be there when I got back. Turning, I said again, not too hard but strong enough to let her know I was looking for a response: "See you later."

From under the hair she mumbled "Yeah" at me.

Good enough. I left.

I left, but I had nowhere to go. I half thought about camping out across the street from my apartment. That way, if Mona—still trying to get used to the sound of that, still trying to make it fit her look and voice—if she skipped,

I could catch her before she got too far. But what was I going to do, stalk her every minute of every day? And what if she just ran out for, say, some smokes and I confronted her like . . . like a guy who'd been stalking her every minute of every day? What would that do but scare her off? If she was going to run, she was going to run, and there wasn't much I could do about it. I came off the idea of watching her and traded it for wandering around instead.

So I wandered and I thought and I went over blueprints in my mind—plans for Jeffty's big score. The first thing was to keep myself alive and out of Dumas's touch long enough for everything to come together. Beyond that, there was getting Mona—it still wasn't working for me—getting her on my side, which was feeling like an easier proposition. She was a girl who had it for money and didn't seem scared to do the things that sent a little her way.

Then there were other items, like getting Mona hooked up—a makeover, some new gear, getting her into the posh locales I needed to place her. That was going to take some serious ready I didn't have.

I felt something creeping up on me. A car. I think I felt it, as opposed to just noticing it. I felt it watch me, analyze me. Maybe I was just being paranoid. Or maybe that's what paranoia was: sensing all the uneasiness that other people took for granted.

The car moved slow, staying behind me. Late-model Ford. Wasn't Dumas and his boys. Dumas and his boys don't drive domestic. Cops. Only cops drive cars so dull and ordinary they stand out same as Woody Allen at a Farrakhan rally. I took a corner to see if it was me they were on, or if they just happened to be doing a slow cruise.

They took the corner with me.

Panic and me got reacquainted again. Things went through my mind. Things like Nellis, and Nellis's body, and Nellis's body getting found and somehow his dead finger pointing back at me.

Or maybe something else.

How about those three piggies from Vegas? How about any number of the people I'd conned over the years finally deciding to do something about me? How about that time in middle school I changed the grade on my report card from an F to a B?

Paranoia was in full effect. Dripping sweat got in my eyes.

Run, or keep walking? To run was stupid. How far could I get, dead broke and on foot, from the law? The only thing stupider than running was to keep on walking, waiting for them to put their hand on my shoulder.

Run.

That's what I landed on. Just take off and don't look back. Maybe I could hop a bus, or get down to Union Station and snag a train to . . . But I didn't have any money, not enough for a getaway. No way I could go back to the apartment. They would—

Behind me, a siren. The squeal of wheels. Too late for anything now. I was going down.

In an instant the siren was on me. . . . Then it was past me and getting farther away by the second. After that it was gone, having blended with the half dozen other sirens that were wailing about the city. Gone to tend to a gang shooting, or a wife beating, or a liquor store robbery-slash-murder, or some other incident that would barely rate mentioning behind all the other daily violence on the eleven o'clock news before being forgotten altogether.

And just like that the world was all good and fine again. As good and fine as any smoggy morning on a too-hot day in LA could be. I wanted to laugh at myself for being so bitchy scared. I wanted to laugh at myself, and I did, for thinking that I was something more than what I was, just another body walking the streets. And no matter what I did, no matter how illegal, nothing would ever change that. Dumping Nellis's body didn't mean a thing to anyone. A nobody was dead, and a loser'd covered it up. The world simply didn't care. Him, me, guys like us are too small for people to ever step up and take notice of what we do. Phantoms is what we are—the living dead. We are the fringe, the outsiders, the faces you walk by every day and not even know you passed. As much as I might sometimes want to believe otherwise, that I might want to believe I mattered, this, my nothingness, was fact. There were times I thought I could have dumped Nellis's body in the middle of Hollywood Boulevard and gotten little more than a littering ticket for my trouble.

I worked for a while, took in some forty bucks. Blew ten on drinks at the Regent. But not liquor, just soda. I was on my mission now, and wanted to stay clean. It made me feel good to be able to go without alcohol. Made me feel like I had a purpose, like I was doing something important. Too important to have my mind clouded.

Let 'em all see it, too. All the little people, littler than me even, who spent their days and nights hunched over drinks, all wretched and pitiful, trying to forget how wretched and pitiful they were. Let 'em all take a good look at Jeffty: clean and sober and ready for action. Ready to hit the big time. Look at me, you pugs!

They didn't look. They didn't care. All that any of them saw was a cloud of themselves floating in the bottom of their glasses.

Amber came in. Is that a new dress she's got on? She's got her hair combed, too. Amber looked in my direction and I "Oh, shit"-ed to myself. This I didn't need, not when I was trying to go it sober—Amber coming around pushing her knockoffs on me, sob-storying me into a sale.

But that's all she gave me was a look. Then, over to the bar, to Eddie, where she ordered up a cognac. Cognac, like all a sudden she'd gotten some style, and the money to go with it. She must have stumbled into some somehow. Not that what Eddie poured was four-star, but for the Regent it was gold standard. Amber took her drink and huddled with it in the back of the room.

I watched Amber drink, watched her savor her liquor. Each sip a treasured moment to be stretched as far as it would go. A thought came to me that was kind of funny: Here she is with cash, and what does she do? Dry out, get herself respectable? Not a chance. All she does is buy herself up to being a better class of drunk. She was low end, rock bottom and getting lower by the second, same as Wesker was the little time he had money. They all were, every one of them in the Regent. Did any of them have plans or aspirations the size of mine? And if they did, did any of them have it in them to get things done?

No.

Just that plain. No. They were nothing, less than that, and it felt good, from the lofty perch of my mind, to look down on the lot of them.

I enjoyed my superiority through another soda, then went home.

Mona was gone when I got back to the apartment. Her backpack sat prominently on the couch, so I didn't freak much, as I figured she wouldn't leave permanently without that. Right? I thought maybe she'd left it there for me so I would know she was coming back, so I wouldn't go crazy worrying if she'd skipped or not. More likely, she didn't care what I thought and the pack was there because that's where it ended up.

I made some food and ate with the TV on. News. Somebody dead; somebody else won the lotto. Neither of them was me, so it didn't matter much in my life.

The pack.

A game show now. Half an hour of questions. One I thought I knew the answer to, but I was wrong. The woman who got the most right won a combo washer/dryer. Seemed to me she'd done a whole lot of thinking for something she could've just bought at the store.

The pack.

Hard as I tried not to think about it, the pack kept popping back into my head. The pack and Mona, face hidden behind her hair, not wanting to tell me anything about her.

The pack.

Anything I was going to learn about the girl, no matter how insignificant, was in the pack. I moved for it, hands outstretched in anticipation.

It came to me I shouldn't be doing what I was doing. It was Mona's backpack; it was Mona's past. If she wanted to keep things private from me she had a right, and for a moment I felt guilty.

I shoved the moment aside.

The pack in my hands. Me, clawing; a frenzied expectation I hadn't even known I'd carried. I dug through a couple of shirts, a change of jeans, sandals, three joints wrapped in tinfoil, a copy of *Popular Mechanics* . . . What? Yeah, *Popular Mechanics* . . . a toothbrush that was well on its way to being bristles.

On TV, a guy who used to be famous told me how much better life would be if I would just buy the laxative he was pitching.

No ID, no personal effects, no photos. I piled Mona's belongings back in the pack, having gone from feeling guilty, to being pissed the girl didn't have anything more revealing in there.

I went back to the TV, to letting it tell me what was wrong with me, what I needed that I didn't have, what I should have bought that was so much better than what I did buy. All of that between segments of a show about some beautiful young white people without jobs who sat around in a big apartment complaining 'cause they couldn't get laid.

Yeah, TV does make you want to commit violence.

After a few mind-numbing hours, I quit the TV and went to bed. Not to sleep, but to bed. I lay there waiting for Mona to come home.

She didn't.

After it got clear to me she wouldn't be coming home until she was good and ready, I got to thinking about all the places Mona could be. Not on purpose, but as I lay, alone, staring at the shitty paint job on my ceiling, my mind just went that way. Maybe she was at a club. But Mona was too poor and too dirty for that scene. Maybe she was on the street with friends. Friends? Junkies and prostitutes. Can you call them friends?

Sure.

If you're a junkie or a prostie I bet you get along with the rest of the bunch real fine. And the greeting Mona'd given me, the quick negotiation on how much for what, said she was a professional. Not quite professional. Pros do it for the money. Mona did it for food, shelter, whatever. It was to be expected. There's not much else the boulevards offer in the form of getting by. What was of more concern were the joints in her pack. Maybe she was a recreational smoker, you know, like the President.

Maybe.

Or maybe that was just her light stash. Maybe that's what kept her going between needle hits. I worked my mind real hard. Track marks — did she have any?

I got a little nervous. Mona the junkie. I couldn't use a junkie. I'd tried that once. For what was coming I needed a girl who could think straight, not a girl who was going to fall apart in the middle of things 'cause she was getting sweaty for a hit.

And yet, I figured as I thought too much on Mona's whereabouts, that's what she was doing right then: getting high from the money she'd earned one lay at a time. At least that's what I'd convinced myself she was doing. And that would have to change. I could see now I was going to have to get more actively involved in Mona's life. Not too much. I wasn't trying to control her. I knew I couldn't if I wanted to. But, yes, definitely, I was going to have to get involved. It was for her own good. If she was on something, I'd get her off. No more shooting up. . . . Maybe, no more sleeping around, either.

I looked over at the clock: 4:00 a.m. Hours wasted just lying there thinking and outlining on what I was going to do with Mona's life. Almost morning, and not once did I feel myself need a drink. Sometime over the last day or so I'd kicked the need for booze; I'd fought it out of my system. I wasn't sure, but I had the feeling my body was making room for a new craving.

When I woke up later that morning Mona was home. She had slipped in quietly and curled up on the couch in a state between sleep and passing out. I showered, cleaned, made breakfast, and generally lingered hoping she would wake. Hoping I could engage her in conversation and surreptitiously draw out where she'd been last night and with whom doing what.

No good.

She slept and stayed that way until I got tired of waiting around, and my reluctance to admit to myself I cared that much about who she ran with drove me outside. Away from Mona.

Work.

I needed money. Like always I needed it, but this time I needed it for Mona. I needed it to change her, shape her, re-create her in another image. An image that wouldn't come cheap. I halfheartedly ran my usual con at my usual kind of spots. I didn't have a head for small-timing my way through life anymore. There were bigger things that were only a touch away, and impatience was wearing on me. I tried to keep my focus, to keep my mind on the grift, but it didn't much work.

Home.

That's where I wanted to be, and it was plain to me why. I let myself call it a day and rode the Corvair back to Yucca speeding all the way.

When I got to the apartment Mona was gone, her pack left to mark territory same as before. I ate and watched TV and went through the motions of having a life; of not waiting and wondering where my angel was. Same as before. And same as before, evening ran into night, and still she was gone.

I made a sandwich and left it for her in case she was hungry when she came in, then went to bed.

Sound drifting into the bedroom finally woke me around three o'clock. Voices. Guys. Muted. I followed the sound into the other room.

Mona was on the couch watching TV in the dark. Waves of blue light washed over the walls. When I came in she looked at me, not a word said, then looked back at the set. Frankie and the rest of the Summit were strategizing on how to rip off Vegas.

To the TV, not me: "It was his best."

"What's that?"

"*Ocean's Eleven*. It was Frank's best movie."

Something different about Mona. I couldn't tell what in the blue light, but something different. "You're crazy. *Manchurian Candidate*."

"Huh?"

"His best movie. *The Manchurian Candidate*. I don't care what anybody says, Oscar for *From Here to Eternity*, *The Manchurian Candidate* was—"

"I never saw it."

That paused me, then: "How can you say this was Frankie's best movie if you've never even seen *The Manchurian Candidate*?"

Mona didn't say anything to that. I didn't know if it was because she didn't hear me or if she just didn't care about my taste in Sinatra films.

Frank traded lines with Angie Dickinson. He was an ex-con; he cheated on her, drank too much with the boys, but she loved him anyway. That was her sole purpose in the movie: to love Frank in spite of the fuck he was. Why couldn't more women be like Angie?

I said: "I made you a sandwich."

Mona was evidently too into the back-and-forth between Mr. Sinatra and Ms. Dickinson to say anything.

I came again with: "Thought you might get hungry, so I made—"

"Yeah. I saw. Baloney sandwich. I don't much go for baloney. I left it." She didn't say it mean, but she said it without any "thanks just the same" in her tone, and I felt myself hurt a little bit.

Upset because a girl didn't like my sandwich. Lookit me going straight bitch.

On the TV: Frank in Vegas. A chick coming on to him hard. Apparently in the early sixties, in Vegas, chicks dug middle-aged balding guys.

Mona: "That's why this was his best movie." She didn't look in my direction. Took me a second to realize she was talking to me.

Maybe she was.

Or maybe she was just talking and I happened to be around to hear. "He was at his peak—smooth, cool."

"He was standing around boozing it up with the rest of the Summit."

"The . . . ?"

"Summit. The press tagged them the Rat Pack. Frank didn't much dig that. He liked to call himself and the boys the Summit."

"Whatever. They were the most talented group of men ever to walk the planet. They weren't even that—not men. Too groovy to be just men. For my money they were like gods come down from . . . Where's that one place where gods live at?"

"Mount Olympus."

"Yeah. They were like gods come down from there to hang with the rest of us."

"I'm not saying they weren't talented. They were all very talented. Except for Peter Lawford."

She turned finally. What the fuck are you talking about? all over her face. "Peter Lawford didn't have any—"

"Look, Frank could sing; the Bishop could tell jokes; Dino could do both; Sammy could do everything. What the hell could Peter do?"

"Pimp broads for Kennedy."

That gave me a laugh. "Broads. Listen to you. And that's not a talent."

Mona's smile came even to mine. "Maybe not a talent, but it's a skill." For the first time, for the first time since I'd known her, Mona was something besides the rough little street urchin who tough and sexy came natural to. She was something bright, happy and playful. Something that was probably always part of her, but just long buried.

A commercial. The light from the TV changed. I could see what was different about Mona. She'd made use of the shower and gotten herself clean. Her hair washed and still a little wet. The way it kicked the light, it looked like mink draped over her shoulders.

While the commercial played, I said: "Tell me about you."

Just that quick, she shifted. Same as a candle blown out she went from light to dark. Her head dropped, and the only thing that kept her from hiding behind her hair was its wetness. "Why'd you have to do that? We were having fun; then you have to go and do that."

"Because I want to know about you—where you're from, how you ended up on the streets."

Dismissive: "We've been here before."

"Yeah. I remember, but I still want to know."

Mona kept looking down. If I'd never been born, she couldn't have ignored me more.

"How bad could it be?" I asked. "Where you came from, whatever happened to you—how bad could it be you got to keep it buried?"

"You know what it's like outside. You know what it takes to survive. Look at you: Got a roof over your head, and still barely keeping yourself alive. You think you've got it severe? Guess what a good day for me is, Jeffty? A good day for me is when I can suck dick to pay for my crack so I'll have money left over for food. A great day is when my john is so hopped-up he passes out so I can steal the food he's got.

"So how bad do you think my past has to be to make me choose the street over any other way I could live, 'cause that's how bad it was. Go on, think of something awful, something hideous and horrible. Whatever it is you cook up is nothing compared to where I came from. Nothing. And nothing compared to what I'd do to keep from going back.

"So leave the past, okay? For me, the past didn't happen, and the future's just wishful thinking. All that counts is right now."

The commercial ended. The movie came back on. Mona returned her attention to it.

"And right now all I'm trying to do is watch Frank."

I believed Mona when she said for her the past didn't happen. I believed that it was so awful she had ripped it from her memory and buried it away somewhere no one would ever find it. Not me, at least. Not tonight, and probably not ever.

On the TV, Frank sang with Dino and Sammy. A couple of wops having a good time with a one-eyed black Jew who couldn't even stay in the same hotels with them in Vegas. Pure Tinseltown fantasy. There is no more perfect place in the world than Hollywood.

H e hit me.

He hit me, and I took it with equal parts pain and surprise. Pain, because he hit hard, and surprise, because, even though I'd just said "Fuck you" to him, I didn't figure he would hit me. I don't know why I didn't figure that. He was a cop, and this was LA, and that's what cops in LA did. I should have been glad there were no billy clubs and stun guns involved.

I counted my luck as I picked myself up off the floor, only to head right back down there again courtesy of another openhanded slap to the face. That seemed to be his specialty.

I didn't like this guy. Besides the beating he was handing out, I didn't like him. It was Tough Guy Cop, the pretty boy who had busted Wesker. I didn't like his easy good looks and thug-cop manner then. I didn't like him when he had taken Wesker in. I sure didn't like him now that he was bitch-slapping me but good. I didn't like him this morning when he was cruising me in his squad. A good half hour he sat on me. I figured he didn't have any cause to bust me. If he had, he would have done it. He just cruised me to cruise me, to make me sweat. That was his idea of fun.

So I let him have it, his fun. I drove and walked and sat around biding my time. The only thing that was getting on my nerves was that I needed to work, to generate a little cash, and I couldn't much do that with Tough Guy and his partner eyeing me.

Noon or so. I was hungry. Went to the chicken place off Highland at Melrose, where you get so much food for your dough, it makes you think there's something wrong with it. Soon as I'd gotten my order, not a second later, Tough Guy and his partner come strutting hardass in for the brace.

"Jeffty Kittridge?" asks Tough Guy. He knows who I am.

"Yes," I said, polite just the same. I didn't do anything; they don't have anything on me: That little ditty kept playing over and over in my head.

"Police." He pushed back his jacket, flashing a badge clipped to his belt. Eighty-five-plus degrees in LA and Tough Guy's wearing a jacket. He wore a jacket 'cause Joe Friday would have worn a jacket and tie while building sand castles in Aruba, and I'd lay money Tough Guy jerked himself to *Dragnet* when he was a kid.

Partner: "Got some talking we need to do."

Nellis. The sweat from the heat covered my sweat from panic. "Sure. Sure. Whatever."

Tough Guy: "Let's take it back to Division."

"I just got my food."

Words barely out of my mouth and Partner was yanking the tray of chicken loose from my hand. "You can eat later. Let's go." As soon as he set the tray down a homeless guy was all over it.

I worked hard to keep my voice calm and steady; just another innocent guy, like everybody else in the city. "What's this all abou—"

Tough Guy, firm: "Let's go."

Curled fists, four between them, that said, Go on, be difficult. Please, be difficult.

I wasn't. Innocent guys had no reason to start anything. I just went along, back door of their car open and waiting to swallow me, quietly convincing myself: I got nothing to worry about. I didn't do anything.

Hollywood Division. Every cop in the place looked the kind of tired that took years to layer on. Tired of dealing with the spics and addicts and prosties. Tired of going home to a policeman's pay–sized house, and a wife who just got older and more out of shape. It was enough to make you want to beat the head in of the first punk who wise-talked you. I thought about that. I thought very seriously about that.

Tough Guy and Partner kept herding me farther back and down in the building until I didn't think we could go any deeper or lower. Until I didn't think we could be any more removed from humanity, or people who might hear things like the sound of a badly roughed-up guy begging for mercy and medical attention.

Back room. Interrogation room. "The Box," they called it. Dull gray. Table and a couple of chairs all screwed into the floor. On the table a file, a police record. Mine.

Beyond that, it was just me, Tough Guy—whose name I came to find out was Duntphy, Lieutenant or something—and Partner, whose name I never got.

Duntphy flipped through the file. The way his eyes skipped over the papers I knew what was inside wasn't new to him. "Con, grift, bunko. You don't got many aspirations, do you, Kittridge? But you been a bad boy just the same."

"So I've got some time against me? So what?"

Partner leaned against the wall. Fist still curled, still saying: Go on, be difficult.

Duntphy: "Two convictions. You'd probably have more, but who really gives a fuck about a guy like you? You're small-time, Kittridge. Small as they come. The little fish that keeps getting thrown back."

"But what? You're going to change all that? You're putting me away?"

Duntphy snorted a laugh. Against the wall, Partner laughed, too. I was the only one missing the joke.

"Didn't you hear what I said? Nobody gives a fuck about you. You don't even have yourself together enough to commit a real crime, and I don't have time to waste bringing in guys whose idea of a big score is hitting a Chink laundry for change of a dollar. But I could. I could have the time if you don't give me what I want."

I started to ask something.

"Shut up! You know a guy named Dumas? I know you know him, so don't bother telling me otherwise. He's got a lock on the illegal gambling in LA. I want him."

Gambling. Nothing about Nellis, about a dead body. I wanted to breathe easy, but my situation wasn't much improved. I was still where I was for a reason. "What's Dumas got to do with me?"

"You're going to give him to us." That was Partner from the wall. "You're going to roll over on him."

"M-me?" My sputter was genuine. "What do I have on Dumas?"

"You know Dumas. You know his whole setup."

"I don't know anything."

"You're thirty grand into him, he's tired of waiting for you to pay, and he's starting to get rough."

I only wondered for a second how they knew so much about me and Dumas. Wesker. I could picture him sitting where I was, cutting deals, spewing anything he could think of to get himself out of a jam — anything that would make the cops forget what a slug he was and get hot for some- one else's ass. He probably couldn't go soprano on me fast enough. The way Wesker made things sound, I bet I was an intimate of Dumas gone stray. Duntphy and Partner must've thought I knew Dumas's operation inside and out, and with the money as bad blood I would spill my guts if they put the squeeze to me.

From what must have been the next room thudded a noise. It sounded oddly like a head getting slapped up against a wall.

"I don't know what you heard, but you heard it wrong." I looked from Duntphy to Partner and back again. "I got nothing to do with Dumas."

Duntphy looked at me. He looked at me; then his hand shot out to mine. He wrapped it around my broken fingers and went to work on them. My teeth gnashed. I straightened in the chair like I'd just taken a hot poker in the ass.

Duntphy said: "Yeah. You don't owe any bookies. You got your fingers busted up working at the soup kitchen."

Partner picked himself up off the wall. He came closer and brought his curled fists with him. "Why do you want to play things that way? We're trying to be decent with you."

I cradled my bad fingers. Sweat was collecting on my forehead. "I'm not trying to play—"

"Shut up!" Duntphy was all over me again. "You know where I'm from, guy?" The question wasn't meant to be answered. Duntphy kept on rolling. "The Valley. Van Nuys. Used to be nice. Used to be clean. Used to be white. Used to be. First came the blacks, then the Mexicans. Know what rhymes with *nigger* and *spic*? *Gangs.* It's gotten so if you go out at night for a carton of milk, you better be carrying heat with you.

"So now comes along a guy like Dumas—black and a foreigner. The worst of both worlds far as I care. I don't mind so much about his gambling. Between the lotto and the card houses, LA's just that close to being Vegas anyway. And if low-life shits like you want to take your chances and get your fingers fucked up as the back end, that's fine with me."

Duntphy ran his fingers through his hair—reddish—dragging it away from his face even though his buzz cut rendered the action moot. It was a habit, born of vanity, he had never broken.

Duntphy went on: "What I don't like is Dumas's high livin', his snow-white Benzes and his fine, fine clothes. That gets other people thinking the criminal life ain't so bad. It gets them thinking maybe they ought to try it, too. Dumas is bad influence, see how I mean? He's bad influence, and I got a spot for him over my mantel."

"And if I don't help you, then that spot belongs to me. That how it works?"

Duntphy's shoulders went up and down. "Pretty much."

"You got nothing on me; you know that."

"I'll tell you what we got: We got a three-strike law in this state, and you've already got two against you. Don't think a guy like me can't pitch out a nothing like you. You're a worm, Kittridge. You're less than that. You're like an insect I could crush under my heel and not even know I'd stepped on. You feel that? That's my foot coming down on you."

That's when I said it. That's when I said "Fuck you" to Duntphy. And that's when he opened up his hand and hit me. All that time I'd been worried about his curled fists, about what they might do to me. But when he uncurled them, that's when I saw how big his hands were. Massive paws that weren't good for much more than hitting. Openhanded, he bitch-slapped me. His right hand swallowed up the side of my head and rode me from the chair to the floor. He did it hard and quick, and in case I'd missed anything, he did it again.

After a beat, after I was sure Duntphy was through giving away punches, I picked myself up off the floor, head on fire from a pain that soaked through from the left side of my face all the way to the right. I tried to keep that to myself; tried to look tough and angry same as when my father used to beat me. But same as when my father used to beat me, my version of looking tough and angry was getting red-faced and teary-eyed.

Duntphy and Partner looked at me. More laughing. I had that effect on people. I wanted to say something about police brutality and civil rights, but I knew that here—in the back room of a precinct full of sociopaths with shields—talking like that wouldn't buy me anything but some kicks to go with my slaps.

Truth: People like me—people at the bottom of the barrel regardless of race, but especially so if you've got any tint to your skin—the only rights we had were to get shoved around, beaten up, slapped to the floor, then shut up and take it and be happy that was all that had happened to us.

God bless America.

Duntphy stopped laughing. He talked about some things. My face hurt and my ears rang too much to pay attention, but it involved me and trouble and more bitch slaps. For starters.

After that, they were done with me. I asked for a ride back to my car.

More laughs.

I started walking. Every step of the way, and there were many of them, I hoped and wished and prayed whatever jail or prison or penitentiary Wesker was in, right then, at that very moment, he was being fucked as badly as he'd fucked me.

It took a half hour to get back to my car. The sun, the endless traffic noise didn't help my face hurt any less. It was getting on late afternoon. As much as I needed to make money I didn't really have the head for working. I drove the Corvair toward home. After a day such as this, what I really needed was a bath, a meal. Rest. I needed to cocoon a bit, let my mind defecate all the shit that filled it, and focus on a better tomorrow that I had almost convinced myself lay ahead for me.

My key in the lock. I opened the door to my apartment and walked in. Mona was waiting for me. She was waiting for me with a gun—my gun— and she pointed it dead at my face.

was very surprised to find out that when you stare down the working end of a gun, your life really does flash before your eyes. I was unimpressed by what I saw, and depressed that it would be the last thing I would see. The one piece of luck I had working for me was, because of the cops taking me in, I hadn't eaten all day. There was a chance when Mona shot me I wouldn't shit my pants. At the moment of dying you find good in the littlest of things.

Mona's face, what I could see of it as she stared the length of her arm past the gun, was hard and cold and ready to kill. And then, one-half of one second later, all that was gone. Mona was all smiles and giddy—Christmas morning–happy.

"Look what I found." She held the gun up and out toward me in case I hadn't seen it.

I took a beat to start breathing again, then put out my hand. "Give it to me."

"You're shaking," she noted, unclear as to why.

"Give me the gun!"

She did. I waited until I had good possession of it, then cut loose on her.

"What are you doing, huh? *What the hell are you doing?* I don't need this shit! After the day I've had, I don't need to come home and get a face-ful of gun."

"It's not loaded. I took the bullets out."

I cracked the chamber open. It was empty.

"What do you think, I'm going to shoot you?"

"I don't know what the fuck to think. I don't know you."

"You're the one who took me in. If you don't want me around . . ."

It's not where I wanted the conversation to go. "Forget it, okay? But for the future, try and remember I'm not big on having guns pointed at me."

Still excited: "Why didn't you tell me you had a gun?"

"I didn't know it was a selling point."

Mona's eyes changed a little. "What happened to your face?"

I put a hand to the tender flesh. The way that it hurt I might as well have hit myself in the head with a hammer. I figured my trouble with the law was something Mona didn't need to know about. "I . . . walked into a door."

With something like a laugh: "Same excuse my mom used to give after my dad went a couple of rounds with her."

We had that in common.

"Teach me."

"What?"

"Teach me how to shoot the gun."

I shook my head. "You don't need that."

Mona pouted, cute and sexy. It was the kind of pout that could get men to jump from tall buildings. I was no different from your average guy.

"Okay," I said. "Let's go shoot the gun."

Downtown LA, by the rail yards, was littered with abandoned ware-houses. Boarded up and decaying, they were left over from when manu-facturing was a decent way to make a living. Now they weren't much good except as shelter for rats and bums, and to do some practice with a gun. Most people were way too used to gunfire to pay a couple of stray shots any mind.

Someplace that used to make toys, third floor: The building was quiet and eerie with the way the sunlight punched through holes rotted in the walls. Underfoot the pop and crunch of glass. Crack vials. I figured the place might be a smokers' house—hardly an abandoned building in LA that wasn't—and I had the .38 loaded up well before we went inside. Once in, I held it out to Mona.

For a girl so excited about doing some shooting, all I got from her was a stare. "What am I supposed to do with that?" she asked.

"You're supposed to shoot it." I pointed to a vertical that was some forty, fifty feet away. "Shoot it at the pole."

"I don't know how to shoot a gun. That's what I want you to teach me."

"There's nothing to know. Take it."

She did.

"Aim at the pole."

She did that, too.

"Now pull the trigger."

She jerked the trigger. The gun uttered one loud, harsh sound. A bullet spat from it, went wide of the pole, and lodged somewhere I couldn't see.

I said: "It's that easy, like using a doorknob. Except with guns, people get dead."

She fired again. Again she missed. Mona asked: "You ever kill anybody?"

The question struck me as a little odd, but it wasn't really. Mona didn't know thing one about me. And in the world she lived in, we both lived in, murder wasn't much of a stretch for most people.

"Naw," I said. "Never killed anybody."

"Why not?" Now her questions were getting strange.

"Was I supposed to?"

"You got a gun. I just figured maybe you used it on somebody."

I had planned to use it. On Dumas. Hadn't gotten very far with that idea. "I don't think I got what it takes to kill anybody. You've got to have a lot of hate inside of you to pull the trigger on someone; a lot of rage and anger to want to snuff a life. I don't have that kind of hate."

"Or love." She jerked the trigger again. Again the gun barked and spit up fire and flash. The bullet nicked the side of the pole, kicking off some wood chips. Her aim wasn't much, but it was getting better. She looked comfortable with the .38. She looked like it was part of her.

"What's that?" I asked as the echo of the shot rippled off.

"You got to have a lot of hate—or a lot of love—inside you to kill someone."

"Love?"

"Yeah. Love. Passion. Think about all the crimes of the heart you read about. Guy catches his chick screwing around, so—*bang*—he pops her. Or the other way, too: Chick shoots a guy 'cause he's putting his dick where it don't belong."

"That's not love," I cut in. "They're doing it 'cause they're pissed."

"They're doing it 'cause they got burned. They're doing it 'cause the one they loved hurt 'em. And how about this: I read about a guy who was dating this girl, right? Except he didn't want to be with her anymore. Except he loved her too much to hurt her by dumping her. So what's he do? He kills her 'cause he figures her getting a surprise bullet to the back of the head is a lot less painful than her walking around with a broken heart. That's what I think of when I think of love."

"Well, that's messed up."

Mona shrugged. "People say love is a beautiful thing. Maybe. I sure as hell wouldn't know."

You and me both.

"As far as I can see, love hurts, love hates, love kills. Passion's racked up more of a body count than anger ever will."

I thought about what she'd said. Her words were bitter, cold, and empty of hope—a reflection of the place she'd come from and the life she'd led. And because they were such, I understood their meaning exactly.

"Maybe," I said. "I guess love does have a funny way of showing itself."

A quick *tickety-tick* sound on the wood. A rat going out for a little jog. Mona aimed and fired. The fourth shot split the rat in two. Mona was good with a gun, naturally so. And a woman like that, who was smart and tough to boot . . . A woman like that was just about perfect.

Yeah, Mona was ready for what I had for her.

My sore face pained me awake early in the morning. I had to pee, so I got up anyway.

Noise and light from the bathroom, both soft. Mona doing whatever. I should have just gone back to bed, held my water for a while. I could have, easily. Instead, I moved toward the bathroom, toward the subtle sounds that came like a whisper.

A crack in between the door and frame. I angled myself to see through it. Mona was over the sink, water running. She stood, naked except for some men's briefs that looked worn enough to be her only pair, washing herself.

Her body was better even than the bits and pieces of it I'd seen before would've led me to believe. She was plenty tight and lean for a girl off the streets, but maybe it was the streets that kept her that way. Hard living made for a hard body. If that was the case, every chick in America should spend a couple of months a year sleeping on heating grates.

She cupped water and splashed it against her shoulders. The morning light caught it and gave her a gentle glow as the droplets ran down her arms, her chest . . .

Her chest.

Breasts that were full and firm, that didn't sag, but seemed to be sculpted perfectly in a gentle upward curve ending in hard brown nipples. They were the kind of perfection that every reconstructive surgeon, cosmetic surgeon, and plastic surgeon in Beverly Hills had put all their brainpower and all their bad-titted clients' money into trying to build a flawless imitation of. Nothing I'd ever seen had even come close.

The rest of Mona dipped and curved and flowed with firm muscle exactly as woman's body should, and better than most women's bodies ever would. I didn't so much look at her as I did stare, a schoolboy first flipping through a *Penthouse*. But it was more than just a hard-on that kept me gawking. Something like desire held me in place. It was a spark inside me, kindling since first I'd seen Mona, maybe longer, that had grown into a wildfire.

My eyes, done wandering her, came back up to her face. She was looking at me. She was watching me watch her. I felt ashamed. I wasn't sure I knew how anymore, but I felt small and dirty.

A shadow of emotion filled Mona's eyes. She smiled a light smile that said: It's okay. You can look. I don't care. Then she turned away. That was for me. Mona did her best to make me feel not so much like the leering bastard I was, but all her kindness did was make me feel that much worse for peeping in the first place. Shrunk within myself, I finally walked off. The sound of water splashing over her body chased me through the apartment.

Hollywood Boulevard. Same bookstore, same book where I'd found that picture of Pier Angeli. This time, I showed it to Mona.

"Damn," she said. She said it again, then went on with: "She kinda looks like me."

"No, you kind of look like her. More than kind of. Do up your hair some, do up some makeup, you are her."

Not once taking her eyes off the picture, Mona said: "It's not an accident—me looking like her and you grabbing me up off the streets. It's not an accident, so what's it about?"

I ran things down for her, the story of Pier, of Pier and Jimmy, Pier and Vic, Pier after Jimmy, Pier and Moe, and, finally, dead Pier.

"And?" Mona prompted, wanting me to get to what's what.

"This guy, Moe—he's still alive, he's still rich as hell, and I'll bet he's still crazy for Pier. We get you made up, get you looking like Pier, introduce you around so you can meet him."

"Then?"

"Then wait for him to fall in love with you. Not much of a wait, I'm guessing. After that, we put the touch on him; tell him you're in trouble and you need dough. I figure we can hit him up for seventy-five, hundred thousand easy."

"He's just going to give that to us?"

"This guy's spent the last forty years, living day by day, pining away for a chick who never once cared for him, who he never thought he'd see again. Now, you're going to happen; a second chance at everything he ever wished and hoped and dreamed. That in combo with a few things I've got worked? Yeah, he'll give us the money."

After I was done talking, a good half minute after, Mona lifted her head up from the picture of her twin. "I knew when you took me in you weren't no aid society. I knew you had a racket."

"What about it? It's not costing you nothing. You get some new clothes, a new look, and you get to cash in."

"Fifty-fifty?"

"Seventy-thirty."

"How do you figure?"

"It's my con. I'm the one's done all the thinking."

"Some thinking. Get a girl that looks like some other girl. Without me, you don't have a con."

"Look, I owe some people in a big way. No matter how things work out I'm only walking away with part of my take. At seventy-thirty we're both getting out of this about even."

Mona went through the motion of considering things. The fact was, I did need her. The fact was, without her I didn't have a con. She could have pushed me if she'd wanted. She could have gotten herself a bigger piece of the pie. Instead: "Okay. Seventy-thirty. But any clothes I gotta buy don't come out of my cut, and I get to keep them after the job."

Shit, was that all? I went for it, but slow. I didn't want to her to think I was taking a better deal than I would've. "Yeah. All right. I can live with that."

We left the bookstore, first me ripping the picture of Pier out of the book. I needed it but was short on the cash to buy the book with, just like I was short on the cash to buy Mona clothes and makeup. There was overhead to be considered here, more than I could make—and make quick—nickel-and-diming. I was going to have to get some serious money. I had ideas where.

*T*he Regent. New booze-free me skipped the bar and took up a seat at a back table. Eddie didn't much care, me using up space. He had plenty of midday drinkers without my help. I sat and waited, not knowing how much waiting I would have to do before Amber would come in . . . if she would come in.

She would, I assured myself. She would.

Twenty minutes stretched into an hour, all the while me just sitting, thinking, and watching the regulars sedate themselves with glass after glass of liquid denial. Watching them drink, watching them drown in their own pathos made me so happy. Happy because I wasn't like them. Not anymore.

And more than that.

I was happy because I was better and smarter than them, and I was going to cash in for more money than they would ever see in their lousy, most-likely-to-be-shortened-by-cirrhosis lives.

Close to an hour and a half passed. I went outside to a newsstand and got the *LA Times*. Good paper. Easy to read. I took it back inside, and got a Coke from Eddie. He laughed at me when I ordered it.

Let him.

When I sat back down at my table I realized that when I ordered the Coke from Eddie, when he laughed at me and I didn't care, all through that I didn't think once about the body we'd gotten rid of together.

The paper: A war in a country I'd never heard of. I didn't know which side I should root for and, since I'd probably never hear of the country again, I didn't bother picking. A woman killed by a car jacker. They ran a picture of her with the story. She was pretty, and I was sorry she'd gotten killed. I wondered if I would've been as sorry if she'd been ugly. The Fed lowered the interest rate. I cared less about that than I did about who was fighting who in that country I'd never heard of before.

Entertainment section: a story on some alternative rock guy who died in a pile of manure. Choked to death. Weird. But not so weird it didn't happen.

When I was almost out of paper, when I had gotten to the real estate section and was reading about houses I couldn't afford in parts of town where they would never let me live, Amber came in, new clothes and clean. She stopped at the bar, got a bottle of drink, and took it to a table. For a second she looked at the bottle not quite believing it was hers, all hers, and just hers. Enough speculation. She cracked it open and got to drinking. In the time it'd taken me to cross from my table to the one where she sat, Amber'd already put down her third glassful. When I took up a chair, her face glowed with something besides the booze.

"Hey, Jeffty. Whatcha doing, Jeffty? Haven't seen you around, Jeffty. Jeffty, have a drink with me." Amber had a little slur on her words. It wasn't so much from the three shots she'd just swallowed. Hers was a permanent state of inebriation. She wore it like a tattoo.

"No thanks. I'm not drinking much these days."

"Not drinking? That's a waste. Guess I'm drinking for two now." From the size of her laugh, that was apparently the funniest thing Amber had ever heard. But then, drunks were so easily amused.

I said: "That's a nice new outfit you got, Amber."

"You like it?"

"I like."

She fell into me, gave me a drunk's hug. "You're so sweet. Nobody else even noticed."

"I noticed," I said. "I noticed you got yourself a few new dresses."

"Here I am, trying to look presentable, and nobody else even gives a damn." She said that last part loud, said it to attract attention. She got none. People still didn't give a damn. "But you're sweet, and you noticed. Have a drink with me."

"No thanks."

"Well, looks like I'm drinking for two," she said again. She laughed again. She drank again. Then: "I got a buncha new clothes, Jeffty. A bunch. I love clothes. I came out here to do costumes for the movies, ya know that?"

"No, I didn't."

"I did a picture once with Bob Mitchum. Only big picture I ever did. Sorta big, I guess. Bob counts as a star, right?"

"Sure. Big star."

"RKO we did the picture at. *His Kind of Woman*, it was. Jane Russell, she was in it. God, Jane could do things to a dress. They don't make tits like that anymore. Not natural, they don't.

"I used to borrow clothes from wardrobe. Ohhh, they had so many gowns, Jeffty. They were so beautiful."

Dig her getting misty-eyed.

"All silver and gold and shiny. So beautiful, they'd just make you cum."

I was getting tired of Amber babbling, but let her have her memories and feel good for a minute, 'cause in a minute more it would end.

"I used to borrow them, the gowns. I wasn't supposed to, but I did. They were so beautiful."

"So beautiful, they'd make you cum. I know. You said."

"I got caught one night borrowin' 'em, the gowns. They said I was stealing, but I was just borrowin' 'em. They fired me, Jeffty. The bastards fired me, and they put in the fix so I didn't never work again. And Bob didn't lift a finger to help me. He was a big star. He could've stopped them if he'd wanted to. Or he could've gotten me work. That's the part that hurt. I was Bob's dresser, and he didn't do nothing to help me."

Sweetheart, except that he's dead, Robert Mitchum don't even know you're alive.

I said to Amber: "But you got some new gowns now."

"Yeah. They're pretty, huh?"

"Yeah. Pretty gowns like that must cost something."

"They ain't cheap, Jeffty." More drunken laughter.

"So, where'd you get the money to pay for them?"

Amber leaned close. She got all quiet and conspiratorial. "That's a secret."

I whispered back, "Not much of a secret. Wesker. You got the money from Wesker."

Playful smile: "I didn't get no money from Wesker."

"You did when you sent him over to the cops for that bank job he pulled."

Playful smile dropped: "I . . . I didn't turn Wesker in. He . . . he just got caught."

"He just got caught, except the cops didn't know who to look for, remember? Wesker told us the security cameras were out at the bank. He told us nobody else knew about the job. He told us that. You and me. I didn't turn him in, Amber. Mostly because I didn't think of it first."

Amber poured herself a shaky-handed drink that barely got liquid into glass. That was nerves, not booze, working on her.

I reached over, poured the drink for her. I asked: "How much was the reward money?"

"Why you think I got money?"

"C'mon. Those dresses didn't pay for themselves. And except for the money, I don't think you'd much care about pointing a finger at Wesker. Now, how much?"

Amber took the drink, using the time to figure a way out of telling me things. But the liquor didn't make her any smarter, just drunker. She said: "Twenty-five hundred they give me."

"How much you got left?"

Amber grumbled: "I spent about five or six or so.

"Okay. Give me a grand."

Her lips moved, but she didn't say anything.

"That's less than half."

"But . . . but it's my money."

"It's only yours 'cause you sold out Wesker, and when Wesker got with the cops he sold me out, so the way I see things, you owe me."

"I don't got to give you nothing." Amber's white face went flush. "Just 'cause you say so don't mean I got to give you anything."

"You don't have to, but if you don't maybe I'll just spread it around how you were the one who handed over Wesker. How do you think everybody else in here's going to take you being a snitch? How many people you figure to be buying your cheap wares when they know they can't trust you any farther than they can throw a piano?"

Amber stared at me all angry. She stayed angry for a good long beat; then she started to cry. "Why you doing this to me? Why you taking my money?"

Snot formed at her nose and started to bubble with her every short, quick breath. Amber looked pitiful and I almost saw my way to feeling sorry for her, except if it wasn't for her I wouldn't be in nearly as bad a state as I was. I thought, too, about the last time she'd conned me into feeling sorry for her and all I got for my sympathy was taken for fifty bucks. So I didn't feel sorry for Amber. I just wanted my money.

I said: "A thousand dollars is fair."

"It's not fair. It's my money!"

"Okay. It's not fair, but just the same I want it."

Amber went on crying and looking pathetic, but I was immune to it. I just sat and watched and waited, and when she got it in her head I wasn't going anywhere, she reached into her handbag and pulled out a nice wad of bills. She counted out ten one hundreds and leadenly handed them over like if she did it slow enough I might just change my mind along the way.

Nope.

No fanfare. I took the money and shoved it in my pocket.

As I got up from the table Amber mumbled at me: ". . . Not fair. It's my money. It's not fair."

Turning back: "Look at you: First time in your life you ever come into any cash, and what do you do? Sit here drinking it away just like always. Only difference is you got new clothes to do it in. You'd drink yourself dead if you could. I'm doing you a favor."

Amber didn't see things that way. She cried and mumbled on.

I left.

*I*n the eighties, Melrose Ave. passed for hip and trendy.

The eighties are over.

What used to attract assholes in their Beamers, LA chicks in miniskirts, and foreign tourists looking for LA chicks in miniskirts now attracted too many kids who, if they weren't in gangs, acted like they were in the farm club. What brought me there, with Mona in tow, was the fair number of vintage clothing stores.

Vintage.

Just a way of saying old, but not inexpensive. The people who ran the shops would cull though Goodwill centers buying whatever for nothing more than change, then turn around and sell it for upward of a hundred bucks apiece. And there wasn't a chick or guy who fancied themself model material who wouldn't pay through the nose to get the stuff. It's 'cause vintage is what they wear on MTV, and when you haven't got a style of your own you gotta make do with someone else's.

Mona and I hit a couple of places. I didn't know shit about fashion, but I knew the look I wanted for her. A low-cut sleeveless cocktail kind of thing. Big zipper in back that just says: Work me, daddy. Maybe some gloves to match, and pumps sexy enough to drink bathwater out of. I wanted Mona to look like Audrey Hepburn in *Sabrina*, or Audrey Hepburn in *Breakfast at Tiffany's*, or just Audrey Hepburn, 'cause Audrey Hepburn owned the Look.

I—we needed an evening gown, too. Maybe a couple. The way I figured things, Mona would have to get herself a few dates with Moe; burrow her way into his soul slow and gentle, him not even knowing how she got there. That's when we'd put on the squeeze. That's when we'd go for the money.

Mona was easy about shopping. She dug it. I'm guessing she was the kind of girl who'd never had any money to toss around before. There wasn't a window we didn't stop in front of, and each shoe store cost us at least a half hour's time. She begged me to buy her stuff, but I didn't blow any of what little money we had on things we didn't need.

It took us the good part of the day to work our way up the Ave. We found a shop that had about what we were looking for dresswise. A girl who still thought dyeing her hair bright orange was a cool thing to do helped us out; helped Mona try on a few items.

Dress number one was the cocktail thingy. It worked good with Mona's body, the shortness of it showing off her legs and the lack of sleeves displaying her defined arms. With the pumps on she was just about delicious. Mona looked more like Pier now, but not exactly like. There was still work to do with her hair and makeup, but that would come.

Evening gowns. They covered more of Mona, but that only served to make her more mysterious. It made you wish you had X-ray peepers so you could see what was hidden beneath the flowing silk that billowed about her body. Every once in a while, backlit, you could get a pretty good idea. Again, except for the hair and makeup, Mona looked right: sophisticated, untouchable.

She was allurement embodied.

She made my cock hard.

Mona and Orange-Haired Girl returned to the dressing room so Mona could change back into the clothes—the rags—she'd worn in. Her momentary disappearance gave time for my distended member to collapse and breathe.

Behind me, the bell on the shop's front door jingle-jingled. I didn't pay much attention to it. I did to the voice that spoke to me smooth and cool as melting ice.

"It is Jeffty, no? I thought it wasn't, but it is."

Dumas.

I turned to face him. The two great constants of Dumas's life were in effect: He was dressed in white silk, and Ty was at his side. Along with the silk, Dumas wore a smile. There was nothing pleasant about it.

Dumas said: "We were driving by, and Ty said to me, he said, 'Isn't that Jeffty? Isn't that Jeffty shopping?'

"Jeffty? Shopping on Melrose? No, I thought. How could Jeffty be shopping on Melrose when Jeffty owes me money?"

A soft layer of sweat formed on me like dew on a field.

"So we pulled over, and came in, and yes, yes it is Jeffty shopping."

Ty inspected a rack of clothes trying to look unassuming, except there's no way for a man to be unassuming when he's intently looking through a rack of women's clothes.

Dumas: "How is it, I wonder, you can buy things and not pay me my due? Hmmm, how is that, Jeffty?"

A phantom hurt crawled all over my busted fingers. I tried to answer Dumas. I just ended up sputtering.

"Maybe you are holding out on me, do you know? Is that it, Jeffty?"

Ty kept working over the rack of clothes. Looking at it, looking at it, looking at me, looking at it.

"Why would you do something like that, Jeffty? What would ever possess you to do such a thing?"

Mona came out of the dressing room with Orange-Haired Girl. Mona held her dresses up to me. She said: "I want these three, Jeffty."

Ty stopped looking over the rack of clothes.

Dumas dug Mona and got with a smile. "Is she yours, Jeffty?"

I didn't care for the smile, or the question. My hand balled into a fist. So what? I knew I wouldn't do anything with it.

"Friend?" Mona asked to me jerking her head at Dumas.

Before I could answer, Dumas jumped in with: "Sure. Old friends. Haven't seen each other in a while, but dear friends. *N'est-ce pas*, Jefferson?"

I didn't know French, so I stayed shut up.

Ty was just as quiet as ever. It was how quiet he could be that was creepy.

Looking over Mona again, Dumas went on: "I was just speaking with Jeffty about a little financial matter. He owes me a bit of money. Quite a bit. You did not know that? Yes, he does. He owes me money, yet I see him shopping here on Melrose. I wonder to myself, Why is that? Then I see that he is shopping for you. This is what you spend your money on, eh, Jeffty?"

From Mona: "Jeffty, who is this guy?"

From Dumas: "How much does she cost you?"

From me: "She's not like that."

First a little nasty laugh. Then Dumas followed it up with: "Of course she's like that." He got close to Mona. He touched one of his black-black fingers to the pale whiteness of her cheek. "What other kind of woman would waste her time with you except a whore?"

I moved toward Dumas. I didn't even realize it until the action was already begun. I moved toward him fast and hard and determined, and my fist that was so impotent moments before was ready to strike; ready to pound the side of his head until it was soft and gurgled with blood and pulp.

I didn't make two steps before Ty was on me. He hemmed me up good, driving be back, hard, against a wall. Arms pinned, a forearm across my throat. It crushed my windpipe, made me choke and cough spittle.

Orange-Haired Girl stepped up. She started to say: "What are you—"

Dumas shot her a look that sent the woman two steps back and slapped her quiet.

Looks alone, however, didn't do much to shut down Mona. "Hey, dickhead," she screamed. "Tell your bitch-ass gorilla to get off him!"

Fast and accurate, like he'd been slapping women all his life, Dumas turned and shot a backhand across Mona's face, the blow whipping her head to the side.

All I could think was if Dumas fucked up her looks, then he fucked up my chance to collect. "Jesus Christ!" I choked out from under Ty's arm. "Lay off the face."

Mona's head stayed turned for a second, then came back around, cheek swollen, lip bloody, and something else—a smile. Mona was smiling. All a sudden, I knew why she never wanted to tell me before about her past, about where she came from and how she ended up on the streets. A girl who could get bitch-slapped and smile about it has seen some hard things in her life.

Dumas stared at Mona. He had hit her. He had hit her square with everything he had. He had hit her, and she just stood there and took it and smiled.

Then Dumas smiled with Mona, slightly, appreciatively.

Odd the things that will impress a man.

Dumas: "She's too much for you, Jeffty. It's not good for a man to take on a woman her size. She'll be the death of you, she will." To Ty: "Give him some hurt."

Ty, no emotion, like he was reading from a phone book: "Where do you want it, Jeffty?"

I didn't know how to respond. A guy asking you where you wanted to get hurt, I didn't know how to respond to that.

"You want it in the face, or in the stomach?" Ty prompted. "The face hurts less, but it shows. Stomach hurts like hell, but you don't walk around looking like a bitch that don't listen."

I couldn't answer; couldn't talk. My only response was body quivers.

"Where do you want it, Jeffty?"

Did it matter? Someone's going to put the hurt on you, does it matter where?

Dumas getting impatient: "Just hurt him!"

Orange-Haired Girl: scared, whimpering.

Ty got a fist ready. Last time asking: "Jeffty . . ."

Face, or stomach? I didn't believe getting hit in the face would hurt less than in the stomach. I tensed up, got ready to take a shot. "Stomach," I said. Cried, really.

The word not even out of my mouth and Ty was already swinging. All the tensing and getting ready in the world wouldn't have helped me any. Ty drove his fist deep and hard into my solar plexus; the only thing that stopped it was the wall behind me. No muscle where he hit me, just softness. The air shot from my lungs and the world rushed away from me as I dropped down a long, narrow shaft that ended when the floor jumped up and slapped me in the side of the head.

I lay there, on the tile, gurgling spittle, watching Ty's and Dumas's feet glide toward the door. As before, as always, Ty was very, very apologetic.

"Sorry, Jeffty," he said. "Should've let me give it to you in the face."

They were gone.

I looked up from my fetal position, looked up and saw Mona looking down at me. She had been hit and just taken it. Smiled even. Here I was on the floor, teary-eyed and choking on my own stomach juices. Right then I hated Dumas. Not for the things he'd done to me; not for the way he'd hurt me and beat me and used me for his amusement.

Not just for that.

Right then I hated the hell out of Dumas for humiliating me in front of Mona. I wanted to get up off the floor, chase Dumas down, beat him in the middle of Melrose Ave. so all of Hollywood could see him for the bitch he made me feel. I wanted to get up off the floor and humiliate him same as he'd done me. I wanted to get up off the floor, dig out my .38, and drill five or six or a hundred holes in his head.

I got up off the floor and paid for Mona's dresses, too ashamed to look in the eyes of the girl with the orange hair.

I spent the rest of the day hunched over from Ty's punch. He was right: It did hurt like hell. In addition to the pain, my stomach felt queasy, too, like it was filling with blood, or something else that shouldn't be in there.

Mona didn't ask me about Dumas or Ty or why they should want to beat the shit out of me in a store on Melrose for buying a chick a dress. She just took it all at face value. She took it for being a dose of the wigged-out kooky shit that made up my life. She took it quiet; she took it without making a stink. Mona took it the same way she took a punch, and that impressed me all the more.

As I drove, bent in half, Mona said maybe we should go home, put things off for a day or two, or at least until I could straighten up. I told her no. My run-in with Dumas was just incentive to set things in motion so I could pay him off. Besides, we were almost finished with Mona's transformation and, in spite of the intense ache in my gut, the thought of her clean and beautiful and prettied up made me hard with excitement. When it comes to things like that, sexual arousal over pain, I'm pure man.

West Hollywood. The finishing touches go on here. Couldn't afford a Beverly Hills hair and makeup job, but, dollar for dollar, anything I could get in West Hollywood would be just as good. Better, maybe, as WH is where all the fags are. Fags know cosmetics.

Gays, Mona corrected me. She felt soft for them. She must've known some back on the streets.

Okay, gays. Vaginally challenged. Dick-impaired. Whatever, as long as they got Mona looking the way I needed.

And they were all too happy to try. These boys knew plenty about Pier. In their off-hours, some of them probably went around looking more like her than Mona ever would. The way they hopped to their work all giggles and smiles you'da thought I'd brought Liza Minnelli by for a dye job.

I asked how long it would take for Mona to get perfect. The fa . . . The gays all huddled around same as doctors planning open-heart surgery, discussed things, then told me to come back in about three hours.

So I took the time to walk—shuffle bent over—around West Hollywood. Santa Monica Boulevard. Next to Disneyland, the happiest place on earth. Nothing but guys, and guys touching guys, and guys kissing guys. It freaked the hell out of me, but I couldn't stop looking at them. It was like being a kid at the carnival: You're repulsed by the woman who's half human/half snake, but at the same time you can't take your eyes off her.

And they were beautiful, too, all the boys in Boy's Town. Toned and buffed and tan, like all they did for a living was get toned and buffed and tan. From their dress to their hair to their occasional makeup, they were all perfect. No wonder they were gay. As much time as they must've spent looking at themselves in mirrors, they couldn't much relate to anything but other men.

I killed two and a half hours, and I didn't do a very good job of it. First I tried to eat, but the number Ty did on me took away my ability to digest food. I spent the rest of my time on a bus stop bench slumped over and coughing up green/red stomach fluids every few minutes. The heat didn't help in making me any less dizzy.

Over there: a big bum beating up a skinny bum, pushing the skinny bum around, making him lie facedown on the sidewalk, then literally kicking his ass. All around the dirty pair LA life went on. Not that anyone didn't notice a bum trying to break his foot off in another bum's ass; some people even had to step around the two of them, but nobody did nothing about it, either. There wasn't anybody in LA who was going to stick his neck out for a bum. Why should they? What did helping a bum ever get you? Big Bum just kept on kicking Skinny Bum's ass.

I spat up some more green/red stuff, then went on my way unsteady in every step.

Back at the salon. The boys told me they'd need at least another hour with Mona, and went pouty 'cause they didn't want me to see her before they were done.

I was getting anxious. They told me not to worry, got giddy, and asked me to bring in one of the dresses I'd bought for Mona so they could do her up right.

Sure. What the hell?

I got the cocktail number, then cooled my heels reading magazines—*Glamour, Vogue, Elle.* What are the chances they might have a *Road & Track* or a *Sports Illustrated* lying around?

Sitting.

Sitting.

The lack of food, my damaged stomach, the anticipation—it all ganged up on me; made my head feel like it wasn't with my body, but floating over a stadium broadcasting live pictures. Fun-house mirrors reflected everything around me oblong and distorted. All the boys, with their chatter, started to sound sweet and harmonic—a Broadway chorus singing at me from a hundred miles away. I tried to ask for a glass of water, but my lips moved without making a sound. Or maybe the chorus couldn't hear me way far away where they were. Or just maybe with their beautiful voices, they chose to ignore my ugly one.

And their voices were beautiful, and so were they, and that's why you hate them and call them names, isn't it, Jeffty? Because they are so much more beautiful than you could ever be.

Pain. Nausea. Heat. Honesty. This was all too much for me. The axis of the earth seemed to shift a little, revolve at an odd angle.

Then the beautiful boys with the beautiful voices gathered around me, talked at me. It was like trying to understand the language of whales. With a thousand excited hands, they lifted me from my seat and carried me to the center of the salon. A million ecstatic fingers pointed.

From a bathroom, from forty years past, stepped Mona/stepped Pier. Mona looked good. She looked better than good; she looked just right—glamorous in a fifties way. A chick Dino would be trading palaver and sipping highballs with in one of his Matt Helm movies. Mona was reborn a living doll who could wax a floor to a glass shine, fuck like a racehorse, and still make it to the PTA meeting on time.

I took a step toward Mona. I thought I did, but instead I took a high dive toward the floor and nailed it perfectly. The Gay Men's Choir went into heavy singing, and the thousand hands rushed to my aid. As I dropped back into a familiar tunnel, I looked up into the gentle, sweet eyes of Mona—into the eyes of Pier—and knew why to this day, after so many years of watching her love others and so long after she'd been dead, poor old Moe was still crazy for her.

And, more importantly, I knew my little scam couldn't fail.

Love Is a Racket

Moe Steinberg, and how to find him. Not hard like you might think. Even at his advanced age and semireclusiveness, he still had his regular haunts.

Haunts is right.

Now and again he passed through places like a ghost unwilling to lie down and be dead. A ghost who still zombied around looking for the others who'd gone before him—the Mayers and the Zanucks and the Goldwyns—not knowing, not realizing, that they, like him, were deceased. Except they, unlike him, acknowledged this by having the courtesy of vanishing from the earth.

The library. Magazines, *Times* "Style" section, the trades: all pieces of a map that led me to Moe. When he wasn't rambling around his Beverly Hills house, he was rambling around at the Formosa Café, Chasen's, or the Polo Lounge. The Formosa was the wrong setting for the scene I needed to play. Left over from the Golden Age, it was now more of a West Hollywood hangout for hipsters and male prosties. Chasen's was recently closed, though it probably took Moe four or five visits to get that through his head. So that left the Polo Lounge at the Beverly Hills Hotel. My choice was made for me. That would be the place.

Home. Mona on the couch watching TV. She looked at me, then looked back at the television.

I stepped around so I could see what she was viewing. A movie. *Robin and the Seven Hoods*. A Summit flick with Bing thrown in for a bonus, and an okay one at that. But it wasn't so okay that she should be paying more attention to it than me. I stood, stared at her for a few seconds, then went to the set and slapped it off.

That got Mona's attention. She what-the-fucked me. "Hey, don't you see I'm watching that? Sammy was just getting ready to sing."

"Are you ready?"

"Ready for what?"

"Ready for what do you think? Ready for what I've been buying you dresses and getting you made up for."

Eyes rolling: "Is that all?"

"Don't get wise. This is important."

"You don't think I know that? You don't think I want to get paid, too?"

"That's why I'm asking if you're ready."

"Sure I'm ready. You hook me up with this old guy, then I make him think I'm some dead chick. How ready do I got to be for that?"

Mona reached to turn on the TV. I slapped her hand down. She didn't like that, but I didn't much care.

"Listen to me," I barked. "You think this is a game? You think those guys in the dress store were knocking me around for practice? You don't make Moe think you're Pier. He's old, but he ain't senile, and he sure ain't stupid. You try to make him think he's seeing a ghost, he'll smell our play a mile away."

"Then what?"

"The look is just what catches him. The hair, the makeup, the dresses—they're just the worm on the hook."

Smartass: "That's attractive."

"After you get him to bite, you got one job and one job only: Make him fall in love with you. Not Pier, *you*."

Mona looked at me for a beat, then: "Not the dead chick, *me*. Can I finish watching the movie now?"

"You stupid little—"

"What?"

"I got guys wanting me dead, and all you can think about is the god-damn Rat Pack!?"

"The Summit, and I heard you. I gotta make this guy fall in love with me."

Somewhere inside of her Mona flicked a switch. She changed. Without moving a muscle or batting an eye everything about her changed. Where there was hard, now there was soft. What was inscrutable was now inviting. She went from being a rock to a warm, placid pool that begged you to dive in.

Mona floated up to her feet and with equal grace sailed to me. I didn't even notice her placing them there, but suddenly, gently, her arms were around me—a perfect fit. My hands groped her body. They felt inadequate and unworthy of the flesh they touched, but just the same I couldn't stop them from moving over her.

Mona looked deep in my eyes, and I swear when she spoke her voice came from somewhere within me.

She said, she cooed: "What's the matter? Don't you think I can make a man fall in love with me?"

I was on a precipice, a slippery slope, and way down below me was Mona. I was descending, tumbling out of control, and I didn't care.

More than that.

I wanted to beg for the fall to continue. I wanted to dive down and keep diving no matter what was waiting for me when I smacked bottom.

And then it was over. Just as quickly as she had turned it all on, Mona shut it all down and did it with such swiftness she was halfway back to the couch before I realized she was through with me. As if the moment that had just passed had not even occurred she turned on the TV, sat on the couch, and went back to watching Sammy sing.

For me, for an instant, I had felt the burn of a fire and passion I didn't even know lived inside me. For Mona it had been nothing more than a trick—something done with cards to entertain children at a birthday party. I stood, feeling stupid and foolish with my own desire—a little boy who doesn't know the difference between play pretend and reality.

I said to Mona: "Be dressed by eight. Tonight we go."

. . .

Eight o'clock. Mona/Pier was ready. The cocktail number, some long gloves to go with it. Hair done up, and makeup to match. The gays had taught her how to do it. With all of that, she didn't look old-fashioned or like she was going for retro-chic. She looked timeless: No matter where she was, she belonged. I marveled at Mona, at my creation. I had done this—built her, transformed her. I wondered, for a moment, if the reason I had remembered Pier and remembered Mona from the few times I'd seen her was not because of some cosmic destiny to rip off an old man, but because in my heart I'd for so long wanted to fashion a woman so perfect in every way of my own. Pier was not only Moe's ghost. She was my ghost as well.

The dizziness that had become so common when I was around her came at me again, only now I didn't have lack of sleep, or hunger, or a punch to the stomach to explain things away. I wanted to tell Mona/Pier how beautiful she looked. I wanted to touch her and hold her, and I wanted to kiss her. Instead, to the point: "Let's go."

Sunset and Beverly Glen: The Beverly Hills Hotel. Big. Old. Remodeled not too long ago to look new, but it would always look big and old, and the fresh coat of green and pink/beige paint just made it look ugly.

I turned the Corvair up the drive and passed rows of parked cars that chanted a silent mantra of BMW, Mercedes, Porsche. BMW, Mercedes, Porsche. Every now and again the thought was punctuated with Ferrari.

The valets: not the usual. Not Mexicans parking cars for a couple of bucks in tips. Instead, well-to-do white kids who went to nearby UCLA, or very wealthy white kids who went to not so nearby USC. You knew you were in a ritzy joint when they could afford to hire whitey to help out.

And with the white kids came the white kids' attitude. They saw me and my banged-up Corvair, and they looked down on me even though they were the ones running around parking it. They looked down on me, until they saw Mona. A girl like that on your arm, all a sudden I wasn't some kind of jerk driving yesterday's technology. I was some kind of somebody who could attract a girl like that which meant I had to have money, or power, or a good mix of both. Mona was the illusion of success and she played her part well.

Into the Polo Lounge. Low lights and walnut gave the room a dark warmth. Old guys who used to be players like to hide in the dark smoking fat ones. Young guys who fancied themselves players sat around smoking fat ones, too, but they didn't much care for the dark because it made it difficult to be seen, and to a player being seen is everything.

Inside the lounge I set Mona loose. It was no good for Moe, if he was there, to see me with her. That would come later. Mona sat at the bar, her sex in full effect. I took up a table at the back, in the corner, from where I could watch all.

It didn't take long for men to get sucked toward Mona, just like it doesn't take long for little boats to get sucked toward a whirlpool. Every kind there was rolled up on her. The slicked-back hair guys, the "I got a German car parked outside" guys, the "My wife doesn't understand me" guys. But Mona was a good girl. Mona stuck to the plan. Mona sent them all away with a smile and a "No thank you," or, when that didn't take, some harsh words that I couldn't hear but knew were such by the way the man would scamper from her.

A waitress finally got around to asking me what'd I drink. She was young and pretty and cream colored, and was polite, but with a tone that said: Drinks is all you'll get from me, so don't even bother to ask for more. I'm sure that wasn't the tone she always used. I'm sure sometimes her tone was: You look like you've got it going on, so you can trade jokes with me if you want. But I didn't look like I had much of anything going on, so she toned things to me the other way. I ordered a Coca-Cola with just a little ice. She was gone before I'd finished asking for it.

Twenty minutes, half an hour, then forty-five. More men stepped to Mona just to get knocked back.

No Moe.

All the while Mona kept her fire going, undiminished by the passing time. When Moe walked in she'd be plenty warm for him.

An hour. An hour, ten. Twenty. The waitress came back for the jillionth time asking if I wanted something else to drink. I'd managed to nurse the Coke this long, the glass little more than half-empty. I told her no, and she made a show of being more annoyed with me than the last time she'd come around. Bad enough I wasn't drinking hard drinks, I'd just had the one so far. She figured that would cut into her tip.

She figured wrong.

I wasn't about to tip her in the first place.

A few more men tried their luck with Mona. One of them, a guy who still thought sports coats with sleeves pushed to the elbows was the height of cool, wouldn't take no for an answer. He pulled up a stool next to Mona's and did all the talking in a one-sided conversation.

I watched for a while; then it seemed like I was watching Sleeves Guy try to talk his way between Mona's thighs for too long. I was half out of my chair to do . . . something. Partly because I wanted Mona freed up when Moe came in, and partly because I was just sick of this guy trying to make time with her.

Then Mona leaned close to Sleeves Guy, whispered in his ear. Sleeves Guy smiled. For a second. Then the smile went away fast. It got replaced by shock and horror. Not merely a mild revulsion, but a fear that seemed to burn same as if he'd taken a flaming arrow straight to the soul. Sleeves Guy started up from the stool. Mona took him hard by the wrist, her fingers burrowing to his bone. He jerked, jerked, finally jerked free of Mona. Sleeves Guy stumbled, groped, clawed his way from the lounge out into the lobby, a drowning man flailing desperately for beach.

Mona? She smiled. I had begun to notice that she smiled at the oddest things.

An hour and a half turned into two hours, then a little more. My Coke was finally empty, more ice water than soda by the time I'd finished it, and men had finally given up on getting anywhere with Mona. I had given up on the idea of Moe showing.

I went for the door, gave a nod to Mona, and she followed. She passed a table, two guys she'd blown off earlier. One looked at Mona, then to his buddy. One word: *Dyke*.

Outside. Valet. He pulled my car around from where it was parked no more than thirty feet away, then stood by my door waiting for a tip. When I looked up in my rearview mirror as I drove away he was still waiting.

"It's no big deal, Moe not showing up," I said to Mona, reassuring myself by way of reassuring her. "Tonight was like a dress rehearsal, you know? A dry run. You looked great, we know that. All those guys rolling up on you. You sure looked great."

Mona's attention was focused outside the window. It was dark and it was hard to tell exactly what it was she was looking at, but I was pretty sure it was the Beverly Hills mansions that lined Sunset Boulevard.

I asked: "What did you say to him?" I had to ask it again before Mona said: "Huh?"

"That guy, the one who went tearing out of the lounge—what did you say to him?"

"Oh. He asked me if I wanted to fuck. He told me that was his rap, that he just went up to women and asked them if they wanted to fuck. He was supposed to be a no-bullshit guy, and that was his way of showing me he was a no-bullshit guy."

"By saying: 'Hey, let's fuck.'"

"Yeah, like that. So he goes on and on for a bit, Mr. No Bullshit, blah, blah, always getting back around to 'Let's fuck.' Finally, I tell him how happy I am that he wants to fuck me, and he gets all excited; then I tell him the reason I'm so happy he wants to fuck me is 'cause I haven't had sex in six years on account of the lesions."

"Lesions?"

"The lesions on my vagina. Like a leprosy thing."

"Jesus!" Somehow Mona using the clinical term for her privates made what she was saying seem all the more vivid and disgusting. Maybe that was the point.

"I don't really have them."

"Yeah, I know, but . . . Jesus."

"I told him I don't actually get wet anymore, I just bleed. Then I grabbed his hand and told him to feel 'cause I wanted him so bad, and not to mind the blood—"

"Jesus!"

Mona got with her odd smile. "What? You wanted me to make nice with him? You wanted him around when Moe walked in?"

"No, no. You did good giving him the brush; it's just . . . where do you get shit like that—lesions?"

"Where do you really get them?"

"No! That's not what I'm talking . . ."

Mona smiled. She was messing with me. She had a soft smile for such a hard girl.

Mona said: "When you're living on the street and all you got is winos and crackheads rolling up on you all day wanting to break off a piece of what you've got, you learn to defend yourself."

That seemed an odd choice of words. "Defend yourself?"

"Defend, as in: Keep from getting raped."

"Damn, they try to rape you?"

"What do you think, they're asking me out for cocktails and an opera? Yeah, guys've tried to rape me. More than just tried. After it gets done to you three or four times, you figure things out: Don't matter if it's the hoity-toity bar of some big-ass hotel or a slab of concrete behind the Chinese Theater. You tell a man you got a bloody vagina and he can come up with a whole list of other places he can think of to put his dick. He can think of them fast."

Mona rapped like a street-corner prophet. She jammed a lot of years and a lot of living into a very young frame.

Even though we hadn't hooked up with Moe, I thought this evening had been a nice beginning, and it would only be a matter of time before things really got rolling. On the way home I stopped for ice cream. Mona had a banana split which she finished all by herself. I was going to have a scoop of vanilla, but Mona ragged me for being so dull. Instead, I got a scoop of some exotic berry. I didn't like it.

All in all, it was a fairly good night.

Second night. Second time with the valets giving me stinkeye when I pulled up at the Beverly Hills Hotel. Second time with them adjusting their attitude when they saw me with Mona. Second time with turning Mona loose at the bar, and watching the space around her get lousy with guys. Another night of nursing a Coke until it was brown water. And one more night of no Moe.

After a couple hours waiting, me and Mona left. We drove back to the apartment. No ice cream tonight. I talked at Mona a little; told her that it was no big deal Moe not coming around. Again. It was only a matter of time.

Mona didn't much listen. Like the night before, she just stared out the window at the houses along Sunset. It was good that she didn't talk, really. I didn't much feel like talking.

Third night. Same as the other two. We put in a couple of hours at the lounge and when I saw how things were heading, when I saw Moe wasn't going to show, I signaled Mona it was time to leave.

As we drove, like before, Mona stared out the Corvair window at the houses. Elizabethan, workman, architectural. All they had in common was their bigness.

Mona asked me how much I thought one of the houses cost, and I told her I didn't know, and she told me to guess, and I told her maybe a mil. Maybe. Maybe more. And that was for starters.

Mona turned and looked at me. "A million dollars?"

"For starters," I reminded her.

She went back to staring out the window. To her reflection she said, "There're so many of them."

"Yeah."

"If you were like in . . . I dunno . . . if you were in Tennessee, Nebraska . . . some shitty state, and you were where the million-dollar houses were, there'd be one of them. Two maybe. Five tops."

"Yeah," I said again.

Mona nodded her head at the window, at Beverly Hills. "But look at them houses. All those people got a million to spend on houses? On just their houses?"

With her voice Mona made that kind of money sound real far away. Too far away for people like us ever to reach out and grab hold of.

"Don't worry," I reassured. "We'll get a piece of that."

Me, she ignored. To her reflection she said: "They don't even know what they got, do they? They don't even know."

Night number four.

Night number five.

Mona and I were getting to be routine at the Polo Lounge. So much so that the valets stopped expecting tips and took their time bringing my car around, and I had to open field–tackle a waitress to get her to bring me my Coke. The boys of the lounge had been trained to give Mona her space. Now and again a new one would come around seeing what they could get her to buy. Mona schooled them real quick. All that, and we still hadn't seen anything of Moe.

The next night, I told Mona we should take off. Wouldn't do any good to be seen at the lounge too much. Wouldn't do any good for Mona to look like she was waiting to pick up a particular guy, like she was laying bait.

Mona came back at me wondering why we didn't try another spot, why we didn't look for Moe somewheres else.

It was no good changing up, I told her. The night we go somewheres else is the night Moe decides to go to the lounge. It's like roulette: You don't bounce around the table so the ball can land where you aren't. You pick a number, you stick with it.

Night number six.

Night number seven.

Seven tries, and Moe hadn't been around once. And worse, Mona was getting sick of playing dress-up every evening with no payoff in sight. She made that clear on the drive home.

"Chad had money," she said to me, not looking at me, just looking out the window at the houses as she had every night when we went home busted. Mona was talking about a guy at the lounge who'd hit on her. Unlike the others she'd turned away quick, this one she let work his bop for a while. If I hadn't given her the eye and stared her into sending him off she would have let the guy work her all night. "He had money, is all I'm saying."

I could tell she was starting to be distracted by shiny objects the other boys were dangling in her face.

I said: "He didn't have enough money."

"Plenty for me."

"Not enough he was going to break us off any. What the fuck was he? Some low-end studio exec who leases cars outside his income."

"He's an agent. A big music guy. He told me he used to have that one grunge singer. The one that died in a pile of shit. Weird."

About any of that I didn't care. "He'd fuck you and toss you like used Kleenex."

"What if he didn't?"

"He would."

"But what if—"

"Look," I snapped, stubbing her out. "Silk shirts and penny loafers back there don't live in your world, okay? Just 'cause I dress you up nice and let you play in their sandbox don't mean these boys want to take you home to mommy. A guy like that don't care nothing about you. And a guy like that ain't sending a hundred thousand our way."

"Maybe I don't need that kind of dough to get by."

"Maybe I do."

Mona muttered something I didn't like. I called her on it, and she went dumb about having said anything at all. Didn't matter. I heard her the first time. I heard her when she said: "Maybe I don't need you."

In that moment I became newly reacquainted with an old and familiar sensation. It was the feeling of things slipping away from me.

Night eight.

Mona wasn't ready on time like she'd been every other night. When she was, I had to go back over her hair and makeup with her. She wasn't much looking like Pier. She wasn't much trying.

I was running out of time. I had to hook Mona up with Moe soon before Mona gave a big "fuck you" to this whole little scam.

The ride to the Beverly Hills Hotel. My stomach was sick with despair. I broke a sweat I couldn't shake. I was starting to think I'd never find Moe. I was starting to think my grift was nothing but a pipe dream and as solid as the smoke that drifted from it. I was starting to think I was taking the long way down in life. So, why even bother anymore? Why hang on to the idea of taking Moe? Why hang on to hope? Why not just let go and drop to the bottom of my being? After all, it's not the fall that kills you. . . . I was starting to think, also, a drink would taste real good right about then. Taste good, and feel even better.

Pulling up the drive. A valet pointed me to where I could park the Corvair. They were long hep to me and my no-tipping ways.

Me and Mona walked into the hotel, plenty of space between us and not a word shared. I stepped into the Polo Lounge, just one foot through the door.

Truth: There's a feeling you get when you gamble—not when you gamble for fun, or when you gamble to kill time while the missus goes off to catch the Mr. Las Vegas doing the second show at the Luxor, but when you gamble as a way of life, as a way of feeling alive—there's a feeling that comes when you peek under your blackjack hand and get a king and an ace staring back at you. A feeling that pumps like death row voltage all through your body when you look up from the green felt and see that ivory ball has fallen into black thirteen just like you bet it would. That's the most, Jackson. The ne plus ultra. A bigger, better, badder kick than any drug or booze or lay could ever swing you. A high that's such a delight to the blood you'd bet your life, your wife, and your last dollar just to taste it again.

That's the feeling I got walking into the Polo Lounge. Walking in, and looking up and seeing Moe Steinberg working a brandy at a table for one.

M
oe.

Finally he'd gotten around to showing up. I looked at him: old and shrunken like a husk without humanity. He sat at a table alone and drinking. The only thing that sent him out into the world, the only thing that kept him alive for that matter, was a small hope—the hope of finding again what was lost, the hope of discovering something to make what was left of his life worth living—which barely smoldered inside him like fading embers. I knew the feeling, and I knew Moe couldn't be more ready for what I was about to send his way.

Funny. Here was a Joe that had everything and more, and me who had less than nothing. We couldn't be further apart, but our two lives were about to smack together at the juncture where depression met desperation.

Better than that.

Abruptly I realized it had been some producer, in fucking up my script and thereby fucking up me, who'd reduced me to the life I had known for my most recent years. And now by fucking Moe—a producer, a mogul, a Hollywood suit; an icon of my contempt—I was going to hoist myself high to the life I had always wanted. Can't say I planned things this way—consciously or unconsciously—but it didn't keep me from enjoying the irony of ironies, the perfect "screw you, Hollywood" symmetry that layered this exquisite con of mine.

With a nod of my head I hipped Mona to Moe. Dig her: Miss Cool, getting a little nervous. Practice is over; it's game night.

The usual: Mona to the bar and me to my table. The wait was on.

Moe drank. Not heavy, but anytime you drink alone it looks like you're downing more than you should. He was thin and way past balding, and his face was checkered with liver spots. What I could see of it. Most of his face was hidden behind glasses big enough to have been windshields from a couple of Japanese cars. Every now and again some guy just as old as Moe would shuffle over to him, shake his hand, say a few words, then shuffle away. Other than that he didn't mix with anyone, go out of his way to talk to anyone. It was like he wanted to be alone in public 'cause being alone in private had gotten to be too routine. He stared at his tabletop. Stared at it like he was watching a movie. Call it: *The Good Old Days*, or *Where Did My Life Go?* He stared at the table so much he didn't notice Mona when she came in, or when she sat down at the bar, or when she ordered her third drink 'cause she had gone through the first two waiting to get noticed. All he had to do was look up, but he didn't. Why should he be in a hurry to have himself a look around the lounge? Not like he'd see many people he'd know. Most of his friends were dead. Most of the crowd in the lounge didn't know or give a shit as to who he was, or what he did, or that guys like him built this town and "the Industry" just so people like them—the crowd—could drive their German cars home to their big houses to be with their dysfunctional kids who drank during the day when they should've been going to their prep schools.

I wanted to throw my glass at Moe. I wanted to stand up and shout: Hey, you old slug! There's your dream girl at the bar!

Instead, I just sat and waited some more.

Halfway through Mona's fourth drink Moe did it. Just a simple lift of the head. A glance toward the bar. His glass jumped from his hand and shattered on the floor. The room looked.

Heart attack!

That's the first thing I thought. I hadn't figured for that, but I should've. An old man like Moe seeing the love of his life resurrected? In my mind I saw him drop dead, and my hundred grand getting buried in the hole right next to him. I was in the grave one over.

Moe did me the favor of not dying. He only looked like he had. Moe sat frozen, stared hard. He was oblivious to the looks he got from others in the lounge. He made no notice of the waitress who mopped up glass and brandy from around his feet. For Moe the world consisted only of a ghostly beauty from decades gone by.

Moe finally got it in himself to do something. He stood, gingerly walked the lounge to the bar. All his moves were careful, delicate. I almost felt for the guy, the way he was afraid; the way he acted like a harsh movement and this vision might break, splinter, and leave him alone with his useless reality once again.

Almost to her, Moe stopped. His fear hit a high note. Silently, I pushed at him: C'mon, you pug. Finish it. Go to her!

Moe ignored my telepathy.

Mona turned to him. Her face was lit with a smile. Warm. Sweet. Inviting. I'd seen it before. It was the same smile she'd smiled at me. I knew what a lie it was. I knew how powerful it was. I saw that again in the way Moe, thin, scared old Moe, floated toward her.

They talked for a bit, the two of them. I was too far away to hear what about, but Moe smiled and Mona smiled brighter and Moe smiled some more, so I knew things were okay. After a few minutes Moe invited Mona back to his table, an offer she graciously accepted. More talk. More smiles. A big one from me.

A lot of frowns from a lot of guys who had spent a lot of time trying to get next to Mona only to get upstaged by some geezer ancient enough to be their father's father's older brother.

As it got obvious that I was no longer needed, that Mona had things under control, I made my way out of the lounge. I worried, some, if Mona was going to be able to carry things off. She had the look and some skills, but, like I'd told her before, Moe was old and only that, not stupid. If Mona played things at all wrong, Moe could get wise in a second. I should've coached her better. I should've gotten her more prepared. I should've . . .

I took one look back. Moe was laughing at something Mona had said.

This was going to work. Mona was going to do all right. As I left her there I felt like a parent dropping his kid off to school for the very first time. Nervous, happy, and proud all in one.

I hadn't been home for more than two hours when Mona came in the door. First, I was worried some. It seemed like she was back too soon, like her night with Moe should have gone on forever. The devilish smile on Mona's face told me I had no reason for concern.

She fell into a spot on the couch next to me and shook her hair loose from her sexed-up beehive.

"Details, baby," I said, a smile to mirror hers.

"Details," she cooed back at me. "He finally sees me at the bar. Took long enough. Then he sort of creeps over—"

"I caught the early show. Skip ahead. After you went back to his table."

"So I go back to his table, he orders me a drink, we talk."

Eager: "And?"

"And nothing. We talked."

"He didn't make a play for you? Didn't invite you back to his place?"

"We just talked."

Moe Steinberg sees the incarnation of his one true love after she'd been stone-cold dead for more than thirty years, and all he wants to do is talk? I got disappointed again. Scared even. Mona saw that and was on top of my worries.

"Don't get panicky," she purred. "Everything was working like a dream. You should've seen him, daddy. You should've seen the way he looked at me. Like he was looking at that no-arm statue chick. Oh, I had him. I had him right here." Mona waved her little finger at me.

"C'mon," I pushed her. "Spill it all."

"He was nervous, shy. Cute like a little boy. Asked me a lot of questions."

"Like?"

"Like: Where was I from? What was I doing with myself?"

"What did you tell him?"

"I sold him some bullshit. Told him I was from Wisconsin, come out here to go to school and was working part-time at a flower shop in the Valley."

"You couldn't come up with something sexier?"

"This one don't want sexy. He wants sweet, innocent. I'm his vestal fucking virgin."

Before I could finish rolling my eyes, Mona said: "He went for it, okay? He was all over it. No matter how small the detail he was licking it up from wherever I dropped it. It was delicious." She gave a little laugh and more of her devil's smile. Mona was getting off on her own sexiness.

She kept on: "He wanted to know what I was studying, what my parents did, what my favorite color was." Mona grabbed my arms above my elbows. "Can you believe that? My favorite color. Who the hell asks shit like that anymore?" If Mona got anymore juiced up she'd've cum. As it was she could hardly control herself.

Neither could I. I leaned close, lips ready for kissing.

Mona leaned away. She gave a queer look. I thought because of me, because I'd tried to make it with her.

No.

She said: "You think I'm going to have to fuck him?" A shrug. "Oh well. You gotta do, right?"

I gave up on kissing Mona. For the moment. I asked: "So where'd you leave it?"

"Tomorrow again. Same time and place. I'm meeting him for drinks." Mona's grin went ear to ear. "How long before we bleed him?"

"Get your hooks in good and deep. Wait till they touch bone."

slept good; safe, comfortable, and warm. It's how the innocent must feel when they go to bed at night.

The day was filled with waiting for evening. I had Mona to the Polo Lounge by 7:40. I didn't even stick to see if Moe would show. He would show.

Me, back home. More waiting. Every time I looked at my watch, it was: I wonder what Mona's saying to Moe now. Wonder what he's saying to her. Maybe he took her home. Maybe he's fucking her.

I didn't like the picture of that, of Mona getting fucked by this old guy. I didn't like the picture of Mona getting fucked at all by any guy.

I tried to not think about things, to just watch TV. That got to be a chore. I gave it up for reading a magazine, then gave that up to lying around.

A little more than three hours. Mona came home. She breezed in and past me like I was furniture, and furniture didn't need to know how her night went.

Refrigerator. Beer. She sucked it down. To me, she said: "I don't drink in front of him. Keeping up that virgin thing, ya know. Figure every bit helps."

Mona wasn't hopped-up like she'd been the night before. She dropped onto the couch, kicked up her feet, but chased it all with a little smile. She was like someone coming off a hard eight hours' work. Another pull on the beer; then she told me how things had gone.

Mona told me the second she walked into the lounge Moe stood at his table. Stood quick for an old guy, she put it. He ordered brandy; she ordered tea. When he saw she was drinking tea, he changed up his order and had the same. Small talk started things off. Moe asked how she was. Moe asked how school was. Moe asked how the flower shop was. Moe asked how her family was.

She was fine, Mona told him. School was going well. She was studying botany at UCLA. That's why she'd taken the job at the flower shop. Her family was good. Her younger brother would be graduating from high school soon, and hadn't decided where to go to college. Her parents wanted him to stay close to home, but he, like Mona, wanted to get out of Wisconsin. Mona's mother, according to Mona, had just taken up harp lessons.

I told Mona she shouldn't be doing so much lying. Lies are hard to keep straight. Mona told me she didn't have any choice if Moe was going to ask questions, and that I shouldn't worry. She could keep her lies straight.

That I could believe.

The lies she told were most likely visions of the life she wanted and never had. A life that'd been lived before a thousand times in dreams and wishes. Wishing it one more time, out loud for Moe, wasn't going to confuse Mona none.

So the night went on with Moe asking shit and Mona spinning tales. Then, at a respectable hour, Moe put Mona in a cab and sent her home.

"He invite you to his place?" I asked.

"No," Mona answered.

"He try to kiss you?"

"No."

"He want to see you again?"

Mona gave a little "What do you think?" laugh.

"Can't believe he hasn't tried to get in you yet," I scoffed. "Course, old guy like that? His dick is probably so shriveled it's good for nothing besides flossing teeth."

I laughed at my joke. Mona laughed some, too. We talked for a bit more; then Mona said she needed to get some sleep, so I went to the bedroom leaving her the couch. As I closed the door I heard Mona's dress unzip. Soon, I promised myself, very soon I was going to make a play for her.

Third night, and things getting routine already: Me driving Mona to the Beverly Hills Hotel. Mona disappearing into the lobby, all eyes on her. Me waiting at home for a few hours. Mona coming in the door, grabbing booze from the fridge, with the same story to tell.

Her and Moe would sit and rap about all kinds of dullness. It was okay, I guess. It was what Moe had to do: Feel Mona out. Find out what she was all about. I always figured him not as dumb as his age would make him out to be. He'd want to know about her, find out if Mona would be a replacement for Pier in more than just the looks department. He was testing the waters. It was only a matter of time before he let himself go and fell into my girl deep and hard.

Mona drank a bunch, told me more about what Moe had asked or said. She laughed at most everything she repeated to me. First because she thought Moe was corny, but later because she was drunk.

I let her drink on to the point where I thought she would be easy. I wanted to fuck Mona. More than anything now, as if my passion was a poison that would kill me if I did not let it spill out, I wanted to fuck her. But when she was finally drunk enough that I could have fucked her, I realized that wasn't the way I wanted her. I didn't want to have to trick her; I wanted her to accept me willingly. I didn't want to have to take her; I wanted her to freely, almost desperately, give herself as if her body were an offering made at the temple of Jeffty. I wanted Mona to throw her arms around me and smile her devil's smile, and I wanted her to mean it. No lies. No deceptions. No street-corner hustle. I wanted her to look at me and say: You own me, Jeffty. Now and always. I wanted her to speak those words, so until the end of time when I looked at Mona, I could say: I own that.

On the fourth night, Mona's fourth date with Moe, she came home with something wrapped in plastic. Not plastic, a garment bag.

"What's that?" I asked.

Mona sat. She looked a little bewildered, a little lost in thought. She didn't say anything, having not heard me, or maybe just ignoring me.

Again I asked: "Whatcha got?"

Whisper: "It's from Moe."

"No shit? He's giving you stuff already? What is it?"

"We went to his house tonight."

I got up quick and went close to Mona. I wanted a front-row seat for every morsel she laid out. "Four dates, and you're already in the door. You're an operator, Mona. What's his place like?"

"Big. Not big like you might think, not for Beverly Hills, but the biggest house I've ever seen. It was cold."

"Moe too cheap to use a heater?"

Mona looked at me sharp. Her expression told me she was looking at the dumbest fuck on the planet. "Not cold like that. Empty. Lonely."

"Far as I can see, the lonelier the better. Only helps us out."

"His wife left him years ago. He had a son—did you know that?"

Didn't know, didn't care.

Mona went on. "His son died. Must be kind of sad, a parent outliving his child."

"Yeah, my heart's busted. So he takes you back to his place. Then what happened? He get busy with his hands?"

With a shake of her head: "No. We talked."

"More with the talking. About what, his dead kid?"

I could tell Mona didn't like the way I put that, but she let it go. She said: "Yes. Some. Mostly we talked about me. He would . . . ask me things."

"What things?"

Mona stopped talking.

Again, stronger: "What things?"

"What difference does it make?"

"None, so what's he asking you about?"

"You'll think it's stupid."

"This isn't about what I'll think; I want to know what he's asking you."

Mona and me had a little stare-down. Mona saw I wasn't going to let it drop.

Mona said: "He asked me about places I'd always wanted to visit. He asked me what kinds of books I read, and about things I dream of—"

I was laughing before I even knew I was laughing.

Mona threw needles at me from her eyes.

I tried to choke back my laughter. "I'm sorry, but . . . what you dream about? The books you read?" The laughter came again.

"Fuck you. I read a lot of books."

"Like . . ."

Mona stared at me a while longer, then turned away.

"Okay," I said. "So he asked you a lot of stuff. Then what? When did he give you that?" I pointed to the bag in her hands. "Before or after he fucked you?"

"He didn't fuck me. He didn't even try."

I was glad about that. As much as it would've helped things if Moe and Mona had fucked, I was glad for now that they hadn't. But it was an eventuality I would have to deal with sooner or later.

I said to Mona: "Okay, so he didn't fuck you. So . . ."

"So we just talked; then he told me I reminded him of someone. Someone, he said, he cared for deeply, but that she was gone now."

Obvious: Pier.

"He said that he had something for her, something that he'd bought once before she was gone. He'd kept it for years, but he wanted to give it to me because . . . because I reminded him of her."

Mona unzipped the bag. Inside: a dress. A gown, really. Golden silk. Trim and beautiful. Dated, but still high style. Something Jackie O would've worn when Jackie O was alive and wearing things like that. Made the dresses I'd bought for Mona look like Hefty bags with holes punched in them.

"That's for starters. Until we hit money, we haven't even begun to take stuff out of him." I talked like I'd barely noticed the dress. The gown of golden silk, trim and beautiful.

Mona zipped the garment bag shut. "I need to get some sleep, Jeffty."

She did need to get rest. Mona looked tired. Not sleepy tired, weary tired. She wasn't hard like I'd thought. Maybe she could handle hustling for herself on the streets, but a racket like we were working took time and attention, and it was obviously draining her. Still, at the rate Mona was going, a couple of weeks or so and we could put the touch on Moe. Then she could rest. We both could. We could rest somewhere together. Somewhere quiet and secluded where we could be alone together. Eat, drink, and have sex together. And when we had done that, I would buy Mona a dress. I didn't know what kind, or where from, but I would buy her a dress. A dress that made the one Moe gave her look like a rag used to catch oil leaking from under an old car.

Morning.

When I woke Mona was still sleeping. She stayed asleep as I stood over the couch. Five minutes or so passed with me staring at her. The dried saliva on her lips, the crust in the corner of her eyes didn't do much to diminish her near perfection. She moved a little; the T-shirt she wore hitched up, revealing her breasts. I felt like a perv. Five more minutes, and I stopped looking at her tits.

I left.

Occasionally through the day, as I drove or when I was trying to hustle a few bucks to get by on until I cashed in with Moe—having spent my advance from Amber on dresses and such—I would find myself thinking of Mona and her skin and her muscles and her breasts and her nipples. An hour passed with me sitting at the corner table of a little sandwich shop just thinking of her. An hour passed like a second with nothing but Mona on my brain.

A voice snapped me back from my fixation.

"Buddy," the guy behind the counter said at me. "Buddy," he said again in yet another of the seemingly endless forms of accented English that are used in this city. "You can't stay here. You not going to eat, you can't just sit. You're taking up space. You can't take up space."

I looked around. The place was empty. Not a soul. I was the only thing anywhere like a paying customer, and this guy was rushing me along. He had torn me from my mania and for what? For nothing, except so that he could push me around 'cause I looked like the "get pushed around" kind. For one moment I had tried to fill my head with something good and clean and beautiful in my otherwise dirty life, and he wouldn't even let me have that. I didn't know this guy, I didn't know his name, but I hated him.

I got up and went to the counter and looked at the guy and he looked back at me.

"You want something?" he said. He said it all weary like the hustle and bustle of running an empty sandwich shop had worn the substance from him.

I just kept on looking at him.

One more time: "You want something?"

I worked up a smile, hoped it didn't come off as a sneer. "Got change of a twenty?"

Inside of sixty seconds I had ten bucks extra, his ten bucks, in my pocket as I made for the door. Fuck you, I said to him in my head. Fuck you, and your empty place, and your bad sandwiches. Fuck you, and your accent, and whatever little country you crawled here from. Fuck you, 'cause I have your ten dollars. It came to me that this was the benefit of owning a small life: Little things, like somebody else's ten bucks, made you happy.

I went outside into the sunshine, and for the first time in a long time the heat, the light, the still, hot air all felt good. It took a second for my eyes to adjust to the brightness. When they did, I found myself staring across the parking lot at two men: Lieutenant Duntphy and his partner whose name, I thought as they walked toward me, I still did not know.

"Larceny," or something to that effect Duntphy mumbled as he shoved me hard—same kind of hard as when he'd bent my arms behind my back, same kind of hard as when Partner jammed the cuffs on my wrists—into the back of their unmarked. I had asked a couple of times what this was about; why they were taking me in. The mumbled answer was the best I'd gotten. The only I'd gotten. Duntphy must have been on my ass all day, watching, waiting for me to pull a hustle so he could drop down on me.

Maybe.

Or maybe Duntphy had it in his mind he was going to cause me trouble and this just happened to be when he got around to it. True to his word, he was going to squeeze me until I told him what I didn't know but what he wanted to hear about Dumas. He said he was going to pitch me out and I was looking at strike number three.

I rode in the back of the unmarked mouth shut. No trouble, nothing smart to say. There was a lot of talk back at me from the front of the car. The gist of it was I was a dumb fuck and a loser and I'd better start thinking about cooperating. Mostly I didn't pay attention. Mostly I watched Duntphy drum his fingers on the cracking plastic of the dash. It reminded me how big his hands were. My face started hurting again just from looking at them.

The ride, short. Hollywood Division, where'd I been before under only slightly better circumstances. Out of the car, rough with me again, inside. The routine: pockets emptied, fingers printed. Flash, flash, and they had some nice fresh snapshots to go with the update of my record. Belt, shoelaces gone 'cause I might want to kill myself. Holding up my pants like a hobo, feet flopping in and out of my too-loose shoes, I got walked down to a holding cell. More talk at me—an update on my "dumb fuck" status. When I got a chance to get a word in I asked about me being able to make a phone call. Turned out to be a rhetorical question.

The holding cell was plenty big, but filled with people just the same. Not a one of them looked as if they'd ever seen the right side of the law. Cuffs off, I got shoved inside. Two big bunks. One sat four people; a brother tipping the scales somewhere near three hundred pounds took up the other all by himself. There was space on the floor. There was also urine. A wino and a hophead didn't much seem to care and curled up same as if they had beds at the Four Seasons.

A long-haired white guy let us know it was bullshit. It was all bullshit. He never let on what "it" was, but he kept telling us it was bullshit long after we'd gotten the message. A guy with a cocked-to-the-side baseball cap entertained with some rap lyrics.

I leaned up against a patch of wall that was as clean as any spot I'd find. No eye contact. Hands in my pocket like maybe I'd smuggled a weapon. Like maybe everybody should leave me alone 'cause maybe I was a badass. In my head, between working up a tough-guy look and bulking up my hand in my pocket, I tried to figure out which one of these guys was most likely to rape me.

After twenty minutes of standing against the wall I gave up caring about the floor and what covered it. Legs tired, I sat, hands out of my pockets having quit playing badass, too.

Thirty more minutes passed. It's Bullshit Guy let us know that everything was still bullshit.

A cop came around, shook the wino awake and sent him on his way. Cocked-to-the-Side Baseball Cap Guy was let go, too. Me and everybody else got left right where we were.

Time went into the next hour. I had to shit. The toilet sat right out in the open. Stainless steel, caked brown and yellow. No toilet paper.

I held my shit in.

I should have had a field release by now. Petty larceny, me with ID. No way they would waste space on my kind except that Duntphy was trying screw with me. Fine. I could wait him out. An hour more, maybe two. Except that I had to shit, I could wait him out.

It's Bullshit Guy chimed in one more time. We were all sick of him, apparently none more so than Big Fat Black Guy. The big fat black guy struggled himself off the bunk and waddled across the cell. He tried to step over the stretched-out hophead, but like his leg was too heavy to lift all the way up, it caught the hophead in the chest. Hophead rolled into a fresh puddle of piss and went right on sleeping.

Big Fat Black Guy stretched out his big fat left hand. It swallowed up It's Bullshit Guy by the shirt and yanked him close. Big Fat Black Guy's right hand went to work on It's Bullshit Guy's head. For a big fat guy, Big Fat Black Guy had some speed to him. He got in four punches before It's Bullshit Guy could see the first one coming. Each blow was punctuated by an undulation from the blubber that hung like a sack of dead cats under his arm. Big Fat Black Guy opened his hand and It's Bullshit Guy sank to the floor. The pounding didn't change much except now It's Bullshit Guy was going on about how it was bullshit through hands cupped to his blood-spouting nose. I couldn't tell if he was complaining about the same old bullshit or about getting his nose broke.

Big Fat Black Guy went back to the bunk. His bunk. Anybody who thought about taking up a seat there thought again after his little floor show. He sat down, the metal of the bunk groaning for help under him.

Long after the fact, a couple of cops strolled lazily to the holding cell. One took It's Bullshit Guy under the arms and dragged him out. Cheers and catcalls all around.

As the cops headed from the cell I moved toward one of them. He swung around, hand on his billy club, ready to do some head pounding. These guys were fast when they wanted to be. I took a step back.

"When am I out of here?" I asked.

From the cop I got a queer look.

Slowing things down for him: "When am I going to get let go?"

"Go? You're not going anywhere."

"What am I up for but larceny? Give me a field release, or send me up to a judge."

Another queer look. "Five-twenty on a Friday?" He shut the cell door. Locked it. "You got two days to think about it."

Friday. Duntphy had timed my bust. If I couldn't get an arraignment I had to sit things out over the weekend. It was a sweet little "fuck you" to help me see things his way. I sat on the floor. The thought in my head was: This is bullshit.

A round 6:30, cops came for me. I had one phone call owed. I got it, eventually, too late in the day to do me any good. I didn't know if I should try Eddie or Mona. Who would be more help to me? I flipped a coin in my head and called Mona at my apartment. No answer.

I got moved into a regular cell. My luck, slow weekend. I'd only be sharing it with three other guys. Mexicans all of them. Mexican Mexicans, like "just got caught hopping the border" Mexicans. Typical tired, poor, huddled masses yearning to be free, but instead who were getting their asses shipped right back where they came from. They could have been brothers, the three of them: dark skin, black hair, and bellies that stuck out from under too tight, too dirty T-shirts. None of them spoke English, or if they did, they didn't do it in front of me.

I settled into my weekend retreat finally taking the shit I so desperately needed to not much caring anymore about the condition of the fixture or being shy for privacy. After that, I crawled onto my bunk—the only empty bunk—and sat. The blanket was stained. I spent a half hour, maybe more, figuring all the possibilities of what with. After that, I'd run out of ways to occupy myself. And this was only Friday evening. My weekend was just starting.

What came next was a lot of time. Time enough for me to think of the how and whys that had ended me up in this place: a Haitian bookie who used me for perverse entertainment; a strong-arm cop who wanted me to hand the Haitian over to him no matter that it might get me dead; a street girl I desperately needed who moment by moment may or may not still be hanging around. Pieces to the puzzle of my life. I had to make them fit. I had to.

The Mexicans went on and on with each other in Spanish. Occasionally they would stop talking, throw a look my way, say something about me I couldn't understand, then get back to themselves.

Later on, we got food. A baloney sandwich on white bread with government cheese, something like potato salad, and green Jell-O. Not lime, just green. Milk washed it all down.

More time. No watch, no clock, no way to know what the hour was. I was tired but didn't want to sleep. I figured the Mexicans to be fairly harmless. Hardcores would have been sent to the downtown jail for the weekend. Still, they were three to my one, and I wasn't much for pressing their advantage by dozing off for them.

I sat.

They talked. Subtle looks my way. Subtle smiles.

I don't know how much later I jumped awake to one of the Mexicans staring at me from six inches away. Startled, I jerked back, slamming my head against the concrete wall. My hand vise gripped his throat. The Mexican went wiggy, flipping around in my hand same as a fish on a dock. Spanish came squealing out of him.

The Mexican's two friends didn't like what was going on. His two friends got up and started moving for me. I let my Mexican go, let him go hard so that he spilled out over the floor. That didn't stop the two friends from coming at me. I clenched my fists and got ready to start swinging knowing it wouldn't do me much good. Just like it was never a bright idea to get into a knife fight with an ugly guy, it was just as bad an idea to try and beat the shit out of three guys from a dirty country where people got the shit beat out of them on a daily basis.

A sound: wood on metal. A cop banged his billy club on the cell bars. He screamed at the Mexicans, working on variations of the word *fuck*. It was the international language of ass kicking, and the Mexicans got the cop's meaning. They backed up over to their side of the cell and I pushed back to what was now *my* half. I stared at them; they stared at me. After that, I didn't get much sleep.

I think Saturday morning came around. Deprivation of sunlight and rest had messed with my ability to conjecture time. During the night one of the Mexicans had fucked up the toilet. Brown, chunky water seeped from it, but the tilt of the building made it flow toward their side of the cell. Served them right, except they didn't much care about shitty water swirling down around their feet. Far as they cared the cell had all the amenities of home.

Eventually, more food came around. Not different, just more. Another baloney sandwich with government cheese, some more virtual potato salad, green Jell-O, and the milk.

I ate.

After that, I sat, stood, lay down, stood, sat, then lay down again. Time was in no hurry to go anywhere. It was all there for me.

At some point one of the Mexicans, the Mexican I'd woken up to, edged his way toward me. I sat up and made a big show of being ready to fight. But he wasn't coming over to stir up trouble. He held up his hand, and in his hand he held a little photograph. Creased and torn and faded, but through all that I could see the photo was of a girl, seven years old or thereabouts. The Mexican didn't try to say anything to me concerning her; I had no way of knowing what she was to him: daughter, niece, a pre-pube he found cute 'cause he was a sick bastard. But the Mexican's face was sad, so I didn't think he was a sick bastard. I thought maybe he was a dad who missed his little girl.

I took the picture from him, looked at it, matched the Mexican's sad face. Maybe the little girl was back home waiting for him. Maybe she was dead.

I gave the photo back. The Mexican shuffled to his side of the cell. I lay back on my bunk and had all the time in the world to take note of the many interesting patterns formed by the water spots on the ceiling.

Later a couple of cops came for the Mexicans. The cops sign-languaged them into sticking their hands through the bars so they could be handcuffed. After that, the cops opened the door and started herding the Mexicans out. The one Mexican, the one who had shown me the picture, turned back my way still sad in the face. I wanted to tell him good-bye. I wanted to tell him I hoped he got back with the girl in the picture. I didn't know Spanish so I couldn't tell him anything so I just lay there until the Mexicans were gone, never to be a part of my life again.

For a second, I was happy because I was alone, until I realized I was happy about being alone for two days behind bars with a broken toilet that leaked shit.

In the afternoon—I thought it was the afternoon because it was after another round of food—cops brought in a new cellmate for me. He was young—seventeen?—and black, and as angry as any young black kid I'd ever seen. He came in ranting at the cops with "Fuck" this, and "Fuck" that, and "Fuck you muthafuckin' white-ass bitch fucks."

The black kid was shirtless, pants slung low around his waist exposing underwear, as was the style. His chest and body were a patchwork of scars and tattoos that equally preached a thug life. Under those decorations his body was lean and sinewy and cut. It seemed too bad such a good physique should be wasted on someone odds on to be dead in the next three to five years.

As I was staring at the boy, at his body, after just nearing twenty-four hours in jail, it came to me in a curious/sick way just how it was men in prison ended up dicking each other. Fast as I could, I tacked up pictures of Mona inside the walls of my mind.

"Bitch-ass muthafuckas," the kid raged. Maybe in general, maybe at me. "What da fuck? What da fuck smell like fuckin' shit in here?"

It was shit that smelled like shit, but I didn't offer that up.

The kid looked down at his feet, at the brown, chunky water that col-lected under the bunk where he sat. "Ah, fuckin' ass. What kina fuckin' bullshit is dis? Muthafuckas got the toilet all runnin' over and shit. Fuck dat!"

The kid's head came up, and he looked at me. "Bitch, git yo ass up. I ain't sittin' over here in this shit!" He made a move in my direction. "Bitch, I said get yo ass up."

He wanted my bunk. Here's the politics of prison: Somebody wants something of yours and you give it up without a fight, then you really are a bitch and you just sold them a ticket to fuck with you in every meaning of the verb. And if you do fight, then you'd better be good at it, 'cause prison fights usually ended when one person was too dead to hit back. My entire life, at that moment, had culminated in the narrow range of choices between getting myself seriously hurt or killed or being a bitch sitting over a pond of shitty water.

I got up from the bunk, slow as if to make a point of quiet protest about the situation, then crossed the cell to my new home. I splashed to the bunk and lay down. As the gang kid went on about muthafuckas and bitches I thought of Mona, of where she might be and what she might be doing. Then I thought of her as I peeped her in the bathroom with the water running over her body. And after that I thought of her lying asleep with her shirt hitched up over her breasts. I stopped thinking of Mona and her body and her breasts when I started to get a hard-on, which, I thought for a lot of reasons, was not a good thing to be wearing in front of the gang kid.

The gang kid kept up his rant. He went on, angry at everything and talking about all the bad things he was going to do to all the things he was angry at. The cops got around to taking the gang kid away, probably to the downtown jail, which made me think he was as bad as he talked, and he really would do some—if not all—of the things he was going on and on about.

As the kid got marched—handcuffed same as the Mexicans—away, I decided I was glad that gang kids killed each other mostly as all it did was thin their number and we're better off with them dead. I also decided, You know what would be a good idea? If we took all the gang kids and moved them to, like, Idaho or Nebraska or another one of the states we weren't using, gave them a bunch of weapons and let them go to work on each other. It'd be like that one movie where they took all the criminals and put them in New York, or that other movie where they took all the criminals and put them in LA, which was really just the first movie over again but not as good. The only other thing I would add is that maybe all these gang kids in one place killing each other should be on TV. I wasn't sure about that, so I made a plan to spend the rest of the afternoon giving it thought. First I moved from the shitty-water side of the cell back to the other. Home again.

Between lunch and dinner, I got a new cellmate. This one was interesting. Middle-aged white guy, all moneyed up in a suburban way: knit
shirt, khakis, shoes but no socks. He was Simi Valley, Pasadena, San
Marino. Anywhere but from LA proper. His eyes flitted around the cell,
trying not to look at me, but looking at me just the same. He started for
the bunk that was over the shitty water, then stopped, then went and stood
in the corner instead. Todd, I called him, because he looked like a Todd,
stood there for a long time as panicky as you can get without going into
cardiac arrest. Finally, when he got enough nerve, or when he felt like he
had to say something, he said: "What are you in for?" Which I think he
thought he should say because all he knew about jail was what he'd seen
in the movies, and in the movies that's what they always say.

I said: "Triple homicide."

Todd took the next step toward having that heart attack. His body
started to shake and go weak, just like a little girl. He went to the bunk, the
one over the shitty water—but shitty water was the least of his worries
now—and fell on top of it.

Todd said: "I shouldn't be here." As if I should care, he said it again. "I
shouldn't be here." Tears started to fill up in his eyes.

"Don't cry," I said to Todd. For a second he thought I was being sympathetic. Then I went on: "If you cry everybody's going to think you're a
bitch, and they're going to rape you."

That set Todd off. "Oh shit . . ." Newborns should wail as much.

"I mean, they're going to rape you anyway, but you want them to rape
you 'cause they think you're cute, not 'cause they think you're a bitch.
They hurt bitches."

Before I'd even gotten all that out, Todd had become a weeping, quiv-
ering heap. For the first time since Duntphy had tossed me in here I was
having fun. I hoped they didn't take Todd away from me. Although I
could do without the crying and told him so.

"Quit crying."

"Y-y-you . . . y-y—" That's all the more Todd got out between maybe
eight sobs.

"I told you, quit crying."

"You said you were going to rape me."

"I'm not going to rape you."

"You said—"

"I said you'd get raped if you kept acting like a bitch."

"Oh Jesus—"

"I said you'd get raped no matter what, but I'm not the guy who's going to do it."

"I shouldn't be here." Todd went back to that. "I shouldn't be here."

I felt a story coming on that I didn't want to hear, so I said nothing thinking Todd might get it I didn't want to talk.

No go.

"I was just out looking for a little fun, that's all. You know? A little fun."

What the hell, right? I had nothing else to do, so I played along. "You were looking for a prostie."

"I love my wife. I love her. I was just . . ."

"Just looking for some fun. Yeah. You said."

"So, I came down here. . . . I'm not from here, you know. I'm from San Marino."

"No shit."

"I came down here to . . . to find a girl."

"In the middle of the day?"

"I have to go to the Rotary Club dinner tonight. I couldn't come here tonight."

I nodded. "Yeah, well, I guess when a guy's got to have it, he's got to have it."

"S-she was a policewoman."

"The whore?" I asked.

"The prostitute," he answered, as if semantics would make what he had done seem a little cleaner. "She was so pretty. I never thought a woman so pretty would be a cop."

"Forget the movies, guy. Hookers aren't starlets. Good-looking chicks don't run the boulevard giving it up for twenty bucks a shot." Except, I thought, for Mona. But then, Mona was special. Even though she was a runaway street slut who did drugs on the side, she was special.

I said to Todd: "So why don't you just take a field release? A guy like you the cops aren't going to keep all weekend."

"They won't let me go. I don't have any ID. Didn't bring any with me. I thought if I got caught, it would be better not to have ID on me."

"Good thinking." It was bad thinking, but I thought I'd be nice to him just so he wouldn't start crying again. "So why don't you call your wife and—"

Todd got all panicky one more time. "Call my wife? Jesus God, no! Call her and tell her what? 'Honey, I know I should have been home doing yard work, but I decided to drive into Hollywood and have sex with a lady of the evening instead.'"

Lady of the . . . ?

He started crying again. Todd was getting on my nerves. I changed my mind and wished they would take him away.

Pretty soon he got over his misery; then he, like me, just sat quietly thinking about things, figuring things, trying to put together how he'd ended up in a metal bunk over shitty water. I was starting to think there came a time in everyone's life when they wondered that.

After a while I heard something, something like a hiss; like steam squeezing from a pipe. I listened close before I figured it was Todd.

"Excuse me," he whispered. He whispered it again. "Excuse me."

"Yeah?"

"I . . . I wanted to ask you something."

"Ask."

Todd hemmed and hawed, and it took him a good thirty seconds to get around to what was on his mind. "Do they really rape men in prison? I mean, I know they do, but . . . but what's it like?"

"What makes you so curious? Couldn't get it with a woman, so maybe you're hoping to get it with a man?"

"No! No, I'm just . . . I'm just asking."

Never, thank God, having been raped in prison, or anywhere else, by a man—and, unfortunately, never by a woman—I wasn't sure what it was really like, but I'd heard things. I knew stories. I shared them with Todd.

"Prisoners, they got this thing they do called 'the covered wagon.' What they do is string up a blanket from a bunk so the guards can't see into the cell. Then they take fresh ass, a guy like you, behind the blanket and gang-fuck him. One guy in his ass right after the other until there's nothing but blood flowing out of his hole."

"That's sick!"

"Yeah. Of course it's sick. It's prison rape."

Todd was repulsed by what I told him, yet he hung on every word same as a kid around a campfire hearing ghost stories. I gave him more.

"See, when you get to prison, not jail like we're in, but hard-core straight-up prison, you're supposed to blow guys. That's what's expected of fresh ass, like 'Hi, I'm new to the neighborhood; let me suck your cock.' And if you don't . . ."

Todd leaned forward in anticipation of the climax of the tale.

"If you don't, some badass bulls will smack you in the mouth, knock your teeth out so's you have to suck him like it or not, and believe me there's nothing to like about sucking a guy while your gums are bleeding. Then when all the other cons in the yard see you don't have teeth they know you're marked a bitch, and they'll all want to have a go at you."

Todd shivered, but with excitement not fear. Now that he'd gotten over the scare of being in jail he was starting to get into the thrill of it. Here he was in the middle of what was probably the biggest adventure of his white-bread-and-mayonnaise life. It would take him a while to get past the shame and embarrassment of how he'd ended up in the Hollywood jail, but one day, not long from now, when he was on convention with his middle-manager buddies and after he'd had three or four too many drinks, he would recount in great and exacting detail how he, Mr. Whitey McWhite, had survived the worst the urban jungle could throw at him and, more than that, had emerged stronger for the ordeal.

For some reason it made me angry that Todd would be able to take something so dismal and terrible and with it construct a monument to himself. The idea of it made me want to make him cry again while I still had the chance.

The chance passed quickly. Cops came and took Todd away. Unlike the Mexicans and the gang kid, they didn't bother to handcuff him. Why should they? Todd, I'm sure the cops thought, was okay. He was like them. Part of the not so secret club of white guys who ran the world. Okay, so he got out of control for a second and wanted to bang a hooker. So what? Wasn't his fault, right? Probably his wife's fault for not being hot and sexy anymore, for having the nerve to grow old. Or maybe it was the policewoman's fault for enforcing laws that say a guy can't go and buy pussy when he wants. And if they really wanted to stretch things, as white guys are apt, the whole sordid incident was probably the fault of some black guy who was secretly being controlled by the international Jew cartel.

As the cops took Todd from the cell out into a holding area I heard a woman start in with some serious, unrelenting yelling and screaming. Looks like Mrs. Todd found out a few things.

Food came later, same as before except for the color of the Jell-O that was yellow this time. I ate and then, not tired, I went to bed.

Sunday was a very long day made longer by the fact that I woke up what felt like early. It was a long time before breakfast came. I was alone, and would probably remain that way. Sundays are slow days for crime. Even bad guys have to take time off.

At some point cops came and took me out of the cell for a little bit so they could fix the toilet and clean the floor. I was happy for the distraction, and sorry when the maintenance guy was done with his work. After that all I had to look forward to was lunch which took a long time to come, then just served to depress me when it did.

Time, which I had fought for a day and a half, started to work on me like a knife that delivered a thousand leisurely cuts. I thought, which was something I'd tried to avoid over the last forty hours. How does a man end up in the place where he is? Not just a physical place, not just behind steel bars, but how does his life evolve to his final destination?

It was tiny, my life. Everything about it was contemptibly limited by its own insignificance. I lived in a cramped world whose boundaries were west to La Brea and east to Western. I earned my keep five or ten dollars at a time from people who wouldn't know they were being scammed if I told them while I was doing it. I had an undersized apartment, on occasion I drank too much, and the last thing I had that even resembled a relationship with a woman was peeping at a girl through a bathroom door. Now, here I was, sitting in a small cell, not particularly because I'd done much wrong, but because I was the way for one guy to get at another. I was nothing to either of them, less than that, and both would be just as happy if I were dead. Worse. They wouldn't even care.

I don't know many things, and I believe in even fewer. One of the things I know and believe in is something I heard on one of those educational shows where the guy narrating talks with an English accent. He had said something like, a certain constant of nature is that a vacuum seeks to fill itself. It was one of those things you hear and say so what to, but never forget, and then, beyond that, you begin to think about and consider. I

was like that: a vacuum. Empty. My primary pursuit having become trying to fill myself. Religion was no good for someone like me, and gambling and booze had only done a bad job of stuccoing over the holes in
my soul. There was one other thing that might have given me a sense of
purpose: love.

Truth: Say you hate someone. Go on, say it. Not anyone you know in
particular, just pick out some guy on the street. Say you hate that guy, hate
his stinkin' guts, hate his mother and the horse he rode in on, and see if
anyone cares. See if anyone treats you different than normal.

But now say you love that same guy. You don't know him, but you
love him like a brother and care about his thoughts and well-being. See if
they don't tailor you for a suit where the sleeves tie up in back.

Love's an oddity. There's no cornier word, thought, or feeling known.
There's no idea that will get you laughed at faster or looked sideways at
quicker than talking about love. To think about it, even in the quiet soli-
tude of my mind, made me sound goofball to myself.

But I did think of it. I thought: If I've ever been in love, I've never
known it. If I've ever felt it, I wouldn't know who with. Love was without
taste, or physical sensation to the touch. No form, no shape, and even
words couldn't describe it, yet I knew I didn't have it just as sure as I knew
love when I came across it.

In other people at any rate.

I saw it in couples so strange, or ugly, or angry at each other they had
no business being together except that they loved each other. Couples
who when you looked at them, you didn't know which person to feel
more sorry for; then you realized the person you should be sorry for was
you 'cause you'd never have what they had no matter how messed up what
they had was. And if I could never have what they had—the strange,
the ugly, the angry—then how could I ever fill myself? How could I ever
be anything but empty? A vacuum is an unnatural existence. Maybe I
am, too.

I found myself crying. It took me a second to realize it. I found myself
crying, and that shocked/surprised me because I didn't know I any longer
had the capacity to feel sorrow or to experience the sense of human pain.
Most of all, it shocked/surprised me that I could feel those things for
myself. The thought of it, of my own soullessness, made me cry all the
more.

Jesus, I was fucked up.

Two days of isolation, and I was broken. Not by Duntphy or by the experience of jail, but by two days alone—days spent with my own patheticness, like staring into a mirror but unable to see a reflection—which had reduced me to a wailing baby. Two days of quality time spent privately with fact: Never once had I amounted to anything, and never once would I. I was broken all right. It was the cumulative effect, day by day by month by year, of a life lived but not worth living.

And in my weeping I made a sound that was a name and the name was Mona. I called out to her, against myself and with every part of my body I called to her. Suddenly each split second away from her filled me with a growing hurt. No alcohol withdrawal, no detox pain ever hit me harder. I needed Mona. I had plucked her off the streets to save my physical self—to keep me from taking another beating—but I needed Mona to save my spiritual self; to give my life meaning. I needed her to fill the void of me. And what's better, I knew now she needed me, too. As vacant as I was, wasn't she as well? Alone and lonely and living hand to mouth—didn't she need me to help her, to guide her, to protect her? To love her? Life is nothing without someone to share it with, and our lives would be nothing no longer.

Yeah.

Yeah, that was our destiny for each other. I'm serious, and I used that word on purpose—*destiny*. It was our destiny, not just—not merely—to gather together to rip off old men, but to save each other. To love each other.

I had love. If I ever got out of jail, if I ever held Mona in my arms again, I would tell her that: I, we, had love.

I cried and cried and cried.

Morning. Monday.

Food waited for me. The sandwich, the potato salad, the milk, and the Jell-O. I didn't eat. Depression filled me in a way food couldn't. I lay on my bunk. I waited for whatever would happen next.

Then he came in. A cop opened the cell door and let him in.

"Jesus, yalooklike shit. Noffense, butya reallilook bad. Iheard they leftya intha cell all weekend, guessya couldn't shavershower, but . . . ya reallilook like shit."

He had dark hair that looked like it'd been combed by a blender and a suit that didn't know what a cleaners was. He was a big guy, but he hunched like he was trying to hide something, and he talked so fast I had to sit for a couple of seconds and let whatever it was he'd just said sort itself out in my brain.

I asked, "Who are you?"

"Habbish Yerlawyer. You know: Ifyadonothave, or can'tafford, then onewill beappointed for you. I'm the one." He pointed past me to the tray of uneaten food. "Yagonna eat that Jell-O?"

Again I sat and let his words distill themselves in my head. "What do you want?"

"Yagotta hearing scheduled. Wegotta figure out how yergonna plea."

"I didn't do anything."

"Sureyerinnocent. Everybodysinnocent. You, theguyintha next cell. Alltha goodlilboys up at San Quentin waitingta sniff someatha perfume the state's giving away free."

"I'm telling you, I didn't do anything."

Habbish slowed himself down for a second. That was his way of getting serious. "Look, when we go to court, you can lie to the judge, the jury, God, Buddha, your crystals . . . whatever you believe in. But I'm your lawyer. I'm the one you tell the truth to—that is, if you're not too tired of looking at the world from between steel bars."

The truth. Okay, let's try the truth. "I was set up by the cops."

Habbish gave me a bored look.

"You wanted the truth."

"And I'm still waiting. Andryagonna eat that Jell-O or not?"

I didn't have the energy to fight this guy. I didn't even try. I just laid things out. "There's this cop, not exactly crooked, but he's not straight, either. He wants to take down this bookie. And he wants me to be the guy to point the finger at him."

"Yzat?"

"This other guy the cop busted, a guy who knows me, I think he told the cop I know the bookie."

"Do you?" Habbish had peeled off the lid of the Jell-O and was working on its contents.

"Yeah, I know him, but not like the cop thinks."

"So the cop puts you in here to give you some time to ruminate, some time to see things his way."

"But there's nothing I can do. I know the guy, but not well enough to send him over."

"Then get to know him. Or get something on him you can give to the police." As Habbish talked his mouth flapped Jell-O down onto his shirt. It made a green stain that blended with a red one already there.

"The bookie's barely letting me breathe as it is. I hand him over to the cops, he kills me for sure."

"He do the job on your fingers?"

I nodded.

"So help the cops out; then get out of town. LA doesn't seem to be doing much for your love life."

Get out of town? There was a problem with that.

"There's a problem with that," I said. "See, I've got some money coming in . . . sort of."

"Sorta?"

"It's not like I got a dying aunt who's leaving me a fortune."

"It's not exactly legal, this money. Thatwhatyasaying?"

"Yeah. I give this bookie over to the cops and I've got to run, then I can't collect the money."

"But if you stick around for the money this cop's gonna put you down for the third time, and third time's the charm."

"You can see my problem."

"Sure. You got a job you're desperate to pull, and why give it up just 'cause no matter what you do you're gonna get yourself burned?"

Habbish tossed the empty Jell-O container back on the tray. He was through with it, and with me.

"So what do I do?" I asked.

"You're looking at misdemeanor larceny. Small, but I'm betting your friend can make it stick. That marks you for a habit. Ifigerya'll spend the rest of your life in jail."

"Yeah, okay, but what do I do?"

"Tell the cop you'll cooperate; I'll arrange that. Buy yourself some time, then get the hell out of Dodge." Habbish got up from the bunk and yelled for the jailer.

As he came to open the cell door, I asked: "What about the money?"

"Yeah, sure. Pull your job and get paid. The way I see it, you won't be alive or outta jail long enough to spend dime one."

After that he was gone.

Maclient's willinta cooperate ifyerwillinta cooperate."

Habbish talked too fast for me, so I know he talked too fast for Duntphy. Watching Duntphy figure out what was being said to him, and looking dumb doing it, made me glad Habbish was my lawyer.

We all sat at a table in the Box, Duntphy, Habbish, me. Good to his word Habbish had gotten Duntphy to call off the arraignment. If Duntphy bought what I was selling I might be able to put off doing time all together. For now.

Duntphy said to me: "So you admit it? You got inside information on Dumas."

"Maclient admitsta nothing."

I cut in: "I don't have anything on Dumas."

Duntphy started to get up. "You must have liked it inside, 'cause that's where you're going back."

"No, wait. Wait." I tried to keep the desperation out of my voice, but it found a way in. "I don't have anything, but I can get stuff on him."

Duntphy came back down to his chair. "How?"

"I'm into Dumas for thirty thousand. That's good money to a guy like him. Hell, it's good money to anybody. So, I go to Dumas, hook him on a scheme to get paid back, something not too legal. When he bites, you move in for the kill."

"What kind of scheme?"

"That's my worry." I tapped my head. "But I'm already working on it."

Duntphy thought.

Habbish talked. "Maclient's makina good-faith gesture. It'swhatya wanted. Solet's cut the bullshit angethim back out on the street."

Duntphy didn't much like Habbish. Habbish didn't much care what Duntphy or seemingly anyone else thought of him. Still, to keep things civil, he said to Duntphy in a relatively polite and much slower way: "My client certainly isn't much use to you behind bars."

Duntphy took the opportunity to lean close and get in my face. "If you're even thinking about trying to fuck me—"

"I'm not. Dumas never did me any favors, and if I can get him and you out of my life at the same time, I vote for that."

Everybody took a breath for a second. I bit at a nail. Duntphy leaned back in his chair. Habbish went to work on some Jell-O he'd lifted from a food tray on the way in.

When Duntphy was done working things out in his head, he said: "You got one week to give me something on Dumas."

I took that about as well as a rod in the ass. "One week? Are you crazy? I can't put anything together in a week."

"Sure you can. It's easy."

"Easy for you to say. All you got to do is sit there and wait for me to toss him to you. I'm the one's got to do all the heavy lifting."

"How long?"

"I need at least four."

"Four weeks to figure out how you're going to get out from under my thumb? Fuck that."

"Three weeks," Habbish chimed in. "Defer the arraignment for three weeks; then see what he's got for you."

Duntphy went back to thinking. I went back to working on my nail. Habbish scooped a fresh glob of Jell-O from his shirt and popped it into his mouth.

Finally, Duntphy: "Two weeks. But if you even smell like you're thinking anything funny, I'm going to kill you first, then put your body on trial."

Habbish jumped up. "Well, that's that. Thanksferalyer help, Officer."

"Lieutenant," Duntphy corrected. It didn't much matter. Habbish was already out the door.

Outside. Sunshine. Fresh air. LA-fresh, anyway. It felt good to be a free man again, or at least to pretend I was free since the feet of at least two different guys were pressing down on my neck. I had rented myself some time from Duntphy, but shortly he would be two weeks older and two weeks madder.

Habbish popped on some four-dollar sunglasses. He was quite pleased with how he'd worked things back inside the station.

"Not bad, huh?"

"You did all right."

My response wasn't nearly good enough for Habbish. "All right? I did goddamn unbelievable. You ought to be down for the count; instead you're walking around free as a white man."

"Then why'd you do it? If I deserve to be put away so bad, why'd you get me out?"

"You probably rate going inside for fifty different things in your life. At least that many. But that cop back there was railroading you, and my job is to make sure the law works." He didn't need to, but Habbish gave me a quick look head to foot for effect, then: "Even for small-timers like you."

He was arrogant, dirty, and a prick, but you got to admire a guy who takes pride in his work.

Habbish said: "This town is full of freeways and they all lead in two directions. One of them is out of LA. You got your freedom. Don't waste it."

I wanted to make a quip back at him, but Habbish had already started walking away. I thought: If I was an honest man, I would want nothing to do with him. But as I am a dishonest one, I can think of no person I'd rather have representing me.

Home. Finally.

The two hundred bucks it cost to get my car out of impound was just insult to injury.

I stank. Stank of three days in jail. I almost choked on my own smell as I rode up the elevator. But I was home. I was back to my Mona and I knew—after my jailhouse epiphany—that neither personal stench nor anything else would keep her from rushing into my arms. I could feel her squeezing me. I could feel her kissing me. I could hear her saying, Jeffty! You're back, Jeffty! Don't ever leave me again, Jeffty. Don't ever—

My apartment door. I opened it. Mona was in the kitchen working a cigarette over a cup of coffee. I don't know that I'd seen her smoke before. Except that cigarettes smelled foul and turned your lungs to tar, I thought smoking was sexy. Or maybe Mona had a knack for making things seem that way.

She looked at me. "Hey," she said, then was done talking. She went back to her coffee and smoke.

No rush to me—no hug, no kiss. No nothing.

I said: "I'm back."

No response.

I said: "I've been gone for three days."

"Oh."

I said: "You don't want to know where I've been?"

Without looking my way: "Where you been?"

"I been in jail."

"Oh."

"You . . . you didn't notice I was gone?"

"I guess. I mean, I knew you weren't here."

"But . . ." How could I say it without sounding like a little girl? I couldn't.

"You didn't miss me?"

Mona looked at me, the expression on her face like she'd just swallowed a spoonful of Drāno. "Miss you?"

"I'm just saying . . . I was gone for three days, and you didn't notice?"

"You were gone. I figured . . . I don't know, you were gone. I'm not your mother." She stared at her coffee like some deep meaning floated inside the java.

A bottle of Jack was on the counter. I got it. I spun the top off. I took a swig, then another. "How are you with Moe?"

"I've seen him every night." Her voice was halting. "We meet at his house now. The other night, we went out to dinner. The Ivy. It's nice in there—fancy, but like old-fashioned. He likes it because—"

Details. I didn't have time for details. "Is he into you?"

Mona said nothing.

"Is he into you or not?"

"I think he loves me."

Another swig of Jack. "All right, listen to me. Things have changed. We gotta put the touch on Moe. Now. In the next few days. It's sooner than we should, but we got to do it."

Mona sat just as quiet as she'd been since I'd walked in the door, only more so. After a second she got up and zombied into the living room.

I followed, watched her sink into the couch. "What?"

Her mouth opened and closed a few times.

"*What?*"

"Jeffty . . . I . . . I can't do this; I can't con Moe. I can't do it."

Now it was my mouth that flapped open and closed.

"He's a sweet man; he's lonely. He loved Pier so much. You should hear him talk. If you just spent ten minutes listening to him . . . He's lost everything. When Pier died, it was like . . . it was like his soul died. He couldn't love anything, anyone else. His wife left him after that; then his son died. . . ."

Fire danced inside me. The heat of it made me blind, and the sound of it burning filled my ears. I couldn't hear Mona, but instead was fixated on what she had first said. "Can't, or won't?"

"What?"

"You can't, or you won't go through with this, Mona? Which is it?"

"Jeffty—"

"Which?"

"I . . . I love him."

A brick to the head would have been more gentle. It would have caused me to swing and sway less. It wouldn't have hurt as much.

Mona went on. She tried to explain the unexplainable. "He talks to me. I mean, he asks me shit about myself, my family—"

"Family? You don't have a family!"

"He's always asking about what I want from life, what I want to be. . . . He cares about me."

"He was supposed to fall for you, not the other way around. He was supposed to fall for you!"

". . . He's kind. . . . He gives me gifts."

"What about me? I never did anything for you? I took you off the street; I cleaned you up. I gave you food and booze and something softer than the ground to sleep on."

"You didn't do anything for me where you couldn't get something in return." Mona matched my tone and put a little more on it. "You took me in 'cause you had a racket to work. Would you've done it if my face was different? Would you have done it if my hair was white instead of dark?"

We both knew the truth of it, so I didn't bother answering the question. Instead: "I got people who want me dead. I got cops who want to put me down for good. I got one chance of getting out from under it all, and you want to blow it 'cause you've gone simple for the first guy who pays you some attention?"

"For the first guy who cares about me."

"He doesn't care about you."

"For a guy who never hurt anybody!"

"*He doesn't care about you!* He cares about a dead girl who never gave a fuck about him in the first place. You think he loves you, huh? How much do you think he'll love you when he finds out you're not from Wisconsin, you can't even spell UCLA, you haven't got a brother or a job at a flower shop? How much you think old Moe'll love you then?"

That was the blow that staggered her. That was the punch that made her know I was fighting for real. "How . . . how's he going to find that out, Jeffty?"

A crooked smile was my answer.

"*How's he going to find it out?*"

"You think Moe will dig you as much when he comes to know you're nothing but a street whore who got herself made up just so she could put the touch on him?"

"Jeffty . . ." Dig the whimper in her voice.

I laid things out plain and simple for Mona. "I've done all right these years nickel-and-diming it. I've gotten by. But for the first time I got a shot at something good: money that doesn't disappear before I can get it all the way in my pocket. Money that doesn't melt in my hands. I got a chance to buy myself a life. You don't get to blow that, Mona. Not for Moe, not for the fucked-up affection he sends a dead chick by way of you, not for nothing. I go down, I don't do it alone."

Mona shed her fear and trepidation and replaced it with a skin of hate and rage. "This isn't about money, Jeffty. This isn't about me keeping you from getting out from under."

"The hell it ain't."

"You're jealous. You're jealous because I picked that 'old man' over you."

"You don't know what you're talking about."

"I see how you look at me—how you stare at me when you think I don't know, or when I'm supposed to be asleep. You want me. You're just not man enough to take me. And now you're all burned up inside 'cause Moe has a piece of me you can never touch."

"Shut up."

"Never touch!"

Mona got with a smile. Not sweet, not friendly, just pure evil. She reached down, took hold of her shirt, peeled it up and off her body.

Mona hissed: "This what you want, Jeffty? This what you dream about when you jerk yourself at night?"

Hands to her pants now. Snap, zip, then they were down at her ankles. She stepped out of them and toward me.

"What about this? Is this the pussy that makes you sweat? Is it the pussy that makes your cock ache with anger?"

She was all over me then. Breasts pressed against me, nipples poking my chest, hands moving from my shoulders to my arms, to my back, to my ass. And her mouth, her sweet, groping mouth everywhere. Yeah, baby, it's what I had wanted for so long now. But the way she gave herself to me, the contempt with which she touched me, kissed me, fondled me, made me sick with revulsion.

Before I knew what she was doing, Mona's hands were at my cock. She held my limpness and laughed. "Look at that. Even Moe can go hard. You're not man, are you? What do you say, Jeffty? Should I cut my hair and call myself Steve? Could you get hard for me then?"

Anger. Fury. Violence. All together in one instant. My hands clamped Mona's shoulders. My hands threw Mona away from me, threw her to the ground.

"You're a whore," I looked down at her and said/screamed. "And all the makeup and fancy dresses in the world won't do nothing but make you a pretty whore. I'm not hard for you, 'cause I don't want you. All you are to me is the money you can bring in."

I said what I said confident and cool, hard, like a pulp tough guy. But I also said it afraid she'd figure me for the liar I was. In my heart I knew how things were: Mona had found her way under my skin. The hooks meant for Moe she had sunk into me, imbedding deep in the tissue that made me a man. I was long past just wanting to make some friction with her. I needed Mona. Can't-eat, can't-sleep, can't-live-without-her needed Mona. Every part of me had to have her so bad I couldn't stand to be in the same room with her anymore.

I went for the door, literally stepping over the girl. I went out of my way to do it as I could have easily stepped around her body, but stepping over her made the point I wanted. With my hand on the doorknob I looked back at her asprawl on the floor, so bare and vulnerable in her nakedness. She clutched at her knee as if it had caught her fall on the way down. She looked pained.

Good.

I had cared for Mona, and she hurt me with her rejection. I had cared for her, she had hurt me, and now I wanted to hurt her back.

Love has a funny way of showing itself.

The Regent. The bar. An open stool. I sat. Eddie came around and "what'll ya have?"-ed me. A soda, I thought to tell him for a second. Maybe some lemonade. Then my mind clicked back. Me coming into the apartment from a weekend in jail. Mona not knowing, or caring. The bottle of Jack, twisting off the top and sucking some down. I was a drinker again. That quick and easy I was back on the horse I rode so well.

And why not? Being clean and sober had bought me nothing but pain and misery. Life was no better undrunk than it was drunk, just more memorable, and I didn't much care to recall my recent past.

I ordered some Jack and Eddie poured and I drank and Eddie poured some more. With each drink, life returned to a comfortable sameness I had once known. The dark room that fought off the light, the barflies that huddled and buzzed, Eddie with his one arm serving up glass after glass of fermented hope. And me, gone back to being a loser. Ass out, dead broke, and chanceless.

Eddie said: "Girl troubles?"

"How'd you know?" I gestured up with my glass for another round.

While he poured: "You look like you got problems. I know you don't got money or job problems 'cause you don't have either of those. That only leaves one other."

"Fuck," I muttered, chasing it with a hit of the Jack.

Eddie nodded to the sentiment. "Think of it this way: You got good company. Right now, the king of Spain, that rich computer guy in Seattle, the captain of some bowling team—they're all thinking the same. Women: Fuck."

The booze was starting to fill me with a warmness that was like a hug that said: Welcome back, old friend. Welcome back, and won't you stay a while?

Secure in my renewed affair with liquor which returned the affection that was so lacking from others, I said: "A legal drug, that's all they are. Women are nothing but evil." I was channeling Nellis. "They're all evil all the time."

"I wouldn't go that far," Eddie defended. "Women aren't one way, or another. Yeah, they can fuck you up with their crazy shit. They got crazy shit to spare. But they got their good points, too. Women, they're like fire. It's all in who's using it. Kid plays with matches, kid gets burned. Kids don't know no better. Same way in how a man uses a woman. Use her wrong, you end up with scars. See, Jeffty, it's not that women are evil; it's just men are stupid."

"Why you on their side?"

"It's not about taking sides; I'm being straight. Men get stupid for women. Leave their wives and kids for a new lay, set a girl up with a condo and a hot car 'cause he likes the way her clothes hang on her. Doesn't matter what he's got waiting for him at home, if there's a new piece of ass out of the factory a guy wants some of it. Women ain't like that. Women can do without men, and are most times happy to. Sure, a cat's got dough a woman'll pay him some attention, but other than that they're particular. Look at me."

"What about you?"

"You see me with women? Women ain't trying to be with a one-armed guy. If I was the last guy on the planet chicks would just start banging each other, and I'd still be alone with my one good limb.

"On the other hand"—Eddie indicated the other hand with his only hand—"if there's a woman out there with no arms and no legs, then somewhere else there's a guy masturbating to pictures of her in *Stump* magazine. Men just like to get stupid for women, that's all."

An itch on the back of my neck. I looked behind me. Deep in the room, Amber at a table. She stared hard at me. She stared, she stared, she stared . . . then she started to cry. Okay, I took your money. Get over it already.

"Don't get me wrong. It's not that I'm saying they're better than us. Truth is, a man without a woman is like a bird without a cage. I'm just saying they got their good points, too."

I turned back to Eddie. He'd topped off my glass for me. I started to drink, then stopped and checked to make sure I could afford my return to inebriation. Eddie didn't pour out of his love for the drunken man. Keeping the booze flowing was just his racket. Not much in my pockets, but I could cover the drink, so I drank.

"So what the hell's your beef, anyway?" Eddie asked. "What'd this girl do to you?"

"She's in love with another guy."

Eddie shrugged his arm and a half. "It happens."

"He's old, this guy. I mean, like really old. And she's really young."

Again with the handicapped shrug. "I ain't weirded out by that any. He's old; she's young. That ain't much. There's strangeness out there, Jeffty. A whole mess of strangeness. Forget about old/young, or chicks doing chicks, and guys doing guys. That kind of thing is just about normal in this day and age. I'm talking strangeness. I know a guy, has to have beads shoved in his ass before he can cum. He's not queer or nothing like that. But he has to have these beads on a string in his ass, then have the girl pull them out just as he's cuming, or it's no go. Now, if you ask him, he'll tell you that's just as normal as can be—beads in the ass. For my money, it's nothing but strange."

I smiled at Eddie. I wasn't particularly happy, but my body felt like smiling.

Eddie: "Know a girl who's got to have her hands held over her head. You can go down on her; you can do her with a dildo hooked up to a car battery. Don't matter. Her hands ain't over her head, you won't get so much as a shiver out of her. That's normal sex for her, no matter what the rest of the world says.

"Then you got the women who like things rough. I never got that. I got no desire to do things that way with a woman. Not in bed. Sure, a woman gets wise, you might have to straighten her out. I'm saying, you're trying to make love to a woman, what sense does it make to be rough with her? I like to be gentle with a girl, hold her."

I laughed.

Eddie scowled. "You laughing at me? You think I'm a bitch 'cause I like to be sensitive in bed."

"No, Eddie. That's not why I'm laughing. Swear to God it's not." I was being honest. Eddie could be Gandhi between the sheets for all I cared. What was funny to me were his words. What was funny was the idea of a one-armed guy holding a woman. Maybe it wasn't that funny, but the booze made it seem hi-fucking-larious.

"My point," Eddie went on, "is that you can't look at what some people do, or how they live and say it's odd. That's the way they are. And love? That's just got—"

I finished the sentence for him. "It's got a funny way of showing itself."

"Yeah." Eddie nodded. "That about says it."

"I know all that. All I was saying was it's weird; it's not right. I like a girl, and she's gotta go for some old bastard."

"It's only strange 'cause you got it for her, but she don't got it for you. But that ain't weird. That's just the way things are."

The way things are. My whole life had been nothing but one bad gamble after another. If two things had ever once worked out for me, I couldn't think what they were. And even with all that history behind me, I couldn't accept that Mona went for Moe instead of me.

Mona and Moe. Moe and Mona. The very lyricalness of it gave me a nausea I had to wash away the taste of with another drink.

"You know what you need?" Eddie asked/told me. "You need a woman. Nothing gets you past a woman like a woman. Do that for yourself, Jeffty. Go out and have yourself a woman."

Amber skulked for the door. She took her time going past me, then gave me a look like she was laying on a curse. Too late, sweetheart. The world already beat you to it. I smiled at Amber. My drunken self didn't know what else to do. She started crying again and left.

I paid Eddie. For the drinks only. His advice I would take for free. I was going to go out and have myself a woman.

*S*unset.

I was cruising. The hookers dressed outrageous, but in Hollywood all the chicks did. You had to look twice, not hard but twice, to make sure the one you had your eye on was for sale. It didn't take much driving for me to find something I liked. She wasn't bad-looking. Not too fat, and a face I could stand. Short skirt and matching top of white-and-pink check, white patent-leather go-go boots that ran up fairly firm legs.

I pulled the Corvair around the corner onto Stanley, and me and her got to talking. The first thing I asked—what my old white friend Todd should have asked his hooker before she landed him in a jail cell with me—was: "Are you a cop?"

Incensed: "Do I look like a fucking cop? You see a fucking badge?" Her voice was shriller than I cared for, and she didn't answer my question.

I asked again. "You a cop or not?"

"No, I'm not. Okay? You want something, or don't you?"

We got down to negotiating. I started at twenty, she started at fifty, and we got together at thirty-five.

She slid in next to me, asked me if I had a place. I thought for a second and was tempted to take the whore back to my apartment and do her right in front of Mona.

No. I wanted nothing to do with Mona tonight except to run away from her straight into the arms of another piece of ass. I told the whore, whose name I hadn't bothered to get yet, I didn't have anywhere to go.

She told me to stay on Sunset and head east. She knew a place, a motel, we could go for a full fuck job.

I pointed the Corvair east and drove.

THE SUNSET COTTAGE is what the sign said. Truly, the sign said: S NSE COTTA E MOTOR HOTEL, burned-out neon leaving the gaps.

Motor Hotel. I wondered if that had ever been a selling point, if *motor hotel* had ever been a distinguished expression. I wondered if there was ever a time in the history of the world when people had once said: Say, let's take a weekend in Los Angeles, and while we're there let's live right. Let's stay at a motor hotel. Heck, if we're treating ourselves so high, we might as well stay at the Sunset Cottage.

Doubt it.

The whore, whose name, or the name she used, was Sarah as I found out while we small-talked on the way to the S nse Cotta e, knew the guy behind the registration counter. They were downright intimate in that she didn't have to tell him why we were there, or what we needed, or how long we were going to be.

The guy behind the registration counter—fat, unshaved, with a dirty wife-beater T-shirt—mumbled "Ten" at me.

I took a ten-dollar bill out of my pocket and let it float to the countertop. A beat-up key attached to a beat-up green plastic diamond with faded gold numbers landed on the ten.

I took the key.

The fat guy in the wife-beater took the ten.

Room 208 is what the green plastic diamond attached to the key said. Truly it said: 08, the 2 having been worn out from so many sweaty hands rubbing over it. How many guys, I wondered, like me had padded this dirty brown-yellow carpet down this barely lit hallway to Room 208 to get themselves an hour's worth of loving? How many sweaty hands does it take to rub a 2 from a plastic key fob?

Room 208, or oh-eight: as ugly as you'd think, with a little extra dinge thrown on for good measure. The sheets on the bed looked used. The toilet had been and sat unflushed. I got the feeling this was the kind of motel where there wasn't a checkout time. You just stayed until you couldn't stand it anymore.

Sarah turned on a light near the bed. It wasn't strong, just strong enough to show what the dark had hid of her. The skin on her face wasn't as good as I'd thought. The left side from cheek to mouth had a patch of acne that heavy makeup covered, but not well.

I turned out the light. "Let's keep it dark," I said, trying to be sexy; trying to hide the fact I didn't want to have to look at her.

"Whatever," she said.

I started to undress. Sarah gave a running commentary.

"Oh, baby," she faux-cooed. "I like that. Oh, yeah. Take it off. Take it all off and let mama see."

I guess, being a professional, she knew what she was doing. She knew that there was a high percentage of men who got turned on by the "surprise" and "thrill" she registered when her john got naked. I wasn't among them.

Now Sarah did the clothes removing. She did it to the beat of a song that played in her head, and even though she was the only one who could hear it, she danced out of step. Sarah made awkward up/down movements while she stripped and peeked over her shoulder at me.

"You like that, daddy?" she asked. "You like what you see?"

I didn't answer, but the answer was no.

I noticed—I couldn't help but notice—a scar that ran diagonally across Sarah's right shoulder. It didn't seem to bother her, being scarred up. She didn't try to hide it. I wondered where she might have picked it up from. Talking back to her man, or maybe talking back to her pimp. Or maybe she got it someplace really whorelike spicy, like from falling off a bike when she was a kid.

Naked now, I got a look at the rest of Sarah. She was pretty good. She was just about tolerable, except for the shit on her face and the scar on her back . . . and a mole on her tit. To me the mole was the worst of her seemingly endless blemishes. Not much you can do about bad skin, and scars are forever. But a mole? C'mon. Go to a doctor. Get that crap cut off. And on her tit? How did I know it wasn't cancer or something? I know you can't catch cancer like that, but I didn't want to be sucking on a cancer tit.

I had half a mind to pack the girl up and send her walking, but I didn't want to hurt her feelings. I was probably still drunk. I must've been, 'cause it was very funny to me that I should care about the feelings of a thirty-five-dollar lay.

I wished, at least, that she'd put her clothes back on. I wished I'd checked her out more carefully back on Sunset. I wished more than anything that she was Mona. Mona had silk skin and was scarless and had no moles on her tits.

Mona was perfect.

Sarah pouted in what was supposed to be a playful, sexy way. "How come daddy's not hard? Don't you want to get hard for me, daddy?"

Hard for her? I had a better chance of getting hard skimming through copies of *Better Homes & Gardens*.

Sarah did her bad dance over to me. She took my cock in her hands and started to work it around. She did it smooth and gentle. She knew just how and where to touch it, to pet it, to make it tingle and throb and grow. Forget her looks—not for nothing was Sarah a professional.

Sarah stroked me down to the bed, knelt at my groin, and took me full in her mouth.

She did things.

Things that made me clutch at the sheets, and arch and wriggle my back. She did things that made me forget her bad skin and scarred back and moled tit. She did things that made me want to touch her and kiss her and be deep inside her. I made a move to enter Sarah.

Sarah made a move off my groin. "Put your rubber on."

"I don't have one." I said it quick and distracted. I was too busy trying to get myself in her.

Sarah pushed me back. Bored: "You ain't got a rubber, forget about it."

Coming at her again: "I'm clean."

"Gee, and you wouldn't lie to me, would you?" She pushed me back once more and she pushed me like she meant things.

"I'm telling you," I started to protest, "it's okay. I'm clean."

Sarah wasn't trying to hear that. "Hey, check your watch. It ain't 1954. I can do without AIDS, or some shit. I got two kids. I gotta work. I gotta feed 'em. I can't do that when I'm dying."

"You listening? I told you I'm—"

"You listening? You don't cock me without a glove."

That was that, and to prove it Sarah turned on the TV. She sat and watched a talk show starring a fat dyke who America loved even though America didn't much care for fat people or dykes. I sat and watched her watching the talk show and the blimpy gay girl, getting limper by the second.

I got up and got dressed and left the room. Downstairs and past the guy at the desk. He didn't look at me.

Outside and across the street to a 24/7 Mart. Condoms. Prophylactics. Rubbers. Jimmy caps. All behind a locked glass case like they were diamonds waiting to get bought. What did I want? Regular, lubricated, sensitive, lubricated extra-sensitive with a reservoir tip? I thought about getting some that were ribbed (for her pleasure), but then I thought: If I'm paying, what do I care about her pleasure? I settled for cheap. Trojans plain as milk. I paid for them and walked back to the S nse Cotta e. The S nse Cotta e Motor Hotel.

Past the fat guy at the desk again. He didn't look at me again. Back to the room. When I got there, Sarah sat in a chair, naked, still watching the talk show. She checked the clock.

"You got twenty minutes." She said it like a union boss.

"Hold back," I tossed at her. "I might think you love me." I started to get undressed.

"You didn't pay enough for love. At these prices, I'll like you for a while."

Naked again, I went to the bed and lay on it. A bug crawled across the ceiling.

I asked: "How do you do it?"

"What?"

"Make love to guys you don't even know."

"That's how I do it. I don't make love. I fuck."

"We don't mean anything to you—guys like us? You never feel anything?"

"No."

"Never?"

"Never."

"Don't you ever—"

Sarah got short. "You writing a book?"

"Curious, that's all."

"You pay me, and I pretend to give a shit about you. Simple, the way a relationship should be."

Sarah got up and came over to the bed. She reached for the light; I grabbed her hand and stopped her.

"Oh, yeah," she said. "I forgot. You like it dark."

That, and I don't like to look at you, babe.

Sarah's hand went between my legs, and she got back to doing what she does best.

"Now, you ready to get to it?" Sarah smiled. I hadn't noticed how bad her teeth were before.

Again, Sarah got me hard with little effort, and again she took me in her mouth. I thought not of the pleasure I felt, I should've been feeling, but, instead, of how Sarah didn't care about me the same way Mona didn't care about me. She could turn her sex on, or shut it off with the same ease and machinery that Mona used. And this, as it was with Mona, was unacceptable. I didn't care if Sarah loved me; I didn't expect her to. She was a whore, and complex emotions were beyond her kind. But I did expect her to experience a sensation—pleasure, excitement, desire. It didn't matter which. I only wanted to affect her, and in turn know that I could affect Mona.

That's why I was here. I knew that now. I had no interest in the momentary satisfaction of my own internal release. I wasn't here to fuck Mona out of my mind. I wanted to prove to myself I could make a woman, any woman, feel . . . something.

I touched Sarah. My hands went to her and over her, and showed no hesitation as they caressed and traveled her flesh: her breasts, her stomach, her legs and in between them. Then I touched her with my cheek, my lips, and my tongue. I kissed and licked and bit, but gently. Always lovingly. Always mindful of how Sarah responded to each stroke of my fingers and press of my mouth.

Every motion was beautiful, respectful, even romantic. I did not fuck Sarah. I made love to her. She did not cum; she climaxed. It wasn't good; it was ecstasy. All her talk of sex without love, and pleasure without feeling—those were empty words now. She had gone to a place where she had never been—a place of ultimate joy that previously she could only conjure in her mind, and I, with my fingers and tongue and touch, was the one who had taken her there. I was sure of it.

Sarah patted me on the cheek. Twice. She got dressed, took her money and went.

I lay on the bed for a while.

Pretty soon, the fat man banged on the door and told me to leave, or pay more.

I got dressed. I left.

Yucca. Home. I parked and went for my building.

From behind me: "Jeffty."

I turned. Ty was coming toward me from one of Dumas's snowflake Benzes. I started to "Hey, how are ya?" him, but the look on his face told me it would be wasted.

Ty: "Word is you're talking to the cops." Ty's hands: gloved, ready to do some beating. "Word is you're going to sell Dumas out."

"Ty—"

"That how things are, Jeffty? You selling people out?"

I didn't know how it had gotten around to Dumas. Maybe he'd seen the cops bracing me on the street. Maybe he had a guy inside on the payroll. Whatever it was, I was sure he didn't have the full story, just enough to send Ty around to rip off my arm and beat me to death with it.

"It's not like that, Ty."

"You haven't been talking to the cops?"

"No. I mean, yeah, I've been talking to the cops—"

Ty's fists clenched and loosened.

"But not like that. Not like you think. There's this cop, a crazy jagoff, Duntphy. He picked up Wesker . . . You remember Wesker?"

Nothing from Ty.

"So Wesker gets picked up, right, and this Duntphy puts it to him. Wesker has to give him something, so he decides to give him me. He gets them thinking I'm some big operator, so now the cops are leaning on me."

More nothing from Ty.

"That's all, Ty. I swear that's all!" And, except for the part I skipped about how I'd told Duntphy I'd help him take down Dumas to keep myself from going inside for life, that was all.

"And all that time you were talking to the cops, Dumas's name never once came up?" The words got forced out from between Ty's teeth.

"I'm going to sell out Dumas? What does that get me?"

"It gets the cops off you and onto him, and you out from under Dumas's thumb."

"It gets me dead is what. I got problems, yeah, but I don't solve them by crossing Dumas. You think I'm that stupid?"

Ty got with a smile that held neither warmth nor happiness. "Look at you: middle of your life, not a dollar to your name, running scared from both sides of the law, and no place to find shelter. Yeah," Ty said, "I think you're that stupid."

I smiled, too. Just as devoid of feeling and with a little "Fuck you" thrown in for good measure. "Only, maybe I do have a way up from under. And maybe when I play things out my pockets'll be swollen."

The smile slid off Ty's face. "What are you talking about?"

"A score, Ty. *The* score. Enough to pay off Dumas, and buy me a life as well."

"Bullshit."

"It's the truth."

"Bullshit," Ty informed me again.

"Why's it got to be bullshit?"

"Because you're a loser, Jeffty. Big as they come. If losers had a Hall of Fame, you'd be on the wall."

"Fuck you."

"Watch yourself," Ty warned. "Never once have things worked your way, and now you're telling me how you're going to cash in."

"That's the way it is sometimes. Sometimes you just get lucky. There's a parking space waiting for you on a busy street. You bump into a girl at the dry cleaners who gives you the time of day. A hundred grand falls into your lap for no good reason."

Ty showed interest. Interest I hoped he'd pass on to Dumas.

"And when's all this luck supposed to happen?"

"Soon, Ty. Real soon."

Ty shook his head. "Soon is too late. I'm not here by accident. Dumas doesn't like the things he's hearing. Dumas is tired of waiting for his pay-off."

I said/I begged: "I'm not talking a lot of time. I'm just looking to get paid. I get paid, Dumas gets paid. C'mon, Ty."

Ty just rolled his eyes. "Yeah, you want to get your money."

"More than that. Fuck the money. Christ, man, you said it. I've been a loser since I pulled my first breath; wrong more than right, and unlucky as long as I remember. But now . . . I got one more shot at things, Ty. Like finding a dollar bill on a casino floor, I got one more chance to get things right. No more coffee and cake setups. This is the big one. But I need time. That's all I'm asking for, a little time."

Ty was unmoved. Mountains should be as still. He looked me over, his fists still deciding what to do, then shook his head.

"You make things hard, Jeffty. I don't like what I do—I don't like hurting people. I don't get off on that. I know people who do. Serious. I know guys who get hard-ons just beating the shit out of some poor sap; can't get enough of it. I'm not that way. I just want to come here, do my job, knock you around, then go home.

"But you make things hard for me. You give me a sob-sister story about how rough life is, how you got it worse than this guy or that guy, and you get me thinking. A guy like me can't afford to think, Jeffty. All I can afford to do is my job."

"What's it to you? You put the hurt on me today, you do it tomorrow: What's it matter?"

"Nothing to me, but it matters to Dumas. He says take his money out of somebody, he doesn't mean when I feel like it."

"Tell him you did it; tell him you roughed me around some and—"

"You don't get it. Dumas wants to put the kind of hurt on you that never goes away. He wants you dead."

A long and plentiful silence fell on the whole of Los Angeles.

There's a thing peculiar to the city, to Southern California: The Santa Anas. Winds that blow hot. Nobody likes the Santa Anas. They start wildfires and spread them like a disease. The dryness of the air, the heat at night—it drives people crazy. Makes them do things—nasty, hurtful things—they wouldn't do in the cool. The Santa Anas blew tonight. The night was hot.

Didn't matter.

I went like ice. I felt like my body was already on a slab. "Ty—"

"You see how you make things hard for me? Us two, we shouldn't be talking right now. I should be stepping over your corpse."

I could feel tears stain their way down my cheeks. I must have looked pathetic, but somehow that didn't matter much right then.

Through the water in my eyes I could see Ty's hands open, lose their fistlike status.

"I may go for your lines, Jeffty. But, hell, I'm a soft touch. I don't think Dumas is going to see things like that. I don't think he's going to see things your way at all."

And just like that Ty turned and walked back to his—to Dumas's—Benz. He opened the door, stopped, turned back to me.

"Tell me something," he said. "That script you wrote, like I said, it was—"

"It was beautiful."

"Like I said. So tell me how come this; tell me how come you didn't write again ever."

"I tried," I sniffled. "Honest t-to God I tried. I went back, I wrote more, you know, but . . . There was nothing there. Maybe a c-couple of ideas. Bad ones. Then I couldn't even fill up blank pages with that much. Got to where I was so scared of my own shittiness I didn't want to be in the same room with paper and a pen at the same time. Some guys can write a hundred things and they're all great, they're all . . . beautiful. I had one story in me. Barely one . . . if even."

"Maybe. Or maybe, same as the rest of your life, you're just too plain lazy to do what it takes and pull a story out of yourself."

I didn't respond to that possibility.

"You should've tried harder," Ty said to me. "Hollywood beats up writers, but it don't kill 'em."

Ty slammed the Benz's door. He drove off.

Up to my apartment. I could hardly generate the energy to lift my legs over each stair. My life was constricting around me in an attempt to do what booze and dumb luck had been unable to accomplish: kill me. Dumas, Duntphy, Mona and her professed affection for Moe.

Moe . . .

It was funny. Not funny, but, you know . . . I was trying, hoping, to get back at Hollywood for what it'd done to me through Moe. Make some cash for my own use, sure, but as an added bonus get even in my head with the whole of Tinseltown by ripping the old boy off. Punish one, punish 'em all. But at the last possible second, something—something so unexpected that no one, at least not a guy like me, could ever have predicted it—had jumped up and jammed itself between Moe and my plans.

Well, of course something had. Hollywood has a way of protecting its own.

Fucking Hollywood.

My shaky hand put a key to the door. It shook from the fact that, according to Ty, I was dead, just not buried. It shook from the fact that not much long ago I'd slapped Mona to the ground. The linchpin of my self-preservation, and instead of trying to reason with her, I'd roughed her up; hit her with everything I had both physical and otherwise. One of two things happen when you hit a woman. Either she leaves or she stays. And if she stays . . .

I opened the door. Dark. The outline of Mona lying on the couch. She was still, but not sleeping. In her hand, opened up to near the end, was the script. My script: A Kick to the Heart. That thing was getting around. Mona didn't say a word. The wetness of her eyes glistened in what little light there was. I could see them follow me as I passed, as I went into the bedroom. Mona just kept on lying there.

I owned her.

I got undressed and got into bed and stretched out, eyes open but unfocused. What they saw, though, with crystal clarity was a short film starring me and a cast of dozens that featured scenes like a guy getting his fingers broke in a back alley and a Vegas road trip with a cardsharp juice fiend. There was that little bit of a murder mystery when the cardsharp took a bullet, which was followed by romance, intrigue, action, and, most of all, pathos. That, the film had lots of.

I saw the film twice, maybe three times. It was, unfortunately, the only thing showing. The one thing I wasn't sure of, even after multiple viewings, was how the film ended. One time the guy got nailed by the cops; the other time he wound up a hood ornament on a white Mercedes. Didn't anybody ever hear of a happy ending? This was, after all, Hollywood. I mean, that's what the big sign on the hill said. I paid my price to get in, I think I deserve a little happiness when the lights come up.

That's the problem: The lights never come up. It's always dark in my theater.

Mona at the door. She floated into the bedroom without hesitation. Just as smoothly she was in the bed, touching flesh to flesh. Her arms went around my body, but she held on to me more than held me.

She said: "I read your script."

"I saw."

"It made me cry, Jeffty. They loved each other, didn't they, the man and the woman? Even though she stabbed him, tried to kill him, they really loved each other."

"I guess."

"I never knew you could do something like that, Jeffty—write a story like that. I never once thought you would have something so . . . so beautiful inside you."

Beautiful. I made a mental note to myself regarding that thing which had caused me nothing but misery since the day I'd finished it, and more than that since Nellis had reintroduced it to my life: Burn it.

A little pause, then: "I'm sorry."

"For?"

"For getting a little crazy; for thinking there was . . . there could ever be anything between me and Moe. For thinking there could ever have been anything besides me and you."

"You see that now?"

I felt her head nod against my body. "I see that. We're no good for anyone but us, Jeffty. More than that, we deserve each other. We're tied together like that."

Dampness on my skin. Tears from Mona.

"It's no use me trying to figure things anymore." Mona's voice vibrated like a violin string. "That's gotten me nowhere. Just tell me what to do."

I told her. I told her to go to Moe one more time. I told her to act nervous, preoccupied, but to not tell him anything. No matter what he asks, don't tell him a thing. Let him worry; let him wonder until he can't stand it—until he begs to know what's happening.

Then, I said, just when she's about to tell him, leave. Without a word, just go. That would throw Moe into a panic that would slow-cook for twenty-four hours. And that's when we would come back and end the game.

I told her all this and a few other items about the way things would go down, a couple of bits I was going to have to throw in if her and me were going to get away free and clear so we could move on with our new life together. I made her repeat it, everything I'd told her, then made her repeat it again. No room for mistakes. All the chips on the table with one more toss of the dice. I tried to think of fifty ways things could go wrong, and I was sure I was short by two hundred. What would come next would either be the moment of a lifetime or the end of a life.

Just so I could maybe get some sleep I made Mona repeat things once more, and when she had finished, I said: "Okay," and that was all we said for a while.

After a while more, I barely heard her ask: "Jeffty?"

"Yeah?"

"Do you know what love is?"

"That's a stupid question."

"Yeah. I suppose."

Another while passed.

"Jeffty?"

"Yeah?"

"What we've got, the way we are together—you think that counts for love?"

"It's close enough. Close as people like you and me are likely to get."

"I think it counts," she said. "I think . . . I think I love you."

"That's good," I said, flat and even. "That's real good."

After that Mona didn't say anything more. I lay with her clinging to me. Eventually, I fell asleep.

T he beginning of the next day.

I was up early, but Mona was up even before that. I found her in front of the TV nursing coffee while she watched Regis and Kathie Lee. I thought Mona watched too much TV, but didn't say that to her. Instead, I sat and started talking about all the things we could do with the money we were going to get. I told Mona that maybe we could get her more dresses if she wanted. Not too many more 'cause we shouldn't waste the money on dresses, and we needed cash to travel with as LA wouldn't be much welcome to me, to us, anymore.

When Regis and Kathie Lee went away for a commercial break Mona told me I didn't have to try and sell her on the future, she knew everything would be all right.

Okay, so I shut up and watched TV with her, but Regis and Kathie Lee annoyed me out of the room. I ate food and left.

I had things to do. Errands, I guess. As I drove around I caught glimpses of a dull car following. Partner keeping an eye on me for Duntphy. The leash he was giving me was a short one.

Shit! And was that a white Mercedes passing in the other direction?

I pulled over and Partner pulled over, but far enough back to look like he wasn't pulling over just 'cause I was pulling over.

Out of the Corvair. Quick steps back to him. I came up to his window and he just stared me down.

I said: "I need to see Duntphy."

Partner just looked at me like he didn't get English.

Again: "I need to see Duntphy. You want to take me, or you want to watch my tailpipe all afternoon?"

Partner played like a hard guy for a little, but just a little. "Let's go," he said.

I followed Partner to the Wilcox station. Inside, Duntphy's office. Neat. Too neat. The kind of neat that made him either closet gay or obsessed with order, and that last made him a Nazi as far as I was concerned. Hell, he was LAPD. If he had a compost heap in the middle of the floor he'd still be a Nazi.

Duntphy: "What?"

"You gotta follow me all the time?"

"I'm not following you."

"Your monkey is."

Partner: "You must like getting slapped."

Me: "He's been on my ass since you let me out of here. I need some room to breathe."

"What for?"

"To get you what you need."

"How's that?"

"I told you: Let me worry about it."

"You do that, Jeffty. You worry."

I found myself swallowing hard. "Look, I'm almost there, and a lot quicker than that two weeks we talked about. But Dumas has got eyes all around. You're following me, he's following us, and believe me, Dumas is the kind of guy who can smell cop. You want to blow things then you'll keep doing like you're doing. All I'm asking you to do is back up a little."

"Yeah, let me back up off you. And maybe I should get you a first-class ticket to Hawaii, or Paris, or anywhere out of here while I'm at it."

"You asked me to do a job for you. You going to let me do it or not?"

Duntphy thought for a sec, then twisted his lips and nodded his head. "Sure. You go do work for me."

I let things settle a bit, then: "There's one more thing. A girl's involved. I want you to tell me nothing's going to happen to her. When this is over, she walks."

Both Duntphy and Partner got with smiles; they went all grade school.

"Well, Jeffty's got himself a girl," Duntphy said.

Partner was too busy laughing to say anything.

"Just tell me nothing's going to happen to her."

"Sure, Jeffty. Nothing's going to happen to your girlfriend."

"Say it, and mean it."

"Nothing's going to happen to your girl. Anything else you need, Superfly?"

"No." I was already going for the door when the word came out of my mouth.

"Hey, Jeffty," Duntphy called to me. "Maybe if things work out that way I can be best man."

More laughs. Wouldn't be long and no one would be laughing at Jeffty anymore. Never again.

A couple more stops. An actors' studio off Ivar, then a drugstore. Envelopes. I bought two of them. The thick brown ones that can handle being stuffed full of money.

I went by one more place, the Regent. Not to drink, but to see Eddie. Over a bunch of years me and him had shared talk and drink, and beyond that he'd helped me get rid of a body. I could think of no greater bond between two men—hiding the dead—and so before I went off to wher-ever to start my new life with Mona, I wanted to stare at his face over a glass one last time. I didn't tell Eddie any of that; I figured the sentimen-tality would be lost on him. So I just sat at the bar and, like I planned, stared at him over a glass.

We talked some about, oh, just stuff, and after a while, after I'd spent what seemed like enough time to constitute a final visit, I paid up my drinks—tipping well—and said: "Bye, Eddie" with a certain air of finality that he didn't begin to catch.

"Yeah," he said back. "See you tomorrow, Jeffty."

I left.

. . .

Home.

Mona was watching TV as usual. *Sergeants* 3. The Summit doing their swinging take on *Gunga Din*. It was nice finding her in front of the set. It was like our lives were falling into a pattern. I liked the way that felt to me. I sat with her and we talked a little—hardly at all, really—and that was okay, too, because Mona and I communicated on a level now that didn't need a whole lot of words. We understood each other, and that was something that was beyond and better than cheap clack.

I went to bed, early, because the night before I hadn't gotten much sleep, and I knew tonight—the last night of life as I knew it—I wouldn't get much more sleep. I was surprised how quickly my mind emptied, and I was even more surprised when I rolled over and looked at the clock and realized that I'd fallen asleep and stayed that way for a good six hours.

Evening now. I got up. Mona was gone, but the TV was still on. I turned it off and sat in the darkening room. I wasn't worried about where Mona was. Not long ago I would have been. A real short time ago I would have thought that she had left me and run off, and that I was as good as gone because, with her absence, I had no out.

But now I wasn't worried about where Mona was. All the fears I'd had before were just that: before. Before Mona and I'd expressed our love for each other, me by shoving her down and her by staying. Mona will be back, I said once to myself and didn't think anymore of it.

Eleven-twenty-five. Mona, all Piered up, comes in the door. I asked her how things had gone, and she said they'd gone fine. She'd done just like I'd told her; she'd baited Moe with a nervous act, didn't tell him much, but hinted she had trouble, then split quick.

Mona was such a good study. I wanted so much to fuck her.

No.

That's what I'd do to some two-dollar hooker. I wanted to make love to Mona.

I told Mona to go to bed. I could hear the faint rustle of fabric against flesh as she bared herself. I sat listening to her wash off her makeup, clean herself, then the sounds of her body slipping under sheets and covers.

I waited. I forced myself to. I don't know why, what I was trying to prove, but I couldn't go to her. Not right away. I wanted to make her wait.

I wanted to make her want me as much as I wanted her. I wanted to let passion simmer.

But it wasn't quite passion cooking. Not for me. It tasted more like trepidation. I got up and went into the bedroom.

Clothes off. In bed. Mona in my arms. I kissed her, and she kissed me back. I kissed her, and she kissed me back again. I kissed her one more time, and one more time she kissed me. I stopped things there. I could've gone further. I knew Mona would have let me.

I didn't want to. I didn't want to have sex with her. To me—in spite of the fact that Mona was a street whore without a past who sold her body for money, or food, or maybe even less than that—she was pure and perfect and beautiful. I didn't want to believe for a second that a girl like her would ever have sex with a guy like me. How could I respect her if she did?

When I got the money, when finally for once I'd done something right and made something of myself, then I'd be able to make love to Mona. Then and only then would I be worthy of her. I knew I would be.

I knew it.

Moe's house—like Mona had said—was not as big as I would've imagined, which is not to say it wasn't big, because it was. It just wasn't as big as I would've imagined. It was on Canon in BH, sitting off the street, but it wasn't surrounded by one of those imposing metal fences you sometimes see, or expect to see, around these kinds of houses. That was okay. That would make things easier.

I parked the Corvair up near the curb. Mona was Pier. She wouldn't have to look that way anymore after today. Too bad. I was way beyond getting to like it.

Way beyond.

We went over things one more time, tried to go over all the variations of how the situation might play out, but I didn't know for sure what would happen. I had ideas and hopes, but I didn't have a clue as to which way things would end up.

My uncertainty showed. Mona squeezed my hand and smiled.

I was ready.

We got out of the Corvair and walked to Moe's front door. No cars in the drive. I hoped he was alone, and figured he must be. Alone was how he lived his life.

Mona rang the bell and we waited for Moe to answer. As we did, I thought: The money we are about to make isn't going to last forever. It's a down payment on a better life, but that's all it is. At some point I would have to work; I would have to make the monthlies on wherever Mona and I ended up. I decided at that moment I was going to write again. I was at least going to make an effort to see if I had more than that one story in me. Maybe it was like Ty had said; maybe I just had to try harder. Maybe I had to stop being lazy and scared and a slave to excuses. Maybe all I had to do was sit my black ass down and write.

Maybe.

At the very least, I was going to find out. And no more scripts. No more Hollywood bullshit. Books this time. Smart people read books. I wanted to write some shit for smart people.

Yeah, there would be a lot of second chances for me now. There would be fresh starts all around.

I was just about to clue Mona in to my addendum to our life plans when the door cracked open.

Moe.

He wasn't as frail as I first remember seeing him, not as hunched over, or as halting in step, either. It was like he'd gotten a shot in the arm with a needleful of life. It was Mona who had done that to him. Like a healer, the effect of her touch was to restore vigor to where once only weariness had been. I could see that, now, as Moe saw her. His eyes went bright, and I swear his skin nearly glowed. The door opened a little more and Moe caught me. His bright eyes and glowing self dimmed way down.

Mona: "Moe, this is my friend Jeffty."

Moe just looked at me, nervous, like I might try to sell him something. Or worse, I might be a Jehovah's Witness.

Mona: "Can we come in for a minute?"

Moe did more looking at me.

"Please, can we come in, baby?" Mona could sell ice to Eskimos. That last bit got us in the door.

Inside. We didn't get past the foyer, and Moe didn't offer up any hospitality—no drink, or chair. At me he just kept looking.

Mona softened him up some, got up under his arms, hugged him.

Even with all that Moe just maintained his inspection of me like at some point he might consider making a purchase of various body parts.

"Moe," Mona said, "you remember yesterday? You remember when you asked if something was wrong?"

Moe gave away a slow and skeptical "Yes."

"I'm in trouble, baby. I . . . we need help."

"How is he part of things?" Moe's voice had a smoker's gravel and a little cough after every other sentence to go with it.

"Jeffty? He's my friend."

"You said. What does he have to do with anything, and what kind of trouble?"

Mona was to the point: "Money trouble."

Moe took that like a wake-up slap in the face. He knew. Mona looking like his long-lost Pier, Mona showing up at the Polo Lounge, Mona saying and doing all the right things; Moe knew he'd been set up. You could see the weight of the knowledge working on him, forcing his shoulders down and his body into a sag. It was like he was melting. He wasn't. He was just an old man suddenly getting older and deader by the second.

He looked at Mona, the restored life tearing from his eyes. "Why . . ." slipped from him.

That one word caught Mona like a knife between the ribs. The pain was the same.

Mona said: "It's not like you think." Her voice was soft and gentle; it soothed—a breeze on a summer day. The tone of it almost got me thinking she cared about Moe. Almost, but I knew it was just stage stuff, part of the act she so gorgeously played. It was me she loved.

Moe, voice weak: "Why?" he asked again. "I would have given you anything."

"I . . . I don't want anything from you. You have to believe that."

Getting tired of the minidrama, I stepped in. "She's being straight, dad. She needs money."

Moe laughed. He got up all the fire he had left inside of him. "She needs money? Let's try it maybe you need money." After that little show of anger he was burned out and simply running on seventy-plus years of inertia.

I said: "The particulars on the money don't matter. The people owed can't tell the difference between me and her. They don't get paid, it's her hide as much as mine. We need cash, and we need it now."

"What makes you think I even have any here?"

"Everybody knows Moe Steinberg is moneyed up. Cash runs hot and cold from your faucets. I'm betting a smart old guy like you doesn't keep it all in the bank." I broke things down for him just like that, no time to be gentle.

Moe broke down as well. He looked at Mona through the water that pooled in his eyes. Old men and babies—they do a lot of crying. Let him cry. Let him feel hurt and betrayed. Most important, let him be concerned for Mona; let him worry and fear for the safety of the woman he's come to love. Let him say: How much?

That's not what I got from Moe. Still looking at Mona, but talking to me, Moe said: "No."

My lips repeated the word without making a sound. As much as he had loved Pier, as much as he loved Mona, Moe had turned them both down flat. The years had made Moe wise as well as old. Not many men would take cash over a chick even though dough will do more right by you than a woman any day. Sometime between now and the last seven decades of living Moe had come to learn a truth: Love fades, but money's always green.

"Look," I "let-me-spell-it-out-for-you"-ed, "if she'd wanted to Mona could've bled you dry a dollar a day for the rest of your life. She's coming to you on the level."

"Leave," Moe said.

"We're in trouble, and the only thing that's going to make it go away is the kind of money you've got."

"Leave!"

"No." The voice came from behind the three of us, from the open door. "Stay a while. Let's all stick around."

Two guys. Gun-toters with nice clothes. Angry faces. They looked like a couple of Dumas's boys. One was talkative; one wasn't.

The talkative one said: "Hey, Jeffty. This your girl? The boss said she was sweet. From what I can see, he was selling her short."

Moe got ornery. "Who the hell are you?"

"Hey, old man, I don't think I was talking to you." The talkative one made a threatening step toward Moe and Mona and me.

Mona and Moe and me took a couple of steps back.

The talkative one said: "The boss is fed the fuck up with waiting for his money."

I did a heavy show of begging. "Please, I'm close. I almost have it. I . . . I just need a little more time. That's all I'm saying, I just—"

The quiet one shook his head.

The talkative one said: "You sound like a gambler, Jeffty. I need more time. I need more money. I just need an ace and a jack and everything'll be okay. Sorry. You got none of those."

The quiet one made a move for Mona.

"Moe . . ." she cried.

Moe just stood there looking scared, like a guy who's watching a car wreck about to happen and doesn't know how to stop it.

The talkative one was on me now, gun shoved up under my ribs.

Mona, again: "Moe . . ."

Quiet One gave Mona the eye like he was ready to do something nasty, he just hadn't figured out what.

A sense of violence crowded the room.

Talkative One leaned close to me. "Don't worry, Jeffty. I'll give you the needle quick. You won't feel a thing." With a glance toward Mona: "I got something for your girl, too—that is, when the boss gets through with her."

"No!" It was Moe, all a sudden sounding like a man. It didn't last long, just until Talkative One shot a hard look in his direction.

"Excuse me? I don't think you want any of this, pops."

Moe shrunk a little more but stayed in the game. "I . . . How much?"

I started to say something, but Talkative One beat me to it.

"One hundred thousand."

"What?" The word exploded from me like I'd been punched in the stomach. "I only owe the boss—"

"You owe the boss what he says you owe him. Besides"—he looked to Mona—"you're paying for two lives."

One hundred thousand. All my money. My brand-new life.

Moe said: "Wait here."

He turned, started out of the foyer and down a hall.

I called him back. Reaching into my jacket I pulled out one of those envelopes I'd bought. "For the money."

Moe took the envelope, shuffled away, disappearing into a room down the hall.

A long moment. The four of us stood around, quiet, like strangers who happened to be on the same elevator, listening to faint sounds: gears turning, metal brushing metal, rustling paper. Then Moe's shuffling steps as he came back down the hallway.

From a distance I could see the envelope in his hand and the bulge from the money that filled it. One hundred thousand. It almost glowed.

Moe held out the money. Talkative One went for it, but I was quicker.

"Uh-uh," I growled as I jammed the envelope back into my coat. "I take the money to Dumas. All I need is for you to accidentally leave a few thousand in your pocket so I end up taking a bullet."

"What's a matter, ace? Don't trust me?" Talkative One smiled.

Quiet One smiled.

I smiled.

Mona was crying. She went to Moe. Between whimpers: "You did that for me? You really did that for me, didn't you?"

Mona leaned in to kiss him.

Moe turned his head away.

That hurt. Mona's body shook, and she heaved sobs. I'd seen Mona slapped, pushed, abused physically and verbally by me and others. I'd seen her take all that and smile. But I'd never seen her cry like the way she cried now, the way Moe had made her cry with one slight movement of the head.

I knew, though, that she was only acting because Moe couldn't hurt her because Mona didn't love him. She loved me.

"Well, that's that," Talkative One said.

Quiet One finally said something. "Yeah, and nobody even got shot."

Ironic. That's what it was. Ironic, because just as Quiet One—who hadn't so much as uttered a word during this whole situation—soon as he says "nobody even got shot," his head snapped back like he'd just been punched in the face. At the same instant, two things happened: A hole magically appeared in the middle of his forehead bubbling a stream of blood. Simultaneously, the back of his head opened up like a trapdoor, allowing his brains to spill down onto Moe's marble foyer. Quiet One hung in place for a few seconds as if his body couldn't get it through what was left of his head that his skull had no blood or brains anymore; as if, by force of will alone, the body was going to stay alive.

The reality of the circumstances won out. Quiet One's carcass sank to the floor, squishing its own gray matter underneath it.

All of us, those of us still left alive, turned toward the front door. Standing there, backlit like he'd brought his own gaffer with him to make sure his entrance was dramatic enough, was Dumas, smoking pistol in hand. Sidekicking with him, as usual, was Ty.

The two of them came all the way into the foyer. Ty went right for me, came up next to me. He stood, pissed, breath hot and short, his body making halting moves like an invisible chain was the only thing that held him back from snapping my neck. Dumas stood over the now eternally quiet Quiet One.

"Couldn't help it," Dumas said. "When he said no one had been shot, I had to shoot him. It is, how is the best way to say . . ."

"Ironic," I finished for him.

Dumas smiled like I was his favorite pupil impressing him yet again. "Yes. Ironic." He looked right at me. "Now tell me something: Who in the hell was he?"

Moe: "Who the hell are you?" The tone of his voice said Moe was getting sick of people pushing their way into his house. The fact that people had started killing people wasn't doing much for him, either.

"I am Dumas." He stepped heavy to Talkative One. "The man these . . . pretenders are supposed to work for."

Talkative One started to shake and undulate. "Oh man. Oh Christ, you're not going to kill me, are you?"

Moe: "What in the name of heaven is going on?"

Dumas: "Yes, Jeffty. Tell us what is going on."

Talkative One did the talking for me. "He hired us, man." His finger came up and out, pointing dead at me. "He came down to the actors' studio, hired me and Rick—"

"Rick?" Dumas asked.

"Rick! The guy you shot. Oh, Jesus, you shot him!" Gelatin don't quiver as much. "You're . . . you're going to shoot me, aren't you? Christ. I don't want to die. I'm going to die."

"You're actors?" Now Moe was asking questions.

"Yeah, I'm a fucking actor. What the fuck do I look like? I'm not a hit man. Rick's not . . . Oh shit, you shot Rick!"

"Yes. I did. You were saying?"

"He hired us!" Again with the pointing at me. "He told us to come in here and act tough. He said all we had to do was wave guns around, and the old man would give up some money."

Moe looked at Mona.

Mona looked at the floor, looked at the wall, looked anywhere but at Moe.

"Look, man, I didn't know there was going to be any trouble. I just needed the money. You know what it's like being an actor?"

None of us knew. None of us cared.

The talkative one kept talking. "I got a two-hundred-dollar-a-month apartment on Franklin, and it's two hundred too much. I bus tables at night so I can audition during the day, only I never get what I audition for." He took a beat, looked around, made eye contact, tried to wring the moment for every drop of emotion. Even scared and *this* close to dying, he was still just an actor.

He went on, sounding even more desperate than a moment ago. "I shot—" A little laugh at the use of the word. "I did one commercial in the last eight months. A diarrhea ad." Eyes wide, like the gift of wisdom had just been imparted to him: "Oh God. I'm going to die, and all I've ever done is a diarrhea ad."

Wow. A life that was almost as pathetic as mine.

Dumas stared at Talkative-Weepy-Bitchy One for a beat. "You know something?" he said very even and calm. "I hate actors."

One second Talkative One's head was normal; the very next a gun was pressed to his temple and another batch of brains and other internal skull substance were misting across Moe's foyer, making spiral textured designs on the far wall. Talkative One took up space on the floor next to his buddy.

All of us stood surprisingly unaffected by the bodies that piled up at our feet. It was as if what we were seeing was not real, as if these two dead guys were existing in some TV show or B movie that they had always wanted to be a part of. They were characters, constructs, but they were not human and so we did not care what happened to them.

Actors had that effect on people.

But the room was running frighteningly low of people I didn't care about. Dumas was thinning the pack so that he might turn his full attention my way, and one thing I knew with absolute certainty was that I desperately cared about myself.

The sound of the shot had long echoed off. The foyer was quiet. Except for Ty's nose breathing, it was quiet. I got the feeling Ty was worried he wasn't going to have the chance to kill anybody.

He said: "I'm 'bout to be up in yo ass with some serious shit, mutha-fucka!" Rage had driven Ty to a state of ebonics. Ty was one of the few people who almost gave a shit about me, and I'd purchased time to work my con from him with lies and deceptions. He was about to pay me back with his fists. "I'm 'bout to tear yo ass up!"

Like all that had happened was he'd brushed a fly from his sleeve rather than just killed two men, Dumas casually turned my way.

"Is that how things are working, Jeffty? Get your girl all prettied, parade her in front of the old man—"

"Stop calling me old—"

Dumas's gun sprang up. "Quiet, please!"

Moe did as told, but he stayed angry. Despite the fact that he was aged and frail, he didn't scare easy. But then, you don't get to the top of the Hollywood shit pile by wetting your pants every time things get a little hectic.

Dumas got back to spelling matters out. "Then once *the old man* became enthralled with your girl, you touch him for the money. My money. And in case he does not bite all the way, you send in the clowns to sell the show. That about right, no?"

I nodded. "That's about right."

"Well, that is something." Dumas's black-black head bobbed in appreciation. "I never would have thought you with the mind for such complications, Jeffty. Never would have thought, do you know? But you're almost the con man after all." The next word came like a death knell: "Almost."

Next to me, Ty huffed and growled and just about drooled. He was like an animal. If he devolved any further he was likely to grow a browridge and suddenly behold with awe the miracle of fire.

Mona, who'd been long simmering, let her fury fly. "So now we got your money for you. Take it, and get out!"

Dumas looked like he wanted to get physical with Mona, but past experience told him it wouldn't do much good. He smiled, and when he talked, for the first time I could ever remember, he didn't sound sweet.

Dumas said: "Money I have. It's too late for money. Now what I would like is satisfaction."

With that, Dumas flipped his head in my direction.

The first punch Ty dealt my skull was so fast and hard I didn't know he was hitting me until the third or fourth blow. My arms flailed about spastically in some wigged-out, instinctual, race-memory survival response where being spastic actually was a defense mechanism against getting beat in the head. My other bright idea was to drop to the ground and curl up like a little baby. Ty saw to it that I couldn't, gripping me tight by the shirt. He jerked me back into every punch, my head meeting his fist halfway. It was like he was getting two punches for the price of one.

As the blows piled up it occurred to me that I was being beaten to death. I heard a woman scream and it took me a second, as my ears filled with blood, to realize the screaming bitch wasn't Mona. It was me. I was going to die like a scared little girl, and for whatever trippy reason, that bothered me more than merely the fact that I was going to die.

Then both the screaming and the punching stopped simultaneously for which I was very thankful and actually tried to say as much; tried to grovel and bootlick and truckle, but no words left my mouth. They were quite literally choked off by Ty's hands at my throat. I tried to run, but my feet dangled off the ground and weren't good for much more than kicking air. My spasms went into high frenzy as my body caught on that it was moments away from extinction. I was almost glad for it, the dying, as the pain of my smashed face and nearly crushed throat was almost unbearable. It seemed Ty had been killing me forever, and I just wanted the chore to be done with.

Crazy thoughts. But maybe those were the kinds of things that jumped into a brain battered about and starved of oxygen.

My eyes began to roll back into my head. I fought to keep them focused before me. Not because I knew when they disappeared up under my eyelids I would be dead. I'd some time ago quit caring about that. I just wanted to keep looking at Mona. I wanted her to be the last thing I'd see when I died. As it was, she stood at the end of that long, dark tunnel, but this time it had fuzzy edges of blackness that crept closer to her.

To Mona. Mona who looked like Pier.

Pier Angeli. Port of Angels. Path to heaven.

I wondered, in a creepy X-*Files* kind of way, if maybe I hadn't created my own destiny, brought into existence an angel of my own design to carry me to the everlastingness. No, I thought. But only because I wasn't going to heaven. My path led somewhere else.

Mona reached for me, but Dumas held her back, held her at the end of the tunnel. I kept moving further and further away from her. The darkness kept moving closer to her.

One last thought: The darkness wasn't moving closer to her. That was wrong thinking. The darkness was moving closer to me. Then it was on me, all over me.

Then I was dead.

When I came awake, I was lying among the bodies of the two retired actors and Ty, who was not dead, but not for lack of trying by three uniformed LAPD officers. Their batons *wooshed-wooshed* through the air with equal measure of speed and accuracy. I don't know how long they'd been working on Ty, long enough to split his skull and crack his ribs, so that the internal blood that leaked from his mouth flowed into that which came from his head. That need not have been long at all, as the LAPD got particularly high marks when it came to beating black men into submission. Or death.

Ty's body jerked and twitched and generally danced at the end of each blow. I thought two things: I thought that I was glad that being spastic was apparently particular to a bad beating, and not just peculiar to me. I also thought, as Ty's blood mixed with the other pools that spread across Moe's floor and his body stopped responding in any way to the cops' attack, that despite the fact he'd broken my fingers, slapped me around, was in on the murder of a guy who passed as my friend and had tried to kill me, I felt bad about him getting thrashed like this.

The cops stopped with the beating. One of them wiped a hand across his brow and said: "Look at that, would ya. I'm sweating."

I rolled a bit and looked up at Duntphy who was clutching his own fist. Dumas was doubled over, grabbing at his stomach. His white-white clothes were stained with his own vomit. The first time I'd ever seen them dirty. I was sorry I'd been so busy dying I'd missed things.

Duntphy looked down at me. "Get up."

My head felt bloated and lopsided. Blood streaked into my left eye, making it useless for looking with. Breathing was hard as my throat had to get used to working again. Besides all that, I had very little trouble standing.

Duntphy filled the time slugging away at Dumas while Partner held him.

Between punches: "You're lucky, Jeffty. Turns out for a shitty gambler you're lucky after all. Lucky I was keeping my eye on you when you said I should do otherwise."

"Lucky my ass," I rasped. "Like I figured, everybody's watching me. You, Dumas. I figured if I tipped off Ty and pushed things enough Dumas would step in. I figured when he did, you'd be right behind him. I just didn't figure you'd let the bodies pile up before you did anything."

"Murder goes a lot further than extortion. Two killings . . . The DA'll have a piñata party with that. And fuck, Jeffty, they're just actors."

My head hurt. I put a hand to it and staggered. I opened my one good eye and it was filled with a kaleidoscope of blood and bodies, twisted cops and bad men, an old man who just wanted someone to love, a young woman who just wanted a better life.

Mona stepped to me. The fire in her eyes was only partway drenched by the tears that filled them.

Mona said: "It was a setup all the time for the cops, just so you could get yourself square. We never were going to get the money."

I said nothing.

Mona said: "You let me ruin things with Moe, and now I don't even have a dollar to show for it?"

One of the cops nudged Ty with his foot. "Maybe we should call an ambulance or something."

Another cop, casual as breeze: "Maybe."

I finally said something, but I said it to Duntphy. I said: "We had a deal. I help you with Dumas, and you don't touch the girl. That was the deal."

"He loved me, Jeffty." The ends of Mona's words garbled as her voice began to crack.

I kept looking at Duntphy. I couldn't take looking at Mona.

"You made me hurt him, and now I don't have anything. Nothing. *Nothing!*"

Mona's hand flipped out and whipped across my face. The pain went beyond the slap. Mona ran from the foyer, from the house. The cops didn't try to stop her. They were too busy laughing at me.

All this, and nothing changes. People still get their jollies when Jeffty's around.

Moe didn't try to stop Mona, either. Moe looked a lot older than I ever remembered seeing him. Quietly, he did his little shuffle off to another part of the house. A door closed behind him. There came sounds, but I couldn't make out what they were.

"What about me?" I asked.

"What about you?" Duntphy came back with. "I told you you were nothing. Busting you ain't going to do nothing to my life except add paperwork to the day."

One of the cops kept nudging Ty.

Partner gave Dumas a body shot 'cause he thought no one was looking.

Me: "I can go?"

"Yeah. Go."

I turned. I started for the door.

Duntphy: "Wait." Like I'd missed the obvious, he spelled things out with two words in big letters: "THE MONEY."

Sure. The money. I reached inside my coat, pulled the stuffed envelope from my pocket, and handed it to Duntphy. He felt the weight of it.

The last thing Duntphy said to me was a dirty smile that spoke more than words could. He had Dumas, Dumas had consecutive twenty-five-to-life sentences to look forward to, Moe didn't have Pier . . . again, Mona didn't have the money or Moe, and I didn't have the money or Mona.

I walked outside.

The sun was too bright.

I kept walking for a bit. . . .

A bit more . . .

Then I started running. I had to put distance between me and Duntphy before he opened the envelope and stumbled on the third act of this little drama.

See, Mona knew about the deal I'd made with the cops. I'd hepped her to it. Her getting mad about being cut out of the picture, about losing Moe, her storming off, all that was just playacting so no one would get it in their heads that she might be around the corner, the Corvair fired up and ready to go, waiting for me and the envelope stuffed with money instead of the one with cut-up newspaper I'd given to Duntphy.

I whipped around onto Elevado. At the end of the street was where we'd spotted for Mona to meet me all set to lead-foot it out of town and race, baby, race to a brand-new us.

Only, she wasn't there.

Jesus.

Twin beasts of panic and paranoia sunk their teeth into me. Maybe Mona had split. Maybe that part about loving Moe wasn't just an act. Maybe she loved him so much, and hated me so hard for exposing her to him, she was willing to leave me hanging for the cops to scoop up even at a cost of a hundred grand. The beasts ground their canines deeper into my flesh.

And then, just that quick, they were gone, driven away by Mona who came skidding around a corner in the Corvair and stopped up the block. She sprang up in the driver's seat. "You got it?" she yelled to me.

Hand to my pocket. I pulled out the envelope, fat with cash, and waved it in the air. "I got the money, baby! I got our money!"

I moved toward Mona. I flew down the street as much as I ran, my body light and easy. This was what freedom felt like, a sensation new and welcome. It was the way deliverance felt. I would feel this way forever.

Mona smiled bright as sunshine. She smiled; then she did something fairly odd. She raised her hand and pointed a finger at me. The same kind of queer-looking finger I'd seen Dumas point at Nellis's head. Then I saw—or maybe not saw but just knew—that it wasn't a finger. It was a .38—my .38—Mona was aiming at me.

A quick thought: Shot with my own gun. Ain't that a bitch?

Mona's smile went supernova as she pulled the trigger.

Cashing In,
Cashing Out

Truth: When you get down to it, at the end of the long day, there isn't much getting past the fact that love, like so many things, hardly amounts to more than just another con. It's the biggest scam I know. Love has its own give-and-take, back-and-forth. It has its own action. You cut deals with the person you're with: Do this for me, I'll do that for you. You ignore their habits that bug the shit out of you 'cause they ignore your habits that bug the shit out of them. You tell the truth only when you need to, lie when it suits you. You forgive, not to forgive, but because prior forgiveness gives you leverage when you get caught in the lie that you thought had fit you so well.

And in the middle of the deceptions and the cheats and the deals, you forge a relationship with someone and it works and sometimes, even, it's a beautiful thing. You get a house you can stand, a kid that's not as fucked up as the neighbor's, and a life that most times doesn't make you want to stick a gun in your mouth.

Mona and I had that—a beautiful relationship. Except for the house and the kids and the fact that she was in the process of shooting me in the head, we had a beautiful thing. It was beautiful because Mona cared about me. It might seem strange to say under the circumstances, but it was true. She wanted Moe, loved him—not fake like I'd thought . . . hoped. She loved him and she knew, now that she'd lost him, she could never really be with me. Still, Mona cared for me enough that she'd rather kill me with a bullet than hurt me with the truth. That's how I convinced myself of things, anyway.

And I cared for her. Cared enough that even in these final seconds of existence I was glad that Mona would get the money, that she would be able to start fresh and clean somewhere. In that respect my con, my racket, had worked. Knowing for once—for the first, last, and only time— I'd pulled off the big one made dying a little easier.

Yeah, what me and Mona had was better than most people would ever know. We had something that was good and right in its way, and in its way it filled the vacuum of me as my empty, soulless self had never been filled before. We had common ground. We had our own groove.

We had passion.

Passion drove otherwise-placid people to frenzied sex in office elevators, and passion incited men to war over the look and fragrance of a woman. And passion, like Mona had said and I should have been more acutely aware and wary of, had racked up a bigger body count than hate ever would. Mona sent 158 grains of lead-lined passion my way at eleven hundred feet per second.

Love has a funny way of showing itself.

A NOTE ON THE TYPE

The text of this book was set in Electra, a typeface designed by W. A. Dwiggins (1880–1956). This face cannot be classified as either modern or old style. It is not based on any historical model; nor does it echo any particular period or style. It avoids the extreme contrasts between thick and thin elements that mark most modern faces and attempts to give a feeling of fluidity, power, and speed.

Composed by Stratford Publishing Services, Brattleboro, Vermont

Printed and bound by Haddon Craftsmen, an R. R. Donnelley & Sons Company, Bloomsburg, Pennsylvania

Designed by Dorothy S. Baker